Michael Durbin:
AN OLYMPIAN'S TALE

BOOK ONE

Written by: Billy Wetzel

Order this book online at www.trafford.com
or email orders@trafford.com

Most Trafford titles are also available at major online book retailers.

Printed in the United States of America.

ISBN: 978-1-4669-1506-0 (sc)
ISBN: 978-1-4669-1505-3 (e)

Trafford rev. 12/18/2012

www.trafford.com

North America & international
toll-free: 1 888 232 4444 (USA & Canada)
phone: 250 383 6864 • fax: 812 355 4082

CONTENTS

DEDICATION

I dedicate this book to anyone who played an important role into me finally publishing my novel, including my family and friends.

WETZEL'S NOTE

Figuring and planning out a good story is harder than most people think. It requires a lot of time, dedication, and hard work. As a writer, it is my job to see the book until the very end. I understand that it is a representation of me. As the reader, you are going to travel to the capital of China and watch as a teenager quickly transforms into an Olympian.

I got the idea for this novel while I was watching the 2008 Beijing Olympics. I never really appreciated the Olympic Games until that time. That changed my whole mind about it. I started to watch and follow it.

During the conclusion of the Olympics (on television of course), I began to come up with an idea to a story and then it just popped to my head. I can't explain to you why I suddenly came up with an idea; it was just one of those things.

I started to write the beginning of my story in the back of my Social Studies notebook and then transferred it to my writing tablet I got from a store. Then, all my ideas were typed onto a computer.

It took time and effort to write this book, just like it takes time and effort to train for the Olympics. I hope you take time and effort to read my work.

Enjoy *Michael Durbin: An Olympian's Tale.*

PROLOGUE

In the Olympic world, turmoil has struck. The 2008 Olympic Games has been become a disorganized mess and competing countries struggle to figure out what to do or what to make of it.

The Chinese Government hired two notorious twins to lead the Chinese Committee and organize the Olympic Games. It turns out their hatred for the United States has left them unconcerned of what would become of the United States Olympic hopefuls.

Fourteen-year-old baseball pitcher Michael Durbin enters the Olympic world and with the help of his new friends, tries to unravel the mystery behind the disorganization of the Olympic Games which could lead to danger for the Olympian.

PROLOGUE

CHAPTER 1

THE NIGHT MEETING

The moon flashed brightly like a shining star which cast a circle of light comparable to a domed stadium on the street. It was very quiet. No sound was heard but the little fireflies in the distance. A sign near the dimmed lamppost read: Collegeville Road.

A shadow crept over the eerie silent road like a cloud blocking sunlight. It made a huge irregular black shape that looked as though it was about to smother the road completely. It was remarkable how the shadow swallowed the whole road on this peaceful summer night.

Collegeville Road would soon be the road that a normal, humdrum fourteen-year-old boy would become famous on. For now, however, it was silent and the boy was probably asleep in his bed, turning and tossing. The trees were not whistling and the fireflies finally made their appearance, flying through the dark night as fast as cars on the Autobahn.

Why would Collegeville Road become famous? It was just like any other street. However, there was one house, one quiet house that would take a sudden upturn to fame as if it were a car making a sharp turn. The residents of this house had no idea that one member of their family would become famous, but they were going to have to accept it as it was creeping up on them like the shadow that was creeping up the street right now.

The shadow stopped abruptly as if it were at the edge of a cliff. The dimmed lights on the street turned off suddenly, making the street look like a scary Halloween village.

The shadow seemed to slowly turn on the spot and then it suddenly changed shape as if it were a blob of some disgusting muck.

But it was not muck.

Or it wasn't a blob. But it did look like one.

It was a man. It was a tall, intimidating, and huge man with a dark mustache and beard. With his facial hair and stature, he had the uncanny resemblance of a grizzly bear. He must have been almost seven feet tall and the weight of a NBA center. No wonder he cast a large shadow over the little road. He could have blocked out the sunlight from reaching earth by himself if in the right spot.

The man slowed to a steady walk across the road as he looked at the other houses in the vicinity. They all looked exactly alike. It was different than what the man was used to. He lived in the country—in the state of Iowa—and was not used to many houses, especially ones that resembled each other. He walked to his car, which gleamed under the dimmed lights.

It was a nice, white Nissan Sport Concept that looked brand-new. The man took pride in his cars. It was unfortunate that he was only renting this car—his real car was back in Des Moines, probably in need of a wash and wax.

He climbed into the Sport Concept and turned on the ignition, which was the first sound made on Collegeville Road in the night. The car roared into the night and the man pressed his snowshoe-type foot on the gas pedal and drove away from Collegeville Road.

The man turned on his blinker and turned onto a desolate road that led him away from Collegeville Road. With his left hand on the wheel, he used his right hand to fiddle around with the radio. After finding his favorite station and cranking up the volume, he turned his focus back on the road. The man loved listening to loud music while he drove. Many people had told him that it was a dangerous practice and that he would get in an accident eventually, but the man brushed away their comments. He never got in an accident yet, and he knew that he was smart enough to avoid accidents, so he was not concerned with his loud music being a distraction.

It was about a mere half hour or so when he reached his destination and parked his car next to a house overlooking a hill. The house looked as though it were haunted. It was a two-story house that looked as though it had seen better days. The olive-colored shutters were hanging loosely in their places; the paint on the door looked chipped as if someone took an ordinary pocketknife and carved at it; and a fragment of gutter was missing. The man was astounded at how little concern or care his friend took into preserving his home. If he had a house like that, he would be ashamed of himself.

The man grunted as he got out of his car and slammed the door on his vehicle with an extreme amount of force that it became detached with the car and fell right by it with a loud crash.

"No!" the man shouted in anger. Then, he went to examine the damage and crime he had committed to his rental car.

Before he even took three steps, the door of the house swung open and a new shadow—a skinnier one—joined the vast man.

"Oh, Mr. Isol," he replied casually, not noticing what happened to his automobile. "I thought I heard your voice."

Mr. Isol turned to see the smiling face of a new man, the man he had to talk to. He was thin, wore a New York Mets jacket, and had brown, dirty-blond hair that was in a need of a trip to the barbershop.

"Then you thought well," said Mr. Isol gruffly, standing up, after examining the door, which looked extremely woebegone compared to the rest of the vehicle. "Good to see you, Harrington."

Mr. Harrington was not paying any attention. He had just realized what happened to Mr. Isol's car. He studied it closely, biting his lips, urging himself not to laugh. "My God, Lyle, what happened to your car?"

"Don't even ask," he grumbled, looking sour and displeased over at his broken vehicle. Mr. Harrington had no right to talk. Mr. Isol knew that Mr. Harrington never took care of his cars and therefore had no privilege to question how he handled his.

"Well, then, come on in," Mr. Harrington said, briskly and clapping his hands together. "Everyone is already here. We have a lot to discuss. Come on in."

Mr. Isol followed Mr. Harrington up the hill to the door, into the house (he had to duck to avoid hitting his head on top of the doorway) and into the kitchen.

Two other men were sitting there; one was thin, strong-looking with blond hair and blue eyes. The other man was slightly chubby, had black hair that made him look like a gorilla and a perfect N-shaped mustache that made it look as though he glued an upside-down horseshoe beneath his nose. They were grinning at Mr. Isol. They both stood up to shake Mr. Isol's hand.

"How are you, Isol?" asked the skinny blond-haired man. "No problems getting here, I hope?"

Mr. Isol caught Mr. Harrington's eye, and he could have sworn he saw a twinkle of amusement in it, but Mr. Isol decided to ignore him.

"Well, if you don't count me breaking down my car, none, Smith."

The black-haired man laughed as he shook Mr. Isol's hand. "Well, I'm sure we could repair your car. I'm sure you didn't damage it *that* badly."

"It's all good, Oberfels, it's all good an' all."

After all four men had sat down at the table with mugs of coffee between their hands, the subject was quickly turned around to baseball, which was the real reason they were here to begin with. Mr. Isol recalled the phone call that he had with Mr. Harrington the other night before. He was not going to forget it for a while because it was most disturbing.

Mr. Harrington explained to him about the reality of the situation. The Olympic Games were in major jeopardy. From the conversation that he had with Mr. Harrington, Mr. Isol gathered that it was due to the disorganization of the Chinese Olympic Committee. Mr. Harrington could not explain as to why it was, but he did have a theory, and the theory had chilled Mr. Isol as if he was stuck in a freezer.

He didn't know what he would do if he found out that Mr. Harrington's conjecture was correct. It involved two notorious people known as the Ying-Yang brothers. The brothers *did* try out for Mr. Harrington's team when they were barely fourteen for the Atlanta Summer Games, but they did not make it. Team USA knew that they would forever hold a grudge on them for refusing them a roster spot. Mr. Harrington, Mr. Isol knew, felt very uneasy when in their company.

Their father, Ming, ended up sending in an official complaint to the USA Olympic Committee, but his letter was ignored. His sons attempted to join the USA Olympic Committee, but Mr. Isol knew that was not a good idea—what if they screwed things up for their nation, for revenge on not selecting them to compete?

Angry, they sought revenge on them, and if Mr. Harrington's theory was correct, Mr. Isol knew that they would be holding all the cards.

"I hate them," Mr. Harrington exclaimed, slamming his coffee mug down on the table. "Those Chinese people just contacted the United States Olympic Committee yesterday! We need to pick our baseball team tonight or we won't have one!"

"Which I'm sure is convenient for us!" Mr. Isol grunted, sarcastically.

All the coaches there weren't completely surprised by this; reports in the paper about the Chinese having organizational problems in relation to the Olympics had been the major headline for weeks. Most countries really had no idea how to organize their teams or prepare for the competition due to the Chinese Olympic Committee's blunders. The men were very concerned that the Olympics would end up being an international disaster instead of an international friendly competition.

Mr. Harrington coughed. "Anyway, the point is we need to decide who to take on our Olympic team this year. We usually would have it done by now, but *they*"—the other coaches knew he meant the Chinese—"made that impossible. I hope you brought your rubrics for each athlete that tried out. We have a lot to do in so little time."

The other three coaches put a red file folder in the middle of the table, one on top of each other. Mr. Harrington picked up the topmost one—which was Mr. Oberfels's—and opened it up.

"Good, good, now let's see," Mr. Harrington said, rifling through the first one. "Now, these are your picks, Glenn?"

"Yes," Mr. Oberfels answered, gruffly. "I picked twenty athletes all together. I have four outfielders, six infielders, and the rest are pitchers. I included Shields in that, but I also put his younger brother in there; however, he is definitely reserved for the bench. He didn't exactly impress me at tryouts. It was pretty evident that he did not have his brother's talent."

"Okay, that's alright," Mr. Smith commented, taking a quick glance at the list. "But do you think we should have more field players? There are too many pitchers on this list. And, you have one too many fourteen and fifteen-year-old kids!"

"I don't think age should be a factor in our evaluation, Christopher," Mr. Harrington said, reasonably, accepting the list back from Mr. Smith. "One, we need to give other athletes a chance and two, we were horrendous last time, so why not add some new young players that could give us the boost of energy and competitive spirit we need?"

"I think Harrington is right," Mr. Isol commented in his gruff voice. "Anyway, we had those Chinese-American punks last time on our team, they all were . . ."

"Lyle!" Mr. Oberfels exclaimed sharply, warningly. "Watch yourself!"

It was quite apparent that Mr. Isol was an outspoken, prejudiced individual, and those types of people usually struggle to keep their mouths shut. Mr. Isol was no different.

"They all sucked!"

"Isol, my good man," Mr. Smith replied, warningly. "Calm yourself. There is no need to put a grudge on the Chinese. I have many good friends of mine that are Chinese."

Mr. Isol, who was fuming, did calm himself, but he was frustrated. "Yeah, we do! They sent us the damn information at last notice, Smith!"

"Do you have concrete evidence to support that?" Mr. Smith queried.

Mr. Isol looked perplexed. "I'm afraid I don't understand you, Smith. It's all been the newspapers. Harrington's explained it to you. The whole world knows the Olympics are in turmoil. It's an organizational mess. What do you mean?"

Mr. Smith sighed. "I mean that just because the Chinese Committee's e-mail address was on the message doesn't necessarily mean a Chinese person sent the message last minute. It's probable, of course, but many people could just use the e-mail address and send mail through the Internet. Not to mention that the papers aren't always factually accurate. My Asian girlfriend has friends on the Committee and they are all excellent people—"

"That still doesn't fully—"

"Anyway," Mr. Harrington said, loudly, breaking up Mr. Isol's ranting, "we are not keeping any of these people. They were not spectacular. And I don't want to give them the impression that just because they were on the team last time, they can just waltz in and have a spot reserved for them. We have to be more like McDonalds, which always changes their items on the dollar menu. Anyway, Mr. Smith, whom have you included?"

Mr. Smith, still frowning at Mr. Isol, recited his selections from memory as though he was trying to impress them with his memorization skills.

"I included six outfielders, six infielders, and seven pitchers."

"That's not too bad," Mr. Isol replied in a gruff voice. "However, Smith, we are allowed twenty-four players. Maybe we should fill up the list to that number. That way, in case someone gets injured and cries about it, we can replace them with a reliable candidate."

Mr. Smith continued as if there was no interruption.

"I also took note of someone during tryouts for this Olympics," Mr. Smith said importantly. "There was one kid who was not exactly eligible because of his age. That Durbin kid—what was his name again?—Michael, that's it. He was solid but due to his age, I have not included him on the list."

Mr. Isol snorted in disbelief, causing Mr. Harrington and Mr. Oberfels to look at him curiously. Mr. Isol remembered only too well at tryouts that Mr. Smith didn't like Michael Durbin at all; he doubted he would have taken him even if he was eighteen or older and threw over 100 miles an hour.

"Mr. Smith, your concern is natural," Mr. Oberfels said, calmly, as if discussing the weather. "But Durbin's prowess at pitching is too good to ignore. The kid is indeed too talented for us to pass up on him. If we take any chances on younger athletes, Michael is one we do so."

"Nonsense!" Mr. Smith said, dismissively. "He is too young!"

Mr. Harrington spoke in a slightly raised voice to attract the attention of the other coaches.

"I sent a note to my good friend Will Goodwin and he replied back saying it would be okay if they are one day below the age limit. Mr. Goodwin did say that all the presidents and people running this did agree on imposing an age limit that all baseball players must be fourteen by July 30th. However, the Chinese Committee is a mess as it is, so I don't think it'll be that big of a deal. They're always modifying the rules and regulations. Michael is not the only one, though. Will's own daughter, in fact, Sheena, has to sneak in as she has the same birthday as Michael," Mr. Harrington explained. Then he added, "Anyway, she deserves to be in the Olympics. She's very good."

Mr. Smith still looked unconvinced. As far as he was concerned, Michael Durbin and Sheena Goodwin should not be allowed to compete. Even though they were only bending the rules by one day, he still didn't like the fact that they were cheating to augment their chances to win the Olympic Games. But he seemed to be the only one in the room that supported age restrictions.

"I personally don't agree with age restrictions," Mr. Oberfels replied, voicing his opinion. "As long as they have the talent, they should be able to compete for their country."

"Yes, yes, I know Goodwin's daughter and Durbin are so awe-inspiring but can we please push our eyes back into our heads and organize our damn roster?" Mr. Isol growled. "Let I remind you we don't have time to talk about unimportant nonsense right now."

Mr. Smith, however, was not done voicing his opinion about age restrictions as he almost cut Mr. Isol off just to get his views heard.

"Look, Lyle," Mr. Smith said quite fiercely. "It's a matter of just being good sports and abiding by the rules. If we allow Michael to compete, we aren't setting a good example! Just think about it for a moment! By bringing in this boy, we are threatening our country's chances of winning and harming our image as well! We can't just push aside the rules to benefit us!"

"You can be rest assured, *Smith*, that more than likely, the Chinese will push aside some of their own rules aside to fit their wants and needs," Mr. Isol snapped, sounding very annoyed.

"We should now just look at all of our lists now and decide whom we should take," Mr. Harrington said, ignoring Mr. Isol's and Mr. Smith's comments completely. "It is already eleven. If we do not send this in an hour, we have no team and cannot compete."

They spent ten minutes deciding their team with much arguing and debating. Mr. Smith kept attempting to dissuade the three coaches by not allowing any newcomers to be selected. He insisted that it was not a good idea and they would only be a distraction. He also made an argument saying that Michael Durbin was too young, and it would be too risky to try to force him into competing. The other coaches disagreed with him, causing his face to turn beet red as though he was being filled with boiling water. After a half hour of debating, Mr. Harrington copied the roster down and quickly typed an e-mail to the United States Commission so that they could forward it to the Chinese Committee.

"Well, they should get it in time," Mr. Harrington replied, breathlessly. "The Chinese can't screw us this time. I just hope they do not *look* for an excuse to kick Durbin off the team. I have a feeling we are going to need him more than you think."

"What makes you say that?" Mr. Smith asked.

Mr. Harrington sighed, looking extremely exhausted.

"Well, look what happened through the first month of summer. We rejected the Ying-Yang brothers on our Committee, and then, they went to the Chinese Commission."

"Goodwin kicked them out because they made a derogatory statement about fourteen-year-old kids, right?" Mr. Oberfels queried, curiously.

Mr. Harrington nodded.

"Apparently, they did not trust any teenagers on any of our Olympic teams. They thought publicity would not be good for them and they aren't good enough. I had to argue that one. Just because *they* didn't make it when they were fourteen doesn't mean no one else could. Before they left, they said that the only way Sheena and my son would get in is just because we are a part of the Committee. They complained about us being 'soft' and 'ignorant.'"

"Those pathetic morons!" Mr. Isol exclaimed, pounding his fist on the table so hard it almost collapsed; it certainly sank an inch or two, causing Mr. Harrington to give him a reproving look.

"I remember before they left, after they got rejected, they watched our tryouts," Mr. Oberfels reflected. "They criticized everyone but the Chinese-American folks. They didn't think much of Durbin either. They tried to mess him up. I had to tell them to leave a few times, but they think they're above rules."

Mr. Isol didn't need Mr. Oberfels to tell him that the Ying-Yang brothers were good-for-nothing cocky bastards; he already knew that. What he really wanted was for the brothers to be fed to a man-eating shark but obviously, that was out of the question.

"I'm worried for Michael," Mr. Harrington said, speaking to the floor quietly. "At the tryouts, they were . . . er . . . let's say, not afraid to voice their opinion. I think they went over to the China Olympic Committee for a reason. What if they did so to try to put our team out of action, to disadvantage us, just because we liked Michael? Or what if they want revenge on us, for not giving them what they wanted?"

"I don't know if they have that much power to do that," Mr. Isol pointed out. "All we know is that Ying and Yang slow-danced right on over to the Chinese Olympic Committee and were hired. We don't know their position."

"They shouldn't have got hired," Mr. Oberfels said fervently.

"I realized this before we added Michael to our roster," Mr. Harrington began, sipping his coffee, and what he said next was not related to what Mr. Isol and Mr. Oberfels said before. "At the final Committee meeting, the other teams had compiled their list of athletes, and my son and Sheena were the only two fourteen-year-old kids. Now, with the addition of Michael, that is going to make it three."

Mr. Harrington paused for a moment before continuing.

"If I could hope for anything this Olympics, I would like to be the champion on the baseball field. I would like to show the Ying-Yang brothers what a real team is and how age is not a deciding factor of what shapes a good or bad team. I don't give a crap how disorganized the Games are. After the many headlines and news broadcasts about the brothers, describing how they were unappreciated by us and how they deserved better, I want to prove their assertions wrong and make them look foolish to the world."

There was a brief moment of silence after Mr. Harrington clearly stated his mission. This ambitious goal that Mr. Harrington had would set the tone for the Beijing Summer Games. His declaration would define what Beijing would be about for a few weeks.

"By the way," Mr. Isol said, looking at Mr. Harrington and breaking the silence. "How is your son doing? Is he getting better?"

"I hope so," Mr. Harrington replied, gravely. "I hope he doesn't fall into the clutches of the Ying-Yang brothers. I can't believe they were even *considered* for our Committee. That had to be the gravest error the late Mr. McKinnon made as President of the Olympic Committee. They were—"

"They're damn heritage and being born in America helped them," Mr. Isol replied, fuming. "Their father was born in China, but their mom was from Los Angeles from what I know."

"Their mom was very nice and polite," Mr. Smith piped up. "She had no grudge against any team. She was also above-average in terms of looks—"

"Oh, come on," Mr. Oberfels said. "She was a C at best. I saw her in a picture."

"And her decision-making was a D," Mr. Isol added, "for choosing an awful husband. Her looks were pretty much on par with my wife."

Mr. Smith recoiled. Mr. Isol's wife looked just like him except she had longer hair. She was definitely not the most attractive woman out there and Mr. Smith felt that she greatly resembled an overweight goblin.

"That shows you have no confidence," Mr. Smith retorted.

"And let's think, Smith, when have you had a woman?" Mr. Isol asked, rubbing his chin in a mocking way. "All you had was your invisible Asian mistress!"

"Alright, that's enough!" Mr. Harrington replied, though he couldn't help smiling. "To sum it up, Ming's wife was okay and her husband was not."

"He was a ball buster," Mr. Isol replied, heavily. "He always needed to have his way of things. Too bad his sons turned out like that."

"Anyway," Mr. Harrington said with the air of one bringing a conversation back to business. "Tomorrow, we are going to need to send out the players' letters. It includes all the information they need to know . . . well, at least the information that we know. Here, I'll type the letters tonight and send them out tomorrow along with their plane boarding passes and other information. I know we usually don't do it this way, but due to the disorganization, it screwed us all up and we are left with no alternative. Anyway, I'll meet all of you at Philadelphia for our flight. The Olympics is only about a month away."

He sounded as though he was reminding a four-year-old to bring his lunch pail to school.

"Have a good one, Oberfels and Smith," Mr. Isol replied, gruffly.

"See you."

"Bye."

Mr. Smith and Oberfels left, draining the last of their coffee before departing.

"Oh, I forgot your car broke," Mr. Harrington said, turning to Mr. Isol. "You can stay for the night in the guest room and tomorrow, we'll fix your car."

"Thank you, Harrington," Mr. Isol replied.

"No problem."

"Harrington, do you think the Ying-Yang brothers will be at Beijing to put our younger athletes out of action?"

Mr. Harrington sighed. "I would be very cautious. I wouldn't put it past them."

Just then, the phone rang. Mr. Harrington put it on speaker to allow Mr. Isol to listen in.

"Hello."

A familiar voice came out of it.

"Matthew Harrington, is that you?"

"Will, great to hear from you, old pal. What's up?"

Mr. Goodwin's tone did not welcome a calm and happy conversation; on the contrary, his voice sounded very tense, as if he just discovered the brothers having nuclear capabilities. "I've got news for you."

"What is it?" Mr. Harrington queried, leaning closer to the speaker.

"I've found out more news on the Ying-Yang brothers. I figured out what position on the Chinese Committee they have. They are the new President and Vice President of the Committee."

"And I'm skinny, right, Goodwin?" Mr. Isol asked.

"No, Lyle, I'm serious. They have obtained those high-ranking positions, something that we were worried about right from the start."

"So that's why the Games have been disorganized!" Mr. Harrington exclaimed. "The Chinese did not have someone in charge at all, though I must say the brothers aren't going to make it any better."

"That should be a real treat," Mr. Isol said, sarcastically.

"Tell me about it," Mr. Goodwin's voice said, bitterly. "Anyway, that's why the notices came at such last minute. The brothers were in charge of making sure that was carried out and they were obviously hoping that we would be unprepared and decide to back out. They basically told themselves that letting us know what's going on isn't a top priority. They are there for another reason, however, one that will deeply interest you . . . according to a government source, the brothers are looking for a sacred object that their father had written for them. Supposedly, it contains a set of instructions for them."

"Why would it be in China?" Mr. Harrington questioned.

"That is where their father hid it," Mr. Goodwin explained. "Apparently, their dad wanted them to accomplish something that he couldn't finish. My guess is that plan of revenge the brothers want to carry out. Remember, their dad was the brains of the family; his sons were pretty illiterate."

"Yeah, their SAT score was comparable to my GPA," Mr. Isol said, gruffly.

"Where exactly is this object?" Mr. Harrington asked, curiously, ignoring Mr. Isol's comments.

"No idea," Mr. Goodwin replied, dispassionately. "We think the object is a scroll, but we can't be sure on anything in this mess. However, whatever it is, it can't be anything beneficial to us as the police are trying to recover it before the brothers do. It looks as if the Chinese want a peaceful Olympics and they certainly don't need this extra problem to be a burden on them. They're extremely tense. The disorganization is what it is because the government is working to thwart the brothers in recovering their father's object that he bequeathed to them. You can thank the brothers for that."

"Thanks for the information, Goodwin," Mr. Isol replied, gruffly. "Good-bye."

Mr. Harrington turned the speaker off and looked at the vast Mr. Isol.

"This isn't good," Mr. Harrington said at long last, heavily. "Those two brothers already have two of the most vital positions on the Chinese Committee, and are looking for something their father wanted done, probably to carry out their plans of revenge on us. You would think the United States would keep an eye on them."

"I know," Mr. Isol replied, shaking his head. "If I had the power to do so, I would keep a constant surveillance on them and not give them that sort of power on the host Olympic Committee."

"I agree," Mr. Harrington replied, exhausted. "But this is not the time to discuss this. We have to get some rest."

"I know."

"Mr. Isol, may you turn off that light?"

Nodding, he turned off the light and they both trooped up the sagging stairs. When they reached the top landing, Mr. Harrington turned to face the vast man.

"There is a guest room right there you can kip in," Mr. Harrington said in an exhausted voice. He batted at his wisps of gray hair from his young face before he continued. "Then, tomorrow, we can attempt to repair your car and mail the letters."

"Thank you."

"You're welcome, Mr. Isol," Mr. Harrington said. "Have a good night."

Mr. Isol bade him a good night and vanished in the guest room, closing the door behind him.

Mr. Harrington got into his room and closed the door. He was pondering all that Mr. Goodwin had said. Ming wanted his sons to finish something for him. But was it a scroll, or something far more sinister? And would it affect Team USA in any way like they expect?

Mr. Harrington may have been drifting into a very uneasy sleep but soon enough, Mr. Isol's snores filled the house.

This would be the start of how Michael Durbin would implant his legacy as an Olympic athlete. This was only the beginning for him and his coaches. He would go through many triumphs, and experience the disappointments people would want. For this young teen, the Olympics were about to become more than just a friendly competition.

They were about to become a competition for survival.

CHAPTER 2

THE LETTER

Michael Durbin was running. He was quite alone. The only other noise was his heavy breathing as he paced himself for the end of the twenty minute jog. He saw his house, which was about 100 meters away. He put on a burst of speed and ended the run on his driveway. He had made it.

Michael thought that a nice run would help wake him up. He was getting used to waking up with the roosters before anyone else. He had to stay in shape, practice his pitching, but he always woke up with the same sequence of nightmares, sweating and shaking.

A recurring nightmare for Michael since he got back from Olympic tryouts was about the events that occurred there. He was only pitching his best and there had been two Chinese people there, who introduced themselves as Ying and Yang. The two of them were pesky like puppy dogs, but they were as friendly as eels. They critiqued Michael constantly and were always keen to criticize him. He remembered his coaches, including Mr. Harrington, demanding them to leave the facility.

But that was not all of it. When he had been dismissed from tryouts, he was taking a drink of water from the fountain, and he found himself in the same hallway as the Ying-Yang brothers. He was so silent that he had overheard them talk about a scroll. They were talking to each other how they must find it, in order to get what they wanted, because their dad wanted them to do it. He ran out of the hallway quickly, hoping they did not see him, but he was afraid they caught a glimpse of him. He did not want them to know he had eavesdropped on them.

Clearing the nightmare from his mind, Michael walked to the backyard and trooped to the back door.

The wind brushed against his face and it felt like it was stinging him like a bee. He was shivering, and even though it was July 31st, he was frigid cold. The wind was not strong, but it was enough that Michael could not get comfortable.

Michael was just like an average fourteen-year-old. He was a model student and always got top marks. He was interested in sports and practiced every day, working on his mechanics or trying out a new pitch. Because of that, he was an extremely talented athlete. During gym class when they picked teams, he was always first or second chosen because of his talent. He did not show-off; on the contrary, he was an excellent team player and was kind to everyone, including less athletic players.

On the other hand, his teachers did not seem to think so. He had to endure many miserable experiences. One time, in math class, the teacher, Mrs. Cogburn, claimed that he was the one who wrote rude words on the blackboard even though he didn't. His teacher yelled at him so harshly (the class covered their ears to block the shrill noise) that the whole class attempted to protest to the teacher that just because he was good at sports, that didn't mean he was guilty for everything. Michael didn't dare protest, even though it was extremely unfair. Had he protested, Michael was ready to bet his baseball mitt and a dozen baseballs that he would have been assigned an in-school suspension. As his punishment for his supposed crimes, he was forced to write lines for four hours each day for a week. Michael knew there would not be another time in his life when his hand ached so much. Not even after pitching.

Another time, in gym class, his gym teacher got mad at him because he accidentally fired a ball and it hit his teacher in the face. His team maintained fiercely that he did not mean to, but it was not a sufficient excuse, as he was forced to stay after school and clean up the gymnasium. His gym teacher, meanwhile, had to recover from a bloody nose ("Well, at least he got him good," Michael overheard one student tell his friend the day after the incident).

Michael never cared what his teachers said about him. He was likable enough because only most of the teachers had an issue with him. All the others thought he was a "sweet little boy," as his pretty, twenty-year-old science teacher always said.

Michael, unlike most of the boys (even though they thought so), had a lot of girlfriends. Girls followed him around everywhere so it was almost impossible for him to get to class on time. Unfortunately, it always seemed to occur during the time he needed to get to math class, which was not only his worst class (even though he had a 93 average), but the class where he was most openly hated by Mrs. Cogburn. If there was one thing that made his math teacher happy, it was being provided with an excuse to disadvantage Michael in some way. His minor punishments were usually five points from his next quiz, but he sometimes was brought to the front of the class and provoked by his teacher.

So at school, Michael was an enemy to the staff. He had all of the students on his side, but it was never enough. Teachers always won the arguments even though Michael never committed any of the crimes he was accused of.

Michael opened the back door and walked quietly into the house. He mustn't wake up his siblings and parents. He got himself a bowl of cereal and made himself some scrambled eggs on toast with orange juice.

As Michael was eating, he suddenly remembered that today was an important day. It was his birthday. He had turned fourteen.

His birthdays were always fun and enjoying. They were also unusual. He never had a birthday party in his life. His mom always offered but he always denied one.

In addition to not having a birthday party, he never got many gifts. He got one from his parents every year, but his other gifts came from relatives or friends. Most kids his age got a mountain full of stuff each year but Michael, on the other hand, said he only wanted one gift each year. He didn't want—or like—to be spoiled.

He suddenly heard a loud, thundering noise and he saw his younger brothers, Isaac and Delbin, enter the kitchen. Delbin was a dirty-blond haired boy and looked a lot like Michael. He had brilliant blue eyes that glittered like diamonds in a mine. He was also small and skinny. Isaac, on the other hand, was the oddball in the Durbin household. He had dark blue eyes with black glasses, which made him look like a nerd. He was tall and was built like a shot-putter. Michael liked his brothers a lot. They also had an adequate amount of talent at baseball as well, but both weren't nearly as talented as Michael. Delbin played second base and Isaac was a left-handed pitcher. They sat down on either side of Michael.

"Happy fourteenth, Michael!"

"Thanks," Michael replied as he swallowed a spoonful of eggs. "Is Mom up yet?"

"Yep," Delbin replied, sitting down by Michael at the table. "And so is Dad. They should be down in a minute."

Isaac looked at Michael exasperatedly, his eyes scanning Michael's plate.

"You know, it's your *birthday*, Mom and Dad could have cooked your breakfast for you."

"That won't be necessary," Michael replied casually as he took a satisfied swig of orange juice.

Delbin was right. His parents came down about a minute later to find their three sons at the kitchen.

His parents wished Michael a happy birthday and all five of them enjoyed a normal breakfast. Michael already had his, but the others wolfed down eggs with buttered toast.

His parents were nice people. His mom had blond hair and blue eyes. She was short and slim like Michael and Delbin. His father had blond hair and blue eyes as well, but he was short and muscular like Isaac.

"Are you ready to open your gifts, Michael?" his mom queried to him, once she took her last bite of buttered toast.

Michael grinned. "You bet I am, Mom."

The family trooped into the living room where Michael let out a gasp at the sight of his gifts.

He observed the pile was a lot bigger than last year. He usually got about five gifts a year but this year he got that *times two*.

Michael felt he could never stop grinning. He walked over to his pile.

Delbin and Isaac stayed with Michael while his parents had to go upstairs to clean up everyone's room. Michael's presents were extraordinary: he received a Phillies sport bag from his dad and a new blue and black glove from his mom.

"I think I know who sent you that," Isaac said, pointing to a large rectangle package. "That's from Tomas and Sara. They were telling me and . . . oh my . . ."

Michael opened their gift and he had to gasp. Inside, he opened to find a custom made Phillies t-shirt with his last name and number on the back (he wore number six). Tomas and Sara were too generous, he thought happily.

"Hey, look there is a note!" Isaac said, pointing it out. "Actually, there are two!"

Michael took both notes and ripped one of them open. It was a typed letter, with a rather untidy signature at the bottom (Michael supposed that it was out of excitement for the sloppy signature) from Sara.

Dear Michael,

Happy Birthday! I'm sorry I'm unavailable to celebrate with you, but I'm very busy at the moment helping my mom around the house and my cousin is in the hospital, having her tonsils removed. All she does is eat ice cream and relax. Lucky girl if you ask me; I'd give anything just to relax and eat ice cream!!!!

Enclosed you'll find your present from Tomas and I. I hope you like it, Delbin and Isaac said you would—I hope they did not give you any vague hints about it!

Have a good birthday and I'll try to swing by later to see you (your mom told my mom that your letter about the Olympics is expected to come in soon). Enjoy your birthday!

Love,

Sara

Michael put Sara's letter down and opened up Tomas's. Michael noticed that his was similar in length, which surprised him: Tomas liked writing and expected him to write him a novel.

Dear Michael,

Happy birthday! I hope you enjoy your birthday with your family. I would come over and hang out with you, but my mother insists on going clothes shopping (ugh!) all morning today. I should be able to stop on by later with Sara (as I understand it, her mom is torturing her as well).

As Sara mentioned in her letter, our present is enclosed. I think you'll put it to great use. It actually honestly was partly my mother's idea (as she suggested clothes, of course) but Sara and I thought it'll be better to be a bit more creative with you, Michael, you know what I mean.

Hope your family celebrates with you and I'll come by later to see you open your letter and get selected for the Olympics. I understand that it's very important to you and I want to be with you when you open it.

Your friend,

Tomas

Tomas Isolant and Sara Perkins were Michael's best friends and in his opinion, were the two best friends you could ever have. They always gave each other gifts for each other for their birthdays, or Christmas. They simply were very generous to each other, and would always stick up for the other when their friend or friends got into trouble.

The rest of his gifts were from six relatives. They all gave him a good sum of money, which was enclosed in Michael's birthday cards. Michael decided that all of it was going into his savings account. As he put all of his things aside, he saw Delbin with a package in his hand.

"This is from us, Michael," Delbin replied.

Michael opened his younger brothers' gifts and he gasped louder. His brothers bought him not only a bat but *three* bats. On the bats, there was a signature of a Phillies player: Cole Hamels, Jimmy Rollins, and Chase Utley were the three, and they also happened to be Michael's favorite players.

He could not stop stammering his thanks to his parents and his brothers, who all were pleased to see Michael so cheerful. Michael was never a person who expressed his emotions in front of people very often. He concealed his emotions very well, unlike the average teen. After he placed his presents in the corner of the room, Michael then offered to play video games with Delbin and Isaac to keep them occupied.

Now, Michael did not play video games that often so his younger brothers were quite a competition for him. They all played *Guitar Hero III* and Michael was pleased that he won, though narrowly. He ended up getting seventy-eight percent and his brothers got seventy-seven and seventy-one.

Michael was probably having the best birthday of his life that he forgot to go outside to break in his new glove or to practice his pitching. He was having such a good time that he spent his time with his siblings, occupying them. The only bad part was that he wished his friends would come over. They usually did, but this year, it was unfortunate that they couldn't show up.

Sara and Tomas were loyal friends to Michael. He felt he had two more siblings because it was impossible to see them without him. Sara was a short, tan, and small athletic girl with dark brown hair and big, brown, puppy-dog eyes the size of tennis balls. Tomas, on the other hand, was tall, had dark brown, almost black curly hair, and green eyes. Michael thought he looked a lot like Frodo Baggins from *The Lord of the Rings.*

Michael almost forgot that besides his birthday, he was due for getting an important letter in the mail today. Fortunately, his mom reminded him over lunch, when they had tacos, which was Michael's favorite Mexican specialty.

"Michael, why don't you throw a baseball around?" Mrs. Durbin asked. "It is a nice day out."

"Oh, Mom . . ."

"Give him a break," Mr. Durbin told his wife. "It *is* his birthday, he's earned a break."

"I guess so. However, he should continue to practice. If he makes the team, he could bring us some financial aid!"

Mrs. Durbin was always worried about their money. Michael never considered himself to be rich, but he never thought he was particularly poor, either. His mom continually moaned about their monetary situation, but Michael thought that they were fine. They certainly did not have any wiggle room, partly because of Michael with baseball, but they were doing well enough.

Michael was very keen to not talk about the letter, as he was very nervous. He was told that the letter would be coming, but it had been overdue. Now, with the Olympics being so close away, Michael doubted that he'd get it at all.

"Anyway, if he does not make it, I'm sure he can do something," Isaac replied, bluntly, which was a poor way to reassure someone. "He can be the gopher or a bench guy . . ."

This did not reassure Michael one bit unsurprisingly. On the other hand, it made him feel worse. The little color left on his face drained quickly from it, but he knew Isaac was saying some truth. He wasn't completely confident that he would grab a roster spot. However, he felt it was more his maturity than talent. At the tryouts, he felt infantile compared to the rest of them and more like a middle school kid than an athlete.

"I hope I make it," he replied nervously, licking his white lips. "I practiced every day and night . . ."

"You'll be fine, Michael," Delbin reassured him, looking characteristically serious. "Don't listen to Isaac. He's always pessimistic. I think you will make it. You've definitely put in the hard work."

"Thanks, Delbin," Michael said, suppressing a grin and bolted down the rest of his taco, feeling slightly better.

"*Thanks*, Delbin," Isaac said, sarcastically, rolling up his napkin and chucking it at his brother.

Michael was grateful of Delbin's support but as the afternoon ticked away, he went back to being even more nervous than he was at lunchtime. His mind traveled to his two friends, and he thought about what they must be feeling. He was afraid that his friends might start treating him differently if he was an Olympic athlete. That thought made Michael so cold his bones seemed to freeze up.

True, if he did make it, he would be the first in his town to do it. Michael could not help feeling excited about that. His town really never had received any attention or recognition from outsiders. From that perspective alone, his town was buzzing with excitement and they promised Michael that they would come to see him open his letter.

On the other hand, he felt nervous that the whole town was coming to see him open it. His friends, admirers, and important people like the mayor, whom he never met in his life, were all coming to his house when the mail came. Michael felt he did not deserve that much publicity. It's not like he was the CEO of some huge company.

At four in the afternoon, Michael started to see the mail truck entering his neighborhood and then he saw a multitude of cars parking wherever there was room just to see Michael open his letter. Michael could see people pouring in from all directions walking to his house as though all of them were magnetically attracted to it. Michael would have not believed what was happening if he didn't see it with his own eyes.

His family as well was astonished with the crowd that Michael was attracting despite the fact he may be selected to represent the United States in Beijing.

"The letter came!" Isaac exclaimed, glancing out the window. "I don't believe it."

"Will you look at that?" Michael's father said, peering out the window. "You must be popular, son. Didn't think that there would be this many people."

"This is *unbelievable,*" Michael gasped, as he looked out the window.

And, ignoring everyone else and their mailboxes, the mailman went right up to the Durbin's mailbox and slid the mail in. Then he went to park his truck (which was difficult, as all spots close to Michael's house were taken) so he could watch Michael open it as well.

Michael watched as the whole town gather around the mailbox, leaving only enough room for Michael to open it. Michael saw his friends, Sara and Tomas, their parents, Mayor Hensley, Mailman Nate, his classmates and their parents, the old folks . . .

"Go on, Michael," Delbin replied. "Go get it."

Michael was shaking, pale, and his eyes glittered like stars. His legs felt as if they were turned to jelled cranberry sauce. He could not move. Finally, after what seemed like hours, he walked and opened the door.

He stumbled on his way out the door and as soon as he got on the front lawn, the whole town started to cheer. People from Philadelphia must have heard the loud, cacophonous noises from Collegeville Road because the town was so noisy. They stamped their feet, waved, and Michael saw Tomas try to start the wave, but it never occurred.

Michael felt as though he was walking down a red carpet.

It was a strange, unusual, and very peculiar feeling. The walk to the mailbox felt immensely long, as if he was retracing his two-mile jog that morning. The crowd was so loud; he might have punched his ticket in the MLB.

At long last, he reached the mailbox. The crowd fell deadly silent as Michael opened the mailbox and pulled out a thick letter in black ink that read out his name, his address, and his hometown, Skippack, Pennsylvania. On the corner of the envelope, he saw that a stamp with the Olympic rings on it. How fitting, he thought to himself.

He just stood there, holding his letter. It must have been long because the folks were starting to get impatient.

"Open the stinking letter, kid, or I'll do it for you!" an old man yelled, crankily, brandishing his walking stick at him.

The crowd instantly booed the old man and Tomas flashed him a shut-your-face-before-I-kill-you look.

Sara walked up to Michael, looking anxious.

"Open it, Michael," Sara replied, softly and Michael could see that she was trembling with excitement, but Michael knew she was anxious for the response.

Then, Mayor Hensley walked up to him. "Open it up, Michael. For the sake of . . ."

He never finished. Michael tore open the letter so quickly it must have been magic. Then, with trembling fingers, he opened up the letter, and flipped through the contents of it.

He read it a good few times to make sure there was no mistake. He wanted to be sure before he announced it.

Michael then looked up. He saw the video cameras pointing at him and many people were snapping photos of him. Michael had to blink from the light. He knew as soon as he said it, the crowd would go wild.

"Well, Michael, what is the deal?" the mayor asked. Michael saw beads of sweat glistening from his cheeks. It looked as though he could not take any more suspense.

Michael stood quite still for a moment, looked at the audience, and then threw his arms up in triumph.

"I MADE IT! I MADE THE TEAM!"

Even the military firing their guns could not be louder than the noise outside Michael's house. The town was screaming and cheering so loudly Michael thought he would need a hearing aid like the elderly.

The whole town made their way toward him as he felt people slap him on the back. He was being engulfed by people he never spoken to before. He was having his hair ruffled and his hand shaken many times. He caught sight of his family and friends, who were a loss for words. They just stood there, beaming at Michael as the mayor came over.

Mayor Hensley called for silence and it seemed that he had a gift of keeping crowds silent without much effort. Maybe it was because the crowd was looking forward towards the mayor's speech, because everyone fell silent at once. Then he spoke to them.

"Ladies and gentlemen," he cried in his deep voice. "It is my greatest pleasure to be here, to congratulate one individual on his hard work. It is my great pleasure to present to you, our first Olympic athlete . . . Michael Durbin!"

The crowd applauded but fell silent gradually as the mayor continued.

"Now, Michael Durbin, I speak to you only . . . I offer you my congratulations and for your efforts for achieving this extraordinary goal, I present you with a plaque. I wish you luck in the Olympic Games at Beijing."

"Thank you, sir," Michael replied as he accepted his plaque and shook hands with the mayor.

Cameras were flashing and Michael found himself being interrogated by many reporters and he answered their questions as best as he could, and the noise was increasing every second. "What are you looking forward to most, Michael?"

"Did you expect to achieve your goal?"

"What do you plan on doing next, Michael?"

Michael answered the questions as honestly as he could. After he had answered the last query from the last reporter, he turned to the crowd once more to show them how truly excited he was for his next venture.

"I'm going to Beijing! I am going to Beijing!"

Michael then looked up to the heavens and thought to himself. So *this is what being an Olympic athlete is. This is what I will have to deal with.*

And with that, Michael got the first taste of real publicity as an athlete.

CHAPTER 3

THE TALE OF THE TWIN BROTHERS

Michael's euphoria of becoming an Olympic athlete lasted for the rest of his time in Pennsylvania. He had no time to bask in his own happiness though; he had to get ready.

He had to break in his new equipment and pack his bags for the trip. Michael was spending endless hours packing that he forgot all about his letter. Even though he read it several times, there were a few sentences in his letter that were rather unusual, but he didn't have time to dissect them further because he was busy packing his socks and underwear, along with the rest of his clothes in his suitcase.

The weird part of his letter came at the conclusion of it. He noticed notes that were scribbled as if in a great hurry. It said stuff that was almost like whoever sent it was concerned. Michael was troubled by this one part of the letter.

Congratulations on being selected to represent your country but the Olympics this year will be more than winning medals. Keep cautious and be on your guard.

Days later, an article was posted about him in the newspaper by Mrs. Newman, the local journalist. Michael was expecting an article about what a hero he was but no, it was along the lines of what Mrs. Cogburn would write. For example, the article went like this.

How did Michael manage to make the team at this young age? Was it really because of his effort? Most experts think that he had used steroids to get in and that he was determined to show-off ever since he was born. I mean, how was it possible that he became so good so quickly? Michael Durbin is sure to be an icon for aspiring athletes, especially teens, but before we jump on his bandwagon immediately, we need to consider that Durbin may not be as great of a person as we think.

Michael was able to control his temper, but he had to make sure no one believed the lies in the paper. He spent some of his hours persuading people he never used steroids and never will. Luckily, everyone believed him, and Michael was sure Mrs. Newman talked to no experts and invented an unfounded accusation. Why she did, though, was the part that baffled Michael. However, the article told Michael that as an Olympic athlete now, he was going to have to get used to the press attention, positive and negative.

Since he was extremely busy, it was hard to get a chance to talk to his friends. He was so busy with pitching that he did not have much free time. He only got one chance to talk to them and that was the last day before he left for Beijing.

They were in his backyard, sitting under a large maple tree. Tomas was throwing pinecones at the shed. Sara and Michael had their backs to the tree and were talking.

"I still cannot believe you made it," Tomas replied, chucking a particular large pinecone at the shed. It hit the rooftop with a *thud*.

"Me neither," Michael admitted.

Sara was reading a magazine called *Rising Stars* while they were talking. She had taken out a subscription for years, mainly to look at the guy athletes but with Michael being an Olympic athlete now, she had another reason to read up.

"Hey Michael, you are in here."

"Am I?" Michael queried, dazed.

"My God, is this the tenth article about you?" Tomas questioned. "Dear me, what are they saying about you now, Michael?"

"Just read it," Sara insisted, shoving the article under their noses.

They both looked at it and read:

MICHAEL DURBIN PREDICTIONS AND TRUTHS

Michael Durbin, 14, was a normal boy—until now.
Now he is leaving the beginning stage of his life.
We took a survey about how would people expect him to do in the Olympics. Overall, most would expect a real shocker.

Below, it listed the predictions most writers thought. Michael was pleased to see that over fifty percent thought he would be successful.

"Why did you show us this?" Tomas asked curiously.

"That is not the point," Sara said, sharply. "I wanted to show you that this is the first article I found about Michael that is positive."

"Why?"

"I've read other articles that did not shed you in a positive light," Sara explained anxiously. "How the pollution is so bad that you might not make it out . . . how the press attention might get to your head . . . how girls might interfere with your success . . . and . . ."

"Sounds like macho," Tomas replied, smirking. "I just hope Michael does not pick a girl with dark brown hair and puppy-brown eyes. We have one already."

Michael fought hard to keep his face straight. But unfortunately, he was fighting a losing battle. Also, Sara seemed to catch on and frowned deeply at Tomas to make her look like a puppy pleading for food.

"Please, Tomas listen," Sara whined. "I've read about how going to Beijing might not be safe for Michael. If he goes, he'll be in mortal danger."

"Me?" Michael asked, pointing to himself. "Why?"

"I can't believe you did not get these articles or even have a slight interest in them," Sara answered, shaking her head. "My dad took out a subscription in *World Sports* and it is all about China."

"So it must have explained the upcoming Olympics," Michael replied slowly.

"Precisely," Sara replied, nodding. "It talked about notes from the Chinese Committee. But there was more. You may be in trouble, Michael."

Michael still could not see what was troubling Sara. She looked as though trying to give him a pointer, but he was completely nonplussed.

"So . . . why am I in mortal danger?"

"There is a scroll, Michael. According to the multiple articles I've read, there are two brothers who are looking for a scroll. Apparently the scroll will aid them in some way carry out their revenge plan. These two men have now joined back with their home country and . . ."

Even though Michael had asked why he was in danger, he already knew what Sara was about to bring up, which prompted him to cut her off before she finished.

"Who? Do they mean the Ying-Yang brothers? They were at my tryout, and they did not seem to like me much," Michael said. "They did mention something about a scroll. I overheard them."

Sara's hand flew up to her mouth. "How do you know? What are you talking about?"

With a gulp, Michael suddenly remembered that he had never told his friends about what happened at the tryouts with Ying and Yang. Usually, with important news like this, he would've told his friends everything, but he didn't want to horrify them. He did not want to see their reactions. Sara would fuss even worse than his family and Tomas would flash him a clueless, stupefied look. Before Michael could answer Sara, Tomas interrupted.

"Why are you so *worried,* Sara? Are you afraid that your Mikey is going to get hurt? These guys sound like punks."

Sara glared at him angrily and Michael was disheartened by how lightly Tomas was taking this. Sara usually was worried for a proficient excuse and he could not believe Tomas was not being his usual serious self.

"There was an article about them," Sara explained, gulping and twitching uncomfortably as though she was having a minor seizure. "An article talked about how they were rejected from the United States Olympic Committee. It also mentioned how they then took their talents to China and joined theirs. Apparently, the two brothers had a row with your manager, Mr. Harrington, about allowing young fourteen-year-old athletes to compete."

"Hang on, what does this got to deal with Mikey?" Tomas queried.

"Use your brains, Tomas. Since Michael is one of only three fourteen-year-old athletes at this Olympics from the United States," Sara explained, "do you think that they might give Michael a hard time or possibly try to knock him out of action? Don't you get it, Tomas? They hate him for being fourteen!"

"So are you saying that they want to kill Mikey or something?" questioned Tomas fearfully, finally grasping the sincerity of the issue.

"Oh, come off it!" Michael said, loudly, but Sara looked more worried and serious than ever.

"They might," Sara replied, her voice higher than usual, "which makes me extremely concerned for your safety. I know China has insisted that there are more policemen than athletes, but I don't know how qualified they all are."

Michael pictured himself being defended by a kindergartener holding a gun while the Ying-Yang brothers were marching with the Chinese military right towards him. Michael felt a little worried. What if the policemen were less than satisfactory?

"Don't worry, I'm sure they are genius if they're in charge of ensuring public safety at a large sporting venue like this," Tomas assured Sara.

"What does that blurb say right there, Sara?" asked Michael, curiously, pointing to a section in her magazine.

"I'll read it to you," Sara replied, looking tense as if reading a sentence was as nerve-racking as taking on a giant with a stick.

"*'The Ying-Yang brothers called themselves the Twin Titans,'*" Sara said, disgustedly. "They call themselves that because they feel they are the two most powerful people in China now with their new responsibilities."

"I recall listening to them," said Michael hastily, changing tack at the speed of light. "They seemed rather anxious and serious to be honest."

At this news, Sara changed from tan to milky-white.

"Did they see you?" Sara questioned, now looking as green as a slimy booger.

"They might have caught a glimpse of me, but . . ."

At this, it looked as if Sara had no color left in her. Tomas walked over to her and crouched beside her.

"That is not good, Michael. The United States Committee knows that the brothers are looking for it. The brothers might think that you might be a threat to them, like the Committee, because you heard them talking about it. They already detest you as it is, with you being fourteen and all that. Michael, you've just given them another reason to hate you!"

But her words sparked another memory in Michael's mind. Is this what the unknown writer meant when he wrote that this Olympics *would be more than winning medals?*

Sara's eyes were wide with fear like a dog being reprimanded for stealing people food from the table and she looked close to tears. Tomas was trying to calm her, but he was exceptionally terrible at it. At long last, when Michael reassured them that he would call them at Beijing, Sara relaxed.

"Good. Michael, just be careful, okay?"

"I will," he promised. "The security should be fine, anyway. Like Tomas said, I'm sure the police are roaming around Beijing and are qualified enough to handle large crowds."

They spent the last half-hour talking about random topics like baseball ("The Yankees are getting better," Sara replied while Tomas mimed vomiting on her magazine) and they did not stop until Michael heard his mom calling him from the house.

"Time to come in, Michael! It's time to tell your friends bye!"

Michael bade Sara and Tomas good-bye, even though there was a lot more that he wanted to say to them. He wouldn't see them again until the end of August. Michael really wanted them to come with him to China, but he knew that they probably couldn't afford it.

"Don't let girls get to your head, mate!" Tomas shouted as Sara squeezed him like a python for about one whole minute in a rib-cracking embrace. "And let him breathe, Sara."

Then, he and Sara left ("You better keep in touch, Michael!" Sara said threateningly) and Michael headed back to the house. He was thinking over about what Sara had said and warned him about. Was he really in this much danger? What can the brothers possibly do to him?

He was determined not to mention any of this to his family as he sat down at the dinner table. He knew his parents would make sure he would be safe; they would, of course, be coming with him, though Michael wondered whether his dad had booked boarding passes yet.

At dinner, it was a noisy affair. Michael had all his favorites cooked and his dad brought home a Phillies ice cream cake for him to enjoy.

Through dessert, Michael actually started the family conversation.

"When do I have to get up tomorrow?" Michael asked his father, who was licking his fork.

"Well, we have to drive you to the airport which is about fifty minutes away. You have to be at the terminal for an 11:30 flight so I would say seven in the morning," his father replied.

"I have to be there? I thought you all were coming with me?" Michael asked, confused.

The whole family did not meet Michael's eyes this time. They looked down at their plates of cake (his dad fingered his fork absentmindedly). It took a while for the nasty and woeful truth to sink down and when he finally realized that his parents were being serious his heart sank like a stone in Michael's stomach.

"You aren't coming?"

"No, Michael," his mom replied. "We can't. We are so, so sorry but your dad has a job trip and these two have to go with him and I have to stay and clean the house."

And even though she said it, she sounded unconcerned. Michael almost felt like bursting out with rage but he knew he would sound highly ungrateful, not to mention jejune. He almost could not believe this. He was angry with his family. They would not be coming to support him, as if they don't care. Michael did not want to unleash his fiery heat against him, which for a rare occurrence reached boiling point. He stood up, hoping it would relieve him. Michael knew fully well that his parents hardly ever stayed and watched him play, and that they always made pathetic excuses as to why they couldn't support him, but he felt that they would find it in their hearts to come to Beijing with him. It had always been Michael's dream to pitch for the Olympic team, but he had hoped his parents would be there to see him accomplish what he strived for his whole life.

"Michael, we tried, but we just could not," Isaac replied in an effort to soothe him, but it did nothing.

"Yeah, yeah, yeah, what's new?" exclaimed Michael bitterly, his face uncharacteristically angry. "You guys never come to support me! I was a fool to think that would change!"

With that said Michael stormed out of the kitchen and up the stairs to his room, where he threw himself on his bed, incensed.

Tried! Ha! As if! Michael was an Olympic athlete and his family was not even bothering to make an effort to support him. Michael felt upset but he refused to show it. He was determined to behave like a mature young man at the Olympics, to show the brothers that he was more than just a kid; he was a professional.

It was like an old dream coming back to haunt him. His parents should have done anything just to watch him and this mattered more than anything to Michael. Later that night, he put all of his belongings to the side of his room and was falling into an uneasy sleep when Sara's words came back to his head.

Michael had lost his first line of possible defense. He was not even at Beijing yet—but his spirits were already plummeting through the sewer system. Michael was not prepared to be alone in Beijing.

CHAPTER 4

MICHAEL'S TWO COMPANIONS

Michael, even though he was miserable with the fact that his family would not be showing their faces in China to support him, was too excited to leave for Beijing and woke up early. He could not fall back asleep. He was only dreading the fact that it would be the first time he traveled to an unknown place alone. The thought of that made him feel very lonely. How was he supposed to enjoy himself if he had no one to enjoy Beijing with?

Michael cooked himself some pancakes (due to his frustration, the pancakes turned out slightly burnt) and then he, along with his brothers, helped put all of his gear in the van. As he closed the trunk of the car, Delbin turned to him.

"Send me a postcard, will you, Michael?" Delbin asked. "I'm jealous of you. I wish I was going."

Michael grinned. "Of course I will. And I wish you were coming with me as well."

"With all the pollution in Beijing?" Isaac asked, wiping his hands on his shirt. "I'd rather stay home!"

Michael spent the last minutes in his home relaxing and reading a book. It was sort of a boring day until the Durbin family piled into the car and they were off to the airport.

Michael was listening to his Ipod when his dad started talking to him.

"Are you okay, Michael?"

"I'm alright," he answered. "Just nervous, I guess."

"Of course you are," Delbin replied, not taking his eyes off of his Game Boy. "You are going to another country and you won't be with us. Still, I'm sure you'll make friends in no time."

Michael sincerely hoped that Delbin would be right. Michael wasn't really that social; the only reason why he became friends with Sara and Tomas was because his parents invited them over in an effort to get him to talk.

They arrived at the airport at precisely thirty minutes to eleven. Michael and his family brought his luggage into the airport. It wasn't crowded, but there seemed to be a lot of people from all over the country who were dressed very inexpertly for the weather in Philadelphia: Michael saw one kid around his age wearing a parka and rain boots and another teen with three sweatshirts on.

"Where am I taking off from?" Michael asked, turning to his father.

"We are supposed to go find C7," his father replied. "You will be traveling with about thirty coaches and over one-hundred kids to Beijing. All of them are competing."

Michael knew he just said that just to relieve his nerves. Even though it did not soothe his nerves much, he was grateful for it.

There was an extremely long line at the baggage check. A square sign near the back of the line said it would be a half hour wait.

"This is spectacular," Isaac replied in a dry, reedy voice.

Michael almost laughed out loud.

"Well, you kind of could expect this," Michael said, reasonably. "Athletes from all over the country are piling in here. Only thing is how come they did not go earlier? I thought they go a few weeks ahead of the real thing to practice in the environment."

Michael silently answered his own question: The Chinese Committee must be disorganized and the papers must be telling the truth for once.

"Different this year," his mom answered, tersely.

Michael noticed on a big, round clock that he had only twenty minutes until he was leaving for Beijing. Finally, his bags were being checked and he and his family started out to C7.

They almost entered the C wing when Michael's father stopped them. "Let's get a bite to eat before Michael leaves."

They all bought hamburgers and shared French fries and sat down to eat them. The aroma of the food permeated the room and it tempted Michael's stomach. In a matter of a minute, he wolfed down his lunch. As he had only snacked on black pancakes that looked like flattened hockey pucks for breakfast, he was hungry.

"Don't make yourself puke!" Delbin exclaimed. He was laughing as Michael finished his meal off with a sip of soda. "If you get sick, you are screwed for the Olympics."

"And the girls won't appreciate it," Isaac added, laughing as well.

Michael gave him a kick to shut him up.

After the food, it was farewell. Michael said good-bye to his family. Many other athletes were also saying good-bye to their families as well, but their parents were sure to come later and watch them compete. Michael felt a pang of jealousy at the thought.

"Good luck," they all said and turned to leave.

As his family turned their backs on him, Michael saw his brother Delbin stop and walk back to him. Without saying a word, Delbin gave his brother a quick hug, patted his shoulder, whispered, "Just be yourself, Michael," and then hurried back to the rest of the family.

Michael felt sick and was disgusted and hurt by their inadequate farewell, but Delbin's gesture was very thoughtful and kind. He was alone and had no idea where to go. He saw the C7 area and headed down that way. The wing was small and his was at the end. He saw that they were already boarding the plane. Michael had to run down and get in line, almost knocking over someone's suitcase in the process.

He gave them his boarding pass and made his way towards the plane. He could hear the roaring of the engines and the chatter of people. He also heard a low rumble from the plane that vaguely sounded like a stomach growling for food.

Michael entered the plane and made his way down. As he did so, he saw some girls turn to look at him, as if they knew who he was. They all giggled and turned away. He ignored them, feeling conspicuous, and finally found an empty seat.

He stored away his gear in a compartment above him but kept out a bag full of all of his entertainment things for the flight. He took out his summer homework, which was a book report on *The Catcher in the Rye*, and started to write.

Pretty soon, the pilot commanded that the flight was about to begin. Michael was still the only one in his seat. He didn't mind. The flight attendant did say it was supposed to be a full flight, but as Michael was concerned, being the only one in his seat was fine with him for the time being, until he got comfortable.

But he would not be alone for long.

Michael looked out the window and saw that the plane was at the beginning of the runway. He heard the pilot command to buckle up. Michael quickly buckled up.

Unsurprisingly, Michael always was traveling by plane to play baseball so he was extremely comfortable with flying. He was probably the only one that did. When the plane was gaining speed, girls screamed. He even saw one fall off her seat. Michael sniggered to himself, thinking that maybe the girl should have paid attention to the flight attendant's announcement about having all seatbelts buckled and fastened.

Then the plane was slowly tilting backward and he exhaled—they were in the air. Michael watched as the ground became smaller and smaller. At ten thousand feet, the flight attendant announced that electronics could be taken out at this time even though there was no need for the announcement—many people had their laptops and music players out the whole time.

Michael extracted his Ipod out from his bag and started to listen to music. However, he was still aware that the stewards were coming around, asking everyone for their drink preferences.

"I'll have a Coke, please," Michael replied when the steward came to his row.

"Are you the only one in this row?" the steward queried.

"Yes," Michael replied, looking at the steward. "Why? Is there a problem?"

"No, but that is weird," the steward replied, shaking his head. "We were supposed to have pretty much a full plane today. I think one might be in the bathroom but the other one . . ."

After that, he moved on to the next row, shaking his egg-shaped head and looking confused.

Michael sincerely hoped that the two kids missing were either boys with a sense of humor or a cute (but not annoying and giggly) girl.

And he got his wish.

He heard a noise of pounding footsteps and glanced down the aisle to see who it was.

A boy was on the ground, apparently pushed down by a group of boisterous boys sitting right by the victim. Once the boy got up, he began walking down the aisle, but a tall blond boy stuck out his leg and tripped him. The boy came crashing to the floor with a loud thud. The bullies were full of gale laughter, but the victim was beside himself once he gotten to his feet.

"What jerks! Now really, I was only trying to get through the lane. What is the *matter* with you, *honestly*? You think it is all good to trip me because I'm fourteen? You find that funny? You idiots better watch yourself, or I'll give you some injuries to think about! My dad is a coach and he has the privilege to punish you!"

"Aw, does Mattie have a boo-boo?" one of the boys asked, snickering.

"I have a Barbie bandage you can borrow," a black boy offered, his voice full of mock sympathy.

The group of boys just laughed even louder, but did not look like they were mean. They merely looked like they were joking with the boy. The victim turned away from the bullies, looking furious. He saw Michael watching the scene and ambled over towards him. Michael noticed that he was taller than him, had a Mets cap on his head, and had dark blue eyes.

"Oh, hello," the boy said, anger vanishing. "I hope those boys weren't bothering you. They are just trouble on top of trouble. They're usually okay, but I guess they must be a little overexcited. If I wasn't such a cupcake, I would have strangled them."

Michael was glad the kid had a sense of humor. The only downfall was that he had a Mets cap on and Michael disliked them with a passion.

"You can sit down if you want," Michael replied, offering him a seat. "I have two extra seats for some reason."

"Okay, thanks," the boy replied, as he sat down.

The boy sat down and looked at Michael shaking his head. "I really can't stand being pushed around like a helpless toddler. Just because I'm fourteen, they seem to think they could do whatever they want to me . . . ugh, anyway, I'd just stay away from them for a while. My dad is the baseball manager and these guys get away with everything just because they are on his team and are good. My dad is a real practical joker. He thought it would be . . . er . . . amusing to tell me that he was trying to get as many athletes on this plane so some would have to sit in the bathroom. He forced and stuffed me in a gigantic suitcase and presented me as a bag."

"Your dad presented you as *baggage?*"

"Yeah," the boy answered. "He poked air holes so I could breathe, but that was it. He thought it was funny, but I thought the opposite from the start. I ended up bursting out of the suitcase before I was sent with the other bags on that conveyor belt thing. The attendant taking care of us was not too happy about my dad's prank. Anyway, who are you?"

"Michael Durbin." Michael was pleased that he could socialize with this boy normally.

"Oh, so you *are* Durbin," the kid answered. "I should have known that. My dad likes you and mentioned your name numerous times. He expects great things out of you."

"Really?" Michael queried, feeling uneasy. He would rather have people telling him he was going to be garbage than saying he was going to be beast. He didn't want all that pressure on him immediately.

"Yeah," the boy replied. "By the way, I'm Matt. Matt Harrington. Your manager is my father like I said."

"I know," Michael said, truthfully. "What sport do you play?"

"I am a diver," Matt explained, though looked nonchalant about it. He pointed to his cap. "This cap hides my head. Right now, I have to be completely bald because my stupid trainer said so. It sucks to tell you the truth. I had to shave all my hair off. I can't wait until I can grow it all back."

"I'm sure you enjoy that," Michael said, laughing.

"Fun and games," Matt replied, rolling his eyes.

The two boys seemed to have formed a quick friendship bond between them. Neither of them knew that they would not be the only ones in that row. Michael appreciated Matt's company and was pleased to find out that Delbin might actually be right with what he said earlier. Maybe making new friends would not be so difficult.

Meanwhile, the two boys talked, mainly about baseball, which was the only subject Michael felt completely comfortable talking about. To Michael's relief, Matt was pretty interested in the sport as well.

"How can you like the Mets?" Michael queried.

"Ah, shut up. How can you like the Phillies?" Matt answered, disgusted. "And I thought you were all right!"

Michael laughed. Matt was a good-humored person to him. But he was not the only one . . .

"Excuse me, is anyone sitting here?"

Michael and Matt turned to see a girl standing in the aisle. With one look at her, Michael almost gasped but stopped himself in time. She was extremely pretty. She had beautiful golden-brown hair that was tied up into a ponytail. She had bright blue eyes that glowed like diamonds. She was also short and skinny like Michael, probably only an inch shorter than him. She had a Yankees sweatshirt on and was looking at the two of them curiously as though they were on display.

"Yes. Every seat is taken, Miss," Matt said, trying hard not to laugh.

Michael knew instantly that Matt must know this girl based on how the girl's eyebrows contracted in the middle with an amused look on her face.

"There is one seat available," Michael replied, quickly.

"Thank you," the girl said, smiling widely at him, and sat down carefully as though the seat was soaked with water.

Matt was still trying not to laugh. The girl gazed at him sadly.

"Oh dear, don't tell me you've became friends with *this* kid," the girl said to Michael, rolling her eyes. "He can drive you insane."

But her eyes twinkled with amusement, which confirmed Michael's theory that Matt and this girl knew each other.

"*You* are insane," Matt replied, gazing up.

The girl turned back to Matt.

"You know, Matthew Harrington, you would be *very* amusing if you did not play the same jokes over and over on the same person," the girl replied with the air of one showing another up. "I can go straight to your dear father and report you for misbehaving."

Matt finally cracked up. He was laughing so hard he almost knocked Michael's Coke over. Michael was able to save it just before it splattered on the girl.

The girl finally turned to Michael and looked him over as if deciding he was a Matt or not. Then, she looked straight in his eyes, almost studying him as if he were a rather interesting animal. "You're Michael Durbin, are you?"

Michael almost dropped his Coke in surprise. How did this girl recognize him that easily? Surely his profile wasn't in *Rising Stars*? The girl smiled at the look on Michael's face.

"Er . . . yes," Michael replied. He felt his face burning slightly, but he answered her quite steadily. He wondered how she recognized him, but he decided not to ask. Then he looked at Matt. "You know him already?"

"I had the unfortunate chance to meet this kid beforehand," the girl said, sighing deeply. "I have known him my whole life since our fathers are best friends. They both work on the United States Olympic Committee."

"Matt's dad is also the baseball coach," Michael answered, conversationally.

"Yeah, I know," the girl answered, making Michael regret saying that; he should have known that she would have known that piece of information. "Oh, by the way, I haven't introduced myself yet, have I? You can call me Sheena. Sheena Goodwin."

Matt finally poked his head out. "You're Sheena? I'm afraid I don't know you. Unless you're that ugly girl that my dad's friend has for a daughter?" he asked slyly.

"Oh, shut up," Sheena replied, before Michael could speak.

"Oh, I forgot," said Matt in a mock thoughtful voice. "You are *so* tough because you are on the gymnastics team."

"So?" Sheena said, defensively. "And swimming is so manly, is it not? You men *obviously* show off your masculinity by wearing Speedos."

"It's diving, stupid," Matt said obnoxiously as Sheena stuck her tongue out at him.

Michael finally decided to intervene in their argument. "You are on the gymnastics team?"

"Yes," Sheena answered, looking at him. "And it's very fun. Of course, you wouldn't want to do it, not with your prowess at baseball. My teammates are all nice to each other and we have a lot of fun. However, they do have the tendency to talk about the same person constantly. It gets slightly old, but this time, I could understand why they are enthralled by this person."

"Me?" Matt asked, hopefully.

"Shut up, Matthew," Sheena said. Turning back to Michael, she added, "My teammates are all dying to meet you, by the way. But all of them are going to be quite upset when I tell them that I met you first!"

There was a humor glint in her eyes.

Matt was now turning red. He looked annoyed and Michael guessed that he wanted the gymnastics girls to like him, not Michael. Michael suddenly felt uncomfortable. He was almost positive this girl only wanted to talk to him because he was good at baseball, not because she wanted to be his friend. He could take a hint; he picked up the fact that he had been the center of gossip within Sheena's team.

"Anyway . . ." Matt said, without any idea what he was going to say.

"You like the Yankees?" Michael asked Sheena, pointing at her sweatshirt. He was doing anything in his power to keep the conversation off of himself.

"Yeah," Sheena replied, smiling at him and resorting back to her soft voice. "They're a good team."

"Sheena," Matt replied conversationally. "The Yankees suck and there is no point in denying it."

"If any team, Matthew Harrington, is terrible, awful, horrendous, *or* unwatchable, it is definitely your New York Mets," Sheena replied, softly. "My sisters could beat them in their sleep and you know it. Tell him, Michael."

"They are pretty bad," Michael told Matt seriously.

Matt was now livid. "The Yankees can go . . ."

But what the Yankees could go do, Michael had the unfortunate opportunity to find out. He guessed that Matt would not have dared said what they could do in front of people he did not know, and his dad, because his words were quite atrocious.

"You know, Matthew Harrington," Sheena replied in a sweet, girlish voice. "It would be . . . ah . . . pleasant if you did not say those despicable words in front of me. I happen to know your father and I'm sure he would like to hear what you said about my favorite team."

"He wouldn't care!" Matt shouted. "He probably thinks the same!"

Michael secretly resorted back to his Ipod. Sheena, though, saw him and smiled sweetly. Michael realized that she probably guessed that he was extremely shy.

"Are your parents coming to watch you?" Sheena queried to Michael.

Michael took out the headphones from his ears, realizing he was being rude and standoffish. He decided to tell the truth.

"No, they aren't," he said, sighing.

"I feel bad for you," Sheena said, anxiously peering into his face. "Why wouldn't your parents support you?"

Michael looked at her, feeling uncomfortable and shy. He was starting to wish she would stop looking at him. It was making him feel awkward.

"My mother's always talking about me bringing in financial aid," Michael explained, not meeting Sheena's eyes but looking at the velvet carpet under his feet. "She's always says that '*we don't have enough paper in our wallets, coins in our pockets.*' I don't think my parents were willing to spend that much money to come out here. We really don't have much money, which is partly my fault. Baseball has really taken a financial toll on my parents. They told me that Dad has to go on a job trip, but he never had to, so I reckon they lied to me."

Sheena looked desperately sorry for Michael. Michael tried to look nonchalant, but he knew part of him felt slightly hurt for his parent's inability to care. He didn't want to give a sob story to this girl, but everything he told her was the truth.

Michael put his headphones back in his ears and selected a song.

"Where did you get that?" Matt queried. "Your parents must care about you if they bought you an Ipod!"

"That's because my parents didn't buy it," Michael said, trying not to sound bitter; instead, his voice came out low. "I did. I made money over the summer being a Day Camp Counselor."

"You had to work?" asked Matt, downright shocked as if an apocalypse was beginning to form.

Michael looked confused.

"What are you talking about?" Michael asked, laughing. "You never got paid?"

"We never had to work," Sheena replied, quietly, looking embarrassed and extremely guilty.

Michael took her hint. Matt and Sheena's parents were obviously so filthy rich that they didn't need the money. His mother disliked those people with a passion but he wasn't his mother. Matt and Sheena seemed to be ashamed of themselves because of their wealth so Michael felt a little sympathy for them.

Sheena pointed at Michael's headphones.

"Can I listen?"

Michael saw Sheena ask the question and he knew he could not refuse her.

"Of course," he said, handing her one end of the headphones.

"You're sweet," Sheena said, accepting the other end of the headphones.

Matt decided to take a trip to the bathroom while Michael and Sheena were listening through the Ipod. When he came back, Michael noticed that he took his Met cap off and his shiny head was visible. Quietly, Michael saw him place the cap on Sheena's head; she was too busy humming to Michael's song that she did not notice.

When the song was over, Michael and Sheena put the Ipod away and turned to look at Matt. Sheena screamed out loud that caused some people with their seatbelts off to jump out of their seats.

"Why are you bald?" Sheena cried.

"I am a diver," Matt replied. "I have to. I shaved everything off besides . . . a sensitive area . . ."

Michael completely understood what Matt meant by that and could understand why he refused to shave that area bald.

"Then where is your cap, Matthew?" Sheena asked, incredulously.

"I took it off," Matt replied, trying hard not to laugh.

Sheena now noticed that it was on her head. She looked horrified, as if wearing a Mets hat caused cancer.

"Your new favorite team!" Matt hollered, laughing.

Ripping the hat off, Sheena jumped on Matt and started to wrestle with him. Michael thought if he should separate him. No, he thought. Let them fight. Actually, he found it funny that a short girl like Sheena could equally match up with tall Matt Harrington.

After a minute of confused fighting, Sheena got up and left the row, never looking back. Matt, however, had to get the cap out of his mouth, which Sheena had shoved in there.

"Women!" Matt answered, once he removed it. "Where did she go?"

"No idea," Michael said, shrugging.

"She's been like that ever since I met her at the age of one," Matt replied, putting the cap back on his head. Then, he smiled mischievously. "I saw you checking her out the whole time. Do you *like* her, Mikey?"

"Oh, shut up," Michael replied, even though that what Matt said was true.

For the rest of the trip, it was pretty much silent, even when they ate some of their meals the steward provided. Michael was too busy in thought to talk to his new friend.

How did Matt know he liked Sheena? True, he could have guessed, but how was he able to tell? And, Michael thought, Sheena was not upset over the fight they had. In fact, he thought she enjoyed it. She was not upset. He was sure of it. He guessed that she just left to make Matt feel sympathy for her or to go brag to her friends that she met the actual Michael Durbin.

Michael felt rotten. He wanted Sheena to respect him for who he was as a person, not because he could throw a baseball.

The loudspeaker now crackled.

"Folks, we are now over Beijing and we will be landing shortly."

Michael woke up from his nap and looked out of the window. It was difficult to see the city from the clouds. But Michael did not care. He just sincerely hoped that whenever Beijing threw lemons at him, he would be able to make lemonade.

CHAPTER 5

BEIJING, CHINA

Michael heard the plane hit the runway with a thud and stop in a matter of ten seconds. He could not believe he was in Beijing. He was finally at his destiny stop. His goal he had worked for his whole life—he was finally here. Excitement bubbled up inside of him.

However, he was one of the few that seemed unfamiliar with their surroundings. Most of the kids and adults seemed like they were getting dropped off at school. It was nothing new to them. Michael figured their parents or friends worked for the Committee.

Michael made his way out of the plane. As he neared the front, he saw Sheena in her seat with two of her gymnastics friends. They all stared as he approached them, but Michael stopped just behind their seat.

"You three can go," he said, quietly, allowing them to exit the plane.

"Thank you, Michael Durbin," Sheena said, giving him a teasing smile as she passed. The other two girls patted him on the shoulder before following Sheena.

Michael made his way to the baggage claim where many athletes were milling about, waiting for their bags. Michael saw many people from all over the world scattered about, gibbering in fifteen different languages and looking excited.

Matt joined Michael at the baggage claim a minute later, where they waited for their bags.

"This is *unbelievable,*" Matt beamed as he collected his blue leather suitcase off the rack. "I can't believe I'm really here."

"Me neither," Michael admitted.

"Do you know where Sheena is?" Matt queried.

Michael almost forgot about her. He had no idea where she went, and he told Matt so.

"Then where is she?" Matt asked out loud.

They finally were able to collect their bags and then were forced into a long line of Olympic athletes from all over the world. They all seemed to have arrived on the same day and time.

"Damn!" Matt exclaimed. "We're never going to leave this airport."

"We have to wait three hours just so we can get checked by security," Michael groaned, pointing to a waiting sign.

"This is absolutely great," Matt grumbled. "Why did they have to come at the same time? My dad told me the Olympics were a bit disorganized this year but I didn't expect this!"

Michael, too, was pondering the same question. He did not ponder it for long as he turned to see a short girl staring at him from ten yards away. The girl immediately turned to the front again as if she did not want to see him notice she was looking at him.

Matt saw the girl, too, and said, "Why is that girl staring at you?"

"Obviously because I'm a sexy beast," Michael whispered. He was no longer timid with Matt at all. Sheena was another story.

Matt snorted as though he doubted it.

Then, he turned to where the girl was standing and saw the whole woman's gymnastics team, including Sheena.

"Michael, what . . . ?"

"Shut up, Matt, listen!"

Matt understood what Michael was trying to eavesdrop on and fell silent. Though he was not particularly proud of it, Michael seemed to have good eavesdropping techniques and tendencies, which enabled him to overhear Sheena and her friends. The girls seemed to be talking about him. All of them were annoying her with questions.

"You talked to Michael? How is he like?" the short girl asked Sheena.

"He was pretty hot," one girl commented. "I saw him in *Rising Stars*."

Michael felt hot around the collar all of the sudden. He held his breath, waiting for Sheena's reply. Matt seemed to be interested as well, and closely listened.

"He's really sweet," Sheena replied, sincerely, and Michael let out a sigh of relief. "I saw him talking to Matthew Harrington."

"I heard of Matt but never spoken to him. What is he like?"

Now it was Matt's turn to be nervous. The two boys waited for Sheena's reply. Matt seemed to know that Sheena was not going to describe him as sweet.

"I've known him for a while. He is very strange," Sheena answered, nodding seriously. "I've known him my whole life, but that does not mean I think he's nice and normal."

Michael instantly understood what Sheena was doing. Sheena was lying just to get back on Matt for his joke. He wondered whether he should tell Matt. However, the look on Matt's face made Michael smile so he decided against it.

"He's a Mets fan," a black-haired girl said, serenely. "Mets fans are not really nice."

Matt turned to Michael and mouthed a disgusting swearword in disbelief. Michael had to fight himself from laughing. Matt was wearing an expression as though a teacher took five points off his test for no reason.

"He's very ugly too," Sheena added, trying not to laugh, but her eyes were twinkling with brutal amusement. "He vaguely resembles a pizza."

The girls laughed and Michael turned to Matt. He looked at Michael, alarmed. He seemed to think this was going a bit far and looked angry.

"Do I look like a pizza to you?" he questioned Michael, pointing at his face.

"No, you look wonderful," Michael answered back vaguely, still listening to their conversation.

"How about Michael?"

Michael and Matt had to lean in to hear Sheena's answer. "He's a good guy. I definitely can get along with him. I want to be his friend. You see, I found out that no one is coming to support him throughout the Olympics. He sounded lonely. I feel so sorry for him."

"Aw, poor boy," all the girls said. Matt stuck a finger in his mouth as his response to those words.

Michael felt relieved but he kept his face normal. The girls moved up to get their bags checked but Michael caught Sheena's eye and she grinned at him. They both were thinking the same thing: Matt had gotten fooled badly by Sheena's prank.

After another two hours, Michael and Matt got their bags checked and they left to find that all the American athletes were gathered just outside the airport door in which Michael got the first glimpse of China. Many Chinese citizens glared at them as they passed, but Michael assumed it was because they were blocking the whole sidewalk.

He almost gagged as soon as he walked out on the pavement. The polluted air was enough to kill him. Isaac did have a point. Michael knew that Beijing was one of the dirtiest cities in the world but he was not expecting this. He wondered if he would able to survive his few weeks here without going back to America with his lungs shriveled and black.

"Team USA, please follow me!" a big, obese man commanded. "I will lead us to our hotel! Don't stray off; if you get lost, it's no longer my problem! This is one city you do not want to wander by yourself in! Stay together now and follow me! Hey, Ken with the Cookie Monster hat . . . stop pretending to pee on the streets and follow the group!"

"That's Mr. Isol," Matt whispered to Michael. "He is a coach on the baseball team."

"I know," Michael answered. Then he added, "I didn't expect this for the Olympics at all."

"It's disorganized," Matt said as they started to walk along the road. "You can thank the Chinese for that."

The one thousand or so people started to make their way through the cobbled streets of China. Michael and Matt saw Sheena by herself. She was looking at her fellow teammates, whom were all gossiping about Michael still ("He's an attractive boy," one girl replied). Maybe it was just Michael, but he thought he saw a surge of anger and worry flare up on Sheena's face, but maybe he imagined it. It was possible that her face was screwed up in disgust as they were passing a landfill at the time.

Jostling the crowd slightly, Michael and Matt were able to make their way through the crowd to get to Sheena so they could talk to her.

"Sheena," Matt said, tapping her on the shoulder.

She turned around, looking haughty. People behind them were forced to walk around them, looking displeased.

"Hi, Michael," Sheena said, looking bitter. She ignored Matt and the three of them began walking again.

"Hi," Michael said, trying not to laugh.

Looking at Matt's hurt face, Sheena burst out laughing and so did Michael. Matt looked at both of them, nonplussed, with no idea what just happened.

"What is so funny?"

Michael finally stopped laughing. "Matt, she was getting you back on your Mets cap joke."

"I don't believe it," Matt whispered. "If you knew, why didn't you tell me?"

"I had my suspicions, but I didn't tell you because I was not sure," Michael replied, quite honestly, which made Sheena giggle more.

Matt then muttered something very weird, which sounded horribly like, "Kiss up."

Matt was annoyed that he fell for the prank. He looked surly the rest of the way to the hotel and he started to chunter under his breath as Sheena and Michael broke into conversation about Beijing. Michael was fascinated by everything Sheena told him and was astonished when she told him that she took her two sisters for a bike ride around Beijing before. After she talked about that, the conversation switched gears to the hotel.

"My dad told me that our hotel is Blossom Suites," Sheena replied. "It is very nice. He had to stay there once for work."

"That's good," Michael said, conversationally. "I'm looking forward to it."

Matt opened his mouth, perhaps to comment on the hotel, but he elapsed in a coughing fit. Michael reached over and slapped him on the back.

The Americans marched through the crowded and packed streets of China. The adults were making sure everyone was following them and pointed out several buildings to them occasionally ("That's the Wong Bookstore," Mr. Isol said, gruffly. "It sells a bunch of stupid books"). Everyone was cheerfully talking to one another as if they were a humongous tourist group instead of a team.

Then they waited at a bus terminal so that the buses could take them to the hotel. In all, more than six buses had to come to fit the American athletes in them. It was very uncomfortable on the bus since the coaches tried to fit in as many people as possible on each bus. People were standing awkwardly close to one another and some people had to sit on other's laps, causing discomfort to other people.

"The rest of the Americans must already be at the hotel," Sheena said, thoughtfully, as they took their seats.

"Thank God for that," Matt said as one fat athlete brushed against him in order to claim the two remaining seats for himself.

"Why are we so disorganized this year?" Michael queried to Matt and Sheena on the bus. "Things aren't usually this chaotic, right?"

"I know," Sheena sighed. "My dad told me about it."

"Do you really think it was the Chinese Committee that screwed up?" Michael asked them. "It could be just a certain person or two."

By his words, he meant the Ying-Yang brothers. However, Sheena did not seem to catch that.

"Maybe," Sheena replied, thoughtfully. "You should ask my dad that question. He might know."

"Wait a minute." Matt snapped his fingers. "The Olympics was never this disorganized as far as I can remember. I know my dad told me that two people known as the Ying-Yang brothers became the two top dogs of the Chinese Committee. Do you think it was because of them or because of the Chinese?"

"They are on the Chinese Committee now," Michael agreed. "You could be right."

"In the newspaper, it said that the two of them were denied positions on our Committee," Sheena said, knowledgeably. "Then, they went to the Chinese Committee, and were not denied a second time. My dad told me that the brothers were in charge of letting us know updates and information, but it looks like that they decided to throw us off by sending it last minute."

The rest of the bus trip was in silence, and by the time they got the hotel, all the team members were so sleepy that they could barely stay awake, even though they could have slept for sixteen hours on the plane. In fact, Michael, Matt, and Sheena were the very few that were totally awake. Their conversation on the bus prevented them from getting drowsy. Michael, however, felt a little envious that Matt and Sheena were kept updated with everything, and that he had been relying on a small magazine for information.

However, Michael was confused about something. If the brothers really wanted revenge on them, why didn't they completely ignore the United States? Why did they send the information at all?

Still in confused thoughts, he barely noticed that the bus stopped right outside Blossom Suites. The many adults led the athletes into the hotel where they checked in. Then, one adult turned to face all the other athletes.

"Listen up," he commanded. "When I call your sport, please come forward so I can give you your hotel room. You will be sharing a room with two or three people in it, depending. After that, all baseball players must return here to have a conference. Everyone else may go to bed. The Opening Ceremonies are tomorrow, and I expect you all to be punctual. No excuses!"

A conference? Michael thought. He wondered how it would go. But he hurried forward to see where he was sleeping every night.

Before he could take two strides, Matt tapped him on the shoulder and said, "Don't bother. You're with me, in room twenty-five, it's on the second floor, come on . . ."

Hoisting his gear on his shoulder and glad that he was with Matt, Michael followed Matt to a huge vast elevator that could fit about forty people inside it.

"Get in," Matt said, and they climbed in only to be followed by forty other people.

The doors of the elevator snapped shut and there was a sudden movement as the elevator shot like a cork to the next floor.

"What the hell . . . ?"

About half of the people fell to the floor causing a disturbance to Michael. In fact, after the elevator stopped on the second floor, Michael and Matt were the only two standing.

Michael and Matt walked around the stirring crowd and made their way through the hallway and made a left turn and found their room. They stood foolishly by the door.

"How do we get in?" Michael queried Matt.

"Oh, I forgot," said Matt vaguely. He pulled out what looked like a credit card and he slid it through a given slot on the door and the door popped open.

The room was spectacular: it had two good-sized queen beds, a flat-screen television, a sliding door with a balcony, and a bathroom complete with a toilet, bath, and sinks.

"This room is amazing, man," Matt exclaimed, awestruck.

"I know," Michael whispered. Then he traveled to the sliding doors towards the balcony. "The view is spectacular from here."

Matt wasn't listening. He traveled into the bathroom, where he let out a shriek that was feminine.

Michael quickly ran straight to the bathroom, thinking that Matt saw a snake in the toilet.

"Matt, what is up with you?"

"Michael, look . . ."

Michael's eyes traveled to where Matt was pointing. He was now looking at the toilet, which was so huge two humans could do their business in it at the same time—not that no one would try it, however. Michael couldn't see what was so remarkable about it. By the way Matt's eyes were wide with excitement he figured David Wright must have been standing in their bathroom.

"So?" Michael asked, bewildered. "Who cares about a huge throne for you to sit on?"

Matt said jovially, "I can't believe this . . ."

Michael almost thought Matt was on drugs because he looked so happy that nothing better could have happened to him than catch his eyes on a huge toilet. After shaking his head exasperatedly, Michael realized he had to attend the conference and leave Matt to stare at his toilet.

"I'll see you later," he said to Matt, who was staring at the pot as if it was the Mona Lisa or a cheerleader.

Michael ran down the stairs this time and saw a group of people at the bottom, milling about and talking to each other. Michael noticed that one boy was off to the side, not looking socially inclined. He looked to be only two inches taller than Michael and he had blond hair, but most of it was covered by green streaks in his hair, as though he plastered seaweed on his head. Thinking that he could get along with this kid, Michael walked up to him.

"Is this for baseball?" Michael asked the boy, who noticed him, and nodded.

"Yep," he answered. Blond specks streaked his green hair. Michael thought it was meant to attract girls, but he personally felt that girls would be shooed away by the hair. It was a little creepy. "I don't know what they're discussing about, though."

"Is this your first Olympics?" Michael asked the youth.

The boy nodded. "I'm fifteen. I know who you are. You're that Durbin kid, who's such a prodigy, is that right?"

"Yes," Michael answered.

"I'm Daniel Shields, but I am usually known to society as Nitro," the boy replied, pompously, shaking his hand. "My green hair is my trademark."

Nitro was so overly formal that Michael felt he was being introduced to some great ruler of a civilized city-state, rather than a socially awkward fifteen-year-old kid.

"Why do you dye it?"

"Just for individuality," Nitro answered, pompously. "Anyway, I couldn't quite believe it when I obtained my letter. I felt so *jubilant* to be honest with you. My brother succeeded in his endeavor by being chosen for the team, but he made it the last time around, when this event was, you know, organized. By the way, if I had to make a guess about what they're discussing about in that room, it's probably about your status on the team and your rightful position."

"Position?"

"Well, yeah," Nitro replied, confused at the reaction. "They are seeing us separately. They first were going to talk to all of us at once in the cafeteria, but they decided on meeting with everyone individually to get a sense as to what kind of a person everyone is. So therefore, they are talking to us in the lounge."

Just then, a voice boomed out.

"Michael Durbin!"

"Go on," Nitro said, encouragingly. "Hope it goes well for you."

Michael entered the room, feeling squeamish and wondering what his coaches were going to talk to him about.

CHAPTER 6

MR. HARRINGTON'S STORY

Michael might have been extremely nervous, but he was impressed by the appearance of the lounge. It was carpeted and the furniture was arranged nicely. At the center of the room stood a rectangular table where four men sat. There was one with a Mets cap on, who was Mr. Harrington; one that looked like a football player he was so vast, who was Mr. Isol; Mr. Oberfels had dark hair like a gorilla; and last, a blond-haired adult, who was Mr. Smith.

"Hello, Michael. Excited for the Olympics?" Mr. Harrington asked.

"Yes," Michael replied, trying to sound confident.

"Please take a seat. There is no need to be nervous."

Michael sat down and made eye contact with the coaches to show them that he wasn't some nervous, immature kid. He politely waited for Mr. Harrington to start talking.

"Now, Michael, I'm sure you know who we are, based on your appearance at tryouts that day. However, I still want to introduce the other three coaches to you."

Mr. Harrington pointed to the vast man.

"This is Mr. Isol, the pitching coach."

Mr. Isol grabbed Michael's whole arm and shook it with his enormous hand.

Then, Mr. Harrington pointed to the dark-haired man.

"This is Mr. Oberfels, the third base and bench coach, and this is Mr. Smith, the first base coach."

They all shook hands and then Michael faced them again.

Coach Harrington spoke, "Now, Michael, straight to business. We are discussing your position. At the end of the meeting we will give you your uniform. Any questions so far?"

Michael shook his head. Of course there would be no questions. Though he was barely a minute into the meeting, Michael had the feeling that Mr. Harrington wanted to get it done as quickly as possible.

Then Mr. Isol spoke, "You have played in many state championships and made an appearance in the Little League World Series, is that correct?"

"Yeah," Michael replied, nonchalantly.

"Well, I've got something to tell you, kid," Mr. Isol replied. "THOSE VICTORIES MEAN NOTHING!"

"Isol, calm down," Mr. Oberfels said, warningly. "He's only fourteen." Then he looked at Michael. "What Lyle means is that all of that is nothing compared to the Olympics. In Beijing, the competition is going to be a lot higher."

"But they still can help you," Mr. Harrington added, gently. "Those victories may give you the confidence needed to survive in Beijing. In the Olympics, you're going to realize quickly that the winners in this Olympics are the ones with confidence. Also, you're going to find out quickly that the Olympics are more than just winning medals. Now, we are going to discuss your position. Right from the start, I feel you should be in our starting rotation. You did well at the tryouts."

"I disagree," Mr. Smith said, almost immediately.

Mr. Harrington raised his eyebrows. "How come, Mr. Smith?" he queried, politely.

"He is too young, Harrington. He's fourteen. He is not ready for that level yet. Placing Durbin in such a high position would not help him succeed. I feel he should work behind a starter, an experienced starter, and be in the bullpen. He should be used as a middle reliever who could pitch three innings or so if one of our starters can't throw a strike."

"However, Mr. Smith, that will not give him the experience that I feel he needs," Mr. Harrington replied, smoothly. "That will halt him from going any farther in his baseball career, one that has a plethora of potential. I say give him the chance while he is young and healthy, because he can't do it when he is older. It won't have that same kind of an impact. Anyway, why does age matter in any assessments?"

Mr. Smith looked as though as if he wanted to argue, but Mr. Oberfels intervened swiftly.

"May I speak, Matt?" Mr. Oberfels replied.

"You may, Glenn," Mr. Harrington said, nodding courteously.

"I really suggest that Michael should be in the starting rotation. However, might I suggest that he be a starter late in the rotation? He could learn from the other starters by watching what they do first. I feel confident that he has the talent to be a starter, but for his first Olympics, it may be wise not to immediately put him on the spotlight as our go-to pitcher."

"He's going to be in the effing spotlight, anyway, it's the Olympics for crying out loud, Glenn," Mr. Isol grumbled, but Mr. Harrington ignored his comments.

"No, he'll be second behind James," Mr. Harrington said in a finality tone. Then, he explained to Michael, "I want you to learn from him, Michael. He's a great guy, and he has an extraordinary understanding of the game."

Michael nodded. That was fine with him, but obviously, Mr. Smith felt differently. Mr. Smith looked as though he would have dearly loved to argue, but he seemed to know it would be fruitless.

"Now, let's move on," Mr. Harrington replied, briskly. "We want to tell you some information that you need to know. First of all, I realize this is your first time and you must be nervous."

"I am a little bit," Michael confessed, honestly. "The media attention is a different experience for me. But I am more desperate to prove that I belong here, even though I'm only fourteen."

Mr. Smith gave him a dirty look, one that Michael often admired in Mrs. Cogburn.

"I never said a kid your age couldn't do it," he lied brutally. "I just felt that they shouldn't. You know what some of them are like? They usually suck, and have no talent, not to mention they're hardly ever trustworthy. They just cast themselves to be a burden on the team while gloating over their *few* glorious victories!"

Michael thought what he was saying was strictly unfair. It was if Mr. Smith was saying this to his face, even though he did not address him by name. Michael turned to the other coaches, wondering how they were going to handle the situation.

Mr. Harrington still stayed peacefully calm, even though he obviously was thinking along the same lines as Michael.

"Mr. Smith, you are speaking like a Ying-Yang brother. They thought that fourteen-year-old athletes were nothing but hindrances too. Is this what you mean? I am the youngest manager ever. Are you saying I am a hindrance to this team's success?"

Michael felt as though Mr. Harrington had won the argument, looking at Mr. Smith's blank expression. He was such an assertive person, he thought admiringly.

Mr. Smith looked as if he swallowed a lemon. "I . . . I didn't . . . sorry . . ."

"We'll say no more about it," Mr. Isol interjected, which reminded the two that Michael was still in the room.

"Anyway, Michael, we will place you in the starting lineup," Mr. Harrington replied, glancing over at the other three. "We think that is where you belong. We've seen you pitch numerous times and you do have a knack of being a great presence in the locker room. I like high-character athletes on my team and based on what your other coaches have told me, you are one of those players."

Michael nodded, pleased by Mr. Harrington's praise. He was already off to a good start.

"Now, the uniform," Mr. Oberfels replied with the air of one relieved at the prospect of reaching the conclusion of some difficult examination. "Michael, are you alright with the number twenty-three?"

Michael nodded. He could care the least what his number was.

Mr. Isol handed Michael his uniform, which was in a bag.

"Thanks."

"And now, Michael, our conference has ended. Do you have any questions?"

Michael thought hard. Did he have any? He could admit to himself that he wanted to know more about the Ying-Yang brothers, but wondered if this was the right time to talk about it. Michael weighed his options: he could remain silent and go up to bed (which was an intriguing option, as he was extremely exhausted) or learn the truth from a reliable source. Feeling like he needed to know the truth, Michael decided on the second option.

"Coach, my friend found an article about the Olympics. Out of curiosity, who are the Ying-Yang brothers? I know I saw them at tryouts, but my friend Sara read an article about them, and she said that they were rejected for the Committee and joined the Chinese Committee. I want to make sure that her information is genuine as I am kind of curious as to how the whole situation played out."

Mr. Harrington eyed Michael curiously. Then he sighed. "You are a curious child, Michael Durbin. This is really official business. I'm strictly not allowed to tell you anything. Kids aren't supposed to know, but the media doesn't seem to give a damn about the Committee's wishes as it is. However, I guess it won't hurt to tell you the basic picture. I will ask you not to mention it to anyone else. Please keep this to yourself, all right?"

"That's fine," Michael replied, but realized that he would break Mr. Harrington's request. He had planned to call Sara and Tomas and tell them everything he found out.

"Okay, so let's see . . ." Mr. Harrington said, lost in his train of thought. The other three adults left the room noticing the end of the meeting. "Yes, that's right. Michael, the first thing you should know about the brothers is that they were born in China to an American woman and a Chinese male. They have dual citizenship in both countries. Then, they moved to the United States when they were young and were educated in America. They had a sort of affection to the Olympics and they both had an ambition to become a part of the Committee."

"When they were young?"

"That's right," Mr. Harrington said, smiling. "The Ying-Yang brothers were well-rounded, and everyone loved them. Most people thought they would get on the baseball Olympic team. They had a tremendous amount of talent, but I really did not think they were anything impressive. They were good—there was no doubt about that—but everyone else who tried out was slightly better. They did try when they were your age, but were unsuccessful. I actually refused to let them in."

"No way!" Michael replied.

"Yes, it's true. But Mr. Isol, Mr. Oberfels, and I did not think they were capable of being on our team. However, we did encourage them to try again next time."

"What about Mr. Smith?"

"He joined our team last year. This is his first Olympics. Now when they got rejected, they decided not to try for it again. They started a grudge against the three of us (Michael knew he meant Mr. Isol, Mr. Oberfels, and himself) and about young kids. But they didn't do anything wrong . . . well, yet, anyway. Then, many years after they were rejected, they put forth to be put on the Committee. At that time, the President of the United States Olympic Committee said he would consider them. However, the old president died in a car accident before he could make up his mind. So, Will Goodwin took his place."

"You mean Sheena's dad is the President of the Olympic Committee?" Michael asked, shocked. Sheena didn't tell him that, but maybe it wasn't so surprising; after all, he only met her hours ago.

"That's right. The first week that Mr. Goodwin took office the Ying-Yang brothers organized a meeting with him. They wanted him to put them on the Committee. Well, Mr. Goodwin did not tell me very much on how the meeting went. It was odd, because I've known him for a long time, and he usually tells me everything. Anyway, it must have not gone well, because the Ying-Yang brothers were not chosen for the Committee. The reasons why are still unknown to everyone but Mr. Goodwin. Then, they quickly joined the Chinese Committee as your friend Sara said, and Mr. Smith joined our team shortly afterward."

"How come Mr. Smith seemed to think I was incapable of being a starter?"

Mr. Harrington shrugged. "Don't take it personally. That's just his opinion on the matter."

Michael was trying to comprehend everything Mr. Harrington told him. "The Ying-Yang brothers didn't like young kids because they did not make it when they were young?"

Mr. Harrington smiled. "I think that might play a role. But we can never be sure. However, it is one of the more likely reasons."

"Unworthy just because they did not make it and I did?"

Mr. Harrington nodded. "Any more questions?"

"Yes. I overheard them at tryouts talking about a scroll. What is the scroll about?"

"Alas, I am sorry but I don't know," Mr. Harrington replied, solemnly. Michael had a feeling Mr. Harrington wasn't being truthful. "But I have a theory. My theory is that the scroll is extremely important or else they wouldn't be trying to find it. Why it is important, I do not know."

Michael nodded. "Do you think your theory is right?"

Mr. Harrington laughed. "Any guess is as good as mine. You sound like Mr. Goodwin. Oh, and speaking of him, ask him about the scroll. He might know about it more. You met his daughter Sheena, right?"

"Yes," Michael answered, wondering how Mr. Harrington seemed to guess that he quickly befriended her.

"That's good," Mr. Harrington said, vaguely. "It is time to go, Michael. I'll tell you our baseball schedule tomorrow, but you need rest. A hard practice awaits you tomorrow."

Michael nodded and turned to leave. Just as he was close enough to open the door . . .

"Michael!"

Michael turned around to see Mr. Harrington's face lighted up, and his eyes were twinkling with amusement.

"If I were you, I would keep my eye on that Goodwin girl."

CHAPTER 7

FIREWORKS FACTORY

Michael found it hard to find his way to his hotel room that night. He was still finding it hard to digest everything Mr. Harrington told him. He had his questions answered, and he decided he would call Sara tomorrow and explain everything to her.

He located his hotel room and knocked on the door. It wasn't Matt, but Sheena who answered it.

"Oh, there you are Michael, come on in," Sheena said, smiling at him. Michael walked into the room.

They both turned to Matt, who was in concentration and playing a video game. He looked as though he was in the middle of relieving himself of the burden of a soccer ball-sized egg. Michael fought to keep his face straight.

"What game are you playing?" Michael queried.

"*Guitar Hero III*," Matt answered. He stopped the game to address Michael. "I'm having a competition with Sheena to see who could get the highest percentage of notes hit on Expert level. Sheena got ninety-four."

"Ninety-four!" Michael exclaimed, shocked, turning to Sheena. "I can't even get that on Easy level!"

Sheena laughed. Matt resumed the game and started playing it. Michael wanted to tell them about everything Mr. Harrington said, but he reckoned they already knew and even if they didn't, he couldn't bring himself to do it—not when they were so happy playing video games.

"I'll be outside," Michael told both of them and he traveled to the balcony. He wanted some fresh air.

He found two seats on the balcony and took a seat in the one farthest to the door. He wanted to view the sight of the whole city and think over what Mr. Harrington said. He wanted to tell his friends, but he was not sure whether he should or not.

It was weird how Mr. Smith came the day after the brothers left, Michael thought. Usually, it'll take weeks to find one. How did he catch a person that quickly?

Mr. Isol looked shifty, too. He looked eager to leave the room when the discussion was being held and the other two followed suit. Could all three of them be working together and trick Mr. Harrington? They all disagreed with him on the same decisions.

But Mr. Oberfels had no grudge against young people, Michael argued with himself. Mr. Isol had no comment and Mr. Smith thought I should be in the bullpen. Aren't they possibly working for the Ying-Yang brothers? The brothers could have placed them there to see what Mr. Harrington was doing.

But that X's out Mr. Isol. He was there for a long time, but Mr. Smith on the other hand . . .

"Michael?"

The soft voice came to his ears, which made him disrupt his thinking. Michael looked up and saw Sheena, looking at him with concern. She sat down in the other chair carefully and turned her body to face Michael.

"What's up?" Michael asked, sitting up straighter in his chair.

"Nothing much," Sheena said, fixing her ponytail. "It's hard to believe that we're really here. I'm nervous, too. I hope I could have the day off tomorrow. I'm not sure I'm ready to compete, Michael."

She didn't sound upset, but she sounded like Sara when she was voicing her concerns about Michael under the maple tree that day before he flew out to Beijing.

"I'm sure you're more than ready to compete," Michael said, reassuringly.

"I hope so," Sheena replied, fervently, playing with her hair.

"And the Opening Ceremonies are tomorrow," Michael added as a thought just occurred to him. "Wouldn't you just go to that and get a day off?"

Sheena shook her head. "I don't think my trainer and coaches would give me a day off."

Michael then made a quick decision. "Sheena, I had a conference with my coaches, and . . ."

He supplied her with his suspicions and conversation with Mr. Harrington. It was okay to tell her; he was sure her father told her everything as it was. When he finished, he looked up at Sheena, waiting for her response.

"I don't know what to think of it," Sheena said, frowning.

"There definitely is something unusual about that, though. I'll bring you to my dad tomorrow, and you can talk to him. I can't promise he'll tell you everything, but he might be willing to tell you one thing or another."

"I hope so—" Michael began, but Sheena interjected.

"Listen, talk to my dad tomorrow and he may fill in the missing pieces," repeated Sheena, slightly sharply, which took Michael by surprise. He had not expected that tone to come from Sheena.

Michael's heart sank like a stone; he'd been stupid not to expect that as a response. Then, without warning, a blast of spectacular fireworks started to burst, showering the sky with beautiful red and gold plumage.

"The Fireworks Factory always does that," Sheena replied, brightly. "They're so beautiful."

"Yeah."

The two friends leaned on the balcony to watch the fireworks. Michael looked at his friend. She was watching the fireworks with interest. A content smile slowly formed on her face as a loud purple firework made its appearance with a loud bang.

He stared back at the fireworks and the two of them just watched the fireworks and said nothing to each other. It was remarkable how the spectacular display of the colorful fireworks captured their eyes instead of each other. Michael had to admit that he would have been content just staying here for the whole night, watching the fireworks with Sheena. He had to admit that it had been a good day. He had met a few people that he liked and was finally supplied with some information.

"Hey! Sheena! Michael! Come and see this!"

Michael and Sheena stood up abruptly.

"What's he shouting about, Michael?" she queried.

Michael shrugged.

"I don't know," he responded. "Let's find out."

Sheena and Michael instantly dashed back into the hotel room to find Matt doing a victory dance—he just got ninety-six percent of the notes hit.

"Ha!" Matt cried, pointing at her as if announcing her under arrest. "I beat you, Sheena!"

"So?" Sheena asked, sitting down on the bed. "I don't care. It's only a video game. If this is the biggest triumph in your life, Matthew, then my pity for you is exponential."

Matt was too busy doing his victory chant that he accidentally hit the PlayStation 2 and it shut off automatically.

"Damn it!" he swore and hastily cleaned it up.

"You should not use profanity," Sheena said, softly.

Matt then gave Sheena a very violent and obscene gesture that Michael was sure he wouldn't do it to anyone but her. Sheena just laughed and so did Michael. Matt even joined in the laughter.

After they were able to calm down, Michael decided to tell Matt about the conversation he had with Mr. Harrington and his suspicions. Matt thought it made sense.

"It does! I think you should blame Smith. It all fits!"

"No it doesn't. It has some holes in it. And we don't have much proof to offer."

Michael then spoke, "I'll talk to Sheena's dad tomorrow and see if he could answer the questions."

"You never met Mr. Goodwin. How can you?" Matt questioned.

"I'll be okay," Michael replied. "I'll try not to sound terribly nosy."

"Yeah, but you aren't going to go to his door and say 'Hello, Mr. Goodwin, sir, my name is Michael Durbin. I was wondering if you could tell me about the Ying-Yang brother's scroll,'" Matt replied seriously. "Yeah, that's a great start to a conversation."

Sheena seemed to be tired of the conversation because she said, "Look, both of you. Listen to me. You are jumping to conclusions. You are trying to frame someone for no reason. Anyway, we have no proof. No . . . anything. Michael will talk to my dad tomorrow and see if he could fill in the holes to Mr. Harrington's story. My dad is the president; he will be able to tell you more about it."

She glared at both of them as if they were being stupid on purpose.

"But since your dad is the president," replied Matt with a cautious air, "he may not want us to know. We kind of are nosing in on information that we don't need to know about."

"Well then he doesn't," Sheena said, firmly. "The last thing I expected today was to meet the baseball pitcher Michael Durbin and literally hours later be dragged into this scroll business."

"I'm just curious, Sheena," Michael said, shrugging. "Anyway, my friend back home also wants to know to and she would like the information."

Sheena raised her eyebrows.

"Is she hot?" Matt queried, suddenly interested. "Is she blond?"

Sheena scowled at him.

Sheena decided to leave and get to her room so she bade the two boys good-bye and left the room.

"We should go to bed, too," Matt replied to Michael, and he agreed. They needed their rest for what would come next over the next few weeks.

Matt took the bed closer to the balcony and Michael the closest to the door. Then they climbed into their beds and Michael turned out the light.

Matt fell fast asleep as soon as the light was turned off, but Michael sat up in his bed. He wasn't at all tired. He wished he could talk more about the conversation. He had to admit he was being a bit obsessed with it, but it seemed so important to him to know as much as he could about the two brothers. He felt as if it was necessary to know everything.

He watched Matt sleeping in the other bed. He seemed interested in Sara. He wondered whether Matt had befriended any other girls besides Sheena. But he really didn't want to think about that.

All in all, Michael was pleased that he learned about the two most important figures in the Olympics that were not athletes. He hoped that he would find out more, and uncover the secret that hung over his country. He would have all of his questions answered, and he would be meeting the President of the United States Olympic Committee.

Like many of the Olympians, they experience two emotions: triumph and disappointment. There are favorites and underdogs. From a sport view, Michael was an underdog not only due to his inexperience at the Games. He was an underdog to be successful in getting comfortable with his new friends.

However, as Michael turned over on his side, his mind traveled to the thought of the growing fear that Sheena might not appreciate him for who he was as a person.

CHAPTER 8

THE GOODWIN CHINA HOUSE

There were two shadows in the distance. They looked quite eerie. Not only because it was dark out but because they were identical. They had the same black hair, fair skin, and olive-colored skin.

They walked down a narrow alleyway in the middle of the crowded city to find a huge building that resembled a bird's nest. The two men were supposed to meet someone there but there was one slight flaw: the door was padlocked.

"No problem," one of the men replied and he took out an ordinary hairpin, and picked the lock easily.

"That's one great thing about China," one man remarked. "The security is inconsistent."

The two men made their way through the circular stadium to find a tall guy in the middle, apparently waiting for them. The two men walked up to him.

"There you are, both of you," the man said, greeting them in a professional voice.

There was something peculiar about that voice . . .

"Moron, the boy that overheard us is here at the Olympics. He made Harrington's baseball team."

"No excuses. That is a horrible mistake made by my old friend. We should deal with him later, but first the kid."

"That kid is trying to find out everything about us," the men both replied. "He'll know everything."

"No, he won't. I will kill him before he does, before the Closing Ceremonies. He does not know about me. I promise you both that."

"But he'll find out about you too."

"No he won't. Not if I can help it. I'll take care of the nosy kid."

Then, the men departed and left in two different directions, leaving no trace that they were there.

Michael woke up to the sound of rushing water—Matt was taking a shower. He got up and waited for Matt to come out of the shower.

"Go ahead," Matt said, fully dressed, walking out of the bathroom.

Once Michael had taken a shower, the two boys walked down to the main lobby. There, they saw Nitro, who apparently knew Matt, because he greeted both of them.

"The chow hall is past those doors," Nitro replied, pointing behind them. "By the way Michael, Coach is passing out the schedules."

When he left, the two boys entered the room and saw Sheena sitting at an empty table. Michael and Matt took seats on both sides.

"Good morning," she replied, cheerfully.

"Same to you," the boys replied in unison.

Sheena then took two packets of paper out from underneath her chair and handed them to Michael and Matt. "That is the schedule of all the United States teams. Every single one so you know when you have to go. It also gives you an opportunity to see any other sporting contest when you're off. My dad wanted to supply all American athletes with this."

Michael looked and saw that he was expected at one in the afternoon until five in the evening. Michael suspected that the practice was to determine close calls for positions, or just to get used to the playing field.

"This sucks!" Matt cried out loud, looking at his schedule. "I'm expected to come to the pool at six tomorrow and have to be there today two times for five hours!"

Michael couldn't see how Matt would be able to use ten hours of diving. In Michael's opinion, Matt's trainer was a stick in the mud for forcing him to spend practically the whole day in a swimming pool.

"Well, Matt, that sounds like one friendly trainer," Michael said, sarcastically. "When does he plan on giving you a lunch break?"

Matt laughed, even Sheena grinned.

"I have some practices today," Sheena informed the two of them. "I'll see you two at lunch. Oh, and by the way, I told my parents about you two—well, they know Matt—and they invited you two over for dinner. That is when you can ask my dad about your questions."

"Okay," Michael replied, feeling elated. He was glad to have something to look forward to. "Anyway, when is your practice?"

"I have to be there at ten, but it starts at eleven. After I finish, I go to lunch and I have the rest of the day off."

"Good luck, Sheena," Matt replied, standing up. "I have to go now to meet my jackass for a trainer."

And he left without further ado, scowling.

Michael was looking forward to a conversation with Mr. Goodwin, but it made him feel nervous. He was going to talk about a serious topic with the President of the Olympic Committee who happened to be Sheena's father. He didn't want him to think he was nosy or interfering.

He abandoned the breakfast hall and set out with Sheena, who was heading to the gymnastics arena. He decided to accompany her and watch her perform, since there was nothing else to do. Sheena was quick to notice that, and was certainly surprised by Michael's decision.

"You should go and explore the complex," she advised him. "It's more exciting than watching me do flips and such."

They were walking to Sheena's gymnastics arena when she said this.

"What's there to look at?" Michael asked with the air of one expressing his boredom at a museum. "Anyway, I think I should support my friend, even if it is only a practice."

Sheena laughed. "Spoken like a true friend and a Goodwin, Michael Durbin. I've never met someone quite like you before."

Michael sincerely hoped that was a compliment, but even so, it made him uncomfortable. Michael decided to change the subject abruptly.

"They give you marks on how well you do your flips, right?" Michael asked, as though asking for a clarification.

"What? Oh. Oh yeah, they do. That's the only bad thing about gymnastics. They might judge you because of your appearance or what they want, you know their *gut instinct*. It's a bit stupid, really."

"Well, if their judging by appearance, you'll be sure to get full marks," Michael answered, slightly bemused.

Sheena turned to face him, which made Michael distinctly hot in the face. He knew what he just said was wrong, even though it was a compliment. He didn't mean to let his true opinion out. Michael looked at Sheena nervously, expecting her to shoo him away. However, to his immense surprise, Sheena laughed.

"You are just like Matt, are you?" she asked, laughing. "You are also desperate to impress and compliment a girl."

Even though she was laughing, Michael wanted to do nothing more than disintegrate into the ground. He didn't mean to say that, but his nerves and Mr. Harrington's words made him force his opinion out.

They made their way to the stadium where Michael bade her good-bye and traveled into the stands. There were many people there, all wearing their country's colors proudly and cheering loudly. He found a seat in the middle of the arena and sat down. No one was really near him.

He was occupied by looking at the billboard flashing advertisements (*Visit Wong Bookstore: The Best Books for the Best Price!)* until Matt came and took a seat right by him. He looked unhappy and furious.

"I skived off," he explained, seeing the look on Michael's face.

"Why did you? Won't you get in serious trouble?"

"Only if the trainer babbles to Mr. Goodwin," Matt replied scathingly. "Anyway, I could care in the least."

"What happens if he does?" Michael asked, curiously.

"Then I'm screwed. But it really does not matter," Matt said, airily.

Michael still didn't understand. "Why are you skipping training if you know you are going to be in major trouble?"

He said it in a tone of someone trying to inject his friend with common sense.

"My dad is on the Committee," Matt answered, "and all of his friends as well. I may not get in as much trouble."

"It doesn't sound like you want to be here."

"I do," Matt replied, defensively. "It's just that I hate the training that comes with it. It's annoying, and I have a bastard for a trainer. You'll be surprised how far connections with the top people can get you. I'm not that worried."

Michael focused his attention back to the stadium—it was about to start.

"I hope Sheena is done quickly with her practice," Matt said, surprising Michael. "I hate gymnastics, period, it's worse than my trainer, if you want my opinion, but I'm only here because Sheena is my friend and you decided to come."

"It looks like she is going first," Michael said, staring down at the arena.

It was indeed Sheena. She was wearing her gymnastics outfit, which was midnight blue with yellow stars on it. Michael had a sudden inspiration of the midnight sky.

"I don't mean to be mean or anything," Matt said, unexpectedly. "But I think the gymnastics outfits are kind of stupid. I mean, why can't they wear like shorts and a t-shirt instead?"

Michael privately agreed, but focused on the arena, where Sheena was about to do her routine. He was curious as to how good she really was.

There was a whistle and the crowd fell silent. It was only then that Sheena began to do her routine. Michael was thunderstruck to see how amazing Sheena was. He could definitely see why she was chosen for the team. She had a graceful move that awed Michael but he wasn't the only one. The crowd and Matt were gaping as well, which was saying something—it was obvious from when Michael first met Matt that he didn't think highly of the sport.

To conclude, Sheena did two flips and landed right back on the ground without stumbling. She grinned and waved at the crowd, smiling widely.

Someone in a neighboring country must have thought a nuclear explosion happened in the stadium—the crowd cheered as loud as they could muster, Matt and Michael included. The cheering only stopped when the people working for crowd control yelled into a huge megaphone and shouted, "Shut up!"

Michael nudged Matt once everyone quieted down. "Let's see if we can find Sheena," he whispered.

Matt frowned. "You mean . . . wait for her by the locker room?"

"I guess," Michael shrugged; he didn't decide where they should meet her. "I think they are allowed to leave after they're done."

Matt shifted uncomfortably in his seat. "Don't you think it's a little bit odd to wait by the locker room door for a girl?"

Michael looked at him with a flicker of amusement on his face. "What, are you still afraid that they think you resemble a pizza?"

Matt said nothing. It was evident that he did not appreciate that remark.

Michael laughed. "Come on, let's congratulate her."

So they two left their seats and wandered down to the locker room door. However, they stopped abruptly in front of a sign that said:

Gymnasts only!
DO NOT ENTER or else face the consequences!!!!

Matt bit his lip. "I forgot about that. Maybe we shouldn't, Michael. I don't like to think what the consequences will be if we wait by a girl's locker room."

Michael did not seem troubled by the sign. It only said that they could not go in. They were just waiting by it, so he could not find a problem with that. There was nothing illegal about waiting for a friend.

"We're not trespassing," Michael pointed out.

"It doesn't say trespassing on the sign!" Matt answered back, nervously. "It says we'll have to pay the consequences."

"*Wow,* I *wonder* what the consequences are," Michael replied, sarcastically.

Matt gave a shaky laugh.

In the end, they decided not to wait for Sheena outside the locker room door. Matt did have a point of how it would look extremely creepy but Michael gave in after thinking that Sheena's teammates adored him, and he preferred not to be put in an awkward situation by them. Also, he did not want to find out how Matt would feel if that happened.

Matt and Michael were sitting out side at a table when she came out of the stadium. They were conversing in low whispers about the Ying-Yang brothers. The only reason Michael had brought the subject up was because that was the only thing he could think of talking about, even though it was for the umpteenth time.

"My dad told me everything he told you," Matt whispered, "but Michael, did you ever think of what might be on the scroll?"

"Maybe a plan," Michael suggested. "It must be something dangerous and beneficial for the brothers or they wouldn't waste their time looking for it."

Matt opened his mouth to speak. He seemed to be on the verge of agreeing when there was a creak that came from the door.

Sheena came out with her whole gymnastics team and all of them were giggling. Michael could not stand giggling girls; he least expected Sheena to giggle.

"Why do girls have to be so mental?" Matt whispered in Michael's ear.

⋆ ⋆ ⋆

It was lunchtime, and Michael was eating lunch by himself. Matt had to go to diving ("My trainer is going to kill me," he said, sadly) and Sheena was nowhere to be found. He had about forty-five minutes until he had to go over to the stadium written on his schedule for baseball practice.

He and Matt did not think it was the best idea to talk to Sheena in front of her teammates ("Those other girls might get sensitive," Matt warned). In case Sheena saw them, the two decided to dive into a bush by them and escape on the other side. Michael had to admit it was foolish, but fun and exciting all the same—especially when Matt banged right into a pole with a sickly crack. It was fortunate that Michael covered up Matt's mouth before he let out the swearword and the girls found out something was odd.

Michael abandoned his lunch and decided to see if Sheena was in her room. He had no idea where her room was but luckily he found her in the hallway on his floor.

She was trying to get in her room when he saw her, and he made a beeline straight for her.

"Hi, Sheena," he said, stopping right by her.

"Oh, it's you, Michael," Sheena said, happily. Even though her tone was happy, she did not look all right. She looked rather troubled and Michael noticed that there was something forced in her smile.

"Are you alright?" he questioned her curiously.

"Yes, I'm fine," Sheena answered, though Michael knew that was untrue. "I was just . . ."

Michael knew she was hiding something. Even though Michael did not know her for long, he knew that she was hardly ever depressed.

"I know you're hiding something, Sheena," Michael replied, seriously. "What's up?"

Sheena opened the door and turned to look at him.

"You're not going to drop it, are you?" she asked, smiling slightly. "It's . . . kind of weird . . . here, come in and I'll tell you about it."

Michael steeped over the threshold and followed Sheena into her room.

It was evident that Sheena took pride in the appearance of her sleeping quarters. The bed was made neatly and there were no spare clothes on the floor. To cap it off (as far as Michael could see), there were no crumbs or garbage on the floor. Michael knew that a maid usually came in to tidy up but it wasn't their job to pick up crumbs or other personal belongings.

"Nice room," commented Michael, looking around.

Sheena gave him a small smile. "Thank you. My parents always made me make my room look nice, so I'm well used to cleaning."

Sheena closed the door and sat down on the bed while Michael remained standing. He looked at her.

"What is it that you wanted to tell me?"

Sheena sighed. "It's . . . weird," she finished lamely.

"What happened?" Michael queried. "Is it about the Ying-Yang brothers? Have you seen them?"

Sheena laughed.

"No, of course not, silly boy," Sheena said, smiling. "The brothers will probably not show their face in public with Americans swarming left and right. They're not exactly popular with our country at the moment."

Michael had to agree with her. However, Sheena was not done talking.

"I did not see them," Sheena continued, "but I did hear them."

Michael was astonished. He least expected the brothers to make the appearance public this quickly. It was only the first day. The Opening Ceremonies did not even take place yet.

"Where did you hear them?" asked Michael, curiously. He yearned to know everything Sheena heard.

"I was busy changing back into my normal clothes when I heard snarling voices outside the locker room door," explained Sheena. "My dad played a recording of their voices for me one time; the voices outside the locker room sounded exactly like the recording."

"You reckon you heard them outside the locker room door?" Michael asked, surprised. He and Matt were there, too. Did the brothers just miss getting Michael?

"Yes," Sheena answered. "Like I said, I recognized their snarling voices. They were talking about you, I think. They said . . . 'that kid is just going to be a hindrance. We must find him.'"

"That has to be about me," Michael answered, slowly, resigned to the fact that they caught a glimpse of him at tryouts. "After all, I overheard them talking about their plans at my tryouts. They are going to think I'm a little bit of a threat."

"They do," Sheena answered, patiently. "But that was not all, Michael. Then, they came in barging into the locker room!"

"They—WHAT?"

"Yes, I know. They came in and asked if any of us knew you, Michael."

"They asked if anyone knew *me*?"

"Yes."

"What did you say?" Michael asked urgently.

"Me? I went back outside to support one of my teammates after I overheard their conversation. I was afraid they might recognize me. They know my dad, and they went in his office before for a meeting, and I was not taking any chances. What if they saw a photograph of me in the office?"

"You are a smart girl, Sheena," Michael answered. "If you stayed, you might have been put in a difficult situation."

"I know I am," Sheena said, cheerfully and proudly. "Anyway, if they think fourteen-year-old kids are bad, why are they bothering to get at you?"

"They think they are untrustworthy," Michael answered. "They saw me overhear them. It's obvious they think I might do something about it."

Sheena looked worriedly at Michael.

"Are you worried at all?"

Michael shrugged. "I had a feeling I might face this. I honestly don't know."

Sheena made a sudden movement as though she was going to put a hand on his shoulder but resisted. When she spoke, she sounded small and terrified.

"Michael, you don't think they might try and kill you, do you?"

"Kill me?" Michael asked. "I doubt it."

Sheena looked taken aback. "What makes you so certain?"

"Look, the only thing the brothers really wanted was a position on an Olympic Committee," Michael explained. "Now that they have it, they might be a little cautious of their actions. They might want to get revenge, but they might do it in a way that goes undetected. Killing me would be too obvious and they would be imprisoned."

"But they also wanted to be on our baseball team!" replied Sheena. "Michael, you don't know the brothers that well. They are dangerous. They want to hurt you."

"Yeah, but they won't kill me," Michael replied.

Sheena gave him a penetrating blue-eyed stare. "Michael, the Ying-Yang brothers don't care what they do. They're going to get revenge on us to their satisfaction whether they break the rules or not."

"But how can you suspect that?"

"Ask my dad tonight, I'm sure he will be able to tell you," Sheena replied. "He knew the Ying-Yang brothers for a long time."

"I wouldn't be so sure, Sheena," Michael answered. "He is the president and may want to keep all of that private. It really isn't any of my business."

"My dad will tell you, Michael," Sheena replied firmly. "He'll let you ask questions, I am sure of it. He's fair."

"Your dad knows a lot about it, I hope," Michael replied, staring out the window.

Michael was yanked back into reality when he looked at his watch; it told him it was ten to one.

"I'd better get going, Sheena. I have baseball practice."

Sheena looked up. "I hope it goes well for you."

"I hope so, too," Michael muttered. "Anyway, see you, Sheena."

"See you later, Michael."

Michael hurriedly dashed back to his room, snatched his bag, and hurried to the first floor and out of the hotel, almost crashing into an elderly couple near the sliding glass doors. Panicking, he hurried out onto the streets of Beijing, searching for the stadium.

Michael realized that due to the disorganization of the Olympic Games, and the stress that was put on the coaches, Mr. Harrington completely forgot to provide a series of directions as to where his practice field was. It was more or less a wild goose chase as Michael traveled on street after street, hoping to find his team.

Just as he was getting desperate, he turned a corner and with a sigh of relief, found Nitro walking into the stadium. Sprinting like a cheetah, he hurried inside the stadium, traveled down the rows of seats, leaped over the padded fence, and dashed to his teammates, who were spread out along the outfield.

The team was putting their bags down and taking out their gloves, evidently starting to warm up with a soft toss. Every player turned to look at Michael when he arrived on the scene, panting and clutching a stitch in his side.

"I'm here," he announced meekly, panting.

"Why are you late?" a demanding voice called.

Michael turned to see Mr. Smith bear him down like an angry dog. Michael looked at his watch: it was only two minutes after. Why was it such a big deal? Due to the fact that everyone was either beginning to walk to a bare spot and Nitro was still searching for his glove, he could not have been much later than everyone else.

"Sorry, Mr. Smith, I just—"

"Ah, Michael, you're here."

Michael turned to see Mr. Harrington come over to them, interrupting Michael's explanation and looking pleased to see him.

"Michael, get your glove and start warming up with Nitro over here," Mr. Harrington replied, taking no notice at Mr. Smith's facial expression, which wore an ugly look. It looked like the color of black currant ice cream. "Then, we will go from there."

Michael did as he was told, and soon enough, he was throwing to Nitro. He seemed to be pleased to have Michael as a throwing partner (Michael had a shrewd suspicion the other teammates made fun of his almost-ridiculous, not-attracting, possibly annoying green hair) and soon enough, the two friends were tossing a grass-stained baseball back and forth to each other. Michael realized that he needed the soft toss. He had not thrown a baseball in three days, and felt a little rusty with his motion and mechanics.

After a few minutes or so, Mr. Harrington called the team over. That was when Michael got a good look at his teammates. All of them were very young. It looked as though most of them were no older then eighteen or so. Michael now could see why Mr. Harrington did not like the Ying-Yang brothers; their views were enormously different. Michael was reminded irresistibly of a high school varsity team, not an Olympic squad.

"Now," Mr. Harrington replied, once everyone had taken a knee, "I would like all of you to listen to me, as I need to say a few important reminders for all of you. Whoever has been on the team before must bear with me, because it will be the same stuff I said over and over to you. Understand?"

The team nodded, though Michael saw one black kid whisper to another kid who looked to be about fifteen. Mr. Harrington, who failed to notice, continued his spiel.

"You all are to be at practice or any games an hour early. This would enable us to get batting practice, conditioning, and everything in. Today, I'll let you off, but from now on, I expect you to be punctual."

"Michael," Mr. Smith muttered under his breath, but the whole team ignored him. Mr. Harrington continued as if there had been no interruption.

"Secondly, I like to call this team a player-lead club. Older players, I will be expecting you to help our new guys and make sure they keep up. I, myself, will be overseeing how you guys work together and make sure you are doing your best. And thirdly, I think it is appropriate that all of us should introduce ourselves and talk about something they enjoy doing—besides baseball. I want to get a better feel for who I have on my team. I know it's corny, but you're going to find that, in the Olympics, team unity beats talent if the teams are competitive. So, if you please, I would like all of you to stand in a circle . . ."

The team, grumbling disagreeably, stood up and spread out and the four coaches joined in as well. One kid muttered, "This is so stupid", but as the coaches were making sure everyone was in a good circle, the boy's comments went unnoticed.

When everyone was in a circle, Mr. Isol took control. "Okay, someone please start. And please, keep this rated PG. And I'm talking to you, O' Leary!"

The same blond-haired kid that tripped Matt on the plane shrugged his shoulders, looking as though he had no inclination to keep the game PG rated.

A tall kid with jet-black hair went in the middle of the circle to start off.

"I am Mike Radford, and I like to rock out on my electric guitar, dudes."

He started doing gestures like he was strumming a guitar. Some people sniggered.

"I also like being—" Mike started to say, but the O' Leary kid cut him off.

"A gigantic weirdo," the tall blond kid supplied for him. Michael instinctively looked at the coaches, wondering if they would appreciate the blond kid interrupting their team bonding experience. The whole team laughed loudly, but the coaches did not seem amused.

"That's enough, Mr. O' Leary," Mr. Oberfels replied, sternly. "And how about you go next?"

O' Leary went in the middle and Mike retreated out. Once he was in the middle, he started to rap.

"Yo, dudes, I'm Fred O' Leary and my hobbies are checking out girls and looking at them on Google Images. It brings me great joy. And the Swimsuit Edition of Sports Illustrated is an excellent magazine as well!"

The team laughed loudly again.

"I said keep it PG, O' Leary!" Mr. Isol growled as he shoved him out of the circle. Fred attempted to explain the top seven ways a man could pleasure himself, but he was stopped abruptly as James made his way inside the circle.

Michael had done this before, but it never turned out weirder than this. The players had some weird hobbies that Michael thought that they were obviously making this into a big joke (it was plain obvious that they were trying to be funny). After Fred's spiel, the coaches gave up on trying to keep the conversation at the ten-year-old level.

Besides Mike and Fred, he got introduced to James, who was Nitro's older brother; Pat Arden, whose ambition was to run a marathon in his birthday suit ("No one would want to come watch it," Fred pointed out), was another goof ball; Ken McClaherty, a black kid with an expertise (according to him), of spying on people ("There's strategy to it, it's almost like a sport," Ken said, sincerely); Nitro; Samuel, a black kid who liked girls in bikinis ("My bedroom wall is covered with these pictures," he said. "I call it the Wall of Fame"); Ahmad, an Indian kid who liked Heavy Metal, and had to sing for everything; Harry, who was too modest with his ability and said nothing when he was called on; Ty, who was extremely arrogant, insisted he was the prettiest boy there ever was ("Narcissistic moron," Nitro snarled beside Michael); Phil, a San Diego kid with a tan, who also spent his summer on the beach, looking at girls ("Good thing we got him away from that," Mr. Isol growled); Todd, a big time nerd and apparently did math problems for entertainment ("He is the king of all nerds," Fred said, sincerely); Cliff, a big black guy that enjoyed bragging over everything he owned ("Too bad he has nothing to boast about," Ken muttered under his breath); David, a kid who enjoyed reading ("That is indecent behavior and ought to be fined," Fred said, furiously); Brad and Chad, two troublemakers who were identical ("They remind me too much of the Ying-Yang brothers," Nitro muttered to Michael); Xavier, a dark horse sport star; George Hamilton, a kid who enjoyed peanuts and cracker jacks ("You know what I mean!" he protested when the whole team roared with laughter); Justin, a kid with an oddly wicked arm; Joe, who was as exciting as a bump on a log; Oscar, who was apparently a huge fan of romantic comedies ("It's classic entertainment," he said); Lew, who apparently had a man purse ("It keeps all my things in one spot," he said, fondly while Fred roared with laughter); and Ron, who took pleasure in buying nail polish and made a small income by selling it in his school ("Obviously, it's a black market so the teachers never find out, and I inflate the prices 200 percent so I make something from it," Ron explained).

Michael never met a stranger group of kids before. He thought his friends were an odd group, but these kids made them look completely normal. As practice wore on, he thought that, as strange as they were, he liked his new teammates, who were always willing to help the younger players in the middle of practice.

During the pitching drill, Michael stood behind Fred, holding his puny bat in front of him. Fred stood by him and held out his bat as well, and Michael noticed that his bat was about two feet longer. Fred grinned at him.

"You know what they say about guys with big bats, right?" Fred queried to Michael as he stepped up to the plate.

The first pitch that was thrown to him was knocked out of the park. Fred cheered loudly and obnoxiously as he rounded the bases doing a war chant.

The kids, however, did not get much time to take a break as the four coaches kept them working all day. They made them do several running drills, throwing exercises, catching drills, hitting contests, and, if they were a pitcher, pitching drills.

Michael was exhausted by the end of it and was glad to enter the locker room with the team when the coaches called for the end of practice. He got changed hastily and chatted with his new teammates.

"Tough practice, eh, Michael?" Nitro commented to him as they sat on the bench of the locker room.

"You're not kidding," Michael said, watching Todd duck to avoid getting hit with Cliff's glove.

"Hey, Ken, who are you liking these days?" Fred asked, loudly as he sprayed his body with water to cool himself down.

"Ah, no one," Ken answered, pretending to be embarrassed. "You know no one likes me, come on."

"Then, who do you think is hot?"

Ken thought for a moment. "Well, no one in particular. However, I do like checking out the soccer and gymnastics girls. But that's just me."

Almost everyone agreed, laughing.

"Hear, hear!" Cliff cheered.

"Keep it PG, guys," James said, though he too was smiling.

"Ah, shut up, Shields, you know we have a point," Fred replied.

"I don't worry about girls," Harry said, nervously. "All they want to do is look hot and mooch off my hard-earned money!"

Everyone laughed.

"Even though that is not normal, you do have a point," Samuel commented. "But let me tell you something about women: they want a man who is brawny, not some rich nerd who plays with his TI-83 like Todd."

Todd chucked his cup at Samuel, who ducked, causing it to fly past him and knock his open water bottle down to the ground. Everyone laughed.

"Ah, he fights like a girl, too," Pat mocked.

"Only Pat would know that, seeing him as one," Fred replied smartly.

Everyone laughed harder.

Pat shoved Fred good-naturedly. "Come watch me when I run the marathon, and you'll see that I'm not."

Cliff then turned to Michael. "How about Michael Durbin? Does he like anyone?"

Everyone turned to him.

"Who do you like?" Brad and Chad asked simultaneously.

Michael willed himself to not tell them the truth. He had been stupid not to expect this remark from them. However, as he only had known them for a few hours, he wasn't particularly keen on discussing his personal life with them. He decided it was time to go to the presidential standby: answer the question but not answer it.

"Me? Well, I'm friends with Sheena Goodwin, do you know her?" Michael questioned them.

"Is she that hot gymnast, dude?" Ahmad queried with a musical tone.

"Well, don't you think they all are?" Michael asked, shrewdly.

The team seemed impressed.

"Mikey's shrewd," Samuel replied. "I like it!"

"Hey, he has a good taste of girls . . ." Harry replied, though he looked embarrassed as though it was against his moral code to say stuff like that.

"How would you know, knowing you like guys?" Fred asked. "Remember that kid Mike Andrews? He had feelings for you."

"Andrews had a girlfriend, Fred, as you very well know," James said, loftily. "Just because he got along with him well doesn't mean they had a weird relationship."

"Trust me, their relationship was weird," Fred replied as though he highly doubted his teammate's words. "And as for his girlfriend, I highly doubt that he was telling his truth. He described her as tall, slim, and with long blond hair. I noticed that when our parents came to meet Mr. Harrington and the rest of the coaches, it became clear that he had merely described his mom for us."

Everyone laughed. Apparently, Fred O' Leary was the joker, heart, and soul of the team.

"Anyway, does Sheena *want* some of Mikey?" Ken asked in a mocking voice.

Michael looked taken aback. He liked Sheena for her personality, and he was not sure he wanted to talk about her physical features with this group of unusual boys. After all, he had been Sheena's friend for two days, and he did not want to say anything that she might get upset and angry about. He still was embarrassed by what he told her the other day before she went to compete.

"Nope," Michael said, after a pause.

"Is that *it*?" Fred asked in a mocking voice.

"Reckon so," Michael said, casually.

"Mr. Goodwin's daughter?" Phil asked, overhearing the conversation. "Is she *nice*, Mikey?"

"Get in there!" Samuel cried.

"You know she wants it!" cried Lew. "More than I want my purse!"

These boys were annoying the hell out of Michael. Michael decided to get out of there, after the boys began a series of chants that went, "*Get in there!*" Heaving his bag over his shoulder, he left the locker room.

He made his way to the edge of the stadium to find Matt and Sheena waiting for him at the edge.

"How was practice?" Sheena and Matt asked, curiously.

"Fine," Michael answered. "They made us work."

"How was Fred?" Matt queried, a distasteful look crossing his face. "I hate that kid. He's a moron."

"I think he's pretty funny," Michael answered.

Matt looked at Michael in surprise. "Did he talk about girls?"

Michael decided it was best to not be entirely honest. "No, he was talking about his hobbies."

Matt raised his eyebrows and Michael knew that Matt could tell he wasn't being completely honest but he didn't pursue the subject.

"We're going to my family's China House for dinner," Sheena answered once she stopped laughing. "My dad called me and said we could start heading over there."

"Where is your China House?"

"It is located in a remote forest overlooking Beijing. It's a long walk," Sheena replied.

As they started walking to Sheena's house, the conversation turned to food.

"What are we having over there?" Matt questioned Sheena intently. "You know I like your mom's cooking."

Sheena smiled.

"My parents are making a dinner of London Broil, mashed potatoes, green beans, and baked beans," supplied Sheena, as though as if she planned it herself. "You better eat up, boys. They said they were making a lot of food."

"Wow," Michael said, excited that he was going to have real food for once instead of stale bread and burnt pancakes. "That sounds excellent, Sheena. My parents usually just have leftovers!"

"Why?" Matt asked.

"Our economy in Pennsylvania is not going too well," Michael explained. "Food prices are skyrocketing and I'm not exactly rich."

They now were climbing a huge hill so they stopped talking. Then, after a good ten minutes, they reached the top. Michael for the first time got a good look at Sheena's parents' China House.

It was like a little cottage. Michael could tell that the house was built to model the Chinese architecture. It looked as though there were about five rooms inside of it. It was not what you would call a luxury home, but it was pretty nice for only to live in temporarily.

"This is spectacular, Sheena," Michael whispered.

"Thanks, Michael," Sheena answered, smiling. "It took about a good six months to build. My parents lived here for about a year before I had to go to Beijing."

"You lived in your house for a year without your parents?" Michael asked, shocked.

"Oh no, silly boy," Sheena answered, laughing. "My grandparents came to live with me. They had to watch my younger siblings. I was busy a lot so I couldn't do it. Here, I'll knock . . ."

Sheena knocked on the door of the house and stood back. Michael and the other two had to wait for a few seconds until it was opened. A man with a brown mustache and beard appeared. Michael reckoned that he had to be Sheena's father.

"Oh, it's you three," he said in a voice that proved that he was pleased to have guests. "This is really perfect timing. We've just finished cooking dinner. You can come right in and wash up."

And he stood back to let the three of them into the house. Sheena led Matt and Michael through the kitchen and into the bathroom, which was just outside the perimeter of the kitchen.

The three of them washed up and quickly came to the table. This was the first time Michael got a good look at Sheena's family.

Her father was a skinny man with brown hair and a mustache and beard; Sheena's mom looked exactly like Sheena except she had dark red hair; Sheena's two younger siblings were both girls; one looked almost like a younger Sheena; the other one looked exactly like her mother.

"Hi, Mr. Goodwin," Matt said, shaking hands.

"How are you, Matt?" he asked in a fatherly voice.

"Great, thanks," Matt answered.

Mr. Goodwin then turned his attention to Michael. Holding out his hand, he said, "And you must be Michael Durbin."

"Yes, sir," Michael answered, shaking hands.

"Sheena's told me all about you already, of course," Mr. Goodwin said, pleasantly. "Sometimes, Shawna and Ember have to tell her to shut up!"

Sheena went red, and quickly went to the bathroom to wash her hands a second time. Matt sniggered.

When everyone sat down, the table was quite crowded. Seven people at one rectangular table made it almost impossible for everyone to have room. Michael had to try hard not to nudge Sheena's elbow as he tried to cut his steak politely.

"Michael, where are you from?" Mr. Goodwin asked, looking at him.

"Skippack, Pennsylvania, sir," Michael replied. "It's close to Philadelphia."

"Interesting," he answered, as he chewed his string beans thoughtfully. "I never heard of the town, even though I've been down in that area many times for work and small trips."

After that, there was a few minutes of everyone getting their food after many "please"s, and "thank you"s, and "No, you first"s. The Goodwins were obviously very proper people, and Michael had to like the family. They were all nice and polite and excellent hosts. They knew when to direct questions at Michael or Matt to strike up a conversation and knew when not to.

Then Sheena's mom spoke for the first time.

"Sheena, how is gymnastics going?" she asked after wiping her mouth with a napkin.

"Good," Sheena said, happily. "I think I'll do well."

Michael noticed throughout dinner that the two younger siblings were staring at him the whole time.

"Oh, by the way, Michael, those are my two sisters, Shawna and Ember," Sheena told him. "Shawna looks like me and Ember resembles my mom."

"Nice to meet both of you," Michael said to them politely.

Both of them blushed, but Shawna nodded politely. Apparently, they were a little apprehensive about meeting him.

"What position do you play, Michael, dear?" Mrs. Goodwin asked, as she passed him the bowl of string beans.

"I'm a pitcher, Mrs. Goodwin," he told her.

"What kind of pitches are you good at?" Shawna asked, curiously. She seemed to be a lot less shy than her sister.

"I like my fastball a lot, but I also have some breaking pitches," Michael answered her. "I sometimes resort to a slider or a change-up."

Meanwhile, Matt was arguing to Sheena about the Yankees, a subject that was getting quite old to Michael. Though he enjoyed debating baseball, he wanted to talk about other things with his friends.

"All they have is money!" he answered defiantly.

"They're a good team!" Sheena protested.

"The Yankees make baseball a contest between who has the most money!" Matt persisted angrily. "The Mets are—"

"You like the Mets?"

Ember, the red-haired sibling of Sheena spoke for the first time. Michael was surprised to hear her speak.

"I like the Phillies. They are a good team," she pressed on, making Matt look livid.

"You probably just like the Phillies just because they're winning for once!"

It was obvious Matt knew the siblings just as well as he knew Sheena, because Ember stuck her tongue out at him, but when she saw Michael noticing their arguing, she closed her mouth and went red like the setting sun.

"I'm sure it's not only that," Michael replied, heavily, making Ember blush even more and Matt furious. "I liked the Phillies for a good seven years and . . ."

Mr. Goodwin now joined into the conversation.

"The Mets are an injury-plagued team that can't win enough games. And not to mention that they don't have the . . ."

"Will!" Mrs. Goodwin said, warningly.

" . . . guts to spend some money," he finished feebly, which made Michael understand what he was going to say.

It was such a pleasant dinner that Michael felt at peace with the world. It was hard for him to think about anything bad, even the Ying-Yang brothers.

Dinner ended and everyone started to help clean up and wash the dishes. With everyone's help, it didn't take very long. Mrs. Goodwin said that they didn't need to help, but Michael felt it would be impolite not to do so.

After the table was scrubbed, Michael seized the opportunity to ask Mr. Goodwin about the scroll. He caught Sheena's eye and she nodded.

Michael walked up to Sheena's father.

"Mr. Goodwin, sir, I was wondering if I could have a private word with you. It's about something really important."

Mr. Goodwin looked surprised, but he said, "Sure. Let's go in the study room here."

He led Michael into a room of many file folders and a computer. It was quite nice.

Then, Mr. Goodwin turned to Michael as he sat down in his chair.

"Now, Michael, what was it you wanted to ask me about?"

Michael looked at him straight in the eye, and said, "Well, it is about the Ying-Yang brothers, sir. Mr. Harrington told me there was a scroll that the Ying-Yang brothers are searching for. I was wondering if you knew anything about it."

Mr. Goodwin raised his eyebrows, perhaps to ask why Mr. Harrington told him this, but he made no inquiries about it.

"Are you talking about the Scroll of the Yangtze?"

CHAPTER 9

THE SCROLL OF THE YANGTZE

Michael had to wait a few seconds for the name to absorb into his mind.

"Is that the name of the scroll that the Ying-Yang brothers are looking for?"

Mr. Goodwin gave him a piercing look.

"I want you to understand this Michael because this is very important. Sheena told me about what you overheard at your tryouts. I want you to get the precise facts. We gave the scroll this name because we think it was written in the hometown of the brothers, which is near the Yangtze River."

Mr. Goodwin paused for a moment as though relaying all he knew to Michael was inflicting pain into his abdomen.

"I've known the Ying-Yang brothers for a long time, Michael, and you would have never guessed that they would be involved in any of this. They were hard workers and were determined to do their very best. Most athletes or people on the committee are like this. Doing your very best in sports isn't always a good thing. In fact, it could be really bad."

"Sir, what does this have to do with the Scroll of the Yangtze?"

"I'm getting there. Listen to me, Michael. I know you heard a thousand people tell you the Olympics are a life experience and that everything is all fun and games. I want you to get it out of your head now. This Olympics is the exact opposite of that. It has a mixture of triumphs and good memories, sure, but understand that there will be very few, especially now with the current situation."

Michael had a guess as to why. "That's because the Ying-Yang brothers are on the Chinese Committee, right?"

Mr. Goodwin looked worried. "Listen to me, Michael. I don't how much I can tell you, or should tell you. No one is supposed to know, strictly speaking. I think you already know too much. The information you know is good enough to get you killed. I don't know how much I should tell you. You, Sheena, and Matt know too much. Nothing could be at a greater risk of your life than knowing about the scroll. Promise me you will not pursue to find any more information than I am willing to tell you. It doesn't concern you and you are better off not knowing about it."

"But, sir, if the Ying-Yang brothers already want to get me because I overheard them talking about, it wouldn't matter how much information you give me," said Michael fiercely.

Mr. Goodwin sighed, looking weary but seemed to appreciate Michael's comments.

"I admire your courage and determination, Michael. But your parents would be worried sick if they know you're in this much danger. Sheena has told me you came to Beijing alone. Not to be critical, but that was not a safe decision. If your parents balked at the price of the trip down here, I can understand that but if I had known that the Committee would have worked something out."

Michael sincerely doubted that his parents were concerned as they already decided they weren't going to go and support him, but he felt it would be churlish to say that, and he wanted to make a good impression of himself to Mr. Goodwin.

"I am not going to tell you much, Michael. Most of it is Committee business. But I guess I can tell you a few things. The scroll that the Ying-Yang brothers are trying to find was actually in possession of their father."

"So their father was the one that had the scroll? Didn't he write it?"

"You figured that out already?" Mr. Goodwin questioned, surprised. "Yeah, he did. The Ying-Yang brothers, according to all of us, knew that their father buried the scroll somewhere in China before he died, but the whereabouts are unknown. We also think that it is dangerous to us. Ming vowed revenge on us for cutting his sons from the team. He probably wrote the scroll then. He died before he saw his sons denied a position on our Committee."

"Do you think the scroll might have sentimental value to the brothers?" asked Michael. "Like a memoir of their late father or something?"

"I doubt it. That is what some people think. But if it was a memoir, why are police patrolling the place? Why is everyone always talking about it?"

"I did notice a multitude of policemen patrolling the streets," Michael admitted. Then he asked, "Are you saying that the scroll could be maybe a . . . plan maybe?"

"That is what I think it is," Mr. Goodwin answered. "They swore to get revenge on the baseball team, so it could very well be a plan. With the scroll, they can execute their plan of revenge. However, we don't know how serious the plan may be. They have given us death threats before, so we have to take this seriously."

"Can't they just do other things to get revenge?" Michael queried. "Why waste time trying to find this scroll?"

Mr. Goodwin sighed. "Good question, Michael, but there is a reason behind this madness. The brothers aren't going to walk up to me and shoot me in the middle of the street. They want to plan their revenge in secrecy. They were never good at formulating plans. Their father was. They got what they wanted, so they want to be extra careful when getting their revenge, as they don't want to lose their position on the Chinese Committee. The scroll probably highlights a well-developed plan explaining how to carry out their revenge on us and our country."

Mr. Goodwin was giving Michael a serious look that Michael didn't like.

Michael tried to comprehend this. "I do have another question, and not about the scroll. Mr. Harrington said the Ying-Yang brothers left the team a year ago. He also said Mr. Smith joined the team a year ago. Do you think there can be a relationship between the two?"

Mr. Goodwin pondered it for a moment. "You know, Michael? Your comments are well-reasoned. I think you may have a point, but you could be wrong as well. Problem is you have no evidence that Mr. Smith has done nothing wrong. That is odd."

"Do you know if the Ying-Yang brothers know where they think the scroll is?"

"I know," Mr. Goodwin said, "where they think it might be, but I am not going to tell you. You know too much, Michael. If I did, I might be afraid you might go and try to find it."

Michael could tell by the finality of his tone that the conversation was over. Michael turned to leave, but Mr. Goodwin called him back.

"Michael, I have to warn you before you leave," Mr. Goodwin said, importantly. "Keep an eye on Mr. Smith. He may be your coach, but if your theory is right and the Ying-Yang brothers did leave and put him in their place, he might be trying to get closer to you and harm you. Be on your guard, Michael. Tell me if you find anything else out about Mr. Smith and enjoy the Opening Ceremonies."

"Okay, Mr. Goodwin. And thank you."

* * *

An hour later, Michael was with Sheena and Matt in his hotel room talking about the conversation he had with Mr. Goodwin.

"So he thinks it is a plan of revenge?" Sheena asked as Michael finished talking.

"Yes," Michael answered. "He says it is something we should take very seriously."

"I can't believe your dad didn't question Mr. Smith yet," Matt said, goggling at Sheena. "He's the president, and he could fire him before he might hurt Michael."

"We have no proof, though," Sheena replied, frustrated. "We can't start pointing fingers without any proof."

"Anyway, what do you think is the reason why they're searching for it?" Matt questioned Michael.

Michael frowned, not because he was angry with Matt, but because he seemed to be pondering it.

"They want to get revenge on the baseball team," Michael said, matter-of-factly. "We know that to be a cold-hard fact. What Sheena's dad said makes sense. Their dad wrote it, he'd have a whole plan drawn up for them."

Sheena looked scared. "Michael, please listen to my dad and don't go looking for more information! The Ying-Yang brothers want you dead! Don't give the two of them more reasons to kill you!"

"They already want me dead, so why does it matter?" he inquired, infuriated by Sheena's opinion.

"Let's try to hash it out first," Matt said, quickly. "So, first you hear them talk about a scroll at tryouts . . ."

"Yes."

"And then, you think they might hurt you for overhearing about it . . ."

"Another yes."

"And now that you made the team and are here, they think you are the one that might try to find as much information as possible about the scroll so they put Mr. Smith on you to make sure you don't."

"That's only a suspicion," Michael answered. "But it is possible, yes."

Sheena looked worried. "Michael, my dad cares about you! Don't go looking for trouble!"

Michael looked at her. "I'm not! I don't even know what is on the scroll! If police are policing the place and Committee members are everywhere, it can't be anything good, Sheena! It has to be more valuable than what some people believe! Security wouldn't be everywhere if they didn't think the scroll could potentially be dangerous! All I'm relying on is what your father told me and a few articles in the paper!"

Matt looked at Michael seriously. "You have a point. So what are you trying to do?"

Michael sighed. "Well, first I'm going to call my friends and family back at home and tell them everything I know. Then, I'm going to talk to an officer tomorrow and ask him a few questions. If he cooperates, then I can see about Mr. Smith. If not, I'll have to research it."

Matt instinctively looked at Sheena, wondering how she was going to take Michael's comments. Sheena looked at Michael with the expression of a girl persuading her boyfriend to buy her an expensive piece of jewelry.

"Please Michael, don't. Don't go looking for more information. The Ying-Yang brothers would like to have a reason to kill you. Let the police handle it. Let the Committee handle the problem. This isn't something you should be getting into."

Michael couldn't look her in the eye because he would not listen to her. He was going to look for more information, no matter what.

Minutes later, Sheena said she would meet them outside the hotel ("The Opening Ceremonies, didn't you know?") and left the room while Matt muttered vaguely about needing to ask his dad something. That left Michael alone to call the people he needed to.

He grabbed the phone and halted. Who should he call first? Of course, he thought. My parents.

He dialed his home number and waited with bated breath. The phone kept ringing, but no one came to answer. After the fifth ring, he heard a voice message.

"Hi you have reached the Durbin residence. We are currently away from the house. After the beat, please leave your name and a message and we will get back to you when we can. Thank you."

Michael threw the phone down and his heart sank. His mom said she would be at home all throughout the Olympics. She lied to me, he thought angrily.

He then decided to dial Tomas's number next. He quickly did it, and then held the receiver to his ear.

On the third ring, he had luck, and got an answer.

"Hello?"

"Tomas, is that you?"

"Michael, is that you?" Tomas sounded excited and relieved. "I thought it was a Chinese punk calling me as a prank. I was hesitant to answer."

"No, it's me," Michael said, happily. "Look, Tomas, I can't talk for long. I got to tell you something important."

And he related all the stuff he knew about the brothers and the scroll to Tomas. There was a pause after Michael finished.

"That does sound odd," Tomas's voice said, sounding thoughtful. "But I must say you are crazy for looking for more info. You're not being a bad boy again, are you, Mikey? Sara will fuss worse than my mother. She's already having kittens about you. She thinks you're going to do something really stupid and to me, I must say she has a point."

Michael sighed. Why did Sara always think he would do something stupid? And why did Tomas disagree with his opinion? He had been hoping for support from him (he knew Matt would sooner dance with Fred than Sara allowing him to help the Committee find the scroll) and to not get it was huge personal blow.

"Why shouldn't I look for more information?"

"It's dangerous," Tomas said in the same tone as Sheena. "Anyway, have you met any friends?"

"Yeah, I met Matt Harrington and Sheena Goodwin."

"Harrington? That rings a bell . . ."

"His dad is the baseball manager," Michael explained.

"Oh. And Goodwin rings a bell as well. Isn't Will Goodwin the president?"

"Yes."

"You're in luck, Michael."

"Why?"

"Your best friend is the president's daughter." Tomas sounded almost jealous. "Is she nice?"

Michael made a noise that suggested he did not want to discuss it.

"Enough soppy stuff, then," Tomas said, positively snorting into the phone. "Now, should I call Sara and tell her you called?"

"No," Michael answered, firmly. "I'll call her. I want to tell her this, too."

"I knew you would say that," Tomas's voice said.

"I should call her now," Michael said, making up his mind. "I need to get up early tomorrow."

"I forgot the time is different. It is only about nine o' clock here. My whole family is still in bed. Do you honestly think Sara would be up?"

"Well, I've got to try, haven't I?" Michael answered back.

"Okay, Michael, I'll let you go," Tomas said, laughing, "but by the way, the Perkins were able to get tickets for a flight out to Beijing. We will be there for the conclusion of it. I just hope you're playing a game then!"

"You are coming?"

Tomas laughed at the excitement in Michael's voice.

"Yes, the Perkins felt sorry for you that no one was there to support you. The Perkins planned to go on vacation as it was, so they decided to come and support you. I'll be there as well."

"See you soon, Tomas," Michael replied, hanging up the phone.

Michael looked up and felt happy: his friends were coming to support him! He thought how his parents had refused to support him. With his family neglecting him, this news came as a huge sigh of relief for Michael.

In all of his happiness, he almost forgot that he had to call Sara. It brought him back down to reality. He picked up the phone again, and he dialed Sara's number this time. As he put the receiver to his ear, a cheerful voice greeted him almost instantly.

"Michael! Michael! I knew you would call, I knew it! How are you? I hope everything is okay in Beijing and you've been doing well!"

Michael smiled; he forgot how cheerful Sara could be when she wanted to. "Sara, it's good to hear from you! How's it going?"

"I'll tell you in a minute," said Sara impatiently. "I knew you would call, Michael! How's Beijing?"

"Very polluted," Michael answered grimly. "Anyway, Sara, I called you to tell you something extremely important . . ."

And he told her about everything he knew: the scroll, the brothers themselves, Mr. Harrington's theory, and Mr. Goodwin's information.

Sara seemed to have expected a better welcome from Michael. He could sense the coolness in her voice when she answered.

"I don't understand, Michael."

"It's simple, Sara. The Ying-Yang brothers were rejected from the Committee because they were obviously ambitious and could not be trusted with such a position," Michael answered, excited. "Not after they were already pissed at us for rejecting them from the baseball team. I think the brothers have a connection with Mr. Smith. They share the same views, and he was placed on the Committee as soon as the brothers left."

"No, it does not make sense," Sara answered, her voice hard.

Michael rolled his eyes. He hated her tone of voice. What was he supposed to say to her?

"Yes, it does. And the next part of it does as well. The Ying-Yang brothers joined the Chinese Committee to get what they wanted and try to locate the scroll as well. I overheard them at tryouts, Sara. It's too obvious that they think I'm a threat. The whole world knows about the scroll now, and that the brothers are looking for it! Your magazine had the facts right!"

"But if the Chinese know about the scroll, why are the police watching the city?"

"That's because the police don't want it to be found! The Olympics are supposed to be a friendly competition between countries! Imagine what trouble could happen if the scroll were to be found by the brothers! The brothers will end up using whatever the plan is on there to get their revenge on us!"

"You also have to figure out if the Chinese want it. What's in it for them? Why are they so worried about getting it before the brothers? It's our problem, not theirs."

Michael instantly read her mind. Sara brought up something that he never considered.

"They might want the scroll to see whether it could help them! What if the plan could be used for something else? You know, for better reasons. The Chinese Government might want to see it. They want to keep the Olympics peaceful, so they might be against the brothers! They might want the scroll just to see whether it has anything scrawled on it that's worth anything!"

When Sara spoke, she sounded anxious, and the hardness of her voice evaporated. "Michael, please do not worry about this. It sounds like this is not a thing you should meddle in."

"I'm okay, Sara. Mr. Goodwin said the same thing. As soon as I figure out what is on the scroll, I'll be set! I could then relay this to Mr. Goodwin, and he would tell the swarming police."

Sara sighed. She seemed resigned to the fact that her best friend was not going to be convinced to not try to learn more about the scroll. When she spoke, she diverted the topic away from the scroll.

"Oh, Michael, by the way, we are coming to see you."

"I know, I called Tomas too, and that is what he said."

"However, I am interested in your story," said Sara slowly. "I would like to find out more, but don't get into trouble."

"I won't."

"Find out more about the Ying-Yang brothers' father. It could possibly tell more about the scroll."

"I'll try. And, by the way, thank you for making an effort to come here. I really . . ."

"You're welcome, Michael," Sara said, cutting Michael off. "Have you met any new friends?"

"Yes, quite a few. I met Matt Harrington and Sheena Goodwin. And my teammates are a great group of guys, too."

"How . . . are they?"

"They are both just as nice as you and Tomas! I think you'd love to meet them."

"I wouldn't mind meeting your friends!" Sara said, excitedly.

Michael laughed.

"Anyway," Sara said, distractedly. "I better go, Michael. I need to cook my parent's a breakfast. I'll see you soon."

"Bye, Sara."

He hung up and went back to the bed. He was waiting for Matt to return. It felt weird, but he felt a little isolated, even though his friends were coming to support him. It was a weird, tingling feeling and he never felt it before until now—

The door opened and Matt came in, holding a huge bag of potato chips.

"Do you want potato chips?"

"Sure," he answered, and grabbed a handful.

After demolishing the chips, Matt burped and Michael crumbled up the bag and tossed it into the nearby trash can in their room.

"We should go out and meet Sheena," he replied. "Or else we might be late to the Opening Ceremonies. I forget when it starts."

"Yeah," Michael agreed. "We shouldn't miss that."

The two boys brushed their teeth quickly, and they hurried outside, where they met up with Sheena, and the three friends walked to the Bird's Nest together. Michael didn't know how he was going to last through the Opening Ceremonies; he was already starting to get tired.

"Did you talk to your friends, Michael?" Sheena asked, sweetly as they joined a huge, packed crowd filling into the stadium.

"Yeah I did," Michael answered as they inched with the crowd to the stadium.

"When does the ceremony start?" Matt questioned. "Do you know, Michael? Sheena?"

"It starts at eight," replied Sheena promptly. She took out her cell phone and flipped it up. Closing it, she responded, "We are not going to be waiting for long. Here, we have to go over here to the edge of the stadium. Our delegation is meeting there. We're going to be part of the ceremony!"

Michael, Matt, and Sheena entered the stadium to find it lit with excitement. The atmosphere was that of a World Cup game. The three kids could not help but be amazed at the sights in the Bird's Nest and on the field. They found Mr. Harrington lurking by the entrance of the stadium. He looked relieved to see them.

"Hey!" Mr. Harrington called. "Where have you three been? You were expected down here twenty minutes ago! Come with me now!"

"Where are we going, Dad?" asked Matt as Mr. Harrington led them right back out of the stadium.

"Just follow me," Mr. Harrington said. "Don't you remember that you're supposed to be taking part in it when they announce our nation?"

"We did remember, but we forgot where to go," Matt said, feebly.

Mr. Harrington cleared his throat, looking as though Matt's excuse was lackluster. "I see. Well, you were supposed to go to the edge of the stadium over here where we are assembling. Mr. Isol got us into a spot where you can still watch the Opening Ceremonies."

After a minute of walking, Michael and his friends came upon a huge group of people who were standing outside the stadium near a large entrance, bundled up and looking excited. Michael easily picked out Mr. Isol from the crowd; he wasn't too hard to find due to his vastness.

"There they are!" Mr. Isol grumbled as they approached him and the rest of the United States athletes. "Causing trouble already, are they?"

"My son forgot to give Michael the information," Mr. Harrington said in an undertone to him. "And Mr. Goodwin forgot to tell Sheena."

"Yeah, I'll believe that when the Ying-Yang brothers go up to me and give me a big, wet kiss," Mr. Isol retorted.

Michael, Matt, and Sheena joined the rest of the athletes and made conversation with them. After Sheena's gymnastics friends greeted him and giggled at the same time, Michael found himself engaged in a conversation with Nitro, who was wearing a lime green party hat complete with green pants and a green t-shirt, looking more like an enormous weed than a person.

"This is spellbinding, isn't it, Michael?" he asked, looking star-struck.

"I'll say," Michael replied, honestly. "This is unbelievable."

"You don't know what unbelievable is until you see the Opening Ceremonies," Nitro replied, earnestly. "It's supposed to be a display of prestidigitation."

Michael had no idea what that meant but merely assumed that Nitro meant that the show was good. Michael looked around him. He saw Sheena talking to her gymnastics teammates, who were giggling; Matt was talking to Mr. Oberfels; and Michael saw Fred talking to Samuel and Ken, wearing nothing but a muscle shirt and shorts with a pair of bright green flip-flops.

Meanwhile, Mr. Isol was prowling around the huge group, criticizing people's appearance and coaching them on etiquette. Michael kept noticing that Mr. Isol's eyes lingered on Ken's Cookie Monster hat, Samuel's Tony Hawk t-shirt, which had a huge rip across one shoulder, and on Fred's legs, which were covered in dirt mangled with blood.

"O'Leary! Put on your jacket, you dumb ass! McClaherty, take off your stupid Cookie Monster hat, you idiot!"

Ken sadly took his hat off and stuck it in his pocket.

Then, the loudspeaker crackled and the crowd sat down as the Opening Ceremonies were about to begin.

"Shut the hell up! That means you too, O' Leary!" Mr. Isol yelled at everyone, and they all fell silent.

Matt and Sheena walked over to Michael and they stood on tiptoe so they could see what was going on in the ceremony.

Michael was amazed by how smoothly the Opening Ceremonies ran. With the disorganization of the Chinese Commission already looming over his head, he wasn't expecting much from China, no matter what they were doing. However, to say in the least, the Opening Ceremonies pleasantly surprised Michael. It started off with a drum sequence of thousands of drummers. The drummers then made a formation to represent digits to countdown the final seconds to the Games and start the ceremonies at 8:08 in continuation of the 8/8/08 start time of the Olympic Games.

After that, Michael and the rest of the crowd were subjected to an amazing fireworks display. Sheena explained to him that there were exactly twenty-nine fireworks that were lit and shot up, signifying the twenty-ninth Olympiad of the modern era.

"How do you know all this?" asked Michael in an impressed voice, as what seemed like fairies were suddenly hovering in mid-air by what looked like the Olympic emblem.

"My dad," Sheena said, simply.

Michael was going to talk to Sheena more, but Matt grabbed their attention by pointing at the track, where over fifty young children stood. According to Matt, they were signifying the ethnic groups of China.

Then, Michael was unsurprised to see the China flag being marched onto the field. Michael saw the flag being handed over to the People's Liberation army soldiers, who were so professional it was clear that they had practiced this procedure day-after-day for the past year. They marched slowly to the flag podium, where a choir began to sing Michael supposed was the Chinese National Anthem. Michael wished he knew what they were singing about; he looked very foolish standing there while almost everyone in the stadium was singing along to the anthem. At least everyone on the United States team did not know Chinese. At the end of it, Michael made up for it by clapping hard with the rest of the crowd.

Michael soon realized that the Chinese took their culture very seriously, and over the next few hours, there were many segments in which where the Chinese would show-off their culture. They showed a brief film which showed the making of paper and ceramics, porcelain vessels, and other objects were also displayed.

However, Michael knew that the attention span of some of the athletes was starting to overtake them. There was just no getting around the fact that Chinese culture was not for all people. Fred had started a game of catch with Ken's Cookie Monster hat with the rest of the baseball team while Sheena's gymnast friends began taking turns poking Michael in the back, obviously looking for attention. Michael ignored them, thinking to himself that he was not going to give them the satisfaction that they were annoying him.

"Look! Here comes the Chinese Opera and the terracotta soldiers!" Sheena yelled enthusiastically, pointing them out.

"What are they going to do?" shouted Matt so that he could be heard over the noise of the crowd.

"Watch and find out!" Sheena yelled back as Michael focused his attention to the scene below.

The opera sang for a little bit, and then there was a Silk Road segment that was quickly followed by seven blue men holding oars. Sheena told Michael that it symbolized Zheng He's expeditions.

"Who's Zheng He?" shouted Michael over the roaring crowd to Sheena.

"He's a Chinese explorer!" Sheena shouted back.

Michael could not fall asleep during the Opening Ceremonies as all of it was very entertaining and interesting to hear the reason as to why it was included in the ceremonies. Finally, as the nations prepared for their introductions, Ken's Cookie Monster hat sailed over several people and hitting one of Sheena's teammates. At that point, before Mr. Isol could snatch it and tear it to pieces, Ken hastily stuffed it back in his pocket after offering an inadequate apology to the gymnast.

The parading of the nations began and one by one, each nation strode past the United States team and meandered onto the track, cheering and waving. Michael was desperately waiting for the name of his country to be called so he could go relax.

When the announcers reached Mexico, all the coaches were organizing their players into a sort of rectangle to look more professional. Michael moved automatically towards Matt and Sheena to ensure he had someone friendly right by him.

The announcers reached the U's, and excitement was crackling with not only the players but the coaches as well.

"Any second now," Matt whispered.

Then, at long last . . .

"The United States of America!"

Michael felt as though he was traveling with a stampede of buffalo: with Fred waving the American on a flag at the front of the group, the Americans charged into the stadium, waving flags and receiving cheers from the crowd. Michael waved at the crowd, trying to not completely lose control of his actions like his baseball teammates. Ken chucked his Cookie Monster hat into the crowd, and Michael forced back a laugh as he saw two small boys fight over the hat.

After running on the track and taking in all the cheers from the excited crowd, the United States' athletes and coaches made their way out of the limelight to the edge of the stadium.

"Wasn't that fun?" asked Sheena excitedly to Michael.

"Yeah," Michael said, stifling a yawn.

After more fireworks and a speech, the Opening Ceremonies began to crawl to a close. The torch relay and the lighting of the flame cauldron came and went as the crowd cheered and clapped. Michael's hands were beginning to go numb from clapping. Even more fireworks to amaze the crowd followed, and the ceremonies concluded. The ceremonies ended after midnight, and Michael, Matt, and Sheena quickly made their way back to the hotel, tired but pleased and excited after what had happened. It was hard to panic about anything at that moment—even the Ying-Yang brothers.

CHAPTER 10

THE LAMENT OF TEAM USA

Michael woke up extremely early that morning after a very unsatisfactory slumber. Matt was still asleep; his snores penetrated throughout the room and Michael thought they were capable of flowing through the whole hallway outside.

He got out of bed and glanced at the clock. It was only five thirty. He tried to go to sleep again, but it just would not come to him. He found a note on his nightstand, however, and he picked it up and read it silently to himself:

Our first game is on August 13.
We are versing South Korea at 6 at WKB Field 2.

This did relieve Michael for he would not have to play until four more days, even though he knew that. Smiling, he got up and pulled on a t-shirt and a pair of jeans. After lacing up his shoes, he crept outside the room, his mind on going downstairs to have breakfast.

The cafeteria was locked when Michael approached it: obviously it was too early to get breakfast. Michael decided on the spot to go outside to take a walk, hoping that by the time he was done, the cafeteria would be open.

The air was as Michael expected it to be: suffocating. It felt like trying to hold his breath underwater for a minute. He knew he could not stay out here for too long. He decided just to walk around the building once to get his legs moving. They felt extremely numb after standing straight and tall for hours last night.

So he started, breathing as little as possible. He was happy the building was not too big, and in a matter of a minute, he was heading back to the entrance.

As he was approaching the entrance to Blossom Suites, he heard voices just outside the hotel. He momentarily froze, and hid behind a nearby dumpster, so the people could not see or hear him. He leaned slightly to hear what they were saying and to see them.

"I swear, if you can't capture him, then be ready to face the consequences!" a very angry voice said in a threatening sort of voice.

"I have a plan, I just need the timing . . ."

That voice was awfully familiar . . .

"Well, if you can't find a way to get him to us without anyone knowing then it won't work! We need the scroll! We want the revenge we've been trying to get for the past ten years!"

Even though Michael could only see the backs of the men, he knew that the Ying-Yang brothers were there. Their snarling voices gave it away too easily.

"The boy will do the work for us because we need to attend Committee meetings throughout the Olympics. We'll kill him if he does not cooperate. It's too dangerous for him to be walking around, knowing all of this information."

"Okay, fine, whatever . . ."

"We shall monitor your progress over the next week. We are patient. Make sure it works before the Olympics is over—"

"Yes, I—I will."

He heard footsteps die away so Michael scrambled up and tried to see who the men were to be sure of who was speaking but it was too late: they were gone as if they were not even there.

Disappointed, he walked back into the hotel to find the two people who he felt needed to know this.

★ ★ ★

"So they were definitely saying about you working for them?"

"Yes, Matt."

It was finally breakfast time, and Michael, Matt, and Sheena were at the same table and eating breakfast while Michael supplied them with what he witnessed earlier.

"I think," Michael said, "that those people were the Ying-Yang brothers and Mr. Smith. I didn't see them but I recognized their voices. They seem determined to capture me and use me to find the scroll."

"But why would they want you?" Sheena asked, buttering herself some toast.

Michael leaned in closer and lowered his voice. "From what I heard, it sounds as if they take away me from your father and Mr. Harrington they feel they have a better shot at succeeding. I bet you they're afraid I would tell both Mr. Harrington and Mr. Goodwin. After all, your fathers could probably do something about it. And killing me out in the open is too obvious and since the police are all over the place, their chances of succeeding are thin."

"I think," Sheena said, quietly, "that you need to pay a visit to my dad again. Tell him what you overheard and your theory. Let's see if he can help us figure this out."

"I think you're right," Matt piped up. "But are you honestly sure your dad will accept this? He told Michael not to meddle in this business more than he already has."

"I think he'll still listen to Michael," Sheena said, earnestly. "He might then take the situation in his own hands."

"We also need to make sure that the brothers and Mr. Smith can't hear us and find out what we're up to," Michael replied, slowly. "I don't want them targeting you two as well."

Matt and Sheena just looked at each other with resigned expressions. Michael was baffled.

"Did I say something wrong?"

"No. You must understand that it's too late for that, Michael," Sheena whispered, seriously, her eyes wide with fear. "The brothers want revenge on my dad and the baseball team. They'll be sure to target me and Matt."

"I think Shawna and Ember are in more danger," Matt piped up, thoughtfully. "Your two sisters are a lot younger. They are probably easier to take care of than you."

How Matt worded it was weird, but Michael got the message.

"It's like the strong preying on the weak," Michael replied, slowly. "Matt has a fair point, Sheena."

"Damn right I do," Matt said, chucking his apple core into a nearby trash receptacle.

"But in the meanwhile," Sheena said, "we need to concentrate on our sports. Michael, you have to understand that you are here to pitch, not play detective and investigate the Ying-Yang brothers."

"I'm not playing detective. I don't have a game or practice today."

"I don't care, I'll breathe freely again when those two are in jail," Sheena said with tone of such finality that Michael could not reply.

"Why don't you come with us?" Matt said. "You can watch me kill myself on the diving board."

"Okay."

Sheena looked at Michael. "Try to forget about the scroll. We don't need anymore pressure on us than we already do."

⋆ ⋆ ⋆

The next three days for Michael were mixed in with some strenuous practices and a disaster of a conversation with Mr. Goodwin.

Michael did go and try to talk to Mr. Goodwin about what he witnessed. However, Mr. Goodwin did not find it intriguing. He was shocked at the fact that Michael observed this and thought of it as a great miracle, he told Michael, that he was not seen.

"You need to be more careful, Michael," said Mr. Goodwin sternly as Michael sat at the kitchen table, guilt bubbling up inside of him. "They could have just nipped you right there! Anyway, what you overheard gains us nothing. It really is not important, especially since you don't know for sure who was speaking."

Then what was important? Michael had no answers: all he had were questions. And, on top of that, he didn't know how to answer any of them without arousing suspicion of the Ying-Yang brothers, Mr. Smith, and Mr. Goodwin (for he knew he would not be impressed by it).

Baseball seemed to be unimportant now and every practice, Michael could sense that the coaches were beginning to sense his lack of attention to the game, which he usually loved, but the scroll put it out of his mind. Only Mr. Harrington had confidence in him now, and since most of them feared his inconsistency, he was abysmally flunking in practices and he was moved out of the starting rotation. Michael could understand the move even though he didn't like it: he certainly wasn't pitching with the urgency that the coaches were expecting him to pitch with.

"Michael, you need to *concentrate*," Mr. Harrington said, in a tone that suggested urgency after he beamed his third hitter at practice.

Michael was finding it hard to concentrate. He couldn't get the picture out of his mind of what the Ying-Yang brothers might do to him, and the families of his two best friends. Somehow, he thought that it was his destiny to find the scroll. Baseball was merely a distraction for a larger issue that needed to be solved immediately. However, it only seemed like Michael really felt the urge to quickly stop the growing threat that was the Ying-Yang brothers.

The only two players that seemed to think Michael still had starter material were Nitro and Fred O' Leary. Nitro just said Michael was in a bad slump and would get back in a groove after the first game. In contrast, Fred thought his excuse was from a disruption between his personal problems.

"He is worrying about that Goodwin girl too much," Fred replied, after the end of the last practice before the game. "Harry is right after all, girls can cause trouble."

Michael had to appreciate Fred not thinking other horrible things to make up for his performance. He was having enough trouble as it was and the constant *"Get in there!"* chants did not make Michael's life any simpler. He found it irksome more than anything.

Meanwhile, Matt was not having great luck either. His dives were less-than-inspiring to say the least. At the pool, he managed to fall off the board by accident and had to twist in mid-air like he was having a seizure. He was so bad his trainer called his dad and told him if he continues diving horribly, there would be no Olympics for him.

"Then I'll have to be bat boy," Matt muttered to Michael when he told him this.

Sheena, unlike the other two, was looking towards a successful Olympics. She did well in her competitions over the following days, and the judges seemed impressed by her talent. Out of the three of them, Sheena was the best at letting go about the scroll and only concentrating on what she was here for in the first place. The only way Michael figured out that she was not herself was when he overheard her trainer talking to Mr. Goodwin.

"She's never happy during practice, but I don't know what's wrong with her. She's performing the best I've ever seen her, yet she's always quiet."

Michael could understand why Mr. Harrington was concerned about his performance. He wanted to prove to the Ying-Yang brothers that young athletes could succeed. However, he was disheartened that Mr. Goodwin did not seem to find any of Michael's information interesting. Michael guessed that he already knew, but he wished that Sheena's father could tell him that. Then, he wondered if Mr. Harrington told him not to tell him anything so that Michael could get back on track with pitching.

Finally, at long last, it was the day of the first baseball game. Michael understood that this might be the only chance he may have to prove he was a good pitcher and get back in the rotation. He needed to be focused.

He had breakfast with Matt and Sheena, who were trying to boost his confidence. Once they learned about his lack of concentration, the two of them had been taking turns to throw a baseball with him outside the hotel when he was not practicing the last few days. However, Michael had a shrewd suspicion that they were doing it to distract him from the scroll.

"How are you, Michael?" Sheena asked as he sat down.

Michael nodded sleepily. Sheena did not take that as an adequate response. She snapped her fingers in front of his face.

"Hello? Michael, am I speaking to myself?" Sheena asked. She took her half-eaten donut from her napkin. "I need you to be focused and prepared!"

And without hesitation, she shoved the donut into Michael's mouth. He choked, and with great difficulty, swallowed the donut while Matt looked at Sheena as though he was seeing her in a whole different light.

"Sheena!" he exclaimed, downright shocked by her actions.

"Are you focused yet, Michael?" Sheena asked, sharply. "Are you awake and alert?"

"Yes, Sheena," Michael replied, weakly. "There was no need for that."

"Since you could not answer me, I think there was a need for it," Sheena said, calmly. "I don't want you walking out onto the mound with an empty stomach and no focus."

"Good luck, Michael," Matt replied.

"I hope," Michael said, in a voice unlike his own.

And, within no time at all, he had to join his team in the locker room where they were changing into their uniforms. They looked up when the door cranked open.

"There's Michael," Cliff greeted him, as he entered the room. "He's the kid who has nothing to boast about anymore."

"You say that about anyone," Samuel replied.

Michael joined Nitro in the corner where he stood.

"Are you ready?" Nitro asked him.

"I think so," Michael responded back.

Then, the coaches came in. They had uniforms on as well and were looking serious.

"Team, huddle up."

The whole team crowded around the coaches. Then Mr. Harrington spoke, "I have decided on the lineup for this game. I would like you all to look at it."

The whole team huddled around the lineup, which was so big everyone could see it. Michael read through it:

RF Xavier
SS Ty
CF Ken
2B Harry
1B Fred
LF Cliff
3B Todd
C Mike
P James

Reserve Fielders:

Nitro 3B, Phil 3B, Lew 1B, Samuel LF, Brad SS,
Chad SS, George 2B, Ahmad RF

Reliever Pitchers:
David, Michael, Joe, Ron

Other starters:
Justin and Oscar

Michael finished reading the lineup and looked to find that the team was making its way to the dugout. He followed, wondering if he would get to pitch at all. He really wanted to show that he deserved to play—to prove to the brothers that fourteen-year-old kids could succeed on the big stage.

While everyone was discussing about the lineup, George passed everyone gum.

"Chew the gum, it'll help," he told everyone. "It relieves your nerves."

Meanwhile, Ty was swearing, annoyed that he was not leading off. Unfortunately for him, Mr. Harrington heard him and knocked him off the starting rotation and decided to put Brad in his place.

"Coach, you're wasting my talent!" Ty cried at him like a baby. "I deserve to be first in the lineup!"

"Xavier is leading off, whether you like it or not!" Mr. Harrington said, loudly.

"Xavier is good but he's no starter," Ty said, dismissively.

The whole locker room went silent. Michael glanced at Xavier. He looked exceptionally angry, but Michael could tell he knew that it was best to hold his tongue and leave it for the coaches to sort out. Mr. Isol took charge.

"Ty, you better SHUT UP now or leave the team for good!" Mr. Isol bellowed at him. "I've had it with your poor attitude! Unless you want to be shipped out after the game, cut the crap!"

The locker room was deadly silent. Michael knew that no one dared argue with Mr. Isol. The man was intimidating already as it was due to his vastness. Ty looked defiantly and insolently at the vast man, and then stamped to his locker, bristling with fury.

"Nice decision, Coach," Brad muttered, grinning, which made Ty go even redder.

"Brad, be quiet," Mr. Harrington whispered.

No one in the locker room spoke after that. Most were avoiding Ty's gaze, wary of what he might do. Michael sincerely wanted to get out of the locker room—he hated the quiet atmosphere.

Soon enough, the South Korean team was warming up, and Xavier was doing practice swings. The crowd was cheering, and Michael was with the pitchers and Nitro in the bullpen, watching the game. Since he wasn't playing, Nitro had been giving the task of warming the reliever pitchers up when they were called.

"I hope we get an early lead," Nitro said to him. "James is a great pitcher, you watch."

"He's your brother, of course you think he's great," Michael said, laughing.

Xavier led off the inning nice with a bunt single that just skirted down the third base line. Then Brad came up and he flew out to center field after three pitches.

"That's okay, though," Nitro said. "Xavier is going to steal, watch."

And sure enough, Xavier did steal and was successful. The crowd cheered hard, Michael and Nitro with them.

"Ken is good, right?" asked Michael as Ken was next to bat.

"He led our team in homers last time," Nitro answered, without taking his eyes off the game. "James told me."

Ken, however, struck out, making it two outs with a guy on second.

"He better not strand him," Michael replied.

"Harry is good, he won't," Nitro replied confidently. "He'll hit a double I bet you."

Nitro was right—for the second time. Harry delivered on a 2-1 pitch and drove it to the right field wall and he got the United States on the board with the lead 1-0.

Cheering hard with the crowd, Michael asked, "How can you guess this stuff?"

Nitro smiled. "I'm just amazing like that."

Nitro indeed did have a knack of guessing things correct and was right when he said Fred would walk and the next batter, Cliff would fly out to right field to end the inning.

"That's a decent start," Michael replied to Nitro, who was watching his teammates trot back to the dugout.

"Let's hope we don't blow it, though," he replied, biting his lip. "We always had a tendency to do that."

James was dominant for the first inning and two-thirds and got all of them out and struck out four of them. However, he suffered a base hit and then the next batter hit a two-run shot in the bottom of the second.

"Damn it," Nitro said, chucking his glove at the bench. "There goes our lead. James never gives up homers."

"We can get it back, though," Michael assured him, not worrying about it. From where he sat, Michael thought James was handling himself well. He did not brood over the fact that he had given up a homer—he was only concentrated on rectifying his mistake.

He finished the inning but the Korea team got another run in the third and the United States could not score making it 3-1 after three whole innings. The fourth inning was very short and James was able to strike out the side, totaling now up to seven strikeouts in four innings.

"That's pretty good," Michael said, as he pointed this out.

"Yes but he gave up three runs," Nitro replied, unhappily.

Team USA got to tie the game in the fifth by a Harry double and Fred went yard to get both of them in. It was 3-3 and James was back on the mound for the bottom of the fifth.

"Oh no," all of the pitchers groaned in the bullpen but Michael.

"What's wrong?" he questioned them. He couldn't understand their morose expressions on their faces; they were acting as though women were wiped from the world completely.

David spoke to him this time. "This is the inning we were dreading. Every Olympics, in the first game, in this inning, someone gets injured. It is never a good one for us. We lost three guys in this inning last time."

Michael sincerely hoped this was not the case, but was surprised that his teammates were being so superstitious. He couldn't see what was going to be a problem.

And it did not look like it was. James got another strikeout and a ground out for the first two batters. Then he was 3-2 on the last guy. James got in his wind-up, looking at Mike.

"Come on, James," Nitro pleaded.

The crowd was silent too as if they knew this inning was monumental for the Americans. James threw a pitch right over the middle and batter took a mighty cut at the sailing ball.

Clang! The ball ricocheted back at James who had no time to avoid it. The ball beamed right into his chest. James was lifted into the air and fell backwards, and moved no more.

The crowd gasped in shock at what they just saw. Harry tried to underhand the ball to Fred but it was too late. The batter was safe by a half a second.

"See? What did he tell you?" demanded Ron to Michael. "James will be lucky if he's still alive!"

"Gulping gargoyles!" Nitro screamed. "That ball flew as fast as a falcon! I hope he's not seriously hurt!"

"Me too," Michael whispered. "Man, did that look bad . . ."

The medical crew on the team plus Mr. Harrington, Mr. Isol, and Mr. Oberfels was on the field while Mr. Smith grabbed the phone.

"He's calling for a pitcher," Nitro said matter-of-factly.

Michael did not care; he just hoped James was all right. There was a five-minute wait while the coaches and medical people were examining James.

The phone rang and Mr. Smith's voice echoed in it.

"Get David out here. He's pitching."

David got his glove and hurried out onto the field without further ado. When he got to the mound, Michael watched as the crowd cheered: James got to his feet and was being escorted off the field by the coaches. Though he was standing, Michael could tell that Mr. Harrington and Mr. Oberfels were supporting him completely. Michael wondered whether Mr. Harrington was trying to show the Chinese how tough his players were by not calling for a stretcher.

David could not finish the inning very well. He gave up two walks and then a three-run homer before he could finish the inning. The crowd booed him as he walked off, looking displeased with his performance.

The United States were able to get one more run in the sixth thanks to Mike's single. As soon as he reached first base, the phone rang in the dugout. Nitro answered it quickly.

"Get Michael warmed up," Mr. Harrington's voice said. "We should have had him out earlier."

Nitro warmed Michael up and as soon as Mike jogged back to the dugout, Michael grabbed his mitt and entered the field from the bullpen door in the outfield.

A ray of orange sun obscured his vision at first and it took him a second to realize that the crowd was on their feet, cheering. Feeling elated, Michael slowed to a walk as he reached the infield and acknowledging his teammates, Michael bent down and scooped up the ball right at the edge of the mound.

It was 6-4 when Michael first stepped on the mound. He felt as if his destiny was waiting for him. He stepped on the mound and Mike gave him the sign from the plate as the first batter stepped up.

Michael looked up and saw Sheena and Matt holding a sign that read: Michael = Team USA Hero. Michael could not help smiling.

Michael felt like yelling to his friends but he knew he had a job to do. Staring his batter down, he got a signal from Mike telling him to throw a fastball. He went into his motion and pitched a fastball on the outside corner as the batter watched it sail into Mike's glove.

Strike one.

The crowd cheered as Michael got the ball back. He then worked quickly into throwing another fastball right level with the letters. This time the batter swung under the rising fastball.

Strike two.

The crowd was on their feet. So was the dugout of his team, cheering. Mike gave him a nod, which meant—*use your hang glider.*

Michael nodded. He went into his motion and crossed his middle and pointer finger on his throwing hand before he let it go and the crowd held its breath.

Michael watched as the ball spun fast and it dropped at ankle level and the batter swung over it.

"HE STRUCK HIM OUT!" Fred yelled, interrupting the umpire.

The crowd was cheering hard, but by the end of the inning, it was deafening. Michael struck out the next two batters in six pitches. The batters just could not seem to make contact with any of his pitches which made Michael's goblet of confidence fill itself to the brim with excitement.

Michael walked back to the dugout with his team and sat down on the bench when Mr. Harrington came up to him.

"You will be back on the starting rotation," he said quietly.

"I am?" Michael asked, perplexed.

"Yes, I think so," Mr. Harrington replied earnestly. "By the way, you're going out in the next inning too, so don't get comfortable."

"Okay," Michael said, taking a sip of Gatorade. Then he added, "How is James?"

It was not Mr. Harrington that answered but Mr. Oberfels and Mr. Isol who did. They had come over to congratulate Michael as well.

"He's okay, but he'll be out for all of the Olympics," Mr. Oberfels replied, sorrowfully. "He's lucky to live that to tell the tale."

"I guess you will replace him after all, Durbin," growled Mr. Isol. "Anyway, that was some damn nice pitching out there."

Out of the corner of his eye, Michael noticed Mr. Smith leaving the dugout and went down to the locker room. Michael wanted to pursue him and see what he was up to but thought better of it as he had to pitch the next inning. He would deal with him later.

The next two innings went almost as perfect as the first one for Michael. He got three more strikeouts and was able to keep the ball on the ground, preventing the baseball from getting past the infield.

When the top of the ninth came around, Michael was in the dugout, spitting out sunflower seeds when Mr. Smith came out of the locker room and into the dugout. He saw Michael looking at him and went over to him.

"Are you done pitching?" he asked, curiously.

Michael felt like pointing out that as a coach he should know those things but he thought it best not to do so. He would have also liked to tell him that he was partly responsible for those three runs in the fifth inning but desisted.

"I think so," Michael replied, conversationally. "Mr. Harrington called down for Ron to get loose."

"You're surprising me, Durbin," Mr. Smith said, abruptly. "I would have never thought you would be this good. Keep it up. You're even surprising the Chinese."

"You mean your Chinese buddies, Ying and Yang, right?"

The words were out of his mouth before he could stop himself. He shouldn't have said that. He still had no explicit proof that it was Mr. Smith talking to them outside Blossom Suites that morning. Michael waited with bated breath for Mr. Smith's reaction. Surprisingly, he smiled, but it was more like a leer, and Michael didn't like it.

"Yes, that's exactly what I mean, Durbin," Mr. Smith said, softly and left Michael sitting there, taken aback.

The top of the ninth went smoothly and the USA got their lead back to 7-6 by three RBI doubles by Xavier, Ken, and Harry. The crowd was shouting themselves hoarse. Most of them wanted the Americans to win.

"It's not over yet," Mr. Harrington muttered, and the other coaches smiled. They seemed to think there was no chance for their team to blow the game.

Ron came in the bottom of the ninth for the USA. He got a fly out for the first out but then he suffered two straight walks.

"Ron's making things interesting," Mr. Oberfels said, grimly.

"This kid needs to calm down!" Mr. Isol answered gruffly. "I'll go talk to him."

Mr. Isol went out and had a discussion with the catcher and pitcher. Michael watched Ron nod and Mike went back to home plate.

"I told him to calm down and just throw the damn baseball like he means it!" growled Mr. Isol to the other coaches.

"Let's hope so," Mr. Harrington replied, nervously.

But luck did not suit Ron for he gave up a RBI double the next batter that tied the game at seven. There was a man on second and third with only one out. A sacrifice fly would bring him in.

Mr. Isol turned to Michael.

"We should have you on the mound. This kid sucks period," Mr. Isol said, gruffly. "I don't even remember why I picked him. Probably just so he could entertain the crowd by making every one interesting."

Michael had to bite back a laugh and he turned his attention back to the game. Ron was about to send another baseball to Mike.

The next batter for Korea ended the game with a single right up the middle that scored the winning run. Ron and the rest of the team slumped off the field, angry as the Korean team charged out onto the field to celebrate.

"Damn it!" Mr. Isol yelled, chucking a Gatorade container at the dugout wall.

"It's okay," Mr. Harrington said, though Michael could tell he wasn't at all happy. "We better change, let's go."

If there was anything worse that could have happened, it was this: their best pitcher was now out for the whole Olympics, and their bullpen blew a game that they should have had. As Nitro and David had said, the looming terror of the fifth inning had torn through them, and now they walk off the field as a loser and Michael couldn't help wondering if this was only the beginning.

CHAPTER 11

THE FIRST CONFRONTATION

The locker room atmosphere was not very pleasant as the whole team changed out of their uniform. No one said much as the team changed out of the navy uniforms. After Michael changed out of his uniform, he left the locker room, pleased by his performance, but disheartened at the result.

They had lost.

We had lost.

There was nothing more to it, Michael thought. We lost. And now we must make game two a victory.

Michael was walking out of the park when he spotted two Chinese men loitering right outside the field. They spotted Michael walking out and their eyes seemed to bulge out of their skulls. They immediately walked towards him and blocked his path. As they stopped in front of him, Michael looked up at them and recognized the two men.

They had coal-black hair that almost went over their eyes. They had fair skin and blue eyes and were very skinny and short. With a horror, Michael could tell that these two men were not taking a stroll around the city. They were the Ying-Yang brothers—the last two people Michael wanted to talk to now.

"Ah, you must be Michael Durbin," the one on the left said in a fruity, unctuous voice. "The excellent pitcher, remember, Yang, at the tryouts?"

"Oh yes, I remember all right," Yang said, in a falsely casual voice. "Remember, Ying, this kid didn't even make the age limit. Bless him."

Michael looked around. There was no one around. This wasn't a situation that played in Michael's favor. If the Ying-Yang brothers wanted him, this unfortunately could be the perfect time to take him away. He had to get away from them before they could harm him.

"Sorry, I have to go—" he started, and walked away from them.

The brothers moved to the right blocking his path. Michael gulped nervously.

"Not so fast, Michael Durbin. Tell us, Michael," Ying said, "whether Harrington told you why he made such an eccentric decision—"

"—In putting you in such a high role. Starter, I tell you, honestly—"

"—Too much of a huge responsibility to put on such a—"

"—Small, nosy, young, and inexperienced boy—"

Michael gulped nervously again. Even though he thought he already knew it, the Ying-Yang brothers obviously knew it was him that overheard him, and the tone of their voices did not soothe Michael. They were obliquely referring to him eavesdropping on their conversation that day at tryouts. The word "nosy" gave it away.

Michael looked at his surroundings. There was still no one near him. Getting frustrated at the sudden lack of people in the vicinity, Michael could do nothing but listen to Ying and Yang bully him right in front of his eyes.

"I saw you pitch," Yang said, leering over Michael. "You are good, but not as good as me."

"Yes, he is not—"

"—As good as Harrington thinks he is—"

"—He is Harrington's favorite, and of course, the precious little snowflake on the team—"

"—Even putting him on the team—"

"—Utter madness, I tell you—"

"—Overrated, I call it—"

"Michael!"

"*Michael!*"

Michael looked around them and saw Matt and Sheena dashing towards him, looking worried. They stopped right by him and then looked at the Ying-Yang brothers, shocked.

"Ah, is it Harrington's son—?"

"—And that Goodwin daughter—"

"—Oh, she's a cute one, isn't she, Yang—?"

"—Oh, bless them—"

Michael found his bravery at last and could not stop himself to ask a question. "How come you two are strutting around in Beijing? Don't you have better things to do than to harass precious little snowflakes like me? Or are you so unimportant on the Committee that you don't need to be at any of their meetings?"

Sheena gasped, Matt looked shocked. The Ying-Yang brothers did not seem to mind. They exchanged a long, amused glance with each other before turning their attention back to the three friends. Their gleeful expressions did not completely hide their surprise at Michael's words.

"Dear me, Mikey, there's no need for those words—"

"—He's different for a fourteen-year-old—"

"—Different than the *average* fourteen-year-old—"

What did the brothers mean? Michael thought. He did not like the emphasis on the word "average." And where were his coaches and teammates? They should have walked out of the locker room by now. Matt faced the brothers defiantly.

"Get out of our way!" Matt said, loudly.

"*MICHAEL! MATT! SHEENA!*"

This time, it was Mr. Harrington, Mr. Isol, and Mr. Oberfels, who were walking towards them. Michael could have laughed in relief. They were safe. He knew that the brothers would be stupid to try and abduct Michael right now, especially with Mr. Isol being present, who was big enough to devour them.

"Ah, look who it is, Yang. It is Harrington," Ying said in a smooth voice. He held out his hand. "We ran into your son, his pretty friend, and baseball's new tragic hero. We were going to show them the way back to Blossom Suites, but it looks like we don't need to do so now."

"I overheard you speaking to these three," Mr. Isol snarled, with the air of one about to slit one's throat. "You two still speak like weirdos, I've noticed."

Ying and Yang ignored him and turned to Harrington, obviously waiting for his reaction. Mr. Harrington did not shake Ying's hand, but only gazed at them coldly, which only showed the hatred Mr. Harrington had for them.

"Ying," Mr. Harrington said, nodding coldly. "Yang. Outside for a stroll, are we?"

"Outside to see your team lose," Ying retorted. "How does it feel like to get rejected from something you desire, Harrington?"

"Yeah, how do you feel, Harriet?" Yang said, smoothly. "However, truth to be told, your loss was not so surprising due to the little league lineup you put out there to compete in vital games such as these."

Mr. Harrington's lip curled. He obviously didn't appreciate being called "Harriet" and the criticism involving his team.

"I've got a *very* different idea of a little league lineup, Yang," Mr. Harrington said, aggressively.

"Manners, Harriet, or I shall have to call the police on you," Yang said tauntingly. "You forget how grudgingly we allow you to stay in our country."

Mr. Isol clenched his fists tightly and Mr. Harrington glared at the brothers. Ying continued to taunt him.

"All these idiotic decisions you make, Harrington," Ying said with the faintest hint of a snarl, "proves that you are a very poor coach. Tut tut tut, Harriet. I thought the program you ran could sink no lower but clearly, I was wrong."

In less than a second, Mr. Harrington extracted an aluminum bat and pointed it at the brothers while Ying pulled out a pistol and pointed it at Mr. Harrington.

"Dad!"

Mr. Oberfels and Mr. Isol also pulled out bats at them, too. The other brother pulled out another gun, laughing.

"You honestly think you can beat us with baseball bats?" Yang asked, laughing.

"Coach, please—"

"You touch my son and his friends and you will be very sorry indeed, Ying and Yang," snarled Mr. Harrington, waving the bat threateningly at them. "You'll be crying for your daddy once I'm done with you two!"

"Dad, you can't start a feud out in the middle of Beijing!" Matt cried. "The Olympics are supposed to be about world peace!"

"World peace my ass," Mr. Isol snarled. "All of that is thrown to the dogs when these morons are in my reach!"

Mr. Isol gripped the bat tighter. Matt attempted to dissuade his father again.

"Dad, put the bat down!"

"Keep out of this, Matt!" Mr. Harrington said, loudly. Then, he turned to the brothers. "Make one more crack about my team and I'll bash your brains in!"

Ying smiled. "So, tell me, Harrington, why did you place Mikey on the team? Surely you must be second-guessing your decision after he blew the game today."

"For your information, he did not blow the game," Mr. Oberfels replied, angrily.

The Ying-Yang brothers shrugged. They kept their guns pointed at the coaches. Sheena looked scared and worried about what might happen; Matt was shocked, appalled to say anything; and Michael was glaring at the brothers. All the coaches held their bats steady as if waiting for what the brothers were going to do.

Finally, the brothers put their guns back into their pockets and turned to walk away.

"You wait Harrington—"

"—You will pay—"

"For what?" Mr. Harrington queried, coldly. "Not putting you on the Committee?"

They just merely glared at him, which was answer enough for him.

"Who'd want losers like you?"

Ying acted quicker than Michael could have imagined. Ying pulled out a gun and pointed it at Mr. Harrington. Michael pulled

Sheena down with him and the bullet flew over him and made impact at the wall behind them, causing birds to leave their feast of leftover hamburger buns and fly chaotically away.

"See you soon, Harriet."

Then, with a flash, the brothers disappeared.

Mr. Harrington put the bat away while Matt helped Sheena to her feet. She was shaking. Michael turned to his coaches.

"Thanks for that," Michael replied.

"How did you three end up with them?" Mr. Harrington asked them, looking serious.

"I left the locker room and they found me. They started saying about how I am overrated so I tried to escape but they blocked my path," Michael explained. "I don't know how they found me so quickly, but they did."

"Then we saw Michael talking to those jerks," Matt said. "We went to get him and found him with those two brothers. They were just keeping us there."

"But why would those gits just keep you there? Having a friendly little chat, I suppose?"

Michael cleared his throat. He felt that it was time for him to tell his coaches what he had been concealing from everyone for weeks. He answered Mr. Isol's question.

"I found out a lot of stuff about them. They want to kidnap me and use me so that they can obtain the scroll without doing any work. I overheard them at tryouts talking about it."

Mr. Harrington turned white. He looked more anxious than Michael ever saw him.

"Are you sure?" Mr. Harrington asked, looking shocked.

"Dead sure," Michael answered, firmly.

The coaches glanced at each other quickly before turning back to the three athletes.

"It was as Mr. Goodwin feared. Beijing is no longer safe for you, Michael, or my son and Sheena. Mr. Goodwin has told me about you three. He seems to think that you three fancy yourselves as investigators. You need to drop this now. I'm serious. It is of no importance to any of you."

"I don't think it matters anymore," Michael said, shrugging. "I already know too much."

"You trying to be noble will get you murdered!" Mr. Isol growled irritably. "Get your head out of your ass and smell the fresh air, Durbin! These brothers are not brainy, but they can manipulate you. They are not to be messed with. We brought you here to throw a baseball, not play Sherlock Holmes!"

All three coaches glared at him. Then Michael continued to speak after an awkward pause. He wasn't done with everything he had to say and he had no interest in being told off by Mr. Isol.

"Mr. Harrington, I don't think our team is safe."

"How come?"

Michael knew they would probably not believe him but he had to say it. No one was safe from the current situation and all guesses and theories were as good as anyone else's.

"I have the growing suspicion that Mr. Smith may be involved with the brothers in some way."

And he told all of them about his theories and the information that supported it. He also told the coaches about the conversation he overheard at Blossom Suites.

Mr. Harrington looked at Michael critically.

"I can't believe Mr. Smith would listen to the brothers. I know him, Michael, and he is a nice guy. I know he was a little pessimistic about you being on the team, but he admitted that he was wrong."

Michael sighed. He was not completely convinced by Mr. Harrington's assertion. Mr. Isol and Mr. Oberfels looked unconvinced as well, annoying Michael.

Sheena then spoke. "Mr. Harrington? Michael does bring up a point that is worth considering. It could be a coincidence, but I think in this situation you have to look at all possible outcomes."

"You could have a good point, Sheena," Mr. Harrington replied. "But it is not for you three to look into. It'll be the Committee and your father, Sheena, that will."

"They will," Mr. Isol replied, gruffly. "Or I'm not Lyle Isol!"

Mr. Harrington turned to Michael, Matt, and Sheena. "I want you three to concentrate on your sports. We need to prove the Ying-Yang brothers wrong. We need to show how young people can have success in these events. That is what you could do to help out."

It was now Michael's turn to be unconvinced. However, Michael decided to feign understanding so as not to infuriate his coaches anymore.

"So that is why Mr. Goodwin keeps telling me finding more information is unimportant. He wanted me to prove the Ying-Yang brothers' opinions wrong, to show them their views were ridiculous and to show everyone else that they are the bad guys!"

"Yes," Mr. Harrington replied, smiling, completely fooled by Michael's deception. "The scroll is still a mystery to us, but the Chinese and the brothers know about it. But the Chinese know that the brothers are strictly against young athletes. If you three could prove them wrong, it can help things a lot!"

Michael was about to reply that it would be as helpful as a damp log, but Sheena, who seemed to have read Michael's mind, kicked him gently in the ankle to prevent him from speaking.

"Now, I think it is time to get you three to bed," Mr. Isol replied in a gruff voice.

"Yes, and goodnight," Mr. Oberfels replied.

Michael, Matt, and Sheena bade them goodnight and started walking back to the hotel. During their walk, Sheena and Matt were discussing everything that they knew and were trying to piece it together. Michael, however, was not paying much attention to them. He was still deep in thought about what Mr. Harrington told him. He knew it was jumbled up, but as he neared the hotel, he knew it was only a matter of time until the puzzle was solved.

There were three hooded figures walking down the alleyway and they were not noticed by anyone. They were talking in angry voices, like an angry goose would say to her baby if caught in the wrongdoing . . .

"No—"

"It's your job to get him, not ours!"

"You had the chance and you blew it!"

"I know—"

The bickering drove the three men up a wall. The men exited the alleyway and onto the baseball field—

"Michael."

Where they stood unnoticed, hovered like an overgrown bat.

"We will succeed."

The hooded figures looked around the field and they knew what to do. They had to make the field as unsafe as possible.

"MICHAEL!"

"What?"

Michael was jerked out of his reverie to find Sheena holding the door for him.

"I've been holding the door for fifteen seconds," Sheena said, looking anxious. "Matt is waiting in the lobby."

"Oh, thanks," he replied as he walked in the hotel.

The three friends walked upstairs quickly to Michael and Matt's room. Matt decided that he wanted to play *Guitar Hero*, but Michael was not in the mood for it. He felt tired and a little unwell. Therefore, he contented himself with watching Matt and Sheena compete against each other.

After losing slightly to Matt in one song, Sheena turned to Michael.

"You don't look good. Are you alright?" she asked, slightly concerned.

Matt glanced at Michael as well, wearing a peculiar expression on his face. It looked as though he was studying his friend closely, trying to detect signs of an illness.

"I'm fine," Michael said, rubbing his forehead with his knuckles. "I'm just exhausted."

"You've had a long day," Sheena said, sympathetically. "It's not surprising."

Michael suddenly sat up straight. He turned to his two friends. He was very white.

"You don't think that Mr. Harrington is right, do you?" Michael questioned both of them. "He says we can help by succeeding in our sports. How does that help? I only answered the question because I knew he would get mad at me. For me, I don't think I could be satisfied with just being a pitcher."

Matt looked at him as though he thought Michael was a hallucination.

"You mean you want to do something about it? Michael, you must be mental!" exclaimed Matt. He was wearing bemused expression on his face.

"Look, I'm in enough danger as it is," Michael insisted. "I don't want your families to get involved. I'm going to put my efforts towards trying to figure out the location of the scroll *and* baseball. I'm going to find it before the brothers can get their hands on it."

Sheena looked as though she wanted to argue with him. Brushing her hair angrily out of her face, she stood up straight and glared at Michael defiantly.

"So you're telling us that you plan on making it easier for the brothers to kill you?" Sheena asked, incredulously. She was giving Michael a death stare, and Michael was surprised not to see beams of light shining right out of her eyes.

"No," Michael exclaimed, stunned. "I plan on finding a solution to stop them!"

"And what do you expect to do, Michael? Huh? What do you expect to do?" Sheena demanded.

"That's why I plan on working out a solution," Michael retorted, knowing full well Sheena was going to argue back.

"Didn't your confrontation with the brothers today have *any* affect on you?" Sheena asked, exasperatedly.

"Of course it did," Michael shot back at her.

Sheena didn't seem to want to hear Michael's explanations. She stamped her foot angrily, as if she was a five-year-old denied of a cotton candy at a zoo.

"Michael, they'll kill you!" Sheena cried, very angrily. "Don't be so stupid! Just stick to pitching. You seem to be very good at it, anyway."

She glared at Michael once, said goodnight to Matt, and walked out of the room, closing the door behind her.

Matt turned to Michael.

"You two are really cute when you argue with each other, you know that, right?"

Michael ignored his comment. He was looking at the door, stunned to hear the anger in Sheena's voice. He had least expected her to snap; on the other hand, he had expected her to agree with him and voice his own frustrations. Michael turned back to Matt, shaking his head.

"Look, if she wants to see the brothers get the scroll and carry out their terrible plans on her father and his Committee friends, then that's her deal," Michael said, not unkindly, ignoring Matt's comments. "She just doesn't see this the way I do."

"I don't either," Matt replied. "I think you're being thick, but you do have a point. I don't want anything bad to happen to my father, but you are going to need more help. You can't expect yourself to beat the Ying-Yang brothers on your own. I'll help, and Sheena will, too, once she realizes that you are not going to change your mind."

Michael looked at Matt.

"Do you think the brothers will do anything to get revenge on us?"

Matt nodded, looking deadly serious. The event that occurred today seemed to have stiffened his resolve.

"I think the brothers have enough ambition to achieve their goals no matter what the consequences are for themselves."

CHAPTER 12

THE DEPLETION OF TEAM USA

Michael woke up the next morning, waking up through a series of nightmares that he was glad he did not tell Matt about. One involved the Ying-Yang brothers executing him and the other one was with Sheena calling him a bunch of horrible names, while complimenting Matt as the whole gymnastics team swarmed around him.

Sheena was waiting for them down by the breakfast hall with two napkins with toast in them. She greeted Matt cheerfully, but she spoke to Michael in a tone that suggested she was fairly annoyed at him.

"I brought you two this," she told them. "Want to go for a walk to my parents' house?"

"Sure," Michael said, gratefully. "How come you've decided to go to your parent's house?"

Sheena narrowed her eyes.

"Because I said so," she said, irritably. "And I wasn't speaking to you, Durbin."

"Let's just go," muttered Matt. He seemed to be fed up with Michael and Sheena's bickering.

The three of them had a silent hike to the Goodwin household. Sheena led the way, still tut-tutting under her breath as Michael and Matt trailed behind her. Once they reached the house, Mr.

Goodwin welcomed them inside. It instantly became clear why Sheena suggested a hike to her parent's house.

"Dad, did you hear what happened yesterday?" asked Sheena as Mr. Goodwin gave them each a glass of orange juice.

She then flashed Michael an I-got-you look that greatly annoyed him.

"Oh, I heard all right," Mr. Goodwin muttered, looking sternly at the three of them.

"So what do you think about that?" Sheena asked, pressing her advantage. Michael glared at the floor.

"You're lucky you weren't killed, any of you!" Mr. Goodwin said, sternly. "And how did the brothers find you so quickly?"

"I don't know," Michael said, his head hanging; he could not meet Mr. Goodwin's eyes. "It's all a mystery."

"Sheena, you are to drop this," Mr. Goodwin said, looking older and Michael saw the concerned parent look in his eyes, not the serious, presidential look. "I am not in charge of you two, but I advise you to do the same."

"Yes, Dad," Sheena said, flashing Michael her you-know-my-father-is-right look. "But Michael's being stupid and not listening to your advice. He's not listening to me, either."

Mr. Goodwin raised his eyebrows after Sheena spoke at Michael, but it was a peculiar expression, not with anger or impatience. He chose to ignore his daughter's words and instead turned to Matt.

"Anyway, Matt, your father did say that he does not want you to find out any more information. I talked to him this morning."

Matt looked annoyed, but he did not say anything and merely nodded his head respectfully at Mr. Goodwin.

Michael knew that since his two friends were now being watched in case they tried to figure out any more information, he was the only one left. It was up to him to figure everything out. And Sheena and Mr. Goodwin or even Mr. Harrington wasn't going to stop him. He was pleased that the three of them seemed to truly care about him, but also impatient at them thinking that he wasn't capable of handling anything too important.

The three of them went outside for a little bit and played a super violent handball game between Michael and Shawna and Matt and Sheena. Ember watched while she was watering the peony bushes.

Sheena absolutely refused to be on Michael's team. Matt kept on tackling Michael that once he accidentally punched him on the nose, causing it to bleed.

"You moron, Matt," Michael said, stopping the flow by pinching his nose.

"That's God punishing you for being stupid," Sheena said, curtly.

Shawna whispered something in her sister's ear, and Sheena looked away from the group, embarrassed. Michael felt a wave of satisfaction after that.

After the game which ended in a Michael game-winning goal, the three headed back to the complex, where Michael had to get ready for the next baseball game against the Netherlands. He felt excited and not nervous because of his success in the first game.

Sheena and Matt had no competitions so they decided to come and watch him play. Michael appreciated their decision even if though Sheena was in no mood to be agreeable.

"Let's hope I even play," Michael told them as he put on his cap.

"I'm sure you will," Sheena replied in a tone that still suggested her anger and annoyance with him.

Matt raised his eyebrows, but he wore a peculiar expression on his face, not unlike the one Mr. Goodwin wore when he was trying to dissuade them for getting involved.

"After your performance in the first game," Matt said conversationally, "my dad has to pick you."

Michael had to be there early even though the game would start at eight o' clock at night. Mr. Harrington had sent a text to Matt to tell Michael to arrive almost three hours before the game.

So, at five o' clock, Michael bade his two friends see you later (Sheena ignored him) and he went to the locker room. There he found an unpleasant surprise.

There was hardly anyone there. The four coaches were there as always but the players—Michael gasped as he only saw a little more than ten players, counting himself. All of them were looking as though they were at some dreadful funeral.

"Yes, I know," Mr. Harrington said, as if reading Michael's mind.

"What happened?" asked Michael, his throat tight. "Where is everyone?"

"Lost nine more players due to injuries," Mr. Harrington said, bitterly. "Mr. Smith drove six of them back from the last game to the hotel, but they got in an accident. The other three got hurt playing a card game on a picnic table. You're the only pitcher left, Michael. You've got to last the whole game."

Michael gulped. Part of him was still in disbelief that half his team got hurt but another part of him was scared of the mounting pressure and heat that he had to contain in his personal crucible. He never had this much pressure on him, not even in the Little League World Series. He had to last the whole game or the team would have to forfeit. The stakes were never that high for him.

"Who's left?"

"We have only Harry, Fred, Ken, and Mike left as our original starters," Mr. Isol grumbled. "Then, we have Chad, Ahmad, Phil, Brad, Samuel, Lew, and Nitro."

"Are we having this lineup the rest of the Olympics?" Michael asked, hoping the answer was no.

"No," Mr. Oberfels said. "We get Xavier, David, and Ron tomorrow and then everyone else besides James will come back the day after that. We have to win this game, though, or forget getting any medals."

Michael looked towards Mr. Smith, who was wearing a grimace on his face that Michael did not like to see. He thought Mr. Smith purposely had the car crash to hurt the team, and deplete the lineup. If Michael's suspicions were correct, then Mr. Smith's motive for doing what he did was absolutely clear.

"Mr. Harrington—?" Michael started to ask, but the coach just shook his head violently. He knew what Michael was about to say, and it was apparent that he did not want to hear it.

★ ★ ★

At ten o'clock, Michael, who now regained his nervousness due to the fact he had to last the whole game, was on the mound warming up. It was easier to get loose today as Mike, the catcher, had formulated an innovative way to assist Michael. Mike had painted his nails different colors the day before, and that helped Michael understand the signal of what pitch to throw.

"If I give my blue one, throw a change up," he had told him. "If I give you red, throw a fastball. Purple is a slider, Green is a—whatever you called the pitch—hang glider, and yellow will mean a split finger."

The hang glider was a pitch that Michael had invented himself. He usually used it to fan his more annoying batters and it was a pretty effective breaking pitch.

And speaking of effective, Michael thought that Mike was actually being smart with his out-of-the-box plan. It would be hard for the other team to steal Mike's signal. They would only wonder why someone would be so weird as to paint their nails. But that's what Olympic athletes do—they do what they must, and without worry that people might think less of them.

Michael now looked at Mike, who gave him a red finger, which was a fastball. The batter for the Netherlands came up to the plate and immediately got into his stance. After a second pause, Michael let the first pitch go. It was strike one on the inside corner.

As the inning wore on, Michael noticed between pitches that Mr. Smith would leave the dugout and reappear a few minutes later. Could he possibly be talking to the Ying-Yang brothers? The only problem was that Michael could never get the chance to see what he was up to.

Michael was able to get through the first inning decently, combining a total of two strikeouts and a ground out. He left to the dugout where he was congratulated by Fred.

"Nice job out there, Mikey," Fred replied, winking.

"Thanks, Fred."

"Hey, did you notice how Mr. Smith keeps leaving the dugout?"

Nitro had joined into the conversation. He leaned in, his green hair in his eyes. He had a bat ready in his hand.

Fred was confused. "What do you mean?"

Nitro looked at him with a quizzical look. "I mean that he has been leaving the dugout for minutes at a time. It's as if he was doing something he didn't want Mr. Harrington or the other coaches to find out. It's definitely unusual, because coaches hardly ever exit the dugout."

"Where is Mr. Smith now?" Michael asked.

He looked around the dugout. Mr. Smith was nowhere in sight. He must have left while the few minutes between the top and bottom of the inning.

"He's gone. Nowhere to be seen," Nitro said. "Anyway, I have to get in the on deck circle, I'm batting third."

And Nitro left. Fred turned to Michael.

"Fancy hearing what he's up to?" he asked, as if reading Michael's mind.

"I would like to find out what he is up to," Michael said, slowly. "But are you saying—?"

"What I think you're saying?" Fred said. "Yes, I do. And I think I have a plan that would enable you to have time to see what he's up to."

"What is your plan?" Michael asked, thinking how great Fred's plan would actually be.

"When I come up to bat, I'll make sure I hit it," Fred said with the air of one declaring him the president. "And then, when I'm running the bases, I'll fake injure myself."

"You mean you are going to pretend you're injured?" Michael questioned, alarmed.

"There is no other way," Fred said, smoothly. "If I don't, the coaches will realize you're gone. This will help them give the attention off of the dugout and onto the field to make sure I'm 'okay.' You, meanwhile, could check what old Smith is up to."

"There is something in that."

"Yes, and I could do it this inning," he explained.

"How?"

"I saw one of us get on base," Fred explained. "I'm batting fourth. I should be on deck now."

As soon as he said it, Mr. Isol shouted, "O' Leary! Get in the on deck circle now! You're batting fourth, idiot!"

Michael cut to the essentials. "How much time would you be able to give me?"

"I can definitely give you . . . let's say, about five to ten minutes easily. Anyway, I better go before Mr. Isol rips my head off."

Fred left the dugout, so Michael focused his attention back on the game. All he had to do now was sit and wait for Fred to fake hurt himself.

Fred made the plan seem easy but Michael thought it was really risky. He seriously hoped that Fred would be a good actor. If he wasn't, the plan would disappear like sand through a funnel. This, Michael thought, was pushing the limit and he thought he was most likely going to be caught. However, this was the only chance to see what Mr. Smith was up to so he had to take this opportunity. He sincerely hoped that Mr. Smith would stay down there long enough for him to eavesdrop.

He saw Nitro draw a five-pitch walk, and Fred walked up to the plate. Fred did not look like that at this at-bat, he would not be doing it for the team, but for Michael, and to find out what Mr. Smith was up to.

Michael watched Fred take the first two pitches and the count turned to 1-1. Michael flattened his hair nervously. If Fred struck out, the plan would easily implode.

The next pitch soared above the letters for the second ball. Fred looked calm as he backed out of the batter's box. He turned around and flashed Michael a toothy grin. Michael couldn't share his optimism. Fred was enjoying the suspense way too much, Michael thought.

The next pitch was a corner strike. Fred could not take risks now. He had to swing at anything close.

The pitcher then threw a wild pitch which caused Nitro to dash to second. Michael held himself with bated breath. He slowly inched towards the dugout entrance . . .

The pitcher lobbed a ball right over the middle and Fred hit it down the right field line. He saw Nitro hustle to home plate. Then, Fred seemed to hobble to first, and when he got to first, his leg gave way, and crumbled to the ground but not before Michael saw a flash of triumph on his face.

Instantly, the whole team flew out of the dugout to examine Fred, and Michael, without hesitation, tore to the exit of the dugout and out of sight.

CHAPTER 13

FIVE PRECIOUS MINUTES

Michael found himself in the locker room a few seconds later. A TV was there, showing Fred acting like his leg hurt and the players watching him. Michael was happy to think that Fred was playing his part in the diversion well: it certainly looked like he hurt himself due to the fact that he was pretending to swear in agony on the screen.

Michael knew Fred would only give him about five minutes so he tore to the locker room and stopped abruptly once he got through the doorway.

Mr. Smith was at the opposite end of it and the door was slightly open. The door opened to the street, and Michael saw that Mr. Smith was peering out of the locker room talking to the Ying-Yang brothers. Today, the brothers were sporting coats made of red silk with golden lettering on them. Michael suddenly wondered whether they stole them from someone, though he could not explain why he felt that the brothers were not rich.

Knowing he would probably be captured if they saw him, hid behind a wall and listened to what they were saying. The three men were speaking in angry voices, which was something Michael found as a shock. Usually, if you were working together, you would be friends, but this was different. It was as if they were on different sides.

"I tell you, Smith, we do not appreciate your blunders. We've expected a lot better from you!"

"YOU DON'T UNDERSTAND!" roared Mr. Smith. "I HAVE TRIED, BUT HE IS TOO WELL PROTECTED! WE NEED TO GET ISOL ON OUR SIDE! HE'S THE PITCHING COACH, WHO CAN GET THE CLOSEST TO MICHAEL WITHOUT AROUSING SUSPICION! IT'S YOU TWO WHO HAVEN'T THOUGHT THIS OUT PROPERLY, IT'S YOU TWO MAKING THE HORRENDOUS BLUNDERS!"

Michael never heard Mr. Smith shout like that before. However, as short as Michael knew him, he was known to be an argumentative person. The shouts that erupted from him almost made Michael jump.

The plan was not going well, Michael thought, because they weren't working as a team. They were not following Olympic procedure at all by these secret meetings. Mr. Smith was being deceitful to Mr. Harrington and the brothers were irresponsibly not doing what they should be doing. The Ying-Yang brothers looked angry at Mr. Smith, but they seemed to be controlling themselves. Mr. Smith, however, was beside himself.

"I DON'T SEE YOU TWO DOING ANYTHING, YOU LAZY CHINESE PUNKS!"

"Smith, you have not been helpful—" Ying muttered calmly.

"—Too true—"

"—So you are to be given—"

"—One last chance—"

"—And if you fail—"

"—We will—"

"—Most likely—"

"—Shoot you—"

"—And you will suffer—"

"—Bodily harm."

Mr. Smith seemed to calm down a little bit, but he was trembling with anger that Michael could still sense. Mr. Smith was also trembling with fear, as though he expected the brothers to chuck a battle axe at him any moment. Michael realized with a jolt that this conversation was relevant. Mr. Smith was the brothers' puppet, and forced to do what the brothers wanted him to do. He waited in silence, hoping they would continue talking; Michael knew he only had a minute or two left. He was praying they would say any more important stuff.

"Yes, if you fail, we will get Mr. Isol on our side."

"How? He won't agree."

"If he doesn't, we shall make up a backup plan which would get him out of the way instead."

Michael wanted to know what the plan was but apparently they were not keen to continue the subject as the brothers both shook their heads, smiling evilly.

"You mean you haven't decided a plan yet?" Mr. Smith asked, thrown off by such new news.

"We know what it is," Yang replied, smoothly. "But we don't think you're trustworthy enough. Ying thinks you might join Harrington's side and betray us."

"You know I won't!"

"I wouldn't be so sure," Yang replied.

"After all—"

"—You haven't—"

"—Completed the plan yet."

Michael felt his breathing slow down. This was it. That was the answer. Mr. Smith was indeed hired to carry out the brothers' plans. He was their mole. The only thing that remained was the reason for Mr. Smith's actions. Why would he try and help the brothers? What was in it for him?

Michael knew his time was almost up, so after making sure the brothers and Mr. Smith weren't looking, he scurried out of the room back to the dugout.

Fred was on the ground, looking at the dugout. When he saw Michael, he slowly stood up, receiving a standing ovation; he obviously must have knew Michael was back. Michael saw the medical crew and the whole team come back to the dugout.

Nitro spotted Michael and sat down next to him. "Where were you?"

Michael decided to tell his friend the truth. "I went to find out where Mr. Smith was."

"And did you?"

"Yes," Michael replied. "Fred did a good job. He gave me enough time to hear the important points of their conversation."

"What do you mean by 'their'?"

Michael told him everything and what he had overheard. Nitro listened, but he did not get to finish—the inning had ended and he saw Fred jog back. Mr. Harrington looked displeased; Michael found out that Fred had been thrown out at second for attempting to steal a base to set off high spirits.

"How did it go?" Fred asked, excitedly with the air of one asking about a job interview.

"It was not a complete waste of time," Michael replied to him, shortly, and grabbing his baseball glove and a spare ball to throw.

"It better not had been a waste of time because I deserved an Oscar for my performance!" Fred yelled after Michael.

Michael walked right back out to the mound and as he did, he saw Mr. Smith come back in the dugout and suddenly engaged Mr. Isol in conversation. Casting one last glance at the pair, he turned around and stepped onto the pitching rubber.

This brought Michael back to the conversation that he eavesdropped on in the conference room. He had to warn Mr. Isol, after the inning. He was in danger as much as himself. The evil twins were going to use him as bait, or just because . . . but why did they want him in the first place?

Michael warmed up by throwing ten pitches and then the next batter went up to the plate. The batter looked as though he weighed about three hundred pounds—it was incredible how he was able to get to the base without collapsing. He was pretty much a mound of dough with limbs.

This time up, Michael felt a lot more confident, and he showed that by striking out the side and only wasting ten pitches. He left for the dugout, receiving a huge ovation, bigger than what Fred received. As he walked back, he tried to spot Matt and Sheena in the crowd above the USA dugout but he couldn't find them. He wasn't surprised; the stadium was full to the brim with people.

He sat back down on the dugout bench and helped himself to sunflower seeds and some Gatorade. He drank it all in one gulp. He was so thirsty he could have just drained the whole five-gallon container. As he refilled his cup, Mr. Harrington went over to him.

"Feel alright, Michael?" Mr. Harrington asked.

"Fine," Michael answered, sipping his drink.

"I already told Mike that I do not want you throwing fastballs at every pitch like you did the past two innings. You are going to get tired and only last five innings. We have no other pitcher, so we need you to last. Use some of your breaking pitches. You seem to work well with them."

"Okay," Michael answered back, and he threw out his cup.

"You're looking good, Michael," Mr. Harrington said, and he walked away after clapping him on the shoulder briefly.

Mr. Harrington left and ten seconds later, Michael was talking to Mr. Isol and Mr. Oberfels. Both had come over to offer Michael some advice and compliment his pitching.

"Damn nice pitching, Durbin," growled Mr. Isol. "You're looking good."

"Stay alert, Michael, you still need to last for twenty-one more outs," Mr. Oberfels advised him. "Keep pitching with confidence. You have the advantage."

"Mr. Isol?" Michael said. It was now or never. Michael was going to tell him what he had overheard. Mr. Isol needed to know that he played a part in Ying and Yang's plan.

"What is it, Durbin?"

Michael was about to say what he had overheard but Mr. Smith was looking right at him. He knew Mr. Smith didn't know he eavesdropped, but he seemed to be afraid he might tell his suspicions about him anyway. Michael swore inwardly. There was no way he could say what he wanted in front of Mr. Smith.

"Mr. Harrington said I should use some breaking pitches more often," Michael said, knowing he could not say what he really wanted to. "Do you agree?"

Mr. Isol smiled for the first time ever. "Well, yes I suppose so, Durbin. Don't want you tired before you have to be, Durbin, now do we? Don't want you to piss away this game, now do we?"

"Of course not!" said Michael.

"Keep it up," Mr. Oberfels said, nodding.

Understanding Michael's intentions completely, Mr. Smith kept an eye on Michael throughout the rest of the inning. Michael not only found it extremely irritating, but he knew that during baseball games he would not be able to talk to Mr. Harrington or Mr. Isol about what he had eavesdropped on. In the end, Michael decided to let it go and keep his mind concentrated on the game.

The only good thing to be said about this was that Michael was able to keep an eye on Mr. Smith, too. If he went back down to have a word with the Ying-Yang brothers, he could tell Mr. Harrington and the coaches who in turn could see what was going on and actually intrude on the conversation. Mr. Smith seemed to not be taking risks, however, and did not even look to the stairs of the dugout.

That was not to say Mr. Smith was excused from his duties. Mr. Harrington questioned him about neglecting his base coach duties, but Mr. Smith was able to deceive him with his rather pathetic lie.

"I'm sorry," he apologized to Mr. Harrington profusely. "I can be at first base for the rest of the game. I had to go to the bathroom. My stomach is not feeling well."

Michael felt like ejaculating that he was a huge liar and a fraud but thought better of it. He knew now was not the time to say that, especially since he had to concentrate on winning this game, which was, obviously very important because if they lost, this would make the chances of them winning a medal even lower than it already was.

Michael found himself back on the mound for the third inning and realized that the team had supplied him with a lead. He totally forgot that Fred had hit someone home while he was eavesdropping on Mr. Smith. The team was actually hitting even without many of their star players. But then again, they still had Harry and Fred, who were easily the best hitters on the team.

When he was warming up, he found out that his best friends were in seats right in front of home plate. Michael wondered how he could have missed them in the crowd. He saw Matt and Sheena with the whole Goodwin family. He smiled at them, which made them wave back furiously at him. However, Michael did have to admit that this made him more nervous. It would be hard to concentrate when his friends were right there.

Michael got through the third inning by another two strikeout deal and a spectacular diving play by Nitro to stop a double.

This time when he went back in the dugout, he realized that he had something else to worry about: he was going to have to go out and bat for his team in the bottom of the third inning.

Michael had a helmet on and a nice short bat that was able to generate a lot of power behind it. Out of the corner of his eye, he saw the Goodwins and Matt come down to the edge of the seats to talk to him. Michael was glad that they did so but was also hoping against all odds that no one would grill him like chicken for saying hello.

"You're doing great, dear," Mrs. Goodwin said, fondly.

"Thanks, Mrs. Goodwin."

Matt looked at Michael. "You're batting?"

"I have to," Michael said, twirling his bat. "This is madness, how can they expect me to get a hit? I'm going to strikeout."

"Just concentrate, Michael," Mr. Goodwin advised him. "That is the key to success—concentration. You wouldn't be here if you couldn't hit at all."

Michael was about to say that the team only brought him here to strike batters, but Shawna interrupted.

"My dad is right, Michael," Shawna, Sheena's younger sister, said. "I know you'll do fine."

"You'll be fine, Michael," Ember said, then blushing furiously afterwards.

Michael turned to Sheena, thinking she would say something. She looked as though she was about to, and she looked serious, but a loud voice stopped her before she even started.

"MICHAEL, STOP TALKING TO YOUR DREAM TEAM AND LET'S GET THE GAME MOVING!"

Michael knew he blushed this time as he walked to the batter's box after hearing Mr. Isol's voice. He could hear Matt laughing but it stopped abruptly after a loud slap. Michael figured that Sheena's hand met its target.

"Sheena, don't hurt him, he's only a wee little boy," Shawna said, reproachfully, and Michael, forced back a laugh, gripped his bat, and faced the pitcher.

The pitcher glanced at the American dugout for a brief moment before turning back to Michael, grinning in a way that Michael did not find funny.

"Pitchers are golfing, aren't they, Durbin?" the pitcher taunted Michael, who barely heard him.

Then, the pitcher got into his motion and chucked the ball with all the strength he could muster.

The ball sped at Michael's head faster than a rocket. Michael had no chance to get out of the way. The ball hit the side of his helmet dead on. Michael felt himself stumble and he crumbled to the ground, feeling as though a giant had slammed him through a glass window.

Instantly, an angry crowd of boos filled the stadium, and without hesitation, Mr. Harrington ran out of the dugout right at the umpire. The pitcher pretended to be shocked and apologetic, but Mr. Harrington gave him an angry look as he reached the umpire.

"How come you didn't eject the pitcher?" Mr. Harrington yelled at the umpire, beside himself.

Michael was able to get up gingerly, and saw the umpire's face. He was a bald Chinese guy looking deathly serious. He saw the Goodwin family all looking shocked at what just happened. Matt, however, was swearing at the top of his voice, shaking his fist at the pitcher.

Mr. Isol, Mr. Smith, and Mr. Oberfels came over now to plead their case. They seemed to want an argument as well. Mr. Oberfels, however, first went to check on Michael as the crowd booed even louder.

"Are you all right?" Mr. Oberfels asked him urgently.

"Course I am," Michael said, steadying himself. Mr. Oberfels helped him regain his balance.

He looked at the pitcher. The pitcher was giving him an I'm-pretending-I'm-sorry-but-I'm-not-sorry-at-all look that greatly annoyed Michael. He thought about charging the mound to excite the fans but desisted. Now was not the right time for such antics, especially since he was the only pitcher. The pitcher was obviously instigating to benefit his team. Michael gave him a hard glare before turning back to his coaches and the umpire.

Mr. Harrington was arguing with the umpire. It was incredible how the umpire could turn a blind eye on an almost fatal wild pitch.

"THAT WAS DELIBERATE! I SAW HIM MOUTH OFF TO MICHAEL THAT HE WAS MY ONLY PITCHER!"

Michael never saw Mr. Harrington lose control like this. Spit was flying from his mouth in all directions.

"Dear Harriet, how could the kid even know that?"

The Chinese umpire was deliberately taunting Mr. Harrington with those remarks. Michael could see his coach fuming underneath the baseball hat. And as for the pitcher knowing about the depletion of Team USA, Michael knew what the most probable explanation was.

During the first time Mr. Smith left the dugout, Michael thought savagely. He must have tipped the Netherlands team off.

"I DON'T KNOW, BUT YOU CAN AGREE THAT WAS ON PURPOSE AND THAT DESERVES AN EJECTION!"

But the umpire shook his head. Mr. Isol took charge, bearing down at the umpire like an enraged dinosaur.

"HOW BIASED CAN YOU POSSIBLY BE, YOU FREAKIN CHINESE PUNK?"

And by the reaction of the crowd, Michael knew he instantly went too far. Without hesitation, the umpire did a throwing signal to mean Mr. Isol had been thrown out of the game. The Chinese cheered loudly while the many Americans in the stands booed as hard as they could.

"WHAT THE HELL IS WRONG WITH YOU?"

The umpire then said in a calm voice, as if enjoying the frustration on the coaches' faces, "That is a fine of ten grand, dear Isol, is it?"

"COME ON, MORON, YOU'VE GOT TO BE JOKING!"

"No, I'm not," the umpire said, silkily. "If you do not leave this game right now, it will be fifty."

"That's bullshit!" Mr. Isol shouted. "You can't piss on us like this!"

The Chinese umpire raised his eyebrow.

"We can piss on you, Lyle, if the brothers say we can piss on you. Remember that you are not on your home turf, my American friend," hissed the umpire nastily. "We have authorization to detain any Americans who threaten to screw up what we are trying to do! Now leave or I'll let security know!"

For one moment, Michael thought Mr. Isol was going to chuck the umpire into the stands in anger. However, after a hard look that wished the umpire nothing but ill, Mr. Isol stormed away, his great face red with frustration and anger. He looked more intimidating than ever. Mr. Harrington continued the argument.

"Ump, you can't be serious!" Mr. Harrington complained. "He put my only pitcher in danger! He deserves to be ejected just as much as Lyle!"

"That is true," Mr. Oberfels piped up. "It is only fair."

"If you two do not go back to the dugout right this minute," said the umpire, aggravated, "you will both face fines like your dear large friend."

"It's time you start calling a fair game," Mr. Oberfels retorted at the umpire before turning away.

Mr. Smith and Mr. Oberfels left to head to first and third base respectively, and Mr. Oberfels was shaking his head, disgusted with the umpire's attitude.

Mr. Harrington looked at the umpire, anger written all over his face. His legs were trembling. He walked up straight to the umpire.

"I guess Mr. Isol was right," Mr. Harrington said, softly and quietly, so that the umpire and Michael could hear. "You are just a—"

"MR. HARRINGTON, NO!"

"—Stupid Chinese punk like Lyle said. You are just like the Ying-Yang brothers. They blackmailed you, didn't you? Just to make sure we have as many inconveniences as we possibly can have. Or are you deliberately screwing us willingly?"

The umpire looked at Mr. Harrington as if he were mad.

Michael, realizing trouble, took two strides and blocked the way of the umpire.

"GET OUT OF IT, MICHAEL!" yelled Mr. Harrington in a tone of urgency, not anger. "We are in trouble already as it is!"

"For once, you are speaking truth, Harriet," the umpire said, coldly. "Kid, if you do not get to first base right now, you will face an ejection!"

"Don't you *dare* talk to my player like that!" Mr. Harrington said in a threatening voice.

"I'll talk to him how I want to!" the umpire snarled. "Get to first base now, kid!"

Defeated, Michael walked to first base where Mr. Smith was.

"Good of you for getting out of that," Mr. Smith said, quietly. "The umpire's always win arguments, there's no point in trying to reason with them. This umpire is a nasty one, isn't he?"

"I'm surprised Mr. Harrington didn't get thrown out of the game yet," Michael whispered, just as quietly.

And as he said that, he watched as the umpire made a swift motion and Michael knew Mr. Harrington was thrown out of the game. He also saw the umpire put three fingers in the air. Mr. Harrington yelled at him one last time, and then, making as much noise as possible, he entered the dugout, crossed to the stairs, and ran down them, disappearing from sight.

Mr. Harrington's and Mr. Isol's ejection did not deter the team from trying to win. The game started up again and the team was pumped after the arguments, and they not only brought Michael home, but they brought in enough runs to give Michael a humongous cushion. It was now 5-0 their team.

Mr. Smith did have a point, Michael thought sadly. No coach would have a shot of winning an argument with a biased umpire. Especially a Chinese punk—

Mr. Oberfels had taken over the job as manager for the rest of the game. He gave his team some bad news when he got back to the dugout after having a discussion with the umpire, who wanted to talk to him.

"We lost Mr. Harrington for all the remaining games," Mr. Oberfels said, angrily.

"WHAT?" chorused the team.

"Yes, it's true," he sighed. "Anyway, I will be the manager for the rest of the game and when Mr. Isol comes back tomorrow, he will be the interim for the rest of the games."

"That's unfair!" Brad cried. "When has the umpire been allowed to make those judgments?"

"The umpire said the Chinese Committee granted more power to the umpires in general," Mr. Oberfels replied, frustrated. "But we all know that the Ying-Yang brothers passed that law to screw us over!"

Michael saw Nitro looking unhappy; the whole team was angry. This was getting out of hand. They already lost half their team but now they lost their manager? It seemed impossible for Team USA to even win a single medal. How were they going to win with a group of biased umpires and no manager? And with half the team injured, they might as well pack their bags and go home.

As things did indeed look bad, the team was putting together a nice game. Michael went back out for the next three innings, got seven strikeouts, a loud fly out, and a ground out that was fielded by Brad. Michael was getting plenty of cheers, and was even happier when Mr. Oberfels told him that if he kept up his stellar performance for the rest of the Olympics, he had a shot of becoming the best American athlete.

Even the hitting did better. Possibly it was the determination of making Mr. Harrington happy because in those three innings, they scored three more runs from a two-run bomb Harry lifted over the left field wall and a RBI double by Nitro. The crowd was in disbelief at what was happening, but satisfied and pleased that Team USA seemed to be making up for their blown game last time.

The Goodwin family seemed impressed, and Matt yelled out, "My friend is a freaking beast!" after Michael took to the mound for the next inning.

Michael had another cup of Gatorade which was now an ice-blue color. He drank it happily, but as the seventh inning came to be, he had his worst inning in the seventh.

Michael got the first batter out on a four-pitch strikeout, but then the next batter made it three and two. Michael felt himself being nervous. He had to stay calm. Michael got the signal from Mike, which was a fastball and went into his motion. He did a leg kick and threw the ball near the outside corner.

Clang! The aluminum bat hit the ball and the ball sped back at Michael like a rocket. Michael collapsed to the ground and put his glove up, but it sailed one-hundred miles an hour past him and out of the infield.

He had given up his first hit as an athlete.

Michael looked over at first in disbelief. How did he use an aluminum bat? Michael remembered Mr. Harrington telling the team at tryouts that aluminum bats were illegal. How could their opponents get away with breaking rules when they could not?

His teammates seemed to think he might lose confidence after the hit, because Nitro, Harry, and Fred came to the mound while Brad waited.

"Calm down, Michael, it is okay," Nitro said, as if he was the mother of a two-year-old who just dropped his ice cream.

"There had to be the one time you had to give up a hit," Fred replied, seriously.

"You did the right thing, Michael," Harry said, earnestly. "There was no chance you could catch that. If you tried, you could have been dead by that ball. You would have joined James on the DL."

"They are allowed to use aluminum bats?" Michael asked. "I thought Coach Harrington told us we weren't allowed."

"They aren't," Nitro said, biting his lip. "I don't understand why they were allowed to."

Mike and Brad now joined them on the mound.

"I thought aluminum bats are illegal," Brad said, thoughtfully. "They ruled out aluminum bats for this Olympics, everyone knows that. And besides, the coaches told us so."

"How do you know that?" Fred asked in amazement, as if he just noticed how observant Brad really was.

"We were told, but you were too busy fooling around with Ken to realize," Brad responded.

"Guys, the umpire is coming; you better get back to your spots," Michael said, urgently.

"Good luck, Michael," Nitro whispered, and the team scattered.

The umpire stopped at the mound and faced Michael.

"There will be no more mound meetings," the umpire said, nastily to Michael. "Make sure your friends know that."

"Sir, how come the Netherlands team can use aluminum bats?" Michael dared to ask. "They were outlawed by the IOC, weren't they?"

"No they weren't, kid. Just keep your mouth shut before I send you back to the locker room for the rest of the Games!" the umpire snarled before turning away and walking back to home plate. Michael sneered behind his back. This umpire really was an idiot.

Michael got back into his groove after that by striking out the next two batters in nine pitches and he got out of the inning unscathed. He left for the dugout where his team was looking happier than they have been all day.

"Almost there, dude," Harry told him, and helped himself to Gatorade.

"I know," Michael replied.

"This game is going to be a shutout," Phil replied. "I know it."

Lew tossed Michael a large piece of gum. "Take this. It helps."

"Thanks, Lew."

Michael chewed the gum and observed the bottom of the seventh. Unfortunately, the score was 6-0 at the end of the seventh as no runs were able to come home and they stranded one.

Michael had two more at-bats between the time he batted first and now, but grounded out both times. Now he had to make sure he held the game for his team because his bat was not going to save them.

Michael, in seven innings, combined for fourteen strikeouts and Nitro told him he would break James's first start record if he got three more. He desperately wanted to eclipse that mark and be in the conversation about being similar to James for he had nothing but respect for his ability.

Michael was due up second to bat in the top of the eighth.

"Hit a sacrifice, Michael!" Matt yelled.

Michael heard and agreed with him. That was a good idea. Michael showed a bunt signal.

The pitcher fired a ball that was outside and Michael put his bat in front of the ball just in time.

The ball flew about three feet in the air and Michael dashed to first. The bunt was really good because Michael beat the throw by the third baseman by a step.

He had his first hit as an Olympic athlete. He was now one for three with a walk. That was really good for a pitcher, Michael thought. He took a slight lead off the bag and waited for his teammate to come to bat.

The next two batters got out and then it was Harry. Michael slowly inched farther down the baseline. The pitcher delivered a fastball to Harry, who followed the ball with his eyes perfectly, and he swung with all his might at the ball. He made contact and hit the ball to the right field corner.

Michael hustled around second and went for third. Mr. Oberfels gave him a signal to go for home as the crowd cheered wildly.

Running, he concentrated only at home and saw the ball being thrown right at the catcher. He had to hurry or else he would be out. He moved his legs faster, urging them on. Fred was on deck, watching the play and looking excited.

"SLIDE, MIKEY!"

Michael did as Fred yelled and the tag missed him by a hair. He was safe and it was 7-0 USA.

The crowd was cheering harder than ever. The excitement in the stadium was palpable. Michael slapped Fred a high-five and then retreated into the dugout to sit down on the bench and rest his legs.

Fred made the last out of the inning and now, it was the bottom of the eighth. Michael only needed three more outs and the game would be over. With only three more outs, Team USA would win against all odds.

When he came back to the mound, Michael saw that the Goodwins and Matt shifted to the left so they weren't behind the net. They smiled and Michael grinned, knowing there was no way possible he could blow this game.

"Finish them, Michael," Fred said, as he passed. "There's a fraternity party tonight with a bunch of chicks at it that I don't want to miss!"

"One more inning, Michael," Mike replied softly. "Let's finish them off!"

When Mike crouched behind home, Michael yelled to him.

"COME ON, MIKEY! LET'S GO!"

The first batter of the inning stepped up to bat.

Michael threw four pitches to strike him out, ending it with an upstairs fastball. Now he needed two more outs, one to break the record James had set.

Now the second batter had come up. He was a weedy kid who looked extremely nervous. However, Michael did not take him lightly.

Michael got two strikes right off the bat. The kid saw Michael throw his third pitch, which was a change up, but it was just low. The count was 1-2. Michael saw Mike give the signal for a hang glider. Michael nodded, knowing it was the perfect spot to throw it. He faced the batter.

He let it go early, and it seemed to loop on the inside corner, and the umpire called strike three.

The crowd was making a deafening noise, and now all Michael had to do was get through one last batter.

He could see that the crowd was cheering for him. He got into his wind up, and let the pitch go, and the batter swung, and missed.

Strike one.

The crowd cheered harder than ever and Matt was shouting, "Push the roof!"

Michael was now smiling, and he could have sworn he saw the batter give a smile like he was laughing. He couldn't seem to believe how good Michael really was.

But the next pitch wiped it off the batter's face. Michael pitched a slow one right down Broadway and he was lucky it was not knocked out of the park.

It was now 0-2.

Michael thought he couldn't take much more suspense, saw Mike give him the nod. Michael took that as Mike wanted him to use his hang glider. That pitch already fanned about half of his batters for strikeouts thus far so he thought it would be a good idea to use it again.

Michael nodded and got ready to deliver. The crowd was now rising to their feet. The Goodwin family cheered. Matt took off his shirt and started waving it until he saw Sheena look at him; his team started clapping; and the fans roared, stamping their feet. Michael knew it was time to finish the job.

Michael pitched his last one from the stretch and he saw it sink and the batter went after it, missing it and he heard the crowd roar. The batter hurried back to the dugout, humiliated that he missed a ball as slow as it was.

Michael struck out the side to end the game.

He first saw Matt and Sheena run over to the United States dugout to join his teammates, all of which were running towards him. Michael turned to see them running, but not for long, as Sheena was hugging him so tightly he thought he was getting squeezed to death by a huge python.

"I'm sorry about what I said earlier," Sheena whispered in his ear quietly.

"It's alright," Michael whispered back, as Sheena hugged him tighter.

Matt screamed, all dignity forgotten. Then Fred, Harry, and Nitro joined the huddle. Then the rest of the team joined the pile, followed by Mr. Oberfels. Then came all the Goodwins and the whole group sank down, in a many-armed hug, back to earth.

Michael let go of Sheena, who was grinning and shouting. Matt was wolf-whistling; Fred was chanting *"Get in there!"*, but for once, Michael didn't mind. He showed the Ying-Yang brothers what a great pitcher he truly was.

Nitro kept screaming, "He struck him out, he struck him out!"

"GET IN THERE!" Ken shouted to Michael and soon enough, the whole team was chanting that besides him and Fred.

Mr. Goodwin was jumping up and down, all dignity forgotten. Mrs. Goodwin was crying happy tears, and Sheena's siblings were overjoyed, cheering excitedly.

The Netherlands were leaving the field and Michael saw, out of the huddle, that the Ying-Yang brothers were sulking near the edge of the ballpark with Mr. Smith. They made eye contact with Michael for a moment before disappearing amongst the departing crowd.

Michael was in the middle of a huge celebration, and it was better than even making the team. His new team and his new friends were sharing this experience with him, and Michael knew he would never forget it.

To Michael's big surprise, Mr. Isol and Mr. Harrington hopped the dugout stairs and raced out of the dugout and as they reached the huddle, picked up Michael, and carried him on his shoulders around the infield with the rest of the huddle looking on.

As soon as he was brought back to earth, Michael fully appreciated why he should have worried about baseball more than the Ying-Yang brothers. However, there was still one thing for certain. Even after this game, even after his success, he, Michael Durbin, baseball hero, still had to uncover the mystery that still put Beijing down as a dangerous place for him.

CHAPTER 14

THE SECOND CONFRONTATION

Michael's euphoria of the stunning performance to win the game for the USA lasted for the next days to come. Michael was in the middle of all the gossip and conversations. They mostly were all impressed with his skills. Most were comparing him to Tom Seaver who, Michael learned from Matt, was one of the best pitchers in history. Even though he was pleased with the adoration he was getting, he found out that, after a while, it grew old quickly.

However, there was one little group that thought the exact opposite. The Chinese were furious that the USA won as they were anxious to see them beaten, so they started up a huge lie that was spread around Beijing like wildfire. The Chinese released an unfounded accusation that Michael took steroids in an effort to suspend him indefinitely. Michael did not get any criticism from anyone, but he did not get as much support as he would have liked.

Mr. Goodwin responded for Michael, though. He sent a message to the Chinese, explaining why their lies were false, and then, he spread that to the public, who listened with interest. After hearing what Mr. Goodwin said, most felt sympathy for the young athlete, and Michael was grateful for Mr. Goodwin's support. He was glad that Mr. Goodwin seemed to have taking a liking to him.

The Goodwins were also reprimanded for running out onto the field. However, the Chinese decided to let it slide as they were not doing anything wrong. Though surprised at the verdict, Mr. Goodwin told Michael that they were not going to do anything rash like that again.

"We don't want to abuse the Chinese's generosity," he said, seriously.

The USA got three more players back early today: Xavier, David, and Ron, which gave the team another two pitchers. Their injuries ended up not being as severe as the team feared. By the time the team played Cuba, all their players would be restored to full health and be ready to compete. Michael was thankful that their next game was days after their last game. Justin was scheduled to start for the team today against Cuba. Fred also gave the team some news in an effort to rally his team. He had spied on the Cuban team for the USA, and reported to Mr. Harrington that they were nothing spectacular but had an amazing ability for reaching bases in three seconds.

"We are going to need to attack the ball for ground outs," Fred told Mr. Harrington, when he told him this, and he agreed, though a little surprised that he had spied on the Cuban team.

At breakfast one morning, Matt was playfully teasing Sheena at breakfast how she seemed to forgive Michael for his idiotic determination.

"You're jealous, are you?" Sheena asked, laughing.

"Of course he is not," Michael answered, taking a drink of milk. "He'd turn red like a tomato if some girl started hugging him in public."

"Really, I'm not that fussed," Matt replied, and Sheena laughed. "I was waiting for more, but I guess you two don't have the nerve yet, do you?"

Sheena dumped her glass of orange juice on his head for revenge. Matt was not too happy about it.

Michael, Matt, and Sheena spent the morning before the game outside walking around the complex. During that time, Michael had recounted the story about what he had overheard. Matt was shocked and impressed, while Sheena looked thoughtful.

"I'll have to thank Fred," Sheena said, seriously. "He helped you out a lot."

"The stupid git faked getting hurt!" Matt exclaimed.

"He is not a stupid git, Matt."

"You only like him because he's funny!"

"Excuse me, Matt?"

But Matt only sniggered. Sheena aimed a kick at him, but missed as Matt leaped out of the way.

"What interests me most," Michael said, as they walked, "is how they don't seem to trust Mr. Smith, which is making me think he was . . . let's say, he didn't agree to this, but was forced. What do you think?"

"I don't know, Michael," Sheena said, sighing. "Maybe we should visit my dad again. Tell him all of this, and let's see what he makes out of this."

So the three of them walked to the Goodwin's temporary house, where they found Sheena's two siblings watering the plants outside the house. They came over to them when they saw them.

"Hello," Shawna replied, who was a little red from the work. "Come to visit us again?" she added, looking hopeful.

"Actually, Shawna, we came here, I mean, Michael needs to ask Dad something. It's very important."

"Dad's inside," Shawna said, quickly. "He's on the computer. Here, we'll come in with you."

The five of them walked into the house to find it sparkly clean.

"Wow!" Matt said, awestruck.

"Dad is in here," Shawna said, pointing to a room right next to a bedroom. "He's busy, but I'm sure he'll talk with you guys."

"Thanks, Shawna," said Michael, and he opened the door to the room.

Mr. Goodwin was busy typing on his computer when they came in. Sheena cleared her throat and said, "Dad."

Mr. Goodwin stopped typing and turned around. "Oh, I should have known it was you, Sheena, and your two friends. What brings you here today?"

Michael noticed that Mr. Goodwin looked weary, as if he had not slept throughout the night.

"Well, it's just that I eavesdropped on an important conversation . . ."

And he recounted the diversion that was planned between him, Fred, and Nitro; the conversation he overheard; and Mr. Smith's reactions. Mr. Goodwin listened intently, and when Michael finished, Mr. Goodwin rubbed his chin, apparently in very deep thought. Michael looked at Mr. Goodwin apprehensively, expecting him to berate him for getting involved in this deadly business but to his surprise, Mr. Goodwin smiled slightly.

"I see you are not going to be dissuaded to stop investigating," Mr. Goodwin said, rubbing his forehead, but his eyes twinkled with amusement. "You said Mr. Smith shouted at the brothers that they needed to get Mr. Isol on their side?"

"Yes."

"What interests me," Mr. Goodwin said, thoughtfully, "is why Mr. Smith said they need to get Mr. Isol on their side, which I think might suggest that Mr. Smith did not do this job voluntarily. I reckon he was probably forced in some way."

"That's what I said, sir!" Michael exclaimed. "And I really think—"

"I am right," supplied Mr. Goodwin. "I believe you are correct, but we can never be sure. It also could mean Mr. Smith wants to help them, but does not want to do the job that they want him to do. But, why he was forced . . . that's curious . . ."

Michael felt a twinge of anger at Mr. Smith now. He now knew Mr. Smith's true character. And it was nothing positive.

"He's nothing but a coward!" Michael burst out loud, making everyone jump. "He can't defend himself! No wonder he fell into the brothers clutches so easily!"

"So then that still does not explain why Mr. Smith said they needed Mr. Isol," Matt replied. "I mean, we know it could be because he did not want to do this job, but why would he suggest Mr. Isol and not just anyone else?"

Mr. Goodwin looked at Matt. "I think the same reason applies for both, Matt. Mr. Isol is a much better man than Mr. Smith could ever be, and obviously the brothers were expecting more from him. Anyway, if there is the possibility that we are right in saying that Mr. Smith was forced, I think I have a plan that could change his mind."

There was now a determined look in Mr. Goodwin's eyes as he finished speaking.

"What is it, Dad?" Sheena queried, looking curious.

"We need to arrange a meeting with him and find out the truth," Mr. Goodwin said, calmly. "At that point, we'll ask him to tell us everything. If he confesses, we'll find a way to stop the brothers, and alert the authorities. If he lies, we'll explain the evidence that we found to him. As you said, Michael, Mr. Smith has proven to be a coward, so if we tell him what we're sending after the brothers to stop them, he'll join our side."

"But, sir," Michael said, "the brothers said that if he fails, he would be killed or suffer—what was it, oh yes—bodily harm."

"We could prevent that if that situation does indeed arise," Mr. Goodwin replied, calmly. "For now, though, and for the first and hopefully last time, I finally see that there is no chance to distract any of you from this. So, I am going to give you a mission."

"Are you serious, sir?" Michael asked, shocked by what Mr. Goodwin had said.

"Yes, I've thought about it and changed my mind," Mr. Goodwin said, pleasantly. "However, you need to complete this with extreme caution. I don't want any of you to take any risks. This is to be done in your free time only. I still want to see the three of you take home a medal or two. You understand me?"

"Yes, sir," Michael replied.

"Definitely," said Matt.

"I will, Dad," Sheena said, looking serious.

"Okay, then," Mr. Goodwin said, looking as if going against his better judgment. "I need you three to get Mr. Smith when he is not by the brothers. Give him the message that I want to talk to him. Bring him to this house. I'll call the Committee members when you collect him. Do you think you can handle it?"

It was easier said than done, Michael thought. But he did think with the three of them, anything was possible to complete. Michael looked at Mr. Goodwin, and knew it would be quite a task, said, "Yes."

"Good," Mr. Goodwin said, placidly. "Now I believe you have a baseball game today, Michael, right? Don't do it, then. He probably has Ying and Yang right by him, they could just take you, and the plan will spectacularly fail. Wait until the Ying-Yang brothers are not in sight."

"Yes, Mr. Goodwin."

"Thank you for telling me this," Mr. Goodwin replied, stroking his beard. "It was a very important piece of information. This may be the clue we need to stop the Ying-Yang brothers from doing something terrible."

"No problem, sir."

Michael, Matt, and Sheena went out of the study and outside into the backyard. They sat down on a very long bench, where Shawna and Ember were sitting, apparently taking a break.

"How did the conversation go?" Shawna queried curiously.

"Very good," Michael answered, happily, and he told the two girls about the whole conversation he overheard, and the mission Mr. Goodwin assigned them. Their eyes were round as hubcaps when he finished.

"Our dad gave you a mission?" Ember asked, awestruck. "Do you think that's wise?"

"Surprising it is," agreed Matt. "But I think we're old enough to handle the responsibility."

"What was the mission again, Michael?" Shawna asked.

"He wants us to convince one of my coaches," Michael said.

"How will you be able to accomplish that?" Shawna asked. At that moment, Michael just realized how very much she was like Sheena: interested in everything, happy, nice, and curious. He knew that she physically looked like Sheena, but it was only until now that he fully registered that she was *exactly* like her older sister.

"We're going to get Smith on his own without the brothers," Michael replied to her, "and we are going to give him the message that your father wanted to speak with him. We'll bring him to this house, and then we'll go from there."

Michael knew he did not fully explain the plan, but he was not sure that Mr. Goodwin would want them to know the plan. They were still pretty young, especially too young for this Committee business. If Mr. Goodwin thought he was too young, Shawna and Ember definitely were.

"I think it's terribly risky," Ember replied, thoughtfully. "Michael, there are so many things that can go wrong in that plan, you know that, right?"

"Every plan is risky Ember, but we have no choice."

"What's so risky about it, Ember?" Shawna said, as she stopped laughing.

Ember took a deep breath and looked wiser beyond her years as she spoke.

"Look, what are you going to do when Mr. Smith refuses to go with you to see Dad? If he is already being suspected for teaming up with the brothers, I don't think he'll be very willing to go see the President of the Olympic Committee."

Michael was impressed by the little girl's thinking. He knew she had a great point. Mr. Smith and Michael did not get along as it was, as they disagreed over so many things. What if he did not listen to them? And he totally didn't consider that Mr. Smith may not want to see Mr. Goodwin due to his actions. Michael turned back to Ember.

"I don't know, Ember, but I'll think of something reasonable," he assured her.

"I think it is about a safe a plan as you are going to get, Michael," Shawna said, earnestly.

"Hey Michael, did you check the time while we were in there?" Sheena queried. "You have a baseball game today still, or have you forgotten?"

Michael had not forgotten. He checked his watch and was shocked to see that time was moving quicker than he thought. He turned to his two friends.

"We should start heading back," Michael said, standing up. "I don't think Mr. Isol would be pleased if I was late to the game."

So the three of them said good-bye to Shawna and Ember and they started their hike down back to the hotel. Michael, Matt, and Sheena brainstormed ideas out loud to each other, and Michael never remembered doing anything like this before. This was a level up on an ambitious homework project—the only difference was that the reason was more serious.

They passed the Bird's Nest as the sun started to peek out hopefully between the dark cumulus clouds. However, as they started to walk down a narrow path, still discussing their mission, two people appeared right in front of them and walked right into them. The three of them looked up to see two identical twins wearing blue silk jackets this time and expressions of little boys entering a candy shop.

They met up with the Ying-Yang brothers for the second time in a few days.

The brothers smiled with glee at the sight of the kids. They seemed to be acting as though meeting Michael gave them no greater joy.

"Look, Yang it's the hero—"

"—Of that baseball game the other day—"

"—Good game, that was—"

"—Definitely—"

"—Remember that lard Isol and the Harrington loser—"

"—Yeah, they got ejected—"

"—Shame, but we always knew—"

"—They were right-out fools, they were—"

"My father is not a fool!" Matt spat, making his way towards the brothers, but Michael and Sheena gripped his arms and held him back.

Michael turned to the brothers.

"Mr. Harrington is not a loser and Mr. Isol is not a lard!" he said, his voice quite steady.

The brothers laughed. "Oh, look at him, baseball hero Mikey Durbin is defending his coaches, how adorable."

Michael refused to be taunted like a toddler. He was not going to give the brothers any satisfaction that he hated their comments.

Michael, keeping one firm grip on Matt's arm, said, "Just shut up and leave. You have no business here."

Ying smiled with glee.

"We do have business here, Durbin."

"You see, we are highly important people—"

"—Who are way more intelligent than yourselves—"

Matt laughed as though he doubted it. Yang turned to him with raised eyebrows.

"You find that funny, young Harriet?" Yang snarled at Matt.

"Very much so," Matt replied in a choked voice.

Yang looked at Ying, who was flexing his fingers as though readying for a fight.

"Ah, young Harriet will learn his lesson soon enough," Ying said in a childish voice.

"Yeah, we'll see who's laughing when we take a Goodwin girl," Yang said, cackling, and Michael felt a sense of foreboding.

Matt turned to look at Sheena, whose eyes widened with worry. Michael thought she was starting to have second thoughts about the mission.

"The USA Committee was laughing when you two losers were rejected from the Committee," Michael said, sharply, finally losing his temper.

Ying moved in a flash and slammed Michael into the wall by the throat. There was no trace of any grin on his face now.

"Man, Durbin, your temper—"

"—Is unbelievable—"

Michael was choking, finding it hard to breathe. Sheena and Matt moved forward to help, but Ying let go as soon as they did.

"Watch your backs, Mikey, young Harriet, and Goody Goodwin!"

"Yeah, watch it! Good day to you kiddies."

And the two brothers left, leaving the three of them alone, which took Michael by surprise.

Sheena looked worried, not haughty like she was the last time with Michael.

"Michael, you are heading into serious trouble! Don't wind the brothers up more than you already have!"

"I didn't give them an excuse to hate me, Sheena!" Michael spat, even though he was not angry with her.

"When they are here, you need to do two things," Matt replied, holding up two fingers. "One," he put one down, "you need to keep your mouth shut, and two," he put down the last finger, "is act like a helpless kid."

"If you think I'm just going to let them make fun of your dad and Mr. Isol—" Michael started furiously, but Sheena interrupted him.

"Michael, they are trying to bust your chops, don't let them get to you."

Michael looked up at Sheena with an obstinate look on his face. He noticed that she was wearing an expression of concern on her face. Even in his anger and impatience, he recognized Sheena's expression as a sign that she absolutely cared about Michael, like a true friend.

"I—thanks, Sheena."

She only smiled, and Matt, her, and Michael walked away from the Bird's Nest, and Michael was jumbled up in the thought of how Mr. Goodwin's plan might turn out.

Sheena walked in the middle between the two boys and put an arm around each of them, and they walked back to Blossom Suites. Matt and Sheena started an argument about their favorite football teams (the Giants and Jets) but Michael was not paying attention. He was thinking about what Sheena said to him in his head, relieved that the girl who he cared about finally proved to not only be friendly to him because of his adroit skills on the pitcher's mound.

CHAPTER 15

THE FOILED ASSASSINATION ATTEMPT

Michael's baseball game did not go as planned. The Cubans were able to score two runs after Michael pitched a good eighth, but gave up a solo home run. The final score was 5-4 Cuba, and with their second loss, the baseball team was in a sort of panic now due to their abysmal start.

Justin gave up two runs in seven innings, which was fine, except for the fact that he was taken out of the game with a 2-2 tie. The USA never got close to any runs, except in the eighth when Fred was tagged out on a head-first slide to home, and was fortunate that he wasn't injured on the play.

Michael's reaction to giving up his first run was not positively received by his team. Most thought he was being over-sentimental, and Mr. Isol especially thought so, because he gave Michael the what-for when he got back into the dugout.

"Will you stop blaming yourself?" Mr. Isol growled. "You're a damn good pitcher from what we've seen! Just stop acting like a damp mushroom and concentrate on becoming the best player you could be!"

That was when the game was tied.

Michael left the game after it was tied 4-4 and Ron managed to blow his second game of the Olympics. Justin was downright furious.

"Can't Mr. Harrington put in someone else?" he asked, angrily, in the locker room afterward.

Michael made his way out of the stadium where he saw Matt, Sheena, and surprisingly, the Goodwins.

"Tough game, eh, Michael?" greeted Shawna.

"Tell me about it. I see your family has turned up," Michael replied to Sheena, surveying all of them.

"We decided to come," Mrs. Goodwin answered, abruptly. "And while the game was in full swing, my husband made up his mind. Let's discuss the plan today as Will arranged for it to go into action tomorrow."

Michael glanced at Sheena, who looked downright shocked. Not that they forgot about their mission, but they were surprised by the change of plans.

"We're still going to stick to our original plan for the most part," Mr. Goodwin added. "But I added some more details. I'll explain everything back at the hotel once we get there. Are there any concerns?"

Concerns? Michael could have snorted the word out loud. However, he kept his tongue and nodded like everyone else.

"Alright, then," Mr. Goodwin said, briskly. "Let's get moving."

The seven of them trooped to the hotel. There were not many people inside the hotel and the receptionist at the desk spotted Mr. Goodwin, and called him over.

"Yes, what is it?" he questioned, throwing a confused look back at the group.

"Mr. Smith wanted to give this to Michael for his great performance at the Olympics," the receptionist said, taking out a huge chocolate muffin. "He said he's been giving them out to a lot of people."

Mr. Goodwin took the muffin, looking suspicious. "Er . . . alright."

He walked back to the group and handed Michael the muffin. The group stared at it. Michael was looking at it as if it was a time bomb.

"What the hell is this about?" Matt asked, sounding as if holding a muffin proved you were fruity.

"According to the receptionist, Mr. Smith wanted to give you this, Michael," Mr. Goodwin replied. "But I'm not sure why he would do that, though. Don't you think it is a bit odd if a coach hands you a muffin?"

"Of course it's weird," Matt said, wrinkling his nose in disgust. "It's a grown man giving another guy a muffin."

"I don't know, Dad, but I think it would be best to throw it out," Ember said, thoughtfully. "We can't guarantee that the muffin was not tampered with by Mr. Smith. For all we know, there could be a dangerous chemical mixed in it."

No one in the group said anything, but Sheena and Shawna were looking at the muffin suspiciously. It was clear that they did not like it or suspected that it was not just a muffin.

"If Mr. Smith wanted me to eat this, I'm not going to," Michael said. "I don't trust him as it is."

He broke the muffin in half and inside, he found a small rubber projectile in the muffin. He looked up at the rest of the group. They were all dumbfounded.

"Well, I guess Mr. Smith was up to something," Michael said, grimly, tossing the rubber ball in the trash. "He tried to choke me."

"Choke you?" Mrs. Goodwin asked. "Why would he do that, Michael, dear?"

"That doesn't make sense," Sheena said, puzzled. "I thought they wanted to capture you, not kill you."

Michael knew she had a point. But he also knew that the brothers only wanted to capture him to force him to do the work for him. However, if Mr. Smith was making weak attempts to kill him, did that show that the brothers knew where the scroll was and no longer needed his help?

Michael looked at Mr. Goodwin, and he could tell he was thinking the same thing.

"We'll worry about this later," Mr. Goodwin said, finally. "Why don't we go upstairs and talk about the plan?"

After an uneventful ride up the elevator and passing a guy picking his nose on their floor, they reached Michael's room. Michael took out his card and swiped it through the slot. The light changed from red to green, and Michael grasped the handle and opened the door to his room.

It was neat on Michael's side, but it burst with the extraordinary on Matt's side. It was though as if it was a tornado raced through

Matt's side while he was away. Clothes were scattered all over the place, and Michael saw underwear strewn over the floor. Matt hastily shoved his dirty clothes away (Sheena roared with laughter) while everyone walked into the room.

Michael, Matt, and Sheena sat down on the bed while Mrs. Goodwin, Shawna, and Ember sat on the floor. Mr. Goodwin remained standing.

"Okay, so straight to business," he said, importantly, "I contacted all of the Committee members the other night and told them to meet us in the Blossom Suites dining area tomorrow. I requested that the area be empty for us, so that's all set and done. I plan to do this after your baseball game, Michael, as there will be little activity going on, and that was the best time for the Committee members to attend the proceedings."

"You've informed them about what we know?" queried Michael.

Mr. Goodwin nodded.

"Yes, I have," he replied. "They have a right to know everything—and what we plan on doing."

"What have you changed up?" Sheena queried.

"I've got it worked out," Mr. Goodwin said, pleasantly, soothingly, seeing the stupefied expressions on Michael's and Matt's faces. "Our plan is still going to remain the same, like I previously stated. All the Committee members will be there. I need Michael, Matt, and Sheena to go locate Mr. Smith. Tell him that his presence is required at the hotel."

"What if he refuses?" Matt queried.

Mr. Goodwin held up his cell phone. "Then Sheena is going to call me while you three keep Mr. Smith in your sights. Then, I'll bring a few Committee members with me and we'll bring him in ourselves."

"When are we going to do this?" Michael asked, forgetting the time it will occur already.

"Tomorrow," Mr. Goodwin replied again, "after the baseball game, Michael. That would give us plenty of time."

Michael knew he was right. His baseball game against Canada was at half past ten in the morning. By the time it would end, they would have the whole afternoon.

"Now, after you collect him," continued Mr. Goodwin, "we'll take it from there. If we convince him to not work with the brothers, we'll let him go without punishment. If he refuses, then I'll get the police to take him into custody. I am bringing in three police officers to listen to this. They heard everything I told them."

Michael listened to the plan so far, and he thought it was as good as it was going to get. Mr. Goodwin was obviously prepared for the plan. The only hard part was going to get Mr. Smith to come with them.

Mr. Goodwin continued.

"We'll try to get as much information as possible out of Mr. Smith. I'm hoping the plan will end with the police taking Mr. Smith's information and giving all the proof to the Chinese authorities. Then, the brothers will hopefully be placed under arrest. That is the best case scenario for us."

"What's the worst case scenario?" asked Sheena nervously, but Mr. Goodwin did not answer her and Michael was glad that Mr. Goodwin ignored the question because Michael could honestly say that he did not want to know the answer.

"Dad, what are Ember and I going to do?" Shawna queried. "We'd like to be involved."

"You two along with your mother are going to be used as a backup. If Michael, Matt, and Sheena can't bring Mr. Smith in, you three have to keep your eyes peeled for him. Beijing is a huge city, so having three people also looking out for him will work as well. Sheena will call you as well if they can't get him to come to Blossom Suites."

Michael did not like the fact that Shawna and Ember were getting involved. He was equally worried about them as he was worried about everyone else. They were only ten, and somehow, leaving them with only their mother in the city of Beijing to chase after a guy who was capable of murder (no matter how weak his attempts were) was not the smartest thing to do.

"Mr. Goodwin, I think you might want to consider putting another few people with Shawna, Ember, and Mrs. Goodwin," Michael piped up. He was no longer shy to speak up to anyone.

Mr. Goodwin looked at Michael curiously.

"Why? There's no need. My wife can take care of them," said Mr. Goodwin, looking mildly puzzled.

"That's not the point," Michael said, anger coming to his defense now. "Mr. Smith is capable of harming them and, who knows? What if Mr. Smith ends up right with the brothers and their gang? The three of them will be abducted! I'm sure they have a ton of accomplices!"

Mr. Goodwin leaned back, looked at Michael, frowning at the concern on his face, and Shawna and Ember looked thoughtful, but Mr. Goodwin said, "I'm not too worried about that. You three will be fine to convince Mr. Smith."

Michael was not done talking, though. He was not convinced at all by Mr. Goodwin. Mrs. Goodwin turned to Michael, noticing that he was about to open his mouth to argue.

"Your concern makes me happy, dear, but I can assure you that we'll be fine," Mrs. Goodwin told Michael quite kindly. "It's you three that I'm worried about more."

"Well, anyway," Mr. Goodwin said, clapping his hands together as Shawna, Ember, and Mrs. Goodwin stood up, "I think I've said everything of importance. You three better get to bed. You all have important events tomorrow."

With that, Mr. Goodwin, Mrs. Goodwin, Shawna, and Ember left the room, leaving the three friends alone and looking completely stunned by their abrupt departure.

As soon as the door behind them was closed completely, Michael strode to the door separating the balcony from the room and stared out at the Beijing landscape. Lights were flashing everywhere, but they did not cheer Michael up. His insides were boiling with frustration. Michael was touched by the confidence Mr. Goodwin had in him and his friends, but he thought it was dangerously overconfident to think that they would succeed and plain ignorant to leave a woman and two ten-year-old girls in Beijing by themselves to look for a criminal and not expect any harm to come to them. If they failed, Sheena's sisters and mother might be in huge danger.

Michael couldn't help but feel angry at Mr. Goodwin's reckless plan. He was angry at his plan and he was putting all of his kids in danger. He was angry at the fact that he took it so simply and calmly. He was furious that he thought of the plan as simple but it was not. Not even close.

He felt two people come side by side by him and knew it was Matt and Sheena. He felt a small, comforting hand on his right shoulder and it told him that it was Sheena.

"Michael . . ."

Michael did not answer, and for the first time, Sheena did not comfort or soothe him, but made him feel even worse. She did not get it. As much as Michael liked her, he knew that Sara and Tomas would understand how he was feeling a lot better than she or Matt. Sara and Tomas would decipher his emotions easier and relate to his issues.

Michael shrugged the hand off and he walked away, and around the room. His anger would not keep him in check much longer; he tried burning some of it off by walking.

"I thought it was fine," Matt answered.

"Do you know that it puts us in jeopardy?" Michael asked, willing not to let his anger spill on his friends whom he liked so much, but he knew he had to ready himself for it as he was finding it hard to keep it under control.

"Yes, I know, but . . ."

"Sheena, this puts your sisters in jeopardy," Michael said in a voice of deadly calm. His temper was slowly rising.

"I know, but it's the best diversion we've—"

Michael felt like shouting, but he knew it would not solve anything. He bit back his anger barely, willing himself to not shout at his friends.

"Look," he said, struggling to remain calm, "this is a good plan up to the point of leaving your two ten-year-old sisters with only your mother in the middle of Beijing. I can already sense trouble with this plan just because of that."

"They'll be with my mother," Sheena answered, looking genuinely concerned, but she seemed to understand that Michael cared about her family.

Michael gave a bitter laugh.

"And do you think that will stop Mr. Smith and possibly the brothers from harming them? They don't care, Sheena. I can't believe you won't listen to me, especially now."

Michael looked at Sheena with a pained expression on his face. The conversation between the two friends instantly showed how much the two cared about each other. Sheena's expression looked sympathetic, and it touched Michael more than he was ready to admit, but the fact remained that she was refusing to see it from his point of view. She thought her siblings would be safe with only her mom to protect them in a foreign city. Michael thought that it was unwise to test the security of Beijing.

"Michael," Sheena said, softly. "Why don't you have confidence that we can accomplish this? If we can convince Mr. Smith, you have nothing to worry about. *We* have nothing to worry about."

Michael sank down on the bed, defeated.

"The thing is he won't listen to us, Sheena. As much of a coward he is, he won't listen to us just because of me," said Michael dispiritedly.

Sheena glanced at Matt, who seemed to disappear in the shadows while the two of them were talking. Sheena walked up to Michael with a worried expression etched upon her face. She then bent down, hugged Michael, and left the room, leaving Michael and Matt alone. Matt was staring cautiously at him, as if he was carrying a deadly and fatal germ. Michael wished he would stop; Matt's look made him feel uneasy.

"I know what you mean, Michael," Matt replied, earnestly. "And I respect your opinion. But Mrs. Goodwin has always been a good mother to her daughters—and she's a motherly figure to me as well seeing that I don't have one. They'll be fine."

Michael said nothing. He could not share the same optimism as much as he couldn't share a meal with Ty and the Ying-Yang brothers.

"Let's hit the sack, then," Matt answered, yawning, understanding Michael's silence. "We have a big day tomorrow."

Michael nodded.

It was a very troubled sleep for Michael that night. It was in a mixture of disgust at Mr. Goodwin, who he had liked, respected, and looked up to, but he left Michael in a mess. He was putting too much faith in himself and his friends. Michael couldn't help dreaming that he thought that he would be lucky to see possibly his friends or Sheena's siblings alive again. The plan could put Michael's courage to a real test.

This is my fault, Michael thought. If I didn't show Mr. Goodwin that I wanted to make a difference to my country, the people who I care about would not be in this position. Michael was astounded how quickly Mr. Goodwin had changed his opinion as well: he was warning Michael not to get involved, and now—there was no other word for it—he was not only encouraging him to take up missions, but also was permitting his ten-year-old daughters to play a role in his scheme. He was obsessed with ending the brothers' wrath.

The sun rose up when morning came but Michael's spirits were still damp. He took a shower after Matt and when they were both changed, they trooped down to the cafeteria to get some breakfast.

Sheena was already there in her usual gymnastics uniform (midnight blue with gold stars) munching on a slightly burnt piece of toast. She looked wary as the two of them sat down with their breakfast.

"How many events do you have today?" Michael asked, as he poured milk on his Lucky Charms.

"One," Sheena replied, warily, possibly afraid Michael was going to be bitter again. "I have a competition at eleven. I'm competing on the high bar!"

"We could go watch you," Matt answered, "I only have one event at nine this morning and Michael doesn't have his game until later."

"No," Michael said, shaking his head. "My game is at half past ten, Matt. I won't be able to do much after breakfast. I apologize in advance if I'm not supporting either of you."

"Don't be stupid."

"That's alright," Sheena said with dignity. "But we should be able to see you, Matt. I'm curious as to how diving competitions work."

Matt looked as though having friends come and support him was a form of torture.

"Don't bother. I suck," Matt replied, moodily.

"I'm sure you don't," Sheena assured her friend, looking at him.

"Trust me, I do," Matt said, biting his bagel moodily. "My trainer says I dive like a cow having a seizure. That should give you an idea."

"Matt, if you were terrible, you wouldn't be here," Michael said, trying to inject some confidence into his friend.

Matt looked around the cafeteria. Many people were now sitting at tables, munching on their breakfast and reading the paper. He turned back to his friends with a doom-laden expression on his face.

"Don't say this to anyone else, but there's a good chance this will be my only year competing in the Olympics," Matt replied, turning his gaze to his half-eaten bagel.

"WHY?" Sheena and Michael questioned, alarmed.

"I dive like a sack of dog crap," Matt replied, shaking his head. "It's just not fun. Especially with the tool I have for a trainer. If it weren't for you two, I'd hitch an early flight home."

Michael finished his Lucky Charms, but the marshmallows did not taste as well as usual. Matt's comments had put an awful taste in his mouth. If Matt was not going next time, it would only be him and Sheena. And it was no guarantee that either of them would be going either. Michael could not think about how miserable it would be if Matt did not come with them next time—if there was a next time anyway.

Matt glanced at his watch. "It's time, I need to go. Before my trainer takes out his whip and uses it on me."

"Good luck, Matt," Michael replied, as Sheena patted him on the shoulder. "Try to be positive."

But Matt walked away with the stride of one heading to their family funeral. Michael sighed. The last thing he needed to worry about was Matt's lack of confidence.

Sheena convinced Michael to come support Matt even though it meant cutting his time to get to his game fine. Michael couldn't see how him showing up was going to make Matt any better. In fact, he thought he was doing a disservice to his friend by showing up.

By the time the two of them entered the pool arena, most seats were taken. Michael and Sheena spent ten minutes trying to find seats until a familiar voice called them over.

"Michael! Sheena!"

It was Mr. Harrington. He evidently came to watch his son dive. Michael and Sheena made their way towards him, relieved.

"Are you good to go, Michael?" he asked as they sat down. "How are you, Sheena?"

"Yes," Michael answered, facing him.

"Very good, thank you," Sheena said, grinning.

"Glad to hear it," replied Mr. Harrington. "And I heard about what transpired the other night."

Michael and Sheena looked at him, hardly daring to believe it.

"Mr. Goodwin told me about the plan that you helped him plan," Mr. Harrington replied in a low voice. "You aren't nervous, are you, Michael?"

Michael looked taken aback. "It was *his* plan and it sucks. I certainly did not plan it. And it is putting everyone in danger, including Shawna and Ember."

Sheena gave Mr. Harrington a he-is-too-worried-about-everyone-else look and Mr. Harrington smiled.

"I like your reasoning, Michael," Mr. Harrington replied. "But you care too much."

"And that's a *bad* thing?" queried Michael, but Mr. Harrington paid no attention to his words.

"If his daughters want to participate, then they should. Anyway, it should work," Mr. Harrington continued conversationally. "It doesn't sound too complicated to me."

Michael was about to say he thought it was more complicated than what he thought but Sheena, knowing that Michael was about to continue a pointless debate, interjected swiftly.

"Matt told me he was awful at diving and that he dives like a cow having a seizure," Sheena said, trying not to laugh at the expression. "Is he being pessimistic or honest?"

"Well, let's say the lack of self-confidence has killed him," Mr. Harrington said, heavily. "He isn't enjoying this Olympics at all."

"That's my fault," Michael said, hastily. "If I wasn't obsessed with finding out—"

"Nothing is your fault," Mr. Harrington interrupted him. "I just don't think competing really is his thing."

In a span of five minutes, the crowd was packed and the event started. Michael saw Matt in his very small bathing suit. It was like a loincloth tied around his pelvis, except that it was navy blue. Michael almost laughed. Even from this distance, the facial expression on Matt's face told him that he would rather suck up diarrhea with a straw than be forced to dive almost stark naked on a springboard.

Matt was the third to dive off the board. The other two did really good. The first one did three flips, and the second one twisted three times and switched directions, resulting in them receiving applause from the crowd. Now it was Matt's turn.

Matt walked up to the edge of the board and looked down. He looked like he was about to wet himself.

"How much distance is the board from the water?" asked Sheena.

"I think forty meters, but it could be thirty meters. I'm not sure," Mr. Harrington answered her as the crowd held its breath. "It might be higher, or it might be lower. I have no clue."

"Someone could kill themselves on that thing!" exclaimed Michael. "No wonder he doesn't look remotely calm!"

"My son actually is not a very relaxed person," Mr. Harrington whispered. "He is quite panicky in moments of distress."

"Like right now," Michael said, seriously, turning his gaze back on Matt.

Michael saw Matt swing his arms back and forth for a brief moment, and then he bent his knees, jumped off of the board, and dived. He did two front flips with ease and dived smoothly into the water, barely making a splash when he hit the water. Michael saw him break the surface, looking relieved. It was clear that he was glad his first dive was over. The crowd, however, looked dissatisfied as lukewarm applause headed in his direction as he got out of the water and put a towel around his shoulders.

"That won't be enough," Mr. Harrington replied, gravely in response to the mixed reception the crowd was giving his son. "The others were better. The crowd was expecting more from him than that."

Not the scoreboard flashed a big number in yellow letters, which was his score. His score was worse then the other two, but very close to them. For taking a relatively easy route, he was not that far behind. Michael, Mr. Harrington, and Sheena cheered along with the other American visitors for him.

"That was one of the smoothest dives I saw him do yet," Mr. Harrington remarked to Michael and Sheena. "But he needs to get out of his comfort zone. Playing it safe won't help him here."

"True," Michael admitted, "but it's a start."

"I guess so. Anyway, Michael," Mr. Harrington said, lowering his voice and looking guilty. "We need to get going now. We have a game to play. Remember?"

Michael nodded. Standing up, he saw Sheena looking at him. "See you later. Good luck at your competition."

"You too!" she whispered back.

Michael and Mr. Harrington left the stadium and headed to their game. The two of them passed an army of bicycle riders and reached their stadium. They walked around it to the visitor entrance and Mr. Harrington opened the door.

"Mr. Harrington, I thought you weren't allowed to come back at all," Michael replied. "Didn't the Chinese Committee suspend you?"

"I could care in the least whether they suspended me or not," Mr. Harrington said, angrily, contradicting his words that he didn't care. "There's no ban prohibiting me to watch in the clubhouse."

Mr. Harrington led Michael to the locker room, where the rest of the team was hanging out. All of them were already changed in their uniforms but no coaches were there.

"Coach Harrington, are we breaking rules?" asked Fred obnoxiously.

"Shut up, Fred," Xavier muttered.

"Everyone, listen up!" Mr. Harrington said. "I have some quick, few short announcements."

Before he could say another word, Fred broke into song after doing an ungainly Irish jig.

"Announcements, announcements, Coach has got announcements!
He has them every day! He has them without delay! Whether it's a murder case or lineup change, Harrington's got them all!"

"Shut up, Fred," Joe muttered.

"Anyway, as I was saying before O' Leary decided to act like a three-year-old, I am making a couple of changes to the lineup," Mr. Harrington continued ("I knew it!" Fred said triumphantly). "Since James is done for the whole season, I will be putting Oscar on the mound today for us."

"Thanks, Coach," Oscar said, happily.

"And it is also my unfortunate and painful duty . . ."

The locker room door flew open as the other three coaches piled in.

"Sorry, Harrington," Mr. Isol said, gruffly. "I had to lay a dinosaur-sized egg and Oberfels and Smith were giving me some encouragement."

The whole team laughed. Mr. Harrington even laughed, but became serious in an instant.

"As I was saying, it is my painful duty to inform you that due to a new stupid law voted on by the Chinese Olympic Committee, all baseball lineups have to be twenty-two players or less."

There was an outbreak of muttering at this.

"That's rubbish!"

"That's bogus," David protested. "I thought it was twenty-four!"

"That's cat piss!" snarled Mr. Isol. "The Chinese people just love spitting in our faces! They can't give us the short end of the stick!"

"It was twenty-four," Mr. Harrington replied, heavily. "Anyway, the Chinese Committee sent a message to all coaches saying that in an attempt to reduce complaints from parents and family members of players that their angels aren't getting enough playing time, they are cutting rosters to twenty-two. They recommend we start with the youngest."

There was a silence after this announcement before Mr. Isol spoke.

"I could give a damn what the Chinese recommends," Mr. Isol muttered. "Tell them to wipe their butt with bamboo leaves!"

"That means Michael's a goner!" Mike exclaimed, looking horrified.

"You can't cut Michael! He's our best pitcher now that James is gone!" Nitro exclaimed to Mr. Harrington.

"And this is the Olympics for crying out loud!" Chad exclaimed disbelievingly. "People would *die* just to be on a team whether they play or not!"

"I agree, Chad. And to answer Mike and Nitro, I have no intention in cutting Michael," Mr. Harrington replied, smoothly. "I have to cut someone or else we are eliminated for good. I don't like the rule, but it is what it is. I have no control over it."

"That player is definitely going to be me," said Harry gloomily. "I'm not playing good at all."

"Harry, you probably the best hitter on the team," Fred replied bracingly. "Look on the bright side, even if you were the one to get cut, you'd have more time to obtain some phone numbers from some Asian girls."

"Thanks, Fred," Harry muttered, sarcastically.

"O' Leary, for your information we cut a pitcher because some of you are rotting in the bullpen," growled Mr. Isol.

There was an angry hissing noise at this.

"Why is it always the bullpen?" demanded David.

"Because you guys suck," Fred suggested with mock seriousness.

David sneered at Fred. Michael looked at Mr. Harrington, anger blazing inside of him.

"The Chinese are trying to screw us!" piped up Michael angrily.

"You're probably right," Mr. Harrington sighed, exhausted. "But we can't argue, so the person who is cut, I am going to beg you to not jump down our throats. Anyway, before I forget, I also have another announcement to tell all of you."

"Way to raise the suspense, Harrington!" Fred called.

"Shut up and let him speak, Fred," Xavier told him sternly, but suppressing a grin all the same.

Mr. Harrington cleared his throat.

"Whoever is eighteen or older could declare for the MLB draft," he continued, "if they so wish to. Please tell myself or any of the other coaches if you are interested. We'll take care of everything for you."

Fred looked annoyed. "That's ridiculous!"

"You may think so, O' Leary," snarled Mr. Smith, "but that is the rule."

"However," Mr. Harrington continued, "if you are younger than eighteen, you could always declare when you turn eighteen. Some people get drafted younger than that, but I am absolutely refusing to allow any of you to do that because from what we've seen, you guys are still too immature for the MLB."

"Screw that," Ken muttered disagreeably, but Mr. Harrington ignored him.

"Anyway," said Mr. Harrington, "I should tell you who I am cutting. I looked over the past few games and Mr. Isol showed me every pitcher's stats, and we agreed to let this person go, but will include him on our team again right after the Olympics. I still plan on getting our team into some competitive games and leagues."

"I hope it's Ron!" Justin shouted. "He sucks and blows every stupid game—"

"ENOUGH!" Isol growled, and Justin fell silent.

"The Chinese told me I have to start with the youngest," Mr. Harrington continued, now looking angry. He said bitterly, "But I disagree. If I do that, that would mean I would have to cut Michael like Nitro brought up."

"You can't cut him!" Fred bellowed. "He's one of the best, if not, the best! Mikey is the man! He's also got a cute-looking chick as his best friend!"

Mr. Harrington raised his hand in an attempt to silence everyone but the players were not done stating their views.

"There's no way you can cut him, dude," Ahmad replied. "He's too good."

"But I have told you," Mr. Harrington explained with a bite of impatience in his voice, "I am not cutting Michael."

"Thank God," Michael said, relieved, and everyone laughed.

"No, Michael, we are going to need you," Mr. Harrington said, earnestly. "You are definitely not going."

"Then who is?" Nitro questioned.

"I have decided," Mr. Harrington said as though it was costing him his strength, "that we will be cutting Ron, who has been struggling."

"Yes!" Justin cheered. "Woohoo!"

Everyone stared at him, and Ron looked as if he was going to punch him. Justin seemed to have realized he put his toe over the line because he bowed his head in shame once he received the mutinous glare from Mr. Smith.

"Oh . . . I'm sorry."

Ron was not pleased. "That's not fair!"

Mr. Harrington looked sympathetic. "I'm sorry, Ron, but it's the rule, or our team could be kicked out for the rest of this Olympics."

"You're still good, amigo," Samuel replied.

"Don't think about it as an insult," Fred said, smiling, and everyone listened. "Think about it as taking one for the team. Think about it as sacrificing yourself for our country's pride. And," he added, his eyes twinkling, "Think about it as getting more opportunity to flirt with some Asian chicks."

Everyone laughed. Michael thought that was the most tactful way of cheering Ron up. Fred was a really good guy and always had to be funny. Adding humor in this situation would make it seem less miserable and more light-hearted.

Ron stopped fuming and said, "Can I at least stay and watch?"

Mr. Harrington stopped laughing, too.

"I'm sorry, Ron. But I think your parents aren't planning on staying," Mr. Harrington said apologetically. "I called them to explain the situation. They aren't too happy with me to say the least. They plan on coming to take you home, though I would certainly prefer that you stay and support us. Maybe if you talk to them they can work something out."

Ron looked unhappy, but he didn't argue. He turned back to Fred. "I'll call you later to find out the score of the game."

"Bye, Ronnie," Fred said, as Ron disappeared.

Once the muttering of Ron's departure subsided, Mr. Harrington regained the team's attention.

"Now, I have the lineup. Please look at it and know what is expected of you. Everyone will be in the dugout for this game unless I directly tell you. Let's go."

Shocked at Mr. Harrington's abrupt and brief talk, Michael followed the rest of the team, stampeding like a herd of cows to the dugout. Michael realized that Mr. Harrington and Mr. Isol were in the dugout, disobeying the Chinese Committee. No one looked remotely surprised.

As he was taking a drink of Gatorade, Michael realized that his waived teammate could stay and he quickly walked over to Mr. Harrington. If he was right in thinking that James was out for the rest of the Games . . .

"Mr. Harrington, Ron could stay," Michael said, breathing fast.

"What do you suggest, Michael?"

"I'm suggesting that there's a way to keep Ron on our roster. Look, we had twenty-three players to start the Olympics. James got injured for the rest of the Olympics so that brings us down to twenty-two on the active roster. Ron leaving would make it twenty-one. And that means we only have seven pitchers, three starters. Since we are only allowed twenty-two, we just need to rule James off the roster."

Mr. Harrington's eyes grew wide with comprehension. Then he smiled.

"Mr. Goodwin told me you were intelligent. I did think of that. However, we had hoped James would be back to be the twenty-second person, but that probably is not likely at this point."

"No," agreed Michael. "He probably won't make it back."

"Then, we'll just need to check on James to be completely sure that he won't be back. If he's not in peak physical condition, we'll cut him and bring Ron back. In any case, I'll tell Lyle to book a room for Ron's family; they can pay him back later. Lyle, come over here!"

Mr. Isol walked over and Mr. Harrington quickly told him about Ron. Mr. Isol seemed to agree.

"Yeah, Harrington, at this point Shields won't be healthy enough. I'll take care of Stevens, Harrington," Mr. Isol promised, and he left.

By the time the game started, Michael just realized how important bringing Ron back was. Despite his dreadful start, he was an extra pitcher that could easily snap out of a slump. And due to Oscar's less-than-inspiring performance that was taking shape, Michael felt that an extra pitcher would not go amiss whatsoever.

Michael was bothered by how inconsistent Oscar's delivery was. He could never seem to get comfortable on the mound, despite his enthusiasm in the dugout earlier. He was as unpredictable as the weather when it came to how he pitched, but the Canadians interpreted his pitches clearly. By the time the fifth inning came around, the game was 4-2 to the Canadians after five innings, and Oscar's outing was finished.

"Durbin, warm up," Mr. Isol commanded gruffly.

Michael grabbed his glove and was able to hurry to the bullpen with Nitro to get a few reps in before having to go out on the mound.

Michael felt way more comfortable this time around than he ever did in the Olympics. He felt as fresh as ever, and it showed: he was able to go through three good innings, allowing two hits, no runs, and five strikeouts. When he left, the bats came alive for his team, which produced the Americans not only three runs, but a one-run lead.

"Nice pitching, Durbin," Mr. Isol said, gruffly as Michael sat down. "Robertson, get out there and finish them off!"

David was a more reliable closer than Ron: he threw a good inning, only allowing a measly infield single before forcing the next batter to hit into a double play.

The United States had won the game by a score of 5-4.

Back in the dugout, Fred did a silly dance move so exuberantly that his teammates, Michael included, had to get out of the way in fear of injury. However, he was able to be a hindrance anyway by knocking down the whole team's supply of Gatorade. Mr. Harrington wasn't pleased and Mr. Smith chased Fred around the clubhouse with a wooden bat ("Come back here, you joker!").

With a victorious air sweeping through the locker room, Michael joined in the chatter and fun with his teammates, but understood that his presence was required to complete a more important task than enhancing a party.

Michael met the Goodwin family outside with Matt. They were smiling and congratulated him.

"Nice job, Michael."

"Thanks."

Mr. Goodwin looked at him.

"Feeling ready, Michael?" he asked.

"I'm feeling ready, sir," Michael said, honestly.

"Good," answered Mr. Goodwin. "Let's head back to your room so I can give you the final instructions."

The seven of them hurried to the hotel room, where they were given instructions. The happy air that swelled up inside Michael like a balloon had deflated as he opened his room with the card.

There really was not much to go over which took Michael by surprise. Mr. Goodwin only spent his time reassuring him that everything was all good and everyone was prepared. Michael wasn't stupid; he figured out that the meeting was for his benefit, but he didn't care. It made him feel slightly better to hear that Mr. Goodwin at least respected his fear.

"We made sure we have everything under control," Mrs. Goodwin replied to Michael and Matt. "I've checked with the staff at Blossom Suites, the Committee members, and police. When you have Mr. Smith, bring him back down to the cafeteria here in this hotel. Understand?"

"How—?"

"Never mind right now," Mr. Goodwin said, impatiently. "The three of you could get going as soon as you want. The Committee members and the police will be here soon."

"I'll take the girls outside now, Will," Mrs. Goodwin said. "Come on, you two."

In a matter of seconds the three of them were out of the room before Mr. Goodwin could say anything. Mr. Goodwin turned to Michael, Matt, and Sheena.

"Are you three ready to go?"

"Yes," Michael, Matt, and Sheena said simultaneously.

"Then, good luck to you. We shall be waiting for you three to return."

Michael, Matt, and Sheena walked out of the room, down the staircase, and out the door of the hotel, hoping that the plan will work as smoothly as Mr. Goodwin said it would.

CHAPTER 16

THE GOODWIN LAMENT

Michael, Matt, and Sheena made their way out onto the crowded and dirty streets of Beijing. The air was suffocating, but the three heroes walked on, making their way through the dense crowd. Most were jabbering away to their companions, ignoring the three Americans completely. That suited Michael fine; he did not want people to be staring at him while he and his friends were doing secret work for Mr. Goodwin.

Sheena plucked Michael's sleeve. "Where do you think we should start?"

"How about we start at the Bird's Nest?" Matt suggested. "That's always a popular place for people to go to."

But Michael shook his head. He did not think that was the best place to start. Why would Mr. Smith be at the Beijing National Stadium?

"I think we should start at the baseball field," Michael whispered. "He still may be there."

They made their way across to the field. There were not many people loitering there, and certainly not many adults. Michael saw one kid who he recognized as Ty. He was busy re-packing his sports bag, which looked as though it had been ripped in half by a grizzly bear.

Michael and his friends walked over to him.

"Hello, Ty."

Michael was not fond of this kid very much, as he was known to be quite a whiner. Ty looked up, looking aggravated, as though he was interrupted during the SAT.

"What do you want, Michael?" Ty asked, stuffing his things in his bag feverishly. "Come to brag about your good game the other day, I suppose?"

"Michael doesn't brag about his ability," Sheena defended her friend, but Michael waved her down.

"Actually, we were wondering if you've seen Mr. Smith," Michael replied, pleasantly. "We need to find him."

Ty looked past him. His gaze turned to Matt and he let out a sneer with Matt glaring at him with utmost loathing. Michael guessed that Ty was one of the boys who gave Matt a hard time on the plane. Then, he looked at Sheena and his eyes seemed to bulge.

"Is she the Goodwin girl?" Ty questioned, for once not sounding bitter.

Matt's hands were clenched into fists. Sheena nodded. "Yes, I am. Ty, can you please tell me where Mr. Smith went?"

Ty shook his head. "I have no clue where he went. And, if I knew, I wouldn't tell your stupid friend over there."

"Watch who you're calling stupid!" snarled Matt.

WHAM!

Ty had punched Matt in the head with a quick right hook. Snarling, Matt made his way towards Ty furiously, but Michael and Sheena held him back by his shirt. Michael glared at his teammate. Why did Ty have to punch him?

"Just go away, Ty!" Michael said, furiously. "Why did you do that?"

Ty sneered. "He deserved it."

"Just leave, Ty!" Michael insisted, restraining Matt with difficulty; he was beginning to sweat from the effort.

Ty looked defiant. Then, grabbing his bag, he stalked off, cursing. Michael smiled. He did not like Ty that much. He always thought of him as arrogant and selfish. Michael made a mental note to tell Mr. Harrington that Ty punched his son.

Rubbing his head, Matt said, "Ty is the biggest ass I've met."

"I know," Michael replied. "I dislike him."

"I wonder why," sneered Matt sarcastically. "The kid's a brat."

The three of them looked around the baseball field, but Mr. Smith was nowhere in sight.

"Where do we go now?" Matt asked, as if this was an interesting day trip, not a plan that involves bringing a coach to the United States Olympic Committee. "It's obvious that he is not here."

"I thought he would be here!" Michael said, furiously. "I mean, I thought he would be here because the game just ended and coaches have to stay after sometimes to get more information, or to . . ."

"How about we start heading towards the Bird's Nest, see how the rest of them are doing, and then search by it?" Matt queried.

Michael gave a hollow laugh. "Matt, we don't have time to see how everyone else is doing. We need to find him first. We'll find out what they are doing after we get him."

"So, where should we go, Michael?" Sheena queried.

Michael put his hands on his head. Why did his friends expect him to make every decision?

Matt stared. "But—"

"Let's head down to the swimming area," Michael suggested in an effort to get somewhere. "Let's see if Mr. Smith went there."

"Okay."

The three of them walked over to the swimming area. When they got there, they did not find him, but they saw a whole bunch of Chinese officials there and the place was packed with all different sorts of people. On closer reflection, Michael saw that the Chinese officials were holding guns and looking menacing.

"Uh-oh," Michael said, gulping, "we better not let them find us. They probably would recognize us."

"Here, let's hide behind this wall," Matt replied, pulling him behind a small wall right outside the arena.

The officials were jabbering in rapid Manderin Chinese, which was a language Michael never even learned, and neither did Matt or Sheena.

"I wonder if they're in cahoots with the brothers," Michael whispered to his friends.

"Wouldn't surprise me one bit," Matt whispered back.

This was the worst situation Michael thought they could possibly in. They were by Chinese officials who would be able to recognize them, they couldn't speak English, and they would be able to recognize them. What if they were recruits of the Ying-Yang brothers? Michael did not want to take that risk.

"Well, let's not hide here and hope they don't find us." Michael whispered. "We've got to move."

"Where?"

"Anywhere," Michael whispered urgently, "as long as it's not here."

The three friends inched away from the wall and dashed away from the complex before the Chinese officials caught them.

Michael slowed to a walk when he was about a half a mile from the area. He could feel Matt's short breathing behind him and Sheena gliding along beside him.

"Okay, let's back track," Michael said to them, panting slightly.

Matt looked up, puzzled.

"You mean go to the baseball field?"

"Yes," he answered. "I'm sick of this goose chase. Going to the swimming area was a waste of time."

"But why?" Sheena queried. "We've already checked there."

"I know, but that does not mean he couldn't be there now! And we didn't even look inside the stadium!" exclaimed Michael. "It's worth a try. The coaches usually stay there longer than the players."

The three of them walked quickly to the field. They were about there when they were stopped by a man.

"Hey! Durbin!"

The man addressed him so rudely that Michael was one second away from blowing him off, but he kept his temper in check as he swiveled around to face the man, who resembled some kind of Cro-Magnon.

"Yes?" Michael asked coolly.

"I need to ask you something!" the man said in a loud voice. "Where is the Blossom Suites? I'm supposed to meet my son there."

The man was speaking in a ridiculously loud voice, as if he wanted the whole city to hear what he was asking Michael. Michael instantly knew it was Ron's father.

Michael sighed in relief. "It's over there," he answered, pointing to the left of him. "It's that tall pink building."

The man nodded his thanks and went off.

Sheena and Matt glanced at Michael.

"What should we do now?" Sheena questioned.

"Continue on to the baseball field," Michael replied, simply. "We're almost there."

The three of them walked the rest of the way to the baseball field. They saw that a game was being played at the moment.

"How are we going to get inside the stadium?" Michael asked.

"Easy," Matt replied. "My dad told me of a secret entrance inside this field. The managers are the only ones allowed into the stadium through this secret entrance. They get to come in to hang out in the clubhouse, but we're going to go straight through it and into the stadium. Follow me."

Michael and Sheena followed Matt to the other side of the stadium. Matt led them to a door that read AUTHORIZED PERSONNEL ONLY. He turned back to his friends.

"Watch this," he replied.

Matt took a key out of his pocket and jammed it roughly into the keyhole. He quickly unlocked the door and pulled it open.

"Not many people are allowed in here," Matt explained, "but my dad was able to acquire a key."

"Matt, you're a genius!"

"It's nothing," Matt said. "Let's get inside before we attract attention."

Michael, Matt, and Sheena walked through the door and Michael locked it shut again. They found themselves right inside a room filled with supplies and food packages. Comfortable chairs were scattered all over the place and a huge television was attached to the wall, broadcasting the live baseball game that was going on right now. At the back of the room was a staircase that spiraled up.

"Alright, if what my dad says is true, we should be able to take another door out after climbing that spiral staircase in front of us and be right in the stadium. Follow me."

Fortunately, Matt knew what he was doing and saying. The trio quickly climbed the stairs and found them right in front of the door that Matt had mentioned. He unlocked the door with his key and pushed it open. Quickly closing the door behind them, they walked over to a nearby restroom to talk about what to do next, trying to avoid attracting attention. Thankfully, no one was paying them any attention so they slipped by without being noticed.

"That was easier than I thought," Matt replied. "Anyway, Michael, what's the plan?"

"Okay, we are going to search the crowd, but keep out of sight and don't look too suspicious. Just thoroughly search everyone."

Michael knew that it was going to be hard to look at people and move from section to section without arousing suspicion, but Michael knew that they had no choice.

"Right," Matt said, nervously.

The three walked separately looking into the crowd, trying to find Mr. Smith. Michael took the outfield, while Sheena took the third base side and Matt checked the first base side. As Michael moved through the crowd, he did not see a single glimpse of Mr. Smith, even though he did see some fat, bald guy pick his nose and flick his boogers at the person in front of him. They all met up behind the last row of seats behind home plate.

"No luck?" Michael asked, disheartened.

"I did not see him," Sheena said, shaking her head, her eyes wide. "All I saw was some annoying kid laughing like a hyena because his sister dropped her peanuts."

"Matt?" Michael queried. "Any luck?"

Matt looked excited and scared at the same time.

"I found him announcing to a Chinese guy that he was leaving!" Matt exclaimed. "I saw him start to make his way to the first base exit."

"Leaving the stadium?" Michael queried, loudly. "We need to get to the exit of the stadium or we might not be able to catch him!"

The three raced off to the first base side and ran down another set of stairs. Michael could see Mr. Smith below them. Urging his friends to move more quickly, the kids made their way through the exit just as Mr. Smith was rounding the corner away from the stadium. He was alone, which made Michael more pleased.

"Hurry!" Michael urged his friends.

Mr. Smith caught sight of them at that moment. He stared for a moment, and then started to run away from them.

"Stop right there!" Matt yelled, who seemed to overcome his nervousness.

Mr. Smith, unfortunately, had decent running skills and was able to stay even the distance away from them. He ran into an alleyway on the streets of Beijing between two buildings. Michael, Matt, and Sheena pursued him.

Michael went around one building, Matt at his heels. Michael turned and saw a path where Mr. Smith was coming out of. Matt dived for Mr. Smith, but he was able to nimbly evade him.

Mr. Smith ran over to a crosswalk to cross the street but cars were zooming down the road at fifty miles an hour. Michael and his friends slowed down a little, thinking that Mr. Smith would not dare cross the street, but he was wrong: Mr. Smith had found the courage to dash across the street, causing cars to come screeching to a halt and beep their horns at him.

"Oh, come ON!" Michael yelled in frustration and he sprinted across the street with Matt and Sheena right behind him.

After weaving through a maze of cars, they followed Mr. Smith down the street until they saw him disappear in a supermarket.

"Sheena, cover the back exit! Matt and I will go in and search for him!" commanded Michael.

Sheena obeyed without question and tore away from Michael and Matt. Michael burst through the door first, startling an old lady into dropping her peanut butter.

"Lunatics," she muttered as Michael and Matt passed her.

"Take the right side, I got the left!" Michael ordered Matt. "Yell if you find him."

Matt nodded and he disappeared to the other side of the store.

Michael hurried to the left side, where he entered the vegetable aisle. Jogging down it and receiving looks of surprise from customers, he turned right to hurry down the next aisle, which was filled with cereal.

Michael ran to the next aisle (cat food and dog toys) but was interrupted in his search when Matt shouted to him from the poultry aisle.

"SMITH IS HEADING TO THE FRONT EXIT THROUGH THE SODA AND CANDY AISLE!"

Michael hurried back down to the vegetable aisle, jostling a dazed customer to the side as he scooped up a rolled-up cabbage. Tucking it under his arm, he ran around the corner where he found Mr. Smith running past the cashier, Matt on his tail.

Not for nothing, Michael was arguably the most impactful pitcher at the Games thus far so he had a knack of throwing things with deadly accuracy and incredible speed. So what if it was a cabbage? Gathering up his strength, Michael, on the run, hurled the cabbage at Mr. Smith.

To his delight, the cabbage met its intended target, hitting Mr. Smith in the chest, causing him to fly into the glass cases holding the cigarettes, cracking the glass slightly. Mr. Smith got quickly to his feet in a last attempt to escape.

Matt and Michael were too quick. They got there before Mr. Smith took two strides and caught hold of his jacket. Mr. Smith looked angry.

"You're coming with us outside, Mr. Smith," Michael said, forcefully. "We'll explain everything outside."

To avoid the staring of suspicious Chinese customers, they exited the supermarket with Mr. Smith. Sheena was waiting for them right outside and Mr. Smith finally spoke in a voice of suppressed rage.

"What do you three want?"

"Mr. Smith, we're sorry for grabbing your jacket and beaming you with a cabbage," Michael said, panting. "But Mr. Goodwin wants to speak with you."

"Is it something important?"

"Yes," Michael answered, breathlessly, knowing this would keep him interested.

Mr. Smith looked resigned and gave up quicker than Michael expected. "Fine. Where must I go?"

"The Blossom Suites hotel," panted Michael. "Come on."

They lead Mr. Smith back to the complex where they weaved through many people to get to the hotel.

"Michael beamed Mr. Smith with a cabbage?" Sheena asked Matt incredulously as they entered the hotel.

"Long story, Sheena, but I'll tell you the finer details later," Matt promised her in an undertone.

Mr. Goodwin was waiting for them and so were the other Committee members. Michael saw that Mr. Harrington was there, and Mr. Isol and Mr. Oberfels were there as well. Three police officers were also there, but they were hidden in the back. Mr. Smith turned to Michael, Matt, and Sheena.

"I thought I only was speaking to Mr. Goodwin!" he protested, looking at the three of them.

"Yes, but the Committee members have a right to hear this," Mr. Goodwin said, placidly. "Mr. Smith, I just want to talk to you. Please have a seat."

Mr. Smith glared at Mr. Goodwin, but he sat down in a spindly chair, looking extremely anxious. His legs were trembling uncontrollably. Mr. Goodwin looked slightly sympathetic, but he seemed determined to find out the truth.

"Mr. Smith, I need to ask you about your relationship between you and the brothers. Please tell us as much as you can. If you do, you will not be punished for anything."

Mr. Smith cocked his head to the side.

"And if I refuse?" Mr. Smith said.

"Then I have three muscular police officers who can lead you to a jail cell they have already selected for you," Mr. Goodwin said, calmly.

"Even if I were to tell you anything, how do I know you'll keep your promise?" demanded Mr. Smith.

"You have my word, Christopher," Mr. Goodwin replied, placidly. "In this situation, betraying others will not be frowned upon. Just tell us everything."

Mr. Smith seemed to relax, and he opened his mouth about to speak when Sheena's phone started to ring.

Everyone stared at Sheena as she withdrew her phone from her pocket.

"Hello?"

Sheena listened to the reply, and her face widened with shock and fear. She said, "We'll be over there."

She put the phone away and turned to her father.

"The Ying-Yang brothers and their gang have cornered Mom, Shawna, and Ember near the Bird's Nest!" she cried.

There was a huge commotion. The whole crowd stampeded towards the door. Mr. Goodwin was slammed against the wall as everyone hurried towards the exit as if they were running from an incinerator. Michael grabbed Matt and Sheena and lead the way out of the hotel—everyone was obviously heading to the scene of the crime.

"SHEENA! MATT! MICHAEL!"

It was Mr. Goodwin. He was desperately trying to get to them through the crowd.

"Don't go! Stay out of the way!" he hollered. "We'll sort this out!"

"Not a chance!" Sheena cried.

Michael was with her. He had to help. He felt as if he carried a burden of the responsibility of this incident. He pulled Matt and Sheena out of the way of the crazy crowd.

"Listen, we're going with them!" he said, as the crowd rushed past them. "I don't care what your dad says, Sheena. We need to help."

Sheena looked extremely upset and Matt nodded.

The three of them charged on, worried that they might be too late. The Ying-Yang brothers were not the sharpest tools in a shed, but they knew how to operate quickly.

"Hurry!" Matt urged Sheena on, who had much shorter legs than him and was lagging behind. The Bird's Nest was in the near distance and the three friends were able to get near the front of the crowd to see what was going on.

Mrs. Goodwin was being restrained by about ten Chinese men while Ying and Yang were trying to wrestle Shawna and Ember into the car. Both girls were screaming hysterically. Ying looked up and saw the crowd gaining on them. Turning to his remaining allies, he ordered them to stop the crowd from getting to the car.

"ATTACK!" he shouted.

The gang and the Committee collided about thirty meters from the car and started to bring each other to the ground. Legs were merely blurs of peach light and fists were flying crazily in the air. People around them were just staring at the riot that was going on. Most of them looked too shocked to do anything about it.

Michael did not care about the innocent bystanders. All he wanted to do was get Shawna and Ember out of there. Forcing his way through the crowd, he reached the car after dodging a kick by an opponent.

"Michael, help us!" Shawna and Ember cried through the window.

"I'll get you out of here," he promised, and he opened the car door.

"Get Durbin! He's letting the girls escape!"

"Hurry!" Michael urged Shawna and Ember loudly.

The girls got out of the car, but Ying and Yang both ignored the girls and pinned Michael against the car before he could even move.

"We got you now, Durbin!" Ying snarled.

"Let's get him in the car and get out of here before we have problems!" Yang commanded his brother.

Michael struggled, but the brothers were too strong for him. He was going to be kidnapped . . . This was it . . . There was no hope for his escape . . . unless . . .

There was a loud growl, and Mr. Isol came charging like an angry bull at the brothers. He threw Yang over the car and landed painfully on the road. Ying threw a punch, but Mr. Isol grabbed his fist with his claw-like hand, jerked it right into Ying's face, and tossed him away from the car on the ground.

"Get out of here, Durbin!" he growled in Michael's ear. "Before someone murders you!"

"No! These are my friends! I'm helping them!" Michael shouted.

"I know, it's all very touching, but you need to get the hell out of here!" Mr. Isol yelled at him, irritably, before joining the fray again, throwing a stubby man off of Mr. Goodwin, who was pinned down as though he got beat in a wrestling match.

Michael searched the crowd desperately, looking for his friends. He saw a glimpse of Sheena's golden-brown hair, and he dashed to her.

Before he got close to Sheena, an ally of Ying and Yang noticed him, and tripped him up. Michael fell hard on the road, and felt his nose hit the road hard. It was not broken, but he felt blood coming out of it and dripping into his mouth. Michael spat on the ground to rid his mouth of the blood.

He got up to realize that both sides were separating from each other, and glaring at each other with utmost loathing. Both sides had suffered injuries, but none were severe. The bystanders, thinking that the fight was over, started to disperse.

"Michael, are you okay?"

Michael felt himself being pulled to the Committee side by Sheena. To Michael's enormous relief, she looked fine but thoroughly shaken.

"I'm fine," he answered.

Sheena withdrew a tissue from her pocket and handed it to him. "You need to stop the flow."

Michael did as she said, holding the tissue to his nose and pinching it.

The Ying-Yang brothers and their armada of thirty other cronies were standing in a neat array, breathing heavily and looking at their opponents with hatred. Mr. Goodwin, breathing heavily, looked as though he would like to do nothing but shoot the brothers where they stood.

"How dare you try and kidnap my daughters, Ying and Yang!" Mr. Goodwin shouted at them.

Ying shrugged, looking relaxed.

"It's every man for himself in my game, Goodwin!" Ying shouted back.

"This isn't a game!" he spat. "This is treachery! How can you do this to your own country?"

"The United States was never our country, Goodwin!" shouted Yang. "China was always our true country!"

Mr. Goodwin looked around at all the Committee members and his family before turning back to the brothers.

"This bullshit has to end now!" Mr. Goodwin screamed. "There can be no more of this!"

The Ying-Yang brothers both laughed maniacally.

"This isn't *Deal or No Deal*, Goodwin!" yelled Ying. "You're going to regret not giving us what we wanted!"

"We'll make sure of that!" Yang shouted defiantly.

"The authorities will make sure you two don't attempt this kind of nasty scheme ever again!" Mr. Goodwin screamed. "They'll be here in a few seconds to get you! It's only a matter of time until someone informs them of this!"

Ying let out a nasty laugh. "Too bad the authorities are in our pocket, Goodwin. They won't be coming at all. You see, we used some of our father's inheritance money to bribe the Chinese police! They won't be coming unless they turn out braver than we expect!"

"Enough of this, Will!" Mrs. Goodwin said, pleadingly. "Let's get out of here."

Ying, Yang, Mr. Smith, and their gang blocked any way of escaping them. Michael now knew they were helplessly trapped, but only slightly outnumbered.

"Go quietly is in your plans, woman?" Yang replied, snickering. "I think not. I still want to talk to your idiotic husband."

"Why is that?" Shawna asked, angrily.

"Shut up, girly," Ying replied. Then he turned to Mr. Goodwin. "You are outgunned and outmanned, Goodwin!"

"You have no outlet to slip through or no alleyway to run to," Yang added, smoothly. "But we will give you a chance to buy your freedom from us."

"How so?" asked Mr. Harrington in an angry voice.

Ying smiled evilly.

"Well, you see, we only accept the currency called the Durbin," Ying said, and the gang laughed loudly at this.

"I have a bad feeling about this," Michael murmured to Matt and Sheena.

"So, in exchange for all of you to run along and not get harmed in any way, you must surrender baseball hero Durbin to us. Your crummy team will no longer have a shot for a medal, and we will ensure that Durbin helps us get our scroll," Ying replied, pressing his advantage. "We win, you lose. We only want Durbin. Goodwin, you did what we wanted you to do. You allowed your daughters to roam around Beijing quite unprotected. They were the bait for our plan. We knew Durbin would go to their aid. This was all set up to get our hands on Durbin. Now, you must pay the price for your stupidity. This is what a double play looks like."

Mr. Goodwin looked at Michael, and Michael could tell that he was regretting not listening to him before. And Michael also could tell that Mr. Goodwin was thinking the same thing he was.

Michael knew that if the brothers took him, it was going to be impossible for him to get back to them. The brothers seemed to already know about the location of the scroll if Mr. Smith tried to murder him. They'd kill him.

"We're not going to let you take Michael," Mr. Goodwin said, firmly, "even if you have to hurt us, we're not letting you take him."

Michael was touched by how Mr. Goodwin would sacrifice his body for him, but all the same, Michael felt that it might be worth it so no one else suffers from the brothers.

Michael stepped forward.

"Michael, please!" pleaded Sheena, but Michael ignored her and looked defiantly at the brothers.

"Let's say, hypothetically, I surrender myself to you. How do I know that you'll keep your word and not harm my friends?" Michael asked.

"You don't!" Yang said. "But at least it is not guaranteed that we'll hurt your buddies. If you don't, they will be harmed. I can promise you that."

"Durbin is not for sale, punks!" Mr. Isol said angrily.

"That is who we want, idiot," Ying said, icily. "If you refuse to give him to us, you must pay the consequences."

"You are going to pay for the consequences of your actions later, Ying," snarled Mr. Goodwin. "And you, Yang."

"Why won't you just give up?" Yang asked.

"Because you haven't!" snarled Mr. Goodwin. "You have been waiting for years to get revenge on us. You want to hurt us. Just because you would not be accepted on Harrington's team and you have to start an unnecessary feud. You were too proud, too arrogant. You can never learn from your mistakes."

Yang shrugged. "Well, on your head, Goodwin. So be it."

"Cowardice," Michael said, suddenly, surprising everyone.

"What did you say, Durbin?" Ying growled.

"You both are cowards," Michael said, recklessly, and Matt groaned. "You cornered three women when it was thirty onto three. You guys obviously are *so* brave."

"How dare you?" Ying said, and started toward him.

"Yes, I dare," Michael continued recklessly, making Sheena, Shawna, and Ember moan. "I know more about you than you know about me. You'll be surprised what I can figure out on my own. I'm not a stupid kid."

Mrs. Goodwin looked faint. "Michael!"

Michael did not stop, he couldn't. "You two got rejected for the team when you were fourteen because Mr. Harrington didn't think you were good. It wasn't prejudice; it was for the team's own good. You two would have probably bumped off everyone who was in your way to be the star."

"Michael, stop!" Matt moaned.

"You were angry and livid," Michael continued. "So from that moment on, you two had a grudge on fourteen-year-old athletes that made the team because you thought you two were the best things on the whole planet. That is why you are targeting me, because I am fourteen and made the team. You two are the prejudiced ones. Your arrogance disgraces your country, your pride destroys your family name, and for that you two are going to jail."

Ying bared his teeth. "Who told you all of this, you little runt?"

"I did."

Mr. Harrington stood by Michael's side and faced the brothers. Yang threw him a look of deepest disgust.

"You're a loser like your son," Yang said. "Well, Durbin, you seem to know a lot about us. Too bad you don't know the whole story. I can tell you it, if you were to come with us. You can help us find the scroll and we'll get revenge on these fools. We won't make this offer again."

"Yeah, good try, Yang, because I'll hate to reject you twice. And based on your experiences once was already bad enough for you two, eh? By the way, if you were only trying to capture me, why did Mr. Smith attempt to choke me by sending me a muffin with a rubber thing in the middle?" Michael challenged them.

The brothers turned to Mr. Smith. Their lips were formed into a snarl.

"You idiot! You blew everything!" Ying snarled.

"I didn't mean to!" protested Mr. Smith.

"That means that you do know where it is, or you already have it, and you're just trying to kill me now," Michael replied.

"Join us, Durbin!" Yang rasped. "We can offer you a lot more than what they can! This is your last chance."

Michael thought hard. He tried to glance at Mr. Goodwin, and he mouthed a word that looked like no, but Michael didn't know if that was the right idea. If he did, he was endangering everyone, including himself. If he went with them, he would only hurt himself. But, also, he and his friends were outnumbered.

"Ha!" Michael said, laughing. "So . . . I'll just, you know, walk and help you, and the rest can skip on home, will they? It's not like you won't hurt the rest of them anyway!"

Ying knew he was joking. "You leave us with no choice, Durbin. We attempted at negotiations, but now we must play aggressive. Yang, get him."

There was a scuffle, and Michael was knocked clean off his feet, and found Yang strangling him. He choked, but was rescued by Sheena, who kicked Yang.

"Thanks!" Michael breathed to Sheena.

Ying lunged at Michael, punching him on the nose. Michael screamed in pain. He knew Ying had not broken it, but he could feel blood coming out of it again.

Michael tackled Ying, who was trying to drag Shawna to the car. Shawna fell, but scrambled away fast like a squirrel.

Michael watched Mr. Smith being flown in the air by Mr. Isol and saw Mrs. Goodwin and Sheena knocking away Yang. Michael heard Ying yell.

"Get anyone of them! It does not have to be Durbin! Just get one and let's get out of here before the authorities start being brave, you got it?"

Michael shoved Yang, who was bleeding, and shoved Matt out of the way to avoid getting hit by a gun that Ying had chucked at him.

Mr. Goodwin stepped on the gun and broke it.

Ying roared, and with one punch, he knocked out Mrs. Goodwin, who was protecting her two younger daughters. She crumbled at his feet as her daughters screamed.

Michael hurried over to help, but Ying stuck out his foot, tripping him up. Shawna and Ember ran, but Ying dived, and caught hold of Ember.

"Ember!" Shawna cried.

"Help me!" Ember cried.

Michael and Sheena ran simultaneously at Ying, who grabbed a knife out of his pocket.

Michael took the chance and stole Ember from him, but Ying grabbed him by the scruff of the neck and slammed him against the car.

"Ember, run!" he yelled.

Ying pointed the knife at Michael. "You are to give her to me, or die the hard way!"

"No!" Michael cried.

Ying raised the knife, but Mr. Isol knocked it out his hands. Ying tripped Mr. Isol, and he fell to the ground.

"Yeah, fat boy, look who beat you!" Ying crowed.

Ying then grabbed Ember again, and her screams lit up the fading day. He called Mr. Smith and Yang, who were bleeding, and they jumped into the car while the other Chinese gang members dispersed, knowing that they were about to win.

"No!" Michael yelled.

Michael grabbed onto the car door, and Ember screamed to him.

"Michael, help! Don't let them take me!" she was sobbing, crying her eyes out.

Yang stuck his feet out and kicked Michael in the stomach, and that made him tumble back on the road hard, scraping his hands.

Mr. Goodwin tried to grab the car, but it was out of his reach. Ember was being kidnapped.

Mr. Harrington dived to the car, and was forcing it open, but Mr. Smith took an ordinary crowbar and whacked him across the head with it.

"Mr. Harrington!" Ember cried, sobbing.

Mr. Harrington was then shoved backward by Mr. Smith and he fell on top of his own son's left leg, which bent in an awkward angle and they heard a slight crack. Matt howled in excruciating pain.

The car revved into high gear, and ten seconds later, the rest of the gang disappeared and Ember's hysterical screams died away.

Michael stood up, shaking but he could only stare at the fading car. His prediction came true. The plan, as he expected, failed, and this was the worst failed plan Michael had ever been in.

CHAPTER 17

THE SECOND PLAN

As the brothers' car disappeared into the foggy atmosphere of Beijing, Michael could not grasp the fact that Ember may never be seen again—or that she very well may be killed. They knew that the brothers knew where the scroll was, thanks to Mr. Smith's blunder, so they really did not need Ember.

A tiny molecule in his brain sent a message to his brain and Michael thought in his full confidence that he was at fault. He had made the wrong decision. He should have given himself up, because if he had, Ember may have never been taken from their wake. Now, it would be unlikely if she was seen alive again.

The other people were stirring, and Michael walked and helped them get to their feet. His companions were all hurt, but there were no major casualties or bloodshed.

"Are you all right?" he asked Sheena, when he pulled her to her feet.

"Yes," Sheena said, her face was tear-streaked. "I think so."

Michael for the first time got to see how badly injured his companions were: Sheena had a huge cut near her shoulder and had soot over her face; Mr. Goodwin had a huge rip in his shirt and lost his mustache; Mr. Harrington had about a million tiny cuts on his legs; Mrs. Goodwin was barely stirring, but had black and blues everywhere; Shawna had soot in her hair and face with blood slowly pouring down both cheeks; Matt, barely able to walk, had Michael suspect a broken leg; Mr. Isol, a few nasty bruises; and Mr. Oberfels, who was bleeding from his arm. The rest of the Committee members looked fine, except a few cuts here and there.

"Is everyone okay?" Mr. Goodwin asked, breaking the silence.

Everyone said yes but Michael, who spoke quickly, "Mr. Goodwin, we need to get to the hospital fast."

Mr. Goodwin nodded. "Yes, of course."

"After that, we need to find out where Ember could be," Michael said, "we need to get Ember back."

"Michael, you're forgetting one thing," Mr. Harrington replied. "We need to compete in baseball."

"Baseball is not important now," Michael replied so dejectedly that Mr. Harrington stared. "No, I'm serious, Coach. It was me who got all of us in this predicament so I must be the one who gets us out of it."

Shawna gave a whimper, and Sheena put an arm around her, giving her a reassuring squeeze, yet her face was glazed with tears as well.

"Michael—" Matt started, but he broke off, not knowing what to say next. His teeth were gritted with pain.

Mr. Harrington sighed. "You're right, Michael. But if we want to rescue her, we need to do it when we don't have a game so I could help."

"That's true," Michael admitted.

"We should do it tomorrow," Matt said, immediately while grinding his teeth in pain.

"Tomorrow?" Mrs. Goodwin echoed. "But, Matt, dear, we don't have a plan. It would be risky."

"It'd be risky even if we spent a whole month planning it," Michael said, heavily. "Better sooner than later. And that way, we miss no baseball games. They could just kill Ember whenever; we can't wait."

Sheena sniffed. "Michael's right. Matt is right as well. We all need to trust one another. We all need to help. We need to do it tomorrow. We need to get Ember back."

"In the meantime," Mr. Goodwin replied, "let's get up to the hospital, and treat our injuries. I expect the brothers to want us to come get Ember so that they could try and kill Michael. We need to make sure that we are in decent shape to face whatever they have in store for us."

"Let's hurry," Shawna said, tearfully. The loss of her sister seemed to have a huge emotional toll on her.

And the whole group, Michael, Sheena, Matt being supported by Mr. Harrington, and the rest of them started to walk to the hospital, feeling as if they had lost everything.

* * *

When they got to the hospital, Mr. Harrington told them some good news.

"I can do it tomorrow at any time," he said as they checked in at the receptionist's desk. "Michael's right. We play the day after tomorrow, against China. I checked our schedule on my phone."

The whole group spent the night in the hospital ward, which was agreeable as they were provided with good service. The nurses were excellent at what they did. They did not ask any questions nor let anyone else know what had happened to them. They merely led them to separate rooms and took care of their injuries. Michael could only lie down on his warm bed and stare at the blank ceiling, thinking about his friends and in what condition Ember was in.

Michael received phone calls from Tomas and Sara while he was in the hospital and they told him when they were coming exactly.

"We'll be there Wednesday night," Sara had said.

So Michael, knowing he would see his friends in less than three days, told his Sheena and Matt (over the hospital phone, of course, as he was not allowed to leave his room) that they would need to rescue Ember before Wednesday night.

"I don't want my friends coming over here and seeing me in danger," he had told them.

Next morning, it was August 17th. Michael was cleared to leave the hospital after eating a small breakfast (a sesame seed bagel with a small serving of rice), but he waited for all of his companions to come out first.

All the Goodwins besides Mrs. Goodwin came out about ten minutes later and Michael was pleased to see that they had no serious injuries.

"Where's Mrs. Goodwin?" Michael asked, concerned.

"She's still in bed," Sheena replied to Michael. "The nurse said she needs more rest, and they are not clearing her yet. Mom insisted that we go get Ember without her."

"Can everyone else come?" Michael questioned. "We need all the help we can get."

"Shawna wants to but my mom said no," Sheena replied, grin fading. "And my father tried to tell the police the story, but they refused to believe it. However, my dad thinks it won't remain that way for long. If we succeed today, that might be enough to get the Chinese police to side with us. Ying and Yang weren't lying when they said they bribed them."

Michael forgot about the concerned parent attack, even though he thought Mrs. Goodwin was right. Shawna was much too young to come on such a dangerous mission with them.

"What about you?" he asked.

"My mom says I could make my own decision," Sheena said, drawing herself up proudly. "So I'm coming, and so is my dad."

"How is Matt?"

"Not very good," Shawna said, butting in the conversation Michael and Sheena were having.

Mr. Goodwin joined in too. "His leg is definitely broken, so he can't come. Mr. Harrington is okay, though. He'll be available to come."

Michael was concerned. It was only him, Sheena, Mr. Goodwin, and Mr. Harrington that was going. Who knows how many cronies of the brothers would be there? He could not see any way they could rescue Ember with just the four of them, two of them being five and a half feet or smaller.

The door of the hospital opened and Michael gasped as Mr. Isol came in, holding a file folder.

"Those morons," he muttered, sitting down and taking up the capacity of three chairs. "If they were on fire, I wouldn't piss on them to put it out."

"I know," Michael replied, bitterly.

"Oh, and by the way, Goodwin," Mr. Isol growled. "I'll accompany you on your mission to retrieve your daughter. I feel that you might need me. And Oberfels said he would come, too. He got cleared earlier. He'll meet us back at Blossom Suites."

Michael's spirits soared. They were still low on people, but the addition of two more people definitely helped significantly. And Mr. Isol because of his size counted for about three people.

"At least we are nursing quickly," Mr. Goodwin told Mr. Isol. "Only one of us is seriously hurt."

"Who?"

"Matt."

"Oh yeah, that's right. His leg broke. Is he really hurt badly?"

"Yes," Mr. Goodwin replied. "His leg is broken so he is out for the rest of the Olympics."

Mr. Isol groaned. "Why is it always Harrington getting hurt, or something bad happening to him?"

"Tell me about it," Mr. Goodwin replied.

Sheena and Michael looked at one another. Michael could tell that Sheena was just as concerned for Matt as he was. Will Matt be able to experience a full recovery? That was the main question at hand, something that he or any of the nurses here could answer. Michael, however, was concerned about the future of him and his friends. Matt was done because of an injury, and what if something happened to him or Sheena? Who would finish the work that was needed to be done? He didn't think he could bear to lose both his friends. He longed their company on missions like these.

Mr. Harrington came out of the hospital ward, looking rather annoyed and disgruntled.

"How is Matt?" Michael, Sheena, and Shawna asked simultaneously.

Mr. Harrington looked somber. "He is in critical condition."

"What do you mean?" questioned Mr. Isol, who did not seem to understand.

"His leg was not broken very much, thankfully," Mr. Harrington said wearily. "He needs to have a pair of crutches for only three weeks."

"Well, that is good," Michael said, knowing full well that based on Mr. Harrington's expression, which looked as though he were facing certain doom, that nothing about Matt's injury was positive.

Mr. Harrington shook his head. "It isn't. The break was not too severe, but it is broken in several places. More than I could count to. The damage is worse than a normal broken bone."

"Uh-oh," Sheena said, worriedly.

"That means," Mr. Harrington continued, "that there is a good chance that his leg may not fully heal."

"Well, that's *great*," Mr. Isol growled sarcastically.

Mr. Harrington gave a weak chuckle. "Anyway, if he were to fully recover—and based on the odds that is not going to happen—he still will have a limp. Then, he would have to get his legs working again. That could take another good few months."

"But his leg would heal, wouldn't it?" Mrs. Goodwin asked, looking worried.

"I am afraid," Mr. Harrington replied, now looking grave. "That my son has experienced a career-threatening injury. If the doctors and trainers do not help him quickly enough, he might not be able to walk properly again."

"And?" Mr. Goodwin said.

"His sport career would be definitely over," Mr. Harrington replied, looking at the ground. "He most likely won't be ready for the 2012 Olympics in London, but if the doctors do everything right, he could apply for the 2016 Olympics. But, even that, is still in high stakes. We don't want to take any risks with him. However, from a safety standpoint, it may be better just to call it a career before anything serious happens."

Michael's heart sank like a stone. His first best friend here, injured, threatened for his career, all because of him. Why did he have to get all of them hurt because of an idiotic determination of stopping two Chinese twins? The scroll was more important than ever now. Michael knew they had to get it before the brothers to stop more people from getting hurt—or worse.

"Can we go see him?" Sheena queried, indicating her family and Michael.

"Yes, you could see him, Sheena," Mr. Harrington said, giving her a grateful look. "Here, we'll let you and Michael go first, if that's alright with everyone."

"Of course," Mr. Isol grunted while everyone else nodded.

Michael and Sheena stood up and went to the door, but Mr. Harrington called them back.

"By the way," Mr. Harrington said. "Matt is in ward forty-seven, first door on the left."

The two of them walked down the hallway in search of their best friend in silence. Michael could tell that Sheena was very concerned for her friend and there was no point in striking up a conversation. Yet somewhere in Michael's brain, there was a nagging voice in it commanding him to tell Sheena what he really did not want to admit.

"Ward thirty . . ."

Michael stopped at ward thirty and Sheena turned to him. She tilted her head a little to the side questioningly.

"What is it, Michael?" questioned Sheena, looking distinctly unhappy. "Are you alright?"

Michael looked at Sheena with a look full of pain and anguish. "Sheena, this is my fault. If I haven't—"

Sheena put a consoling hand on Michael's shoulder.

"No it isn't, Michael," reassured Sheena, looking serious. "Even if we never met you, we would be doing this as well. You only help us a lot. We probably would be goners right now if it weren't for you."

"Sheena, I know you think I'm great, but I'm not," Michael replied, disheartened. "Because of me, our best friend has a career-threatening injury and your sister is in the grasp of two evil Chinese twins! She might even be dead for all we know!"

"Don't say things like that, of course she's alive," scolded Sheena gently, but Michael instantly wished he hadn't spoken.

They continued walking towards ward forty-seven in silence. Michael felt as though he were walking through some labyrinth. There were so many hallways, and it seemed to drain more happiness away from Michael as they trudged on. Sheena seemed to understand the pain Michael was going through.

Sheena stopped at ward forty-seven and turned to Michael. Then, slowly, she went right up to him and hugged him and Michael knew he definitely did not deserve it.

"You're my best friend, Michael," Sheena said, putting a hand on his cheek and letting go of him. "That is all I care about. I'm sure you'll help us get my sister back, I know it."

"Let's hope," Michael said, as she removed her hand from his cheek, feeling slightly embarrassed. "Anyway, let's see Matt."

They entered the door where Matt was and found it ajar. Matt was sitting up, but his injured leg was straight forward. He smiled when he saw them. He looked in good spirits despite him having his leg broken in a million places.

"I knew you would come and visit," Matt said, happily. "Got discharged from the hospital, I presume?"

"Are you okay, Matt?" Michael asked.

Matt looked up at Michael.

"I know what you are going to say, Michael. This isn't your fault," Matt said, seriously, as though he read Michael's mind. "You need to stop blaming yourself for everything."

"I've been told," Michael muttered.

"In fact, it's my dad's fault," Matt replied, seriously. "However, I'm not blaming him. It was an accident. He landed on me when he attempted to rescue Ember. He saved me the trouble of doing something I've wanted to do as soon as I arrived at Beijing."

"Which was what?" Sheena asked, sharply.

"I don't want to do diving anymore," Matt answered, sounding cheerful. "I didn't tell my dad anything, or my trainer about what was really battling in my mind, I was too cowardly to do so. Michael, you've really demonstrated to me what it's like to be brave, so I finally told my dad once I got into this bed what I really wanted to do."

"And what did your dad say?" Sheena queried, softly.

"He said that he just wants me to be happy and he supports anything that I plan on doing," Matt said. "So, I need to start thinking about what I plan on doing after I recover from this."

"Then what would you do at the next Olympics?" Michael asked. "You still plan on coming to London in 2012, I hope?"

"I have thought out an alternative plan," Matt answered. "And my recovery does not affect it at all. It doesn't matter how bad my leg is; it will be okay to handle the sport."

"What is it?" Sheena asked, curiously. She was obviously looking confused as to how her friend was able to find another passion so quickly. Michael deduced that he wasn't too motivated to dive. His attitude clearly indicated throughout the Olympics that he didn't want to dive.

"Archery," Matt answered, surprising the two of them. "I'm quite good at it, but not Olympic-caliber. I would just need a little training and I then will be good to go. I just need a good trainer and I need help from the archery coach."

Michael felt a warm, glorious wave of relief. He was glad that his friend was not going to surrender because of his injury and pleased that he was able to find passion behind another alternative.

"I never knew you were interested in archery, Matthew," Sheena replied, looking suspicious.

Matt smiled weakly.

"Even after fourteen years of knowing me you still don't know everything about me," Matt said.

"What would happen if you can't do archery, Matt?" Michael questioned.

"If I can't," Matt replied, "I'm still coming to the Olympics, but maybe I can do something else."

"Not with baseball I hope because baseball is knocked out next Olympics."

Mr. Harrington was back with the rest of the Goodwin family. Mr. Isol cast a shadow over them. Compared to him, the Goodwin family and Harrington were little kids compared to a grown man.

Michael looked at him, befuddled. He heard perfectly well what Mr. Harrington said, but he refused to believe it.

"Did you say—baseball is what?"

"I'll explain later," Mr. Harrington replied, quickly. "Matt, you're fine, right?"

"Yes, Dad," he replied, stretching out his good leg. "I don't feel the pain as much anymore."

"Good."

Mr. Goodwin then turned to his daughter and Michael.

"You two," he said, "since we are all ready, we need to go get Ember now."

"We don't even know where we are going," Michael said, confused.

Before Mr. Goodwin could answer, Sheena butted in.

"How about we learn more about the Ying-Yang brothers?" Sheena queried. "Maybe that will give us a better idea of where we can start."

"Good idea," Mr. Goodwin replied. Michael felt more relieved. He was afraid that they might never figure out where she was.

"She can't be too far from here," Michael said, reasonably. "The brothers would need to stay in Beijing to observe what else is going on."

Mr. Harrington nodded.

"The brothers like to be in the circle of news," he replied, seriously. "They're in Beijing somewhere."

"Speaking of them," Michael said, as a sudden thought had occurred to him, "they are no longer in charge of the Chinese Olympic Committee, are they?"

And Mr. Goodwin's response finally brought good news, but it was a little late.

"No, they are not," Mr. Goodwin said, triumphantly. "Mr. Oberfels went to explain what had happened to the Chinese police. They explained it to the Chinese Committee, and after a contact to the Chinese Government, it was decided that they would terminate both of their contracts. The Chinese police are searching for them as we speak. They finally realize that the brothers aren't tragic heroes."

"How are we going to rescue Ember?"

"I have a bunch of items in a little black case that might be of use," Mr. Goodwin said, holding up the sleek, black case. "I have worked for the FBI before I got involved in the Olympic Committee so I have some items that might come in handy."

Michael was tempted to ask what those items were but resisted. He would be wasting time.

"Anyway, before we leave, I think we should do what Sheena suggested and try to look up some possible places where they might be," Mr. Goodwin said, calmly. "We still don't know where we should try."

"I have a laptop in my room," Sheena said, quickly. "We can use that and maybe find where Ember is."

"Good girl," Mr. Isol growled. "Then, we shall go and kick some oriental ass."

Michael and Matt laughed.

Mr. Harrington shot Mr. Isol a reproachful look. "Well, we better get going, then. It could take a while before we figure out where she is."

Matt tried to sit up. "Can I help somehow?"

Michael stopped. Mr. Harrington, Mr. Goodwin, Sheena, and Mr. Isol looked questioningly at him.

"What do you mean?" asked Mr. Goodwin.

"Is there anyway I can assist?" Matt asked, forcefully this time. "I know I can't go, but I feel bad not helping when I'm safe in a hospital when you guys are in danger."

Michael and Sheena beamed at Matt.

"Well," Mr. Goodwin said, smiling at Matt respectively. "You can try this."

And he gave Matt a radio, which was sputtering.

"Michael will take the other one," Mr. Goodwin said, giving Michael the other one as he spoke. "He'll contact you if we find ourselves in imminent danger. It will be your job to alert the authorities either by phone or getting to the police station."

"I can go to the station if necessary," Shawna said, pointing at herself.

"Good," Mr. Harrington replied. "Your help is appreciated, Shawna."

"Now can we kick some . . . ?"

"Even though you may be exclaiming it as your personal hobby," Mr. Goodwin replied, reproachfully, as Michael and Matt roared with laughter, "I must tell you that you are not setting a good example for my daughter here, Isol."

"It is okay, Dad," Shawna said, quickly. "I'm glad Mr. Isol is excited, actually. No wonder he was so willing to help us. He's only going to be doing something he likes—"

"Shawna!" Mrs. Goodwin said, shocked, but Michael and Matt laughed.

"Anyway, we better get going," Mr. Harrington said. "See you all later."

"Good luck, you two," Matt said, forcing a smile. "I'll get you out of danger if necessary."

"See you later, Matt," Sheena said, smiling.

"Then you will have a chance to rescue Mikey after all," Michael replied in a high voice, making Sheena frown with disapproval and Matt laugh with amusement.

"Go kick some oriental—"

"THANKS, Matt," Michael said, loudly, and him and Sheena, chortling, followed the three men out of the room with Michael sincerely hoping, that this time, that this plan would not crumble like the last one.

CHAPTER 18

THE CHINESE OLYMPIC COMMITTEE INTERNATIONAL COOPERATION

Michael was holding the radio as he ran to keep up with the three men. Sheena was right beside him and not saying a word. Michael supposed she was concentrating on how this could possibly work, or what was the importance of the scroll.

But that was all soon to be solved. They were to make their way to Sheena's hotel room and log in on the laptop. There, they hoped that they would be able to access into a site that can give the group new leads—or even better, how important the scroll is and where could they find it along with Sheena's red-haired sister.

Michael and Sheena didn't speak a word to each other until they reached the hotel lobby where another man stood with Mr. Goodwin, Mr. Harrington, and Mr. Isol, waiting for them. Mr. Oberfels had joined up with them, looking ready.

"So we are rescuing her sister?" Mr. Oberfels queried to Mr. Isol, pointing to Sheena. Mr. Isol gave him a short nod.

"What took you two so long?" Mr. Isol growled.

"We didn't realize you were ahead of us by a mile," Michael said, truthfully, because he had not noticed how far the adults were away since he was deep in thought.

"Well, let's get moving before the brothers blow us all to smithereens!" growled Mr. Isol. "We don't have time to be walking like we're in Candy Land, Durbin!"

Mr. Goodwin replied, briskly, "Sheena, can you lead us to your room?"

"Certainly," Sheena said, and she started to lead them up the stairs. "Follow me."

Michael followed her and the three men were walking behind him. Sheena took the steps two at a time, and Michael was finding it hard to keep up with her despite the fact that Sheena had much shorter legs than him.

As they walked up the stairs, Michael tried to get even with Sheena so that he could talk to her without the adults hearing. However, she was moving at such a brisk pace that Michael felt as though he were in some kind of time trial.

Sheena reached the top and waited for everyone to come up to the top. Then, she led them down the hallway and stopped when she reached her room.

"Just out of curiosity," Michael said, smiling a little as he joined her by her door. "How come do you get a room to yourself when everyone else shares one?"

Sheena shrugged. "I was supposed to share it with one of my gymnastics teammates. But she backed out at the last minute because she was afraid of the pollution here."

She then smiled mischievously.

"Is this it?" Mr. Harrington questioned once all the men reached the door.

"Yes," Sheena replied. "Here, I'll open it . . ."

She took out the credit card and swiped it through the slot. It shone green. Then, Sheena grasped the handle, pulled it open, and walked briskly into the room.

Michael caught the glimpse of the room for a second time, and not much had changed. The bed was made, everything was organized, and nothing was out of place. The four men seemed impressed, and Michael had to be amazed as well, because his and Matt's room burst with the extraordinary, including that huge metal throne Matt was giddy to see.

"You keep your room very clean," Mr. Goodwin said, finally. "I'm impressed, Sheena."

"Anyway, where is your laptop, Sheena?" Mr. Harrington queried, surprising everyone.

Michael observed how Mr. Harrington's body language seemed to be trembling. He supposed he just wanted it to get done and not take all day. For a grown man, he looked rather tense in relation to the situation at hand.

"It's in my suitcase," Sheena answered. "Just give me a second."

Sheena disappeared for only thirty seconds and came back with her bright pink laptop.

"Don't ask," she muttered to Michael, who was about to comment on it.

Sheena propped the laptop on her bed and sat down on the bed. Michael stood to her immediate right; Mr. Harrington leaned against the pillows; and Mr. Goodwin was to her immediate left. Mr. Oberfels sat next to Mr. Goodwin. Mr. Isol looked as though he wanted to sit on the bed, but seemed to think better of it and merely stood in the background.

Sheena turned on the laptop and a blue screen showed up, shortly followed by a cool female's voice, which rang through the tiny speakers on the laptop.

"Please type your name and password located in the box. Then press the ENTER key."

Sheena did so, her fingers moving rapidly across the keyboard. Then, she pressed the ENTER key.

"Welcome Sheena Goodwin. Today is August 17th, 2008."

"We know," Sheena muttered, pressing the ESC button on her laptop.

Her personal settings instantly showed up on the screen, which was the background of the New York Yankees playing a game against a team with ugly throwback uniforms.

"Boo," Mr. Harrington and Michael said out loud. Sheena frowned at them and turned to her father.

"What should I type in?" Sheena asked her dad curiously.

"Go to Bing," Mr. Goodwin replied. "I'll direct you from there. I know exactly where we need to go, but it may be difficult to find."

Sheena typed in the web address for Bing and waited for barely a second for it to load up. Michael was pretty impressed with how quickly her computer loaded; at home, it took a whole mealtime before Michael's computer was able to display the homepage so that he could check his e-mail.

"How did it load up so fast?" Michael asked out loud.

"I just got it about two months ago, so it is quite new," Sheena explained. Then, she asked, "What should I type in?"

"Not long ago, I found a website owned completely by the brothers. I forget how I found it, though. Type in 'The Scroll of the Yangtze'," Mr. Goodwin suggested. "That's what it's called by most people, anyway. We may be fortunate to find the website."

Sheena did so, and pressed the respective ENTER key.

Michael noticed that it was loading rather slowly now, and was moving at a speed relative of Michael's computer. Then, a screen showed up that said the search engine failed to come up with a site.

"Dammit," Mr. Isol growled, and everyone in the vicinity jumped.

"Try Google," Mr. Harrington suggested.

Sheena did so, but it was unsuccessful.

"How are we going to find this out?" Michael questioned, frustrated.

The radio crackled and Michael heard a voice come out from it.

"Find anything yet?"

It was Matt. Michael held the radio to his mouth and then responded.

"Not yet Matt. We are having trouble finding a site."

"Don't try a search engine. Go to a Committee website," Matt said.

Michael looked at Mr. Goodwin, who was rubbing his chin thoughtfully. Based on his facial expression, Mr. Goodwin heard Matt's voice and was considering his advice. "There should be no need for that. I now remember what the web address was."

"What is it?" Mr. Harrington questioned.

"Sheena, please type in COCIC.com. Make sure it has all capital letters in the main address."

Sheena did so and a website popped up instantly.

The headline of the website was so big that everyone was able to see it, even Mr. Isol in the back. The headline read:

Chinese Olympic Committee Inter. Cooperation

The Only Website Where You Can Personally Find Out About Ying and Yang, Who Are The Two Most Amazing People In China!!!!!!!

Michael snorted in disgust. He knew the brothers were arrogant little jerks, but the secondary advertisement made Michael want to vomit. It was unbelievable how immature the brothers were. Ten-year-old kids were known to write stuff like this, not the President and Vice President of the Chinese Committee.

"The Chinese Olympic Committee International Cooperation?" Michael asked, frowning. "What is this?"

"Nice one, Goodwin," Mr. Isol said, appreciatively.

Mr. Goodwin turned to Michael and Sheena. "This is one of the websites of the Chinese Committee that Ying and Yang created, though you probably knew that based on the front page. We might be able to find out something meaningful here."

Sheena looked at the home page and found the word Blog.

"Try that, Sheena," Michael suggested. "Maybe the brothers added something."

Sheena clicked on it, and the Blogs showed up. It was categorized by person, so Sheena clicked on Ying and Yang's names which were near the bottom of the long list.

"Bingo," Sheena replied. "Dad, is this right?"

Mr. Goodwin nodded, smiling.

"I think you've found it, my dear," Mr. Goodwin said.

Then, a bunch of different messages showed up, in which Michael and his friends read:

'Ying,

I am currently forcing the Goodwin girl to finalize the plans.

Yang'

'Yang,

Good. If she does not cooperate, I will do the persuading. I need to know that our plan will work. It is very important, as you ought to know.

Ying'

'Ying,

That is true, Ying. It is important. The scroll will indeed help us on getting back at Michael and his goody-goodies. Finding it would be the essential part. This year is our year. Fireworks Factory is already under our control. All we need is all of China. By the way, how will it help us get back at them?

Yang'

Michael was excited about the messages shared between Ying and Yang. He knew the answer must be in the next message. He tore his eyes to the next message on the page and it only carried only one word on it, but it got the message across:

'Rockets'

Mr. Goodwin looked at everyone else, who had an expression of suppressed triumph on their faces. "This is the answer."

"Rockets?" Michael asked. "They are using rockets from . . ."

And now Michael understood, as a look of comprehension formed on his face.

"That's why they captured Fireworks Factory," Michael said, slowly. "They knew the importance of the scroll was a plan to build . . . I guess some type of rocket that is powerful enough to destroy us. They wanted to get revenge on you, Mr. Harrington! The brothers probably just took over the factory!"

"No, they did not," Mr. Isol growled at Michael.

"What do you mean? Of course they did."

"And I'm telling you they didn't!" growled Mr. Isol. "I can even prove it to you as I know you kids think you know everything!"

Mr. Isol took Sheena's laptop and typed in a few words. After a minute of waiting, he clicked on a tab and showed the computer screen to everyone.

"This page has the history of the brothers' father," Mr. Isol replied. "Since he was very important to the Chinese, he has a big history. It says here that he was the founder of the Fireworks Factory."

"They must have found the scroll after they took Ember," Mr. Goodwin replied, glancing at Mr. Isol. "It was probably in Fireworks Factory the whole time!"

Michael still couldn't believe the scroll was in the factory.

"No wonder they were pissed," Michael replied. "Mr. Smith blew their cover! The brothers wanted to make sure that we thought that they were still looking for it while they built this rocket to destroy us!"

"If only Ember were here," Sheena said, sadly, "she probably would have figured that out earlier than us."

"Uh, I'm not sure that they found it, though," Mr. Goodwin replied. "Look at this line. *'Finding it would be the essential part.'* This makes it seem like they don't know where it is still. Maybe they worded it wrong, but we need to find out whether they made a mistake in saying this or not."

"But I'm still confused as to how the brothers obtained Fireworks Factory," Michael said, gazing questioningly at Mr. Isol. "Did they take it from their father?"

"Obviously they didn't take it or their father wouldn't have tried to help them kill us, now would he? Durbin, I knew the brothers. The truth is their father owned the factory and hired employees to help him sell fireworks and make explosive devices," Mr. Isol explained. "The brothers must have inherited the factory from their father!"

"That's bad," Sheena replied, being Captain Obvious. "But not nearly as bad as posting these kind of messages on a public website."

"The brothers are so stupid!" Michael exclaimed. "Why are they posting their comments of their nefarious plans on the Chinese Committee website?"

Mr. Goodwin had an answer for him. "They are the only two who ever go to that website from the Chinese Committee. Like I said, this isn't the Chinese Committee website, Michael. It's a website created by the brothers. They are the only two who know about it—besides me, of course."

"How did you know about it?" Michael asked, amazed.

"By accident, actually," Mr. Goodwin admitted, honestly. "After I heard that the brothers obtained jobs in the Chinese Committee, I immediately went to search up more about how they got those positions. I came across this website when I did research on the brothers. I then immediately reported my findings to Matt and Lyle."

"You never told us about the website," Mr. Harrington said, accusingly. "You only told us about their positions!"

"I didn't think it was important at the time," Mr. Goodwin said, honestly. "But now . . ."

"Let's go get my sister," Sheena finished for him. "We know where we should try now."

"Are we going to go to Fireworks Factory?"

"I think my daughter has a good chance of being there," Mr. Goodwin said, slowly. "I definitely agree with Sheena. The brothers are most likely there—or at least, Ember is."

"How are we going to get inside the factory?" Michael queried. "You would think that the brothers have some security measures in place, right?"

"We'll think of something once we get a general idea of the security," Mr. Goodwin replied, slowly. "In usual circumstances, I would research the security around the place, but we certainly don't have the luxury of time to look that up. We got to save my daughter."

The radio crackled and Michael answered it.

"This is Michael Durbin."

Sheena laughed at Michael for being so formal. Blushing slightly, Michael waited for Matt to speak.

"Michael, did you find out anything?"

"Yes, we found out that the scroll contains a plan how to build a gigantic rocket to kill us all."

"That's pleasant."

"Now, we are going to save Ember," Michael said into the radio. "We will see you later."

"Good luck. Be safe."

Michael promised Matt that he will and then turned to the others. "Are we ready?"

"Yes, let's go," Mr. Isol said, gruffly. Then he smiled, "I could do with a bit of Chinese to take home as a souvenir."

"ISOL!"

"Only joking, Goodwin . . ."

"We'll go in my car," Mr. Goodwin said, cutting Isol off. It was obvious that he clearly wanted to save his daughter as quick as possible. "It is just right outside this hotel. Follow me."

Mr. Goodwin led the way out; then Mr. Harrington came next followed closely by Mr. Isol and Mr. Oberfels. Michael waited for Sheena to shut off her computer and then walked with her and brought up the rear.

"Your laptop just might save us," Michael replied to her, as they followed the men.

"Not yet," Sheena pointed out, "we need to not be blown up first. And we need to rescue my sister."

"But do they really want to blow us up?" he queried. "They easily might want to use the rocket to destroy something else."

"But it may be part of the plan," Sheena pointed out. "All of this is really confusing. What do they plan on doing with that rocket?"

"It looks as though they have several options but are waiting to see what happens before deciding what to do," Michael replied. "They could probably strap one of us onto it and kill us. They might have done that as a piece of their plan to lead us to Fireworks Factory as a trap. They might be using Ember as bait."

"You could be right," Sheena said.

"The brothers don't seem to make much sense in what they're doing, though," Michael replied, slowly. "If your dad was right in what he said, they'd be wasting their time building it if it was not on the scroll."

"That's why I think your theory is logical, Michael," Sheena answered. "The rocket may merely be there to send one of us into orbit when we rescue Ember. They'll be able to set an example of what happens when we mess with them by blowing one of us up."

"I can't believe we're talking about being blown up this casually," Michael said, grimly.

Sheena laughed.

"Oh, you humor me sometimes, Michael," Sheena said, even though Michael did not understand what she meant by that. Nothing he said was remotely funny.

As he walked outside of the hotel, Michael became convinced that he was right in saying that the brothers did not have the real scroll. The brothers seemed to be just trying to get him to them, taking advantage of his heroics. Their rocket would merely just show them that the brothers were capable of defeating them. However, Michael was ready to confront the brothers on that.

When they got to Mr. Goodwin's car, they realized how much of a problem it was going to be to get to the factory. His car was a tiny royal blue Chevrolet Malibu. All four of them turned to Mr. Isol, thinking exactly the same thing.

Truth to be told, Mr. Isol was roughly the size of a grizzly bear, so fitting him in a five-person car was not going to be such an easy thing. Being as large as a refrigerator, he would take up most of the back seat. Mr. Goodwin sighed, realizing that it was going to be a problem.

"We will be a bit cramped," Mr. Goodwin said, sighing. "I think we might be forced to not buckle up."

"You have to be kidding, Will," Mr. Harrington replied, peering inside the car. "There's no way all of us can fit inside this car. I can get my car and—"

"If we travel in more than one car, we'd look a little conspicuous," Mr. Goodwin insisted. "We need to try to make this work. Even an extra car might raise their eyebrows."

Michael could understand the rationale behind Mr. Goodwin's words. The brothers might think that they were attacking his base if they brought more than one car. And it would be much easier for them to get into the Fireworks Factory premises with one small vehicle.

"Will, I'm not—"

"We have no choice, Matt," Mr. Goodwin repeated, and got into the driver's seat. "We don't want to attract a lot of attention. I know the brothers well, just like you, Matt. Please trust me on this one."

"I can take my car," Mr. Oberfels offered, but Mr. Goodwin shook his head.

"Like I said, it'll look suspicious if more than one car goes," Mr. Goodwin repeated. "I know it's not the greatest idea, but I want to be cautious."

In the end, they ended up sitting in the car like this: Mr. Goodwin was in the driver's seat. Mr. Isol, who was so enormous, that they put him right beside Mr. Goodwin, but he still covered most of the front so Mr. Goodwin had to shift towards the window, his left cheek pressed to the window. Mr. Harrington took the right window spot, behind Mr. Isol. Michael took the middle seat, and Sheena took the window seat to the left and Mr. Oberfels was forced to squeeze in between Mr. Harrington and Michael. It was extremely uncomfortable, and Michael found it as hard to breathe in the car as sucking in the polluted air outside. Mr. Goodwin put on his belt, but no one else could.

"It didn't turn out too bad," Mr. Isol replied in his usual gruff voice. "That's good. I'm not too fat yet."

"Yet being the key word, right, Isol?" Mr. Harrington asked, slyly.

"Shut up, Harrington."

Mr. Goodwin then turned to face the three of them in the back seat. "Okay, are all of you ready?"

"Yes," the three of them chorused.

"How about you, Isol?"

"You know what Goodwin? We need to take a potty break. I can feel a big one coming."

Michael and Sheena laughed.

"Hold it, Isol," Mr. Harrington said, laughing as well.

"Why? I need to go bad, and if I do it right now, the size of my log will break down the car."

Sheena laughed.

"Let's go before that happens," Mr. Goodwin said, quickly, but Mr. Isol laughed.

"Just kidding, Goodwin, I'm fine—"

Mr. Goodwin turned on the car. It made a loud, rumbling noise, comparable to a fat man's stomach, and Mr. Goodwin backed up the car out of the parking place. Then he drove away from the hotel.

"Do you know where Fireworks Factory is?" questioned Michael curiously.

"It is on the outskirts of Beijing," Mr. Goodwin replied as he drove. "It should not be too hard to find."

Michael sincerely hoped so. The expression on Mrs. Goodwin's face when they don't bring Ember back alive was not one that he wanted to find out.

CHAPTER 19

THE EVENING LAKE

Michael looked out the extremely clean and cared for windows, wondering if this plan could absolutely go according to plan. This was an extremely risky plan, and if it failed Michael pictured everyone getting injured and Ember never being seen again. Michael could not bear to think about that possibility.

Sheena seemed extremely anxious and tense, too. Sheena was shaking a little bit, and Michael sincerely hoped it was just nervousness. She was not happy, as she usually was, or loquacious, or laughing. She just stared out the window, lost in thought, and Michael knew she was thinking the same thing he was—what if they come back without her?

"Are you alright?" Michael asked Sheena, putting a consoling hand on her shoulder.

Sheena shrugged, but did not answer. Michael understood.

Mr. Harrington was looking at the two of them with a mixed expression of what seemed like sympathetic and mildly amused. It was he, after all, who had kid around with Michael about Sheena, but Michael had no time to worry about that—rescuing Sheena's sister was of vital importance now.

Matt and the others seemed to be in a far away land in the country, away from them. Matt, Michael thought, seemed disappointed when he couldn't help. Was he feeling as if he let them down? Was he upset that he couldn't rescue his friend's sister? After all, Michael had felt guilty when Ember was kidnapped, even though he was not solely responsible for it. Michael wished that Matt was with him now. He could use his companionship. As much as Michael liked Sheena, he had to admit that Matt's presence was something that he sorely missed and an unhappy Sheena could not replace it.

"We're almost there," Mr. Goodwin announced. "We are about a minute away, so get ready."

Michael stood up.

"Mr. Goodwin, sir," he said, "I think there will be a visitor's gate. We should look for that because we definitely aren't going to be allowed in the other ones, right?"

"We can't do that, Michael," Mr. Goodwin sighed. "I do know for a fact that the only way that we can get inside of it is by trespassing by the other gates. The visitor's gate is only for the center, the visitor's center and museum, and obviously we do not want that."

"That's impossible!" Michael exclaimed. "There's no way we could get through that gate—"

"Shut up, Durbin," Mr. Isol grumbled. "We're not interested in your petty worries, to be honest. We didn't bring Goodwin's wife on this day trip for this reason!"

"Mr. Isol, but there will be security and there might be a password we need to know," Sheena cried out dispassionately.

"Screw that," Mr. Isol said, gruffly.

"We'll be okay, Sheena," Mr. Harrington said, quickly. "Goodwin, is the gate coming up?"

Mr. Goodwin did not answer, but looked at a gate that read:

WELCOME TO THE CHINESE FIREWORKS FACTORY
THE FORTRESS OF THE EVENING LAKE

Mr. Goodwin looked at everyone.

"It's padlocked," Michael said, pointing.

"So?"

"We can't get in," Michael replied.

"No problem," Mr. Goodwin said.

He put the car in reverse and the car slowly backed up away from the padlocked fence.

"Goodwin, are you doing what I think you're doing?" Mr. Isol questioned as Mr. Goodwin stopped the car.

"Yes, Lyle," Mr. Goodwin responded. He turned around to face everyone. "Hang on tight!"

"Goodwin, what are you doing?" Mr. Isol queried.

"Just do what I say!"

"GOODWIN, WHAT ARE YOU DOING?"

Sheena gripped Michael's hand hard. Michael glanced at her but surprisingly, she didn't let go. Michael could feel the circulation being cut off from his hand.

Then, without warning, Mr. Goodwin slammed on the gas pedal and drove straight through the padlocked gate and it fell crashing to the floor. They bumped slightly over the gate and continued on their way down the road.

"What the hell's the big idea?" Isol demanded. "Now those Chinese punks will know they have some visitors!"

"Not if we can help it," Mr. Goodwin said, grimly. "They might be so immersed in their work that they probably didn't notice a thing."

"You're mad, Goodwin," Mr. Isol grumbled.

"We needed to get through, so I found a way through the gate," Mr. Goodwin replied. Then, he added in a business-like manner, "We are going to be traveling through the fortress of the Evening Lake."

"What's Evening Lake?" Michael asked, puzzled.

"I'll explain later," said Mr. Goodwin hastily. "Right now, I need you and Sheena to keep your eyes peeled. Try to find the gate that says, Staff Only, or Workers Only. That's where we need to enter."

Sheena and Michael looked out the window and they were now circling a small body of water. Michael wondered if it was . . .

"No, that is not."

Michael turned to face the three men. "Not what?"

"That's not Evening Lake," Mr. Harrington answered, as if he could mind read Michael. "That's only Signature Outpost, a body of water designed to catch trespassers in the dark."

"How do you know all of this?" Sheena asked, amazed.

"I researched Beijing for a project in college once," Mr. Harrington explained, "so I know quite a bit about this place. I just don't know the security. I only know the history about it."

Mr. Goodwin jerked the steering wheel so hard all of them went to the other side. Sheena's head banged against Michael's temple and he massaged the spot vigorously as the car slowed down.

"Sorry," Sheena whispered, looking apologetic.

"Don't worry about it," Michael said, rubbing the spot.

Mr. Isol was also shaken up even though due to his vastness he barely moved.

"What the hell, Goodwin! Come on, man, that was not cool!"

"Sorry," he apologized. "But I just found the right gate for staff members. It was open, which only makes our job a lot easier. I guess the brothers were a little careless with the security due to their excitement."

Mr. Goodwin drove a little bit more and then he entered a parking area where there was only two cars parked. Mr. Goodwin parked away from them.

"Okay," he said, "everyone, out."

Sheena opened the door and got out of the car. Michael and Mr. Harrington went out the other way. Mr. Goodwin shut his door closed but Mr. Isol, whose door was still open, seemed to be having difficulty getting out of the car. His torso was halfway out of the car, but it seemed as though he was stuck between the car door and the car.

"Oh, crap, this is bad . . ."

With the help of Mr. Goodwin, Mr. Oberfels, and Mr. Harrington, the three men were able to pull Mr. Isol out of the car after several attempts.

"Sorry about that," Mr. Isol grumbled. "I better start snacking on veggie sticks like a rabbit."

Michael, meanwhile, went to the edge of the parking area, and walked up a hill and found something on the other side of the hill that made him gape out in that direction.

It was a lake, and Michael knew it was Evening Lake immediately. Looking out and down from the hill, he realized the reason as to why it was so important. The Evening Lake was magnificent and beautiful. It was the exact opposite of the environment of Beijing: it was a clear blue color and had no trace of pollutants in it. Michael could not breathe much easier due to fumes coming from the factory, but he found the view visually impressive. As he stared out at the lake, he admired it, and it seemed like a reassurance of all of the bad things that had happened in Beijing.

Michael heard footsteps and turned around to see Sheena walking towards him.

"Michael, come on, we need to get in the building somehow. We need to get Ember."

Sheena tugged at his arm, and Michael, recognizing defeat, followed suit, knowing that rescuing Ember was far more important.

The four men were over by a door that had a black slot. Sheena led him over there, and saw that Mr. Isol carried a black case, which he remembered was the one Mr. Goodwin had said they might need.

"Now that you are here, Durbin," Mr. Isol said, gruffly, "we need to figure out how to get through this blasted door."

"We could maybe get a huge pole, and use it as a battering ram," Michael suggested half-heartedly as a vain attempt to kid around. He was trying to take a leaf out of Fred's book and make a difficult situation not seem as bad. Like he knew coming into Beijing, he was going to need to make lemonade out of the lemons that the Ying-Yang brothers threw at him.

"Idiot boy! I was joking! We figured out how."

"Then how?"

Mr. Goodwin said, "In this case, we have equipment that could help us. Isol, open it, if you will please. Michael needs to understand our plan."

Mr. Isol opened the case, and took out a black flashlight with a blue light.

"You see this, Durbin?" Mr. Isol growled. "This is a fingerprint detector. This instrument is used to detect fingerprints on objects so the cops could identify the stupid moron."

"Oh," Michael said. "Right."

Mr. Harrington pressed a red button on the side of the black slot and a keyboard came out of the slot. The action was followed by not a cool female voice that Sheena's laptop issued, but rather a robotic male voice.

"Welcome to Fireworks Factory. Please type in the password on the keyboard directly below you."

Mr. Harrington turned to Michael and Sheena. "We could use this instrument to figure out the keys on the keyboard so we could type in the password."

"Here, Sheena, how about you do it?" Mr. Goodwin replied. "Michael, take a pencil and notepad from the case and write down the letters Sheena says."

Michael and Sheena obeyed, and in a few seconds, Sheena shown the flashlight on the keyboard and Michael had the pencil poised in his hand, ready to write down the letters. Sheena cleared her throat.

"I see an A," Sheena replied, as Michael wrote it down. "Z, N, Y, T, and E."

Michael quickly finished writing them down. As he looked at the letters, he thought that he had a realistic idea as to what the password was.

Sheena clicked off the light. "Do you have all of them, Michael?"

"Yes," Michael said, quietly. "I think I know the password as well."

"What is it?" Mr. Harrington asked. "Or, I should say, what do you think it is?"

"Sheena, try 'Yangtze,'" Michael replied. "That has to be the password."

"No, don't," Mr. Goodwin replied. "It probably is a made-up word. He would not use a real word. That would be way too easy."

"The Ying-Yang brothers aren't exactly the world's greatest thinkers, Goodwin," Mr. Oberfels reminded him.

"Yeah, my goldfish can outwit them," Mr. Isol said, seriously.

"Try it, Sheena," Michael said, stubbornly. "I know this is it. The brothers aren't intelligent enough to remember a made-up word."

"Fair point, Michael," Mr. Goodwin said. "But what if it isn't?"

"Then, we'll try again," Michael replied, determinedly. "But I swear this is right."

"Remember, Michael," Mr. Goodwin said. "If we fail, they would know someone was trying to sneak in and they will find us. We have one chance to get this right without being detected and I know this is incorrect. This password seems to be a little too easy."

"What else can it be?" Michael queried, testily. "Sir, passwords can't be a mix of letters, no one will remember them."

"SHUT UP!" Mr. Isol boomed. "Stop arguing. We're getting nowhere. Try the damn password, and if Durbin is incorrect, I'll kick their asses and we could get in! Don't fret!"

No one laughed. Right now was no laughing matter.

"Go for it, Sheena," Michael whispered in her ear.

Sheena, shaking, typed in the password. Then, she raised her finger above the enter key, ready to send it.

"Sheena, don't!" Mr. Goodwin said, warily.

Too late. Sheena pressed the Enter key.

"Access not denied. Welcome to Fireworks Factory. Ying and Yang wish you a pleasant day."

"Yeah, right," Mr. Isol snorted. "And I wish them hell."

The doors opened and all six of them hurried inside before they slowly shut on them, leaving them in almost complete darkness.

"You worry too much, Goodwin," Mr. Isol replied, solemnly.

"That was luck," Mr. Goodwin said, thickly.

The six of them looked around in the cavernous hallway. There were no doors, so all they had to do was walk down the passageway.

"Come on," Michael breathed to his companions.

He led them down the hallway quickly. No sound was heard but the breathing of his compatriots. He was sure that the passageway was long by the way it was twisting up ahead.

"Michael, look," Sheena said, tugging his sleeve and pointing down.

Michael looked at the ground and before him, he saw a sword. Michael bent down and picked it up. Examining it, he noticed it had a slightly curved blade and had a handle made of gems and gold. It reminded him of the samurai, which he had learned about in his history class. The sword gleamed in Michael's eye and Michael thought it must have been new the way it looked.

"Michael, put the sword down," Mr. Goodwin replied, tersely.

"No, Goodwin, we might need that as a defense mechanism," Mr. Harrington replied. "Michael, hand it to me, please. No fourteen-year-old should carry a sword."

"Let the boy keep it," Mr. Isol grumbled. "He should have the opportunity to play hero with the sword. He never got the chance. Anyway, we are obviously wasting time and if we keep arguing about ridiculous things like who is going to hold a sword, we will never get the Goodwin girl."

Michael held the sword to his side, glad that the argument was over.

"Let's go," he replied.

It felt odd, holding a gleaming weapon in his hand, but he felt braver. Even so, the sword was a little heavy for him, like a heavy baseball bat, but he was able to move it well enough. In fact, he figured Mr. Isol could probably swing it one hundred miles an hour.

"Michael," Sheena asked, looking scared. "You don't think that could be the brothers' sword, do you?"

Michael pondered that possibility for a minute. Yes, he thought it was theirs, but he couldn't tell Sheena that. He could not bring his heart to say so.

"No, I don't."

Sheena looked surprised. He hated lying to Sheena, but he knew he would wound her even more if he told her the truth.

The group walked down the passageway. The lights flashed in a consistent pattern, giving Michael an ominous feeling, as though he were walking on train tracks in the Subway. Michael held the sword out in front of him, just in case someone chose the moment to attack. Mr. Isol's ragged breathing frosted the back of his neck, and Mr. Goodwin was at his heels looking around warily, expecting danger.

There was a glowing light in the distance at the end of the hall like a thousand illuminated lanterns. Had they found where Ember was?

"I think we've found it," Michael whispered to the others.

Mr. Goodwin, however, shook his head. "I would not bet on that," he replied, frowning. "I bet you that will be another room that leads to where my daughter is."

And he ended up being quite right. They entered a room that had what looked like the midnight sky for a ceiling. At one end of the circular room, there were many doors, presumably leading to a possible control room or several other research rooms. At the other end, there was one huge door, surrounded by what looked like a little castle, ten feet high. The room was quite peaceful, definitely in contrast to who ran this place.

"It is so beautiful," Sheena whispered, awestruck, her eyes twinkling like the flashing lights above them.

"It is," Mr. Harrington agreed, "but we need to find the room where your sister could be in. She could be through any of those doors."

"It should not be as hard as you might think," Michael said. He pointed to the huge, castle-embroidered door. "I bet you all my money that she is in there."

"We can try there first," Mr. Goodwin replied.

"Lead on," Mr. Isol growled.

The six of them walked across the room. At the center was a green circle, about ten feet wide on all sides. As they were walking across it, it broke open with a bang.

Michael cried out as his hands scrabbled to grab some part of the edge. His compatriots' screams spread throughout the room. He heard a loud thump, a disgusting swearword, and the floor that was encircled by the green circle crumble down in the deep, dark pit. He heard Sheena's high-pitch scream once again, and a panting noise somewhere to his immediate right. Michael heaved himself back onto the ground, gazing at the huge pit, horror-struck and breathing heavily.

He glanced around the edges where Sheena, Mr. Harrington, Mr. Goodwin, and Mr. Oberfels were all panting. All of them were red and looked as though they had just completed a competitive two-mile run.

"What the hell was that?" Michael yelped, joining his companions.

"A trapdoor," Mr. Goodwin panted. "The brothers must have set up a booby trap for us. They aren't as stupid as I thought. They knew we would figure out where they were."

Then, he pointed upward to the sky where there were two black cameras. They had obviously been seen.

"They must have seen us coming through those cameras," he continued. "They know we trespassed now."

"That's fantastic," Michael said, sarcastically. "Our cover's blown."

"HEY, PEOPLE!"

The four of them peered down and saw Mr. Isol at the bottom of what was at least a thirty foot plunge. He was at the bottom, bellowing to them and flapping his arms.

"IS THERE ANYWAY YOU CAN GET ME OUT OF THIS HELLHOLE?" he roared.

"I don't know, Isol!" shouted Mr. Harrington. "We'll find a way! Don't panic!"

"I'm not some schoolgirl, Harrington, I'll be okay! Go on without me!" bellowed Mr. Isol. "I'll try to find an alternate route out of here somehow!"

"Are you sure?" Mr. Goodwin asked.

"JUST GO! YOU'RE WASTING TIME!"

Mr. Goodwin sighed and turned to the others.

"This makes matters a little more complicated," he said in a low voice. "Mr. Isol's presence will be sorely missed. I wanted him to give the brothers a warm welcome for us."

"Well, that's not happening now," Mr. Harrington said. "He needs to be rescued now."

There was a horrible noise, as if chalk was being dragged on a blackboard. It was very deafening and the group huddled close instinctively.

"What the hell is that noise?" Mr. Harrington bellowed.

"Dad, look!" Sheena shouted, pointing to the center of the room.

A sliding platform, which looked like the original center green circle, was sliding back into position, completely making it look exactly as how they had found it.

"Oh no, not good," Mr. Isol said loudly before the sliding platforms collided with each other and remained motionless, leaving no room for air to come in and out of the hole. There was now no way of escaping for Mr. Isol. He was swallowed in darkness, trapped.

"Well, this sucks," Michael said, breaking the silence.

The three men laughed, even though there was nothing humorous about the situation they were in.

"Thank you for your comments, Michael," Sheena said, her voice uncharacteristically dry. "As always, they are greatly appreciated."

"Michael's right in this instance though, Sheena. This does put us in a huge dilemma," Mr. Goodwin replied, sounding casual, as if they were discussing a simple algebra problem and not whether their friend could breathe in a dark abyss. Then he stopped smiling. "I just hope he could breathe down there."

"Let's keep going," Michael said, "maybe there is a switch or something."

"If there is, the brothers will probably be guarding it," Mr. Oberfels said, reasonably.

"Do you still have the sword?" Sheena asked, abruptly, surprising Michael.

Michael looked. He did not have it.

"I must have dropped it in the hole while trying to cling on to the side."

"That gives Isol a powerful defense mechanism, but he does not need it now," Mr. Harrington pointed out. "However, we have—"

"None," Michael said, fuming.

"We must hope for the best now," Mr. Goodwin replied, gravely. "Let's go through that door, as Michael said, and see if Ember is there."

The five of them walked towards the door. It was huge and it towered over all of them. It had to be a lot more than ten feet. Even Mr. Isol could have fit through this door without difficulty.

The door apparently was a sliding one because it opened just as soon as they were by it. Michael made an attempt to lead the way, but Mr. Goodwin stopped him.

"I'm going to lead the way," he told Michael. "They might hurt the first one who enters it, and you are more valuable than me. The Ying-Yang brothers might expect you to come in first. We must foresee that they will."

Mr. Goodwin led the way through yet another passage, with Mr. Harrington to the side of him, and Mr. Oberfels, Michael, and Sheena following them in the rear. They did not walk very far, because then another sliding door appeared in front of them, which opened.

"Come on," Mr. Goodwin replied.

Then, only a hundred feet away, was another sliding door.

"Why do they have so many doors?" Sheena and Michael asked, simultaneously.

Mr. Goodwin shrugged. "It could be for many reasons. Extra security would be my guess. The doors are opening because the brothers must have lifted the security while they are here."

"But if they know we're here, why don't they shut down the doors and lock us in?" Michael queried.

"Maybe they want to give us a proper greeting," Mr. Oberfels said ominously.

They had reached the last door, which took a little while to open. However, it slid eventually, and this time, as the door opened, the four of them did not find themselves in another passage.

They were now in a huge and brightly lit room. There was a huge rocket at a far corner of the room. It stood about seventy-five feet high and had the Chinese flag painted on it. There were stairs and platforms made of glass. As Michael walked in farther, he found the whole room had firecrackers around the edges. Sparks were flying on them, and emitted noises at some times.

"Oh no," Sheena whispered, gripping Michael's arm, and he turned to see where she was looking at.

On one of the glass platforms, looking frightened, and tied in a chair by a computer, was Ember. She looked a lot different than when they saw her last. Her long mane of red hair was unkempt, she was pale as a ghost, her eyes were bloodshot, which gave her a tired look, her face was gaunt, and her skin was cut open in places with blood. And behind her, there were three people: Mr. Smith and the Ying-Yang brothers. The arrival of their enemies did not surprise them one bit.

"Help me!" she cried to her family and friends.

"How nice of you to join us," Ying replied in a sickly sweet voice, ignoring Ember's screams.

"We've been expecting you losers," Yang replied with the air of a doorman at some foreboding hotel.

"What are you doing to my sister?" Sheena shouted angrily.

"Now, now, there was no need to get angry so quickly," Yang said. "We merely want to welcome you."

"It surprises us that you got past our beast trapdoor," Ying replied. "But no matter: we will rectify that in a bit."

"Knock it off!" snarled Michael.

"Durbin, I greatly advise you to stop acting like the big cheese," Ying replied, in a tone that conceived nobody. "As you can see, you, unlike me, are unintelligent, and are foolish to be provoking two people who very much want to seize you by the throat."

"Yeah, maybe that's true," Michael said, recklessly. "But you, unlike me, are a coward and a jerk, so give us Ember back and leave us alone."

"Jesting, are you, Durbin?" Yang asked.

"Nope, not jesting," Michael said, casually. "How come you've been cooped up in this old building?"

He was trying to keep them talking so his companions could formulate some sort of plan. The others seemed to be thinking along the same lines.

"Well, what an interesting question," Ying said, sweetly. "As you can see, we have been working hard on a great project: a rocket to not only blow someone we hate up in smoke, but to amuse the citizens of Beijing. We were here originally under the impression that our daddy's scroll would be in his files. However, we did not have so much luck in finding it. We need it ever so desperately, and we have endlessly been searching for it."

"It seems as if you rascals have been busy with this rocket," Mr. Harrington snarled, nastily.

"Yes we have, Harriet. Isn't she a beauty?" crowed Yang. "Too bad we're going to be blowing her up momentarily."

"So this rocket was not written on the Scroll of the Yangtze?" Michael queried, feeling relieved that Mr. Goodwin's remarks were correct.

The brothers looked bitter. "We thought it was, Durbin. But our father seemed to have enjoyed making it difficult for us to locate it. When we arrived, we found a scroll lying on his workbench. It had a rocket plan all thought out on it. We hired people to work on it for us because Yang and I are too cool for slave labor like this. However, we figured out that this rocket plan was only meant for the Olympic

Games after reading through many files. You can say we wasted our time. However, we are going to put this to some use. One of you American bitches will test it out. It was one of our late daddy's plans that he never got to complete, so we did it for him."

Michael could not help feeling a bit relieved. They had not found the scroll after all. They thought they had. However, Michael knew the situation they were in was not at all relieving: if it wasn't, the brothers would not be looking so happy.

"You know how important the scroll is, then?"

"No, we have no idea," Michael said, sarcastically. "Was it your birthday card?"

The brothers did not laugh at Michael's joke.

"In that case, we might as well get down to business," Yang replied, leering. "We made a special surprise for you. Just because this beast rocket wasn't on the scroll, that does not mean it can be used to harm you. Our daddy said the scroll would be a strategic plan to rid the world of you fools and take over the Olympic world, but right now it doesn't matter. We got you here to rescue Ginger and now we must move forward with our plans."

"That's enough of your terrible jokes!" Mr. Harrington shouted.

Yang smiled. "So be it, Harrington."

Out of nowhere, a long piece of rope with a loop at the end of it came down and fell directly behind them. The brothers were grinning as though it was the grand finale of some magic show. This had Michael taken aback; he was expecting something much more sudden and deadly.

"Wow," Michael said, laughing. "Is this your defense mechanism? You guys are disappointing us!"

"Michael, stop!" Mr. Goodwin said, warningly.

The brothers merely laughed, which was a warning sign. Mr. Smith was standing there, unsure of what to do it seemed. He was acting as though he was the new kid at some school.

"We have more surprises for you, Durbin!" Ying cried. "Security, seize them!"

About ten people went flying at them out of nowhere from another platform. They had weapons in their hands and looked menacing.

The five of them stepped back, away from them.

"AAAARRRRRGGGGGGHHHHH!"

Mr. Harrington stepped into the rope. It yanked him in the air and swung him back and forth like a pendulum. Ying pressed a button on the platform. Mr. Harrington was then moved across the platform from the ceiling. Looking up, Michael saw that the rope was connected to some metal bar right below the ceiling, which was connected to another wire. Michael thought it resembled a zip-line. Mr. Harrington stopped right by the rocket, dangling helplessly with his foot caught snugly in the rope. Yang went over and tied him up to the rocket. Mr. Harrington tried to fight back, but to no avail. He was stuck on an explosive device.

"As you can see, our slaves did an excellent job in building our secret weapons. Now we can get our revenge on you, Harrington!" Ying shouted. "Ember, you pretty girl, please complete the instructions that were assigned to you."

Ember looked up, wide-eyed, at Ying. Michael realized that one of the brothers' gang members was holding a knife right by her. Michael caught her eye and gave her a small nod.

"Yes, sir," she sobbed. She was sounding terribly frightened, and began typing, crying as she did so.

"This rocket should destroy Harriet, the fool," Yang said, as the ten people surrounded Michael, Sheena, Mr. Oberfels, and Mr. Goodwin, "the plan had the instructions to build the rocket. We'll use the scroll on the rest of you—once we locate it, of course. Ember Goodwin, please set the timer."

Ember realized she had no choice. Two gang members were now by her, holding knives and looking threatening. Sobbing, she set the timer for the rocket and Michael noticed that she lightly tapped a red button and when the guards weren't looking, Michael saw her press it.

"I also noticed that we caught Mr. Isol in our beast trapdoor," Ying said, smoothly, pointing at the computer screen, not realizing Ember did not completely follow his brother's instructions. "The pit is air-proof, so he is going to die if he did not find a way out of there. I hope he enjoyed his last meal because it will be his last."

Michael looked at Sheena. He was about to say something to her, but she stopped him, as if she knew what he was going to say, and took his hand.

"I know," Sheena said, squeezing Michael's hand.

"Listen, Michael, Sheena," Mr. Goodwin whispered to them. "You two need to get out of here. Just leave it to me and Matt and Glenn. We don't need you two hurt."

"If we leave, sir, you, Mr. Oberfels, and Mr. Harrington are as good as dead," Michael said, seriously. Then, he added, "We're not going anywhere. We are staying."

Ying spat bitterly on the ground, looking displeased.

"How very touching . . . but your heroics, Durbin, will result in your *tragic* death . . . guards, take care of them."

The ten guards that surrounded them dived on them. The four of them tried to escape, but it was no use. They were outnumbered about three to one.

Michael tried to radio Matt while fending three dangerous guards at the same time.

"MATT! MATT! HELP US! WE'RE—"

Then, there was a smash, and Michael felt the radio in his hand fly out of it, and it shattered on the ground by him. There was no help of being rescued now. Michael kicked the nearest guard, but a quick jab to the back of the head sent him to the ground. The guards dragged him upright, twisted his arms behind him, and marched him to the control platform where Ying, Yang, and Mr. Smith were.

Michael saw Sheena and Mr. Goodwin tied up and gagged. Michael tried to shout out more, but then he found a wad of material shoved roughly into his mouth. He quickly found himself tied up. Mr. Oberfels shortly joined them, struggling with his bounds.

All four of them were tied were forced into chairs and they were tied to them tightly, to make sure they couldn't move an inch.

"Look at you losers now!" Ying cried. "You are about to go down to us!"

Michael spat the material out of his mouth. "You only won because you outnumbered us about four to one!"

"All's fair in war and games, Durbin," Ying pointed out. "The only thing that matters is the result—it does not matter how we got it."

"This is ridiculous," Michael said to Mr. Goodwin, who couldn't talk due to the handkerchief in his mouth. "How can we beat their army?"

"Is this a confession, Durbin?" Yang queried. "You're giving up?"

"Dear, dear, we see to have defeated them."

Michael, unable to move, watched the clock of the rocket trickle down to five minutes. Mr. Harrington had five minutes—or he would be dead.

Michael watched him struggle, wishing bitterly that he could do something about it. There was no one here to help them, to save them . . .

But he was wrong. There was someone still here, someone who might be volatile to join the brothers, but only if he could convince him, he might save their lives.

Mr. Smith was still there. And even though he sided with the brothers, he was a coward. If they could find a way to look like they're winning, they might be able to convince him. The only chance of them getting out of this was by using Mr. Smith.

A distant noise echoed into the control room. It was the sound of hurried footsteps. The brothers looked towards the door, looking anxious. The footsteps became louder, and then—

BANG!

Mr. Isol knocked the door clean off its hinges and fell to the floor with a shaking crash. He looked intimidating, and angry, standing in front of the doorway. He looked like a grizzly bear denied of a salmon and honey.

Ying and Yang looked shocked. "ISOL! How did you escape?"

Mr. Isol shrugged. "Why do you care? The goddam trapdoor opened up again, and I felt the bottom shoot up and I was free. Someone must have pressed a button that opened the door up and lifted the platform up, saving me. But, it does not matter; you are with me now, fools!"

Ying looked shocked, but then he turned to Ember. "You little brat! You must have pressed the red button to activate our beast trapdoor! You two," he ordered to the two gang members, "Kill her!"

Mr. Isol strode forward quickly and picked up one gang member just before he could hurt Ember. He threw him bodily into the other gang member and they both rolled down the stairs until they reached the bottom, and did not get up.

Mr. Isol flexed his muscles. "BEAT THAT, YOU GODDAM SONUVABITCHES! HOW DO YOU LIKE THAT? COME ON! COME ON!"

All of Ying and Yang's allies flew themselves at Mr. Isol, but they were all no match for him. Mr. Isol slugged each and every one of them before they could puncture him with their weapons. In no time at all were they all unconscious, laying at his feet. Michael was amazed at how unrealistic the scenario Mr. Isol got out of was. If Matt was here, he would have seen just how big of a badass Mr. Isol was.

The brothers looked shocked, but they still were smiling. "You can beat the crap out of my team, but you can't escape from this."

Making sure he was away from Mr. Isol enough, Ying pointed a pistol at him. Now no one looked able to rescue Mr. Harrington.

Mr. Isol shook his head disbelievingly.

"You two are the biggest cowards I know," he muttered, casting a look full of hatred at them.

"We can live with that," Ying said, yawning as though he was bored by Mr. Isol's remarks.

Mr. Harrington couldn't free himself, he was tied to a rocket; Mr. Isol was going to get shot if he tried; Mr. Goodwin, Mr. Oberfels, Sheena, and Michael were bound and gagged, they had no chance of escaping in time; Ember started towards the rocket, but Yang pulled out a pistol, making sure she did not move.

"Don't you dare move, girly, or I will make sure my gunshot is the last thing you hear," snarled Yang, with no trace of a forced grin on his face.

Everything seemed fuzzy; Mr. Harrington tied to the rocket, and them bound and gagged. Michael thought hard, making his head pound with frustration. He needed to use Mr. Smith. If he could only possibly convince him . . . they need Mr. Smith . . . He was their last hope . . .

And unlike Ron in baseball games, Mr. Smith came through for Michael and his friends. Surprised, Michael did not shout out in case it attracted the attention of the brothers, but Mr. Smith was slowly advancing to the rocket when there was one minute left until the rocket took off. Michael saw Sheena's eyes grow wide, and Mr. Goodwin raised his eyebrows, as if he couldn't believe it, but just as there were ten seconds left on the clock, all three of them saw Mr. Smith climb on a ladder nearby, and quietly, untied Mr. Harrington. Ying and Yang turned to the direction of their rocket, a look of complete disbelief on their faces. They were obviously not expecting Mr. Smith to turn on them here—especially since that the brothers had the advantage.

Mr. Harrington leaped immediately as the rocket shot straight up into the air. They heard it explode in the air with a loud, cacophonous bang, illuminating the Beijing sky with a blast of red and orange. Mr. Smith was flown backward with such force that he crashed into the computer and Ember, knocking her to the ground in front of Michael. In one swift motion, Ember, Mr. Harrington, and Mr. Isol untied their friends.

"Ember! Over here!" Sheena called, and she hugged her sister.

"Seize them!"

Michael and his friends all jumped down from the platform and began to dash towards the door they came through. The guards, who seemed to have recovered from Mr. Isol's blows, started to chase them. Michael, who was in the lead, saw a lever near the door, and, without thinking about it, slammed it down hard.

"NOOOOOOOO!"

The brothers' scream was too horrible. It was a loud, retching noise that sounded as though someone was dragging their fingernails on a blackboard. Michael entered the circular room again, running from the guards, and heard the pounding footsteps of his compatriots behind him. The lever had caused them to escape through the circular room and trapped some of the guards in the control room. Michael was not completely relieved, though: it only stopped them momentarily.

"LET'S GO!" he roared, and he led the group away from security, which was still after them.

Through the million passageways they went, and soon enough, they had reached the car. Mr. Goodwin, still running, took his key out, and clicked a button on it. The doors opened automatically and so did the trunk.

"Get in!" Mr. Harrington beseeched them.

The guards were still after them. Mr. Isol stood by the car, not even trying to get into it. He turned to the group.

"I'll hold them off, just get in!" he yelled.

Mr. Goodwin threw himself in the driver's seat, while Mr. Harrington took the seat next to him. Michael, Ember, and Sheena dived into the back seat where Mr. Oberfels squeezed in a second later.

Mr. Isol had his fist flying in all directions, knocking the guards out cold. One managed to get through his defenses and grabbed Sheena, trying to pull her back. Michael and Ember grabbed Sheena's arms and pulled as hard as they could. The guard was winning though. He was a lot stronger than they were.

Just as they thought Sheena was about to leave them, Mr. Isol came and punched him, knocking out a tooth. Michael and Ember pulled her back into the car. The guard, howling with pain, drew a gun from his pocket, and pointed it at Mr. Isol.

Mr. Isol was indeed very vast, and those people generally do not move very fast, but Mr. Isol was the exception. He shoved the gun into the bad guy's face, which made his nose begin to bleed and he howled with pain, and fell to his knees. Mr. Isol, knowing there was no room in the car for him, dived in the trunk, his legs poking out.

"DRIVE, GOODWIN!" Mr. Isol hollered.

Ember shrieked as Mr. Goodwin slammed his foot on the gas, and the car revved in high gear. The guard aimed his gun at Mr. Isol from his knees and pulled the trigger three times.

The first bullet sailed over the car; the second one hit right below Mr. Isol's legs; and the third one hit the back window.

Shards of glass flew everywhere and Sheena and Ember screamed. Michael put his arms over his head, and felt some glass hit his arms, but he was able to avoid injury. Michael looked back through the open window and saw the guard attempt to kill them again, but the fourth bullet fell five feet short from the car, and he was out of reach to harm them.

Sheena and Ember were trembling, and Michael felt himself shaking, too. That was an extremely close call. Not only did they escape death narrowly, but the scariness of being surrounded by a myriad of Chinese people was unreal. Even Michael had to admit they were all lucky to get out of there alive and for the most part, unscathed.

Michael put his arms around Ember and Sheena's shoulders and all three of them trembled like they never had trembled before. His gesture seemed to calm both girls down, and Sheena flashed Michael a grateful glance. Even though none of the adults made a sound, Michael saw Mr. Goodwin's beard twitch with amusement.

Michael looked out the window and looked at the Evening Lake, which shimmered in the sunlight. It looked so beautiful though it was a false alarm to what Michael and his friends just had to endure. Evening Lake might look peaceful, but the base that it surrounded, Michael knew from the experience he just had, was as peaceful as a grizzly bear poked in the eye while it was sleeping.

CHAPTER 20

MR. SMITH'S REFORMATION

No one spoke for the whole car ride back to the hotel. Michael was still thinking about their escape and Sheena was fussing over Ember, who still looked pale and gaunt—he assumed it was out of fear from the brothers and the lack of food she was provided. Michael doubted that she ate anything through the time she was captured.

"You alright, Ember?" asked Michael kindly while Sheena patted her shoulder soothingly.

Ember nodded, blushing to the roots of her hair.

After a half hour of silence, the car stopped and Michael knew that they had arrived back at the hotel.

Everyone got out of the car without a word. Michael knew all of them were feeling exactly how he was feeling: they were exhausted as if they had no sleep the previous night and astonished at how they all managed to escape without so much as a scratch. Michael, who was looking forward to coming to this Olympics, now realized the meaning of what Mr. Goodwin, Mr. Isol, and all of his trusted adults were telling him all along: *This Olympics is more than just winning.*

Michael looked at his compatriots as they clambered out of the car. All of them seemed not to have serious injuries. The adults all had a small cut or two; Ember looked sick; Sheena had a cut across one cheek. He too, felt blood run down his cheek too, but that did not matter to him anymore.

"Is everyone alright?" Michael asked, his voice trembling.

"I think so," Mr. Goodwin replied.

Michael fell to his knees. He couldn't take this Olympics anymore. All he wanted was a peaceful Olympics. He fantasized about being an athlete and competing in games, and having fun, but he never expected—or wanted—any of the past events to happen.

This was all because of the Ying-Yang brothers. They caused all this trouble. If they weren't such proud individuals, they would have taken their rejection professionally. If they did, their desire to get revenge would have never appeared into the limelight. If they didn't hate fourteen-year-old athletes, Michael would be enjoying the Beijing Olympics with his friends with nothing to worry about. Their antics clouded the whole purpose of the Olympic Games—to establish ties with foreign nations.

"Mr. Harrington?"

"Yes, Michael."

Michael hesitated. He felt extremely guilty by confessing what he thought, but Michael felt if he didn't tell someone soon, he was going to explode.

"I don't know if I could pitch tomorrow. I do not feel great at all," Michael said in a flat, emotionless voice.

He hated saying the words in that miserable tone, but it was the most honest way he felt he could convey what was going on inside his head. Mr. Harrington looked sympathetic, but Michael knew he was not going to let him off tomorrow.

"Michael, it is just the shock of these dreadful events. That is why I am going to say this: you are going to pitch. You are a pitcher, Michael. You need to pitch. We need you. The only people to blame for these terrible experiences are the brothers. If we're going to stop them, we need to prove them wrong on their opinions, and we need you for that."

Michael sighed. He knew Mr. Harrington was right, and somehow, Michael felt that he had to stay, as if he might be helpful to stop the Ying-Yang brothers. "This Olympics has not been fun at all, Mr. Harrington. You and Mr. Goodwin were right. It isn't fun. I'll pitch only if we could get those brothers in prison."

"Ying and Yang will pay for this," Mr. Goodwin snarled. "First, they injure as many people as they can, they tried to kill us, they kidnapped my daughter, and they attempted to launch a rocket, a nuclear weapon, to kill us all. I'll need to tell the Chinese Government everything to convince them to detain the brothers."

Sheena's phone rang, and she took it out of her pocket, clicked a button, held it up to her face, and then slipped it back in her pocket.

"I got a text from Matt," she reported. "They are waiting for us inside the hotel."

The six of them trooped to the hotel, only to find Matt and everyone else waiting for them. They were all trembling and seemed relieved at the sight of them. Matt's leg was in a black boot and under his arms were a pair of ordinary crutches.

"Michael, Sheena!" Matt cried, limping towards them on his crutches. "I heard Michael cry for help, but . . ."

"The stupid guard smashed it," Michael replied, grimly. "I couldn't finish my message."

Matt let out a strange noise, almost like a cat hissing at some violent blue jay.

"I see your leg is looking better," Mr. Harrington said, examining his son's injury.

"I was allowed to leave," Matt said, with the air one not inclined to talk about his problem. "I also received good news on it, too. I will make a full recovery. The doctors didn't even say that I needed crutches, but I thought they looked cool, and that I look like a badass with them, so I took them."

"Good," Sheena replied, briskly. "I expect you to be in the pool at London in four years, Matthew."

But Matt shook his head.

"I told you, I'm done with diving," Matt said, seriously. "I lost the spirit to dive. I'd rather try something that looks cool—like archery."

"Why?"

"I told you, I hate all of the training and stuff," Matt replied, shaking his head. "I hate wearing a Speedo and all that as well. I hate being bald. I hate the time-sucking workouts. And I'm afraid I might aggravate my leg if I do diving next Olympics."

"I still think you should do diving," Sheena replied, thickly. "You were pretty good."

"No, I wasn't, I was bad!" Matt protested. He turned to Michael for support. "Tell Sheena I was lousy, Michael."

"You were a genius," Michael replied, making everyone laugh and Matt flush red.

Mrs. Goodwin made the group sit down in the cafeteria and eat some chicken salad sandwiches with rice, but despite being hungry, Michael could barely chew. He was overcome with exhaustion. What he wanted and needed was a good long sleep before dinner.

"I'm going up to the room," Michael told Sheena and Matt, getting up from the table, abandoning his half-eaten lunch.

Mrs. Goodwin looked most upset.

"But Michael, dear, you still have half a sandwich."

"I'm okay, Mrs. Goodwin, but thanks. I'm just exhausted."

Mrs. Goodwin looked sympathetic but highly disappointed, as if she had been denied a real treat.

Michael was waiting for the elevator when a voice behind him made him jump with surprise.

"Michael?"

Michael looked around and saw Ember had spoken his name. She blushed when he looked her in the eye. She seemed more embarrassed than usual; instead of looking at him, she became extremely interested in her shoelaces.

"What is it, Ember?"

"At five o' clock, all of us are going out to eat, okay?" Ember said, quietly. "We're inviting Mr. Isol and Matt and everyone. Meet us down in the lobby."

Michael nodded. He turned to walk into the open elevator, but Ember was not done speaking to him.

"And thank you for rescuing me," she added, going even redder. "I really appreciate it."

Michael nodded again, and he stepped into the elevator. It wasn't long before he got upstairs. He trudged down the hallways, feeling sleepy. He reached his room and unlocked it with his card.

Once he got inside, he collapsed on the bed. He felt sick, as if he was about to vomit. He hoped that if he was going to be sick, he did it now and not tomorrow, because he had a baseball game, and definitely more important, his friends were coming to see him.

The thought of his friends coming to visit him cheered him up, and he couldn't help grinning at the thought as he turned over on his side.

Michael then shut his eyes, and went to sleep.

★ ★ ★

Michael would have slept longer, but he received a loud telephone call from Sheena, telling him to get downstairs so they could leave for the restaurant. Michael, still having a slight headache, had to hurry out of his room and down the stairs, meeting his friends right outside the hotel.

All of them were dressed nice: Sheena was in a red dress, looking (in Michael's opinion) more gorgeous than usual, but he didn't tell her that. Everyone else was wearing a nice polo shirt or dress. Mr. Isol's shirt looked as though he had just got out of the dryer. Michael then self-consciously peered at himself: he was wearing a dirty pair of shorts, and his legs looked as brown as a tree branch. His t-shirt was faded, and his shoes were starting to peel from the uppers. His friends did not seem perturbed by his unprofessional appearance, but Michael felt humiliated that he looked so dirty compared to the rest of them.

"What kept you?" Shawna asked.

"Overslept," Michael said, truthfully. "Where are we going?"

"To a Chinese restaurant," Sheena answered, looking sympathetically at Michael. "It's nice."

"That sounds awesome," Michael said, just realizing how hungry he was. He had not eaten that much since yesterday. The chicken salad sandwich seemed ages ago.

"I know," Shawna replied, shaking her hair behind her shoulders; she was wearing a blue dress. "You should have seen Matt's face earlier, Michael! Matt looked so excited, I thought he was going to—"

"SHAWNA!" her mom warned her.

"Sorry, Mom," Shawna said, however, Michael could not comprehend as to what she was going to say.

The restaurant was twenty minutes away, but even twenty minutes was really bad. It was a very uncomfortable journey. Mr. Goodwin had tried to fit eight people in one small car, but with a grizzly bear and many other adults, there was no way it could have been doable. Mr. Isol and Mr. Oberfels ended going in Mr. Isol's rental car and were forced to take Michael, Matt, and Sheena in their car, which was very small and they kept bumping their heads on the ceiling.

"It'll be worth it, though," Matt said, consolingly, banging his head for the umpteenth time. "The food at this place is excellent."

"And very cheap, too," Sheena piped up. "It is a buffet as well."

"What do they serve?" Michael asked. "Or do they just have anything?"

Sheena smiled, and even though Michael could not see her face due to Matt blocking it, he knew she was grinning.

"Anything," she said.

When they arrived at the restaurant, they were seated quickly by a young man. Michael then excused himself from the table to use the toilet and wash up. Matt decided to go with him.

"Michael, aren't your friends back home coming tomorrow?" he asked.

"Yep," Michael answered, washing his hands, "they are."

"Your friends are Tomas and Sara, right?" Matt questioned.

Michael took some paper towels and wiped his hands. "Yes. But why are you so interested?"

"Because," Matt answered, looking slightly flustered, "I never met any people, really. Before you came, I only knew the Goodwin family. It makes a nice change, you know."

"I guess so," Michael said vaguely, throwing the paper towels away.

"Michael, what does Sara look like?"

Michael looked back at Matt. "Say that again."

"What does Sara look like? Is she blond?"

Michael laughed.

"Why do you care?" he asked.

"Just curious," mumbled Matt, going red. Michael stopped laughing and answered his friend.

"She's about my height," Michael said, perplexed. "She also has huge brown eyes that make her look like a puppy dog. She likes to play field hockey and has dark hair."

Matt looked at Michael. Michael laughed.

"Matt, are you okay?" he asked.

Matt did not answer, but walked out of the bathroom and back to the table. Michael still didn't get it. But he was sure he would find out tomorrow. Maybe he was disappointed that Sara wasn't blond.

Dinner was an enjoyable affair. Since it was a buffet, they were allowed to go and get whatever they wanted from the many tables situated in the middle of the restaurant. Michael, Matt, Mr. Goodwin, Mr. Harrington, Mr. Isol, and Mr. Oberfels all had to go back and get more food at least five times. The other four, on the other hand, were insisting that they were full after one plate of food. Sheena laughed at how Matt and Michael were able to shove down all that food.

"Mr. Isol I knew could, but you two as well?" Sheena asked later when they were in the trunk driving home.

"It's the best restaurant in the world!" exclaimed Matt, with his mouth full of angel hair spaghetti.

"Yeah, it is," Michael agreed, wiping his mouth with a napkin.

"Michael, who are you playing tomorrow?" Sheena queried.

"Chinese Taipei, I think," he answered.

"Would your friends arrive in time to see you?" Sheena asked, curiously.

Michael shrugged. He had no idea, though he doubted that they will arrive in time to see him play. The flight was very long, and getting out of the airport was not going to take five minutes.

"I don't think so," Michael said, thinking hard, "I think they'll arrive later that night."

Meanwhile, Mr. Goodwin was telling the adults about how the Chinese Government insisted that they would do something.

"They believed me, thank goodness," he was telling them. "They plan on setting a good number of policemen to seize control of Fireworks Factory. Hopefully the brothers will surrender."

"The brothers aren't dimwits, they must know that they are being searched for," Mr. Oberfels replied, reasonably. "They might try to book it out of Beijing before they're seen. It'll be harder for them to be detected outside of the capital."

"Why can't the Chinese Government establish road blocks and barricade the city until the brothers are found?" Ember suggested, butting in on the adults' conversation. "No one gets in, no one gets out."

"Because they are so many roads that exit the city and the Chinese can't simply monitor them all," Mr. Goodwin replied, glancing at his daughter. "The Chinese still need the police to monitor the Games. Finding the brothers is important, but the police need to keep their focus on the main event."

"Then why don't they call in extra security from the nearby towns and they can barricade the roads that lead into their towns?" Ember countered. "That way, the Beijing police could concentrate on the Games. The town policemen would be able to prevent anyone from leaving Beijing to their town."

The adults all looked completely dumbfounded.

"There is something in that," Mr. Harrington said, looking mildly impressed at Ember's thinking. "You should let the Chinese know of your daughter's suggestion, Will. As long as the policemen agree to it, the towns should be fine with it and it will help us catch the brothers."

After his third helpings of steak and fried rice, the waistband on Michael's shorts felt uncomfortably tight as he and his friends made their way back to the cars to head back to Blossom Suites.

The group was too tired when they got back to the hotel that all they did was say "sleep well" to each other. Ember thanked Michael again for rescuing her.

"Don't mention it," Michael told her airily, as she did so.

Matt and Michael went up to the hotel and fell asleep almost immediately. Michael could not wait for tomorrow to come for when it did, he would finally see his friends who helped him get here in the first place.

★ ★ ★

Breakfast that morning was a noisy affair. Michael sat with Matt and Sheena and started a conversation about the past events. Though he really was not too inclined to talk about it, he felt happier than he did throughout the whole Olympics which made him forget that they were miserable experiences. It was a cloudy Tuesday but there was no rain to be seen or heard. Michael couldn't see why the sun could not shine down on Beijing; he was getting sick of the constant overcast days.

"You know how Mr. Smith was working for the brothers?" Michael questioned.

"Yes," Matt asked, nonplussed.

"Well, yesterday," Michael said, whispering and bending in closer, "at the factory, Mr. Smith didn't help the brothers. When Mr. Harrington got tied to the rocket, Mr. Smith saved his life and untied him. If he was working for the brothers, why wouldn't he just kill him? I mean, the brothers hate Mr. Harrington."

Sheena looked thoughtful. "I've no idea. I noticed that, too. It definitely was unusual. Maybe Mr. Smith thought that they should honor the real scroll, and the rocket was not written on the scroll."

It was a fair point; Mr. Smith did like to stick with the rules and instructions.

"Still, it is fishy," Michael said. He did not want to sound argumentative. "But I don't think that's quite it. I think it was because he knew he was outnumbered and thought he would be protected by us since we outnumbered them. Mr. Isol's presence certainly helped."

"But we were all trapped to chairs and Mr. Isol had a pistol pointed at him," Sheena reminded Michael.

Matt looked confused. "It is definitely fishy, all right. But I think Sheena might have a point there. Also, Mr. Smith likes things to go his way, from what my dad told me. Maybe he wants the plan to go according to what he wants. And he's scared of Isol. Maybe his presence was enough to help my father, despite him being covered by a gun."

"I'll have another chat with your dad," Michael told Sheena. "Maybe he has his opinion on it."

Sheena did not answer; she was swallowing her Cheerios. Then, she said, "You can talk to him whenever. He knows there is no point in hiding stuff from you anymore. My dad likes it when you are inquisitive. But I would suggest doing it before your friends get here. You might want to do something with them."

Before Michael could answer, Nitro and Fred came over to the table, looking annoyed. They were holding the *Beijing News*.

"Mikey, your name is in the newspaper," Fred said with the air of one pointing out the obvious.

"What?" Michael said, thrown off.

"And so is Sheena," Nitro added. "Here, take a glance at it. Digest every sentence like a fat man gobbling down a burger."

Matt looked at him with a look that plainly said stop-talking-you-weirdo. Sheena, however, gave him a smile.

He placed the paper in front of them and they all read it. It did not contain warm regards.

DURBIN-GOODWIN RELATIONSHIP?

Michael Durbin has already shown us his extraordinary talent, writes Patricia Westbrook. *He has carried the American squad to an improbable tournament run. He has only suffered a few base hits and has looked formidable as a pitcher throughout the course of events.*

And why is that?

It might be just of pure talent, as many admirers feel. They had expected Durbin to be a useful pitcher, but if anyone expected him to carry a team on his back and shoulder major responsibility, they could eat bamboo. Michael Durbin has far exceeded expectations. However, the luck that Michael has been experiencing thus far may soon run out due to unforeseen conflicts on the horizon.

"Michael is just getting lucky," Ty, a teammate, said. "He is getting us wins, which is great for us, but no one ever pitched this good. I think Michael's luck is going to run out sooner or later. I just hope it lasts through the rest of the Olympics. I want to go home with a medal."

Then, your reporter asked Ty why he would run out of luck, and he gave a brief answer.

"He will because like everyone, we are all human and we all have our ups and downs," Ty said briefly. "Durbin is being regarded as some superhero, but he is just like you and me. He has his faults but thankfully for our team, no one has been able to exploit them yet."

Ty also noted to me that Michael's relationship with a girl might have some social issues that might affect his baseball performance in the future. He claims that the social issues right now, are helping Michael survive this Olympics, but he is doubtful that they would in the future.

"I see him rarely out of the company of Sheena Goodwin, who is his best friend," Ty reveals, "I swear the two of them are distracting each other from their sports. If they aren't in a relationship now, they certainly will be in one in a few weeks."

Sheena Goodwin, 14, is a pretty gymnast who, according to everyone, spends time with her best friend constantly. The daughter of William Goodwin (who is the President of the United States Olympic Committee) also has had to shoulder some responsibility to help her team succeed in women's gymnastics. However, Goodwin's performance may also be soon affected by her relationship with Durbin.

Though Durbin and Goodwin would undoubtedly be a cute and perfect couple, Ty questioned whether it would last if it were to happen.

"When you have a job to do, day in and day out, worrying what your lover thinks about you should be of insignificant importance," Ty says, "Michael and Sheena may be able to avoid that, for now, but pretty soon, problems are going to start making their appearance."

Fred O'Leary, 16, who is a teammate as well, defended Michael.

"Ty is a git and has no clue what he is talking about," Fred had said, "Michael is the man, period, and he could have as many friends as he want. Anyway, if he's making friends with cute girls, then that is good for him. Why does the world need to know?"

Danny "Nitro" Shields, 15, who is the third baseman for Team USA, also has expressed his view on the matter.

"If you guys are talking about Michael's relationship with Sheena, then that tells me you have nothing better to do," he said, dismissively. "I don't think this story has any significance whatsoever. It is time you guys start publishing legitimate stories and stop wasting our time."

Fred also expressed his opinion about the gossip.

"Michael will be able to avoid any distractions and continue to pitch well," he said, firmly. "It's time for you guys to find better stories. You disappointed me. I was looking forward to reading well-written pieces but all I'm getting is gossip nonsense. Please choose your topics more wisely next time."

Fred's confidence in his friend is admirable, but Ty's point is worth considering. Michael can start to slide if he spends too much time in the company of Sheena Goodwin.

The article ended here and Michael looked up. He tried to look as the article was a joke.

"Well, if Ty does think that," Michael said, glancing at Sheena, "then I really don't care."

Fred laughed. "Ty is an idiot. Why does he not like you so much?"

"Probably because I'm good," Michael said, shrugging. "I don't like him much, anyway."

"This article is bullshit," Matt said, grabbing it and ripping it in half.

"Michael, Fred brought up a stupendous point," Nitro said with the air of one talking about the scientific method. "Why should baseball dictate the way you socialize with others? Ty is just a malodorous jerk. Don't listen to anything that comes out of his mouth."

"Well, thank you two for sticking up for us," Sheena replied, gratefully. Fred bowed and Nitro nodded.

Matt spoke up, "Ty is ridiculous. And if he wants his opinion being read, he might want to get interviewed for another article, because this article just sucks."

Fred looked thoughtful. "It's just another piece of proof of how eccentric this Westbrook idiot is. Who asked her to squeal on Mikey anyway?"

"I'm sure Ty did," Michael said, "Just because."

"Anyway, Michael," Nitro said, resorting back to business. "We came over to tell you that we need to go to the field now. The coach wants us there earlier today than usual."

"Why?"

"I think he is going lecture us on what is morally right for our team!" Nitro said, looking excited, "which includes not posting unfounded accusations and criticisms in public journalism! Ty is going to get what he deserves."

Sheena spoke up, "Well, that makes sense. That kid Ty does sound stupid and should get lectured."

"Arrogant, more like," Fred said forcefully. "And possibly homosexual, the way he looks at Ken every day . . ."

"Anyway, I better go," Michael said, standing up. "I'll see you two later."

"Good luck, Michael," Sheena said, patting his arm. "And you two, Fred and Nitro!"

She seemed to have developed a great deal of respect for Michael's teammates, which seemed to get Matt a little suspicious. His eyebrows were raised at Sheena in slight disapproval. Fred gave a low bow and departed and Nitro said, "Thanks."

"Kick Ty right in the . . ."

"There will be no need, Matt," Michael said, smiling, and he left with the other two.

On their way towards the field, Nitro brought up conversation.

"Your friend Sheena is very nice," Nitro said to Michael.

Fred sniggered, and Michael replied, "Yeah, she is."

Nitro raised his eyebrows. "You're a lucky man, Michael. Don't you forget what I said either. You're lucky to have her—and Matt for that matter—as your friends."

Once they got their stuff, they met with his team on the field itself. Mr. Smith was the only coach to be seen as they joined them.

"Where are the other coaches, Mr. Smith?" Michael asked.

"They are in the clubhouse," he answered with a smile. "They'll be back in a moment. I got the job of lecturing the team. Have a seat."

Michael sat down with the whole team while Fred and Nitro sat by Ken and Samuel. Mr. Smith then spoke.

"It is my unfortunate duty to say many bad things to this team today," he said in a dramatic voice. "As you all know, an article appeared in the paper today about Durbin and his girlfriend."

"She's not my—"

"Shut up, Durbin," Mr. Smith replied, calmly. "Well, Ty?"

The team turned to Ty, who merely glared.

"The coaches and I are all disappointed that you publicized all of those lies to the paper and especially to that idiotic reporter," Mr. Smith continued, causing Fred to wolf-whistle. "Be quiet, O' Leary, I'm not done yet. Anyway, it is my unfortunate duty to call you up here."

Ty walked erectly to the front, and the whole team was looking daggers at him. Ty was never popular with the team, especially for his porous attitude and selfish actions. Xavier in particular was looking murderous. It was he, after all, that was criticized by Ty, who had tried to remove him from the leadoff spot.

"Ty, for giving lies about Michael Durbin and discrediting him, for bringing the United States unwanted publicity, for violating our code of conduct, and for being a moron and arrogant little jerk, you are to be punished as thus—you will be taken off the active roster for the rest of the Olympics," Mr. Smith replied, with the air of an assistant principal executing one for inciting a food fight.

Michael gasped. It was a harsh punishment, and even he did not think Ty deserved it. Ty did not say anything, but he wore a look that showed Michael that Ty would like to do nothing better than put Mr. Smith in a guillotine.

"That reminds me," Mr. Smith said, speaking to everyone. "I am sorry to say that if anyone else does do anything like this again, you are going to go with Ty. Shields, O' Leary . . . I'd be grateful if I were you. If it were my decision, I'd throw you off the team as well, but the other coaches"—at those words Mr. Smith sneered out loud—"liked the way you defended your teammate, even though you criticized the offender."

"That's okay, Coach," Fred said. "We won't do anything like that again. But I'm not going to let anyone make fun of Mikey. I'm sure all of us will never say stupid stuff to the media again."

"Of course we won't, amigo," Samuel said.

"Definitely," said Todd.

"I am not done yet, so shut up!" Mr. Smith imperiously commanded. "You also may have heard, but there have been rumors swirling around that I have been working for the Ying-Yang brothers. I must confess. I did, but I said publicly I was sorry and I am offering to sacrifice my position this Olympics in order to restore my good name."

Everyone gasped, even Michael. This was odd. Mr. Smith was attempting to make a reformation. Though the team looked convinced, Michael had his misgivings. It was as if the Ying-Yang brothers started to hug Michael.

"I have apologized to everyone and I hope this does not affect any one of you. I also will do community service during this year and 2012, to make up for my actions."

Michael saw the other coaches walk out to the field and stood behind Mr. Smith. They seemed to know where Mr. Smith was at.

"Mr. Smith did indeed work for the brothers," Mr. Harrington said, making everyone jump. "However, yesterday, he had saved my life, and I must be grateful for that, and he has publicly stated that he is not working for the brothers no more and will turn his life around. For saving my life, I am going to let him be a coach on my team. Does anyone have anything they want to say?"

"I do!" Ken said, raising his hand.

"What?" Mr. Harrington asked.

"Why can't we replace Mr. Smith with some model instead?" he asked, causing the team to snigger appreciatively.

Mr. Smith seemed to recognize the humor in it, and smiled slightly.

"Because a model would have the IQ of the brothers, who have an IQ of a salad bar," he replied, grinning.

"Hear, hear!" cheered Fred enthusiastically. The team laughed appreciatively but Mr. Harrington cut them off rather quickly.

"Anyway, let's get warmed up and get ready for this game today!" Mr. Harrington said, impatiently. "We must win today!"

The team practiced until the game started. Michael thought it went rather well. Mr. Smith seemed to be in a better mood than usual, and his teammates were perfect with every drill. Ty ended up sitting in the dugout, chewing on sunflower seeds and spitting them vehemently into the ground.

Once the game was about to start and the crowd settled in, Michael received a surprise from Mr. Oberfels.

"Michael, I am sorry, but Isol wants Justin to pitch today. You'll pitch soon, though," Mr. Oberfels told him.

"That's alright, Coach," Michael said, understanding Mr. Isol's decision. He guessed that Mr. Harrington and Mr. Isol decided to listen to Michael's words after all. He only hoped that his words didn't affect the outcome of the game.

The game ended up to be exciting and entertaining. Michael saw his team win a 4-2 game and Justin pitched seven solid innings. Joe and David closed the game up with two shutout innings to preserve their win. Mr. Harrington was very pleased with how his pitchers played; it made him not regret giving Michael some rest.

The offense for the team was alive as well. Fred hit a home run and Harry hit a three-run bomb to put the game away in the eighth. The crowd cheered loudly as Team USA walked out onto the field to congratulate each other on a good game.

It was a pandemonium in the locker room after the game. Everyone was cheering and the whole team was spraying Gatorade at each other. Mr. Harrington liked the way they played and dismissed them after informing them of their next game.

Michael could not have been happier. However, there was one thing that was circling in his mind. He was not entirely sure that Mr. Smith was honest with his change.

He might be lying, Michael thought. How do we know for sure that he's on our side again? His history certainly does not help his cause. Is it possible that he was still working for the brothers?

And the creature in his chest was roaring its approval at Michael's words.

CHAPTER 21

A 10-YEAR-OLD SURPRISE

Michael was able to get out of the locker room after Fred and Ahmad had laden him down with what seemed like half the Gatorade in the world. He carried his bag out of the clubhouse and walked quickly to the hotel after Mr. Harrington received a text from his own son, telling Michael to meet them there.

Sheena and Matt were waiting for him at the hotel with Mrs. Goodwin, Shawna, and Ember. They all looked disgruntled.

"How come you didn't pitch today?" Shawna asked incredulously, as if Michael had disguised himself as one of the pitchers.

"I just didn't," Michael said, wearily. "We still got the win, though. Justin put on a decent show."

"I suppose so," Matt said, indifferently. Then he added, "Michael, your friends left a message at the hotel."

"They did?" Michael queried. His heart gave an enormous leap inside his chest.

"Yeah, they said they would arrive in three hours or so. Their plane is right on schedule," Matt informed him.

"Excellent," Michael said, happily. He was looking forward to their arrival.

"We were thinking of coming up to my house," Sheena said to Michael, matter-of-factly.

"Yeah, Michael, do you want to play Wii or something?" Shawna questioned.

"That sounds great," Michael said, attempting to smile.

Mrs. Goodwin then spoke up. "If we are, we can come in the car. I know there are six of us, but we will manage."

Michael had a sudden inspiration. "Mrs. Goodwin, do you know where Mr. Goodwin is?"

Matt and Sheena were looking at him curiously. Mrs. Goodwin cleared her throat.

"My husband, dear . . . oh, yes he is at the house."

"Good," Michael said. "I would like to have a word with him. It is something very important."

"He's busy, dear, but I guess you'll be able to," Mrs. Goodwin replied. "He isn't always busy."

The six of them were awfully crowded in the car as Michael and the three girls were stuck in the back. There was a scuffle between Michael and Matt of who would sit in the front, but Matt was bigger than Michael, so he won.

"You may be a beast on the mound," Matt smirked to Michael, as he climbed in the front, "but even you can't beat Matthew Harrington *even* if he's crippled with crutches."

"Oh, shut up," Michael said.

Michael ended up getting a window seat and was sitting next to Shawna. He had the inconvenience of watching tons of bugs hit the window at high speeds, which was pretty bad. It was remarkable how so many bugs could hit the window in so little time.

"You'd think they'd be smarter," Michael grumbled, as Matt laughed maniacally.

When they got out of the car, they entered the house to find Mr. Goodwin entering the room.

"Hello," he said, smiling. "Did you win, Michael?"

"Yeah, it was 4–2, sir," Michael said.

"That's good."

"Mr. Goodwin, I was wondering if I could have a word now."

"I'll call you in a few minutes, Michael," promised Mr. Goodwin. "I just need to take care of something real quick."

Michael, Matt, Sheena, Shawna, and Ember started up a fierce tennis match on Wii. Michael had Shawna on his team and Sheena was with Matt. Ember decided to sit out the first match.

Michael realized just how good everyone else was at video games. Even though he considered himself decent, compared to Shawna and Sheena and Matt, he was a lamentable video game player. The only good thing to be said of this was that he was not alone.

"This is overkill," Ember said, when she joined Michael's team. "We lose. I'm terrible."

After a good ten minutes of tennis, they switched to boxing when Matt and Sheena played against each other. It was very close. When they were playing, it was almost impossible to hear any other noise in the room.

"Get her, get her, she's a girl, you idiot . . ."

"Come on, kill him, he's a midget—"

"Michael?"

Michael turned and saw Mr. Goodwin looking at him. Matt and Sheena were still attempting to knock the other unconscious.

"I can talk with you now, but hurry because I haven't got much time."

Michael followed Mr. Goodwin away from the excitement into the study where he saw tons of papers strewn everywhere in the room. It certainly looked like he had been busy. On the computer, it said that he had about one hundred e-mails unopened.

"I understand why you had been busy," Michael said, pointing to the computer.

"I know," Mr. Goodwin said, wearily. "Being the President of the United States Olympic Committee is not an easy job, trust me. I deal with nonsense after nonsense, it gets quite tiresome. Anyway, what did you want to talk to me about?"

Michael took a deep breath, and explained about Mr. Smith admitting his guilt to the team and his theories and concerns. Mr. Goodwin was a good listener; he did not interrupt, but maybe it was because he wanted to get the discussion over so he could work.

Mr. Goodwin looked thoughtful. "Can you tell me your concerns again?"

Michael said tonelessly, "I don't think he's reformed, sir. What do you think?"

Mr. Goodwin absorbed this information into his mind and then looked at Michael. "Have you ever thought that he might have just done it to—?"

Michael cut him off before he could finish.

"But my theory makes sense! Does it, sir?"

"Well, I must admit, it is pretty suspicious," Mr. Goodwin admitted quietly. "But I do not think it is of real importance of what side Mr. Smith is on."

"Why, sir?" asked Michael.

Mr. Goodwin looked at him. "Michael, the only thing that can hurt us is the scroll that the brothers are searching for. Mr. Smith, evil or not, does not make a difference. He might look for the scroll, but it does not change who is in a further lead into finding it."

Fair point, Michael thought. But Michael was still not convinced. Despite Mr. Smith being a coward, he thought the side that he was on was relevant to the discussion at hand. If the Committee regained its trust in Mr. Smith, they would inform him of classified information. Michael felt that if Mr. Smith was indeed deceiving them into believing he was truly sorry, it would only be easier for the brothers to figure out what their intentions were.

"So, that brings me to my next point," Mr. Goodwin continued, interrupting Michael's thoughts. "For the second time, and I hope the last time, I am assigning you a mission, Michael. I want you to use sources from anything you might think of and find out where the scroll's whereabouts are. I will be doing the same, but you can never assume that I might find it. After all, I am extremely busy."

"You want me to find it?"

"Find out where it is," Mr. Goodwin corrected him. "And when we do find it, I think it would be appropriate to take you to find it with me."

"You'll take me to find the scroll when we know where it is?" Michael asked, stunned.

"I underestimated you, Michael. When I first saw you, I knew you were a good person, but not able to complete such dangerous missions. I feel that you now have the privilege, obligation, and right into looking further into this. My only hope is to find it soon."

"Are you sure everyone will approve of you doing this?" Michael asked, apprehensively.

Mr. Goodwin raised his eyebrows. "I do what I feel is necessary, Michael. If you don't mind, I really need to get back to work, so if you can go back and play with everyone, that would be great."

"Of course," Michael replied, taken aback at the abrupt end to their conversation.

Michael was right by the door when he was called back.

"Michael."

Mr. Goodwin was looking at him weird; it was close to somber.

"Good luck."

⋆ ⋆ ⋆

At a quarter past six, Michael versed baseball on the Wii with Sheena. He was, obviously good, at baseball, but on a video game was much different. He threw pitches over the middle that Sheena was able to nail, and he ended up losing five to two. Matt grilled him for it afterwards.

"I thought you were a superstar, Mikey."

Michael decided to vent his feelings off on Matt by giving him a good kick. After he done it, though, he regretted it, as Matt was limping the rest of the way (he reckoned Matt's right buttock would smart for the rest of the month).

Michael, Matt, and Sheena left the house at almost six thirty to head back to the hotel. It was a little dark outside and a nice breeze was beginning to settle in, but what was important to Michael was that his friends were coming. He could not wait for them to drive up spectacularly to the hotel and see them. Just the sight of Sara's big brown eyes and Tomas's curly hair would be enough for Michael to inflate with happiness.

Michael took no time in telling Sheena and Matt about the discussion he had with Mr. Goodwin. Both seemed mildly interested in it, but were alarmed at the fact that Mr. Goodwin might take him to find it when they did.

"I think that is true about Mr. Smith," Sheena said serenely. "He has to be faking it."

"But that does not explain how he rescued my dad," Matt argued.

"He might like your dad and just dislike me," Michael said, thickly. "You never know. I think Mr. Smith was reluctant to be responsible for the death of his employer."

"My dad wants you find the location of the scroll as well?" Sheena asked Michael.

"His opinion seemed to change," Michael said, quietly. "He confessed and told me he had 'underestimated me.'"

"Your dad can do whatever he wants, Sheena," Matt pointed out. "He's the President of the United States Olympic Committee, you know."

"Yes, but still," Sheena said, her tone was now agitated. "He is putting a lot of responsibility in Michael."

"You don't think I'm capable?" Michael asked, looking at her questioningly.

Sheena looked shocked by Michael's response.

"I'm not saying you can't," Sheena said, bluntly. "I'm just saying that you're only fourteen and this—"

Michael wasn't interested in hearing the rest of Sheena's comments but Matt took care of that for him: he drowned out Sheena's voice with a teasing remark.

"Care about Mikey too much?" Matt queried in a mocking but playful voice. "That's very touching."

Sheena looked as though she might retort back, so Michael cut in.

"Let's hurry back to the hotel. We're moving slowly."

The rest of the way they ran (Matt moved pretty fast with his crutches, he was only a few hundred feet behind Michael and Sheena) and did not say another word to each other. By the time they got back to the hotel, it was almost seven o' clock. Michael knew his friends were minutes away from driving up in front of the Blossom Suites.

"We might as well wait out here for them," Michael said, abruptly as Matt almost went in the hotel.

"Oh, yeah, right," muttered Matt sheepishly, and he walked back to Michael.

Sheena leaned against the wall next to Michael. "Are you going to tell any of your friends all of this, Michael? You know, about the scroll and the brothers and all that?"

Michael considered for a moment. What he planned to do was dangerous, and his friends—Sara especially—would fuss worse than

Sheena. But he felt that his friends had a right to know. They were the only people who would come to support him, as a good friend should. And, Michael thought to himself, even if he didn't spill the beans, the information will leak out anyway—Matt, Sheena, and he could all agree that this was news that couldn't be kept quiet for long.

"I probably would," Michael said, grudgingly. "They are my friends, too, and I feel that they have the right to know everything."

"But, Michael," Sheena said, in a voice of suppressed panic. "The truth would terrify them! Do you think it's wise to tell them?"

"It terrified you, too, Sheena," Michael said, kindly, but firmly. "And you're my friend, and I told you everything, haven't I? How would you feel if I concealed secrets from you?"

Sheena looked shocked and guilty. "I'd feel terrible. I'm sorry. You're right."

Michael suppressed a smile. "It's alright."

"Hey, Michael, is that them?" Matt queried, pointing to a blur that was driving right to them.

Michael looked at where Matt was pointing to. All he could see was a pair of flashing headlights, but the car was definitely turning into Blossom Suites.

"It might be!" Michael said, excitedly.

The blur was driving fast, terribly fast, and Michael looked up to see that the car looked like an extremely nice car. If that was really his friends, he couldn't understand where they got such an expensive car.

Then, there was a loud screeching noise—worse than babies bawling—and Michael saw the car spin perfectly right into a parking space.

"Your friends got style!" Matt said, loudly, impressed.

"It might not be them," Sheena and Michael reminded him.

But, to Michael's utter amazement, it was them. They watched as the doors opened, and out came Sara, Tomas, Sara's parents, and, surprisingly, his little brother Delbin, came out of the car looking as though they just had the ride of their lives. They all looked pleased to see Michael.

"Michael!"

Tomas and Sara ran up to Michael. Sara hugged him, and Tomas clapped him on the back. Matt and Sheena were looking awkward and shy and they took a hesitant step backward, away from Tomas and Sara as though they were afraid they would make them ill.

"Are these your friends that you have been talking about?" Tomas asked, glancing at Matt and Sheena, who looked awkward.

"Yep," Michael answered.

"People have been talking about you," Sara said breathlessly and fixing her hair as she did so. "They were already saying how you already set a record for the strikeout total for the team."

"I might have, but I don't really pay attention to statistics that much," Michael said, beaming. "I've been doing well, though. Delbin, I'm glad to see you, how come you're here?"

"I've decided to come," Delbin said, proudly. "I told my parents I wanted to so I came. It's a long story; I'll explain everything later, but going to another country to see the Olympics? I wouldn't miss that for a sack full of cash, and the tickets and flight cost about that much."

Michael noticed Matt and Sheena's uncomfortable looks and he decided to involve them in the conversation with his other friends. Michael didn't want them to stand there as though they were dummies on display.

"Oh, by the way," Michael said, not wanting to ignore Matt and Sheena, "Sara, Tomas, and Delbin, this is Matt Harrington and Sheena Goodwin."

Matt and Sheena looked relieved that they were being included in the conversation. They said "hi" very awkwardly, but friendly all the same.

"Michael told me about you two," Sara said, looking at both of them.

"Did he?" Sheena said, surprised, and she beamed at Michael.

"It's a surprise then!" Sara exclaimed, laughing. "Yes, he has told me all about you two. Thanks for helping Michael get comfortable in Beijing. He isn't too used to different places and meeting new people."

Michael noticed that while they all talked, Sara was looking at Matt with great interest. It was evident that she did not care about his bald head (his cap was in his pocket). It also could have been that he had a big black boot over his foot and a pair of crutches under his armpits.

"Why are you limping, Matt?" Sara asked, looking anxious.

Noticing Sara was looking at him, Matt hastily put his cap on his head, looking embarrassed.

"My leg got broken a little bit," he said hastily. Michael loved watching him act so uncomfortably around his friend. It almost made him want to laugh.

"How did it get broken?" Sara persisted, and Matt blushed.

"Believe me, Sara, if I told you, you would think I was lying," Matt said formally, going fire-red.

Tomas and Michael, meanwhile, were talking about the car while Sheena and Sara were talking.

"Where did you get that car?" Michael asked curiously.

"This Chinese dude gave us it for a rental car!" Tomas said, excitedly. "It's cool as all hell! This baby can reach up to interminable speeds, and we all were able to fit comfortably inside!"

"Sounds sweet," Michael replied, smirking.

"I know," Tomas said, looking at the car fondly. Then he asked a serious question. "Do you have a game tomorrow?"

"I don't know. I'll have to check."

Michael turned back to the rest of his friends, who were still lingering outside the hotel. Sara and Sheena were still chatting away animatedly and laughing. Michael was relieved that they got along well; he had expected them to be rather testy with each other like most girls at his school were.

"Delbin, how long are you staying here?" Michael asked. "The whole time," Delbin answered, cheerfully. "We leave when you do. We're going to go home on the same flight."

"Then where are you staying?" Michael questioned.

"The Perkins, Tomas, and I have a room in this hotel on the bottom floor," Delbin said. "It will be tough to fit all of us in the room, but we'll manage."

"You can come in with me and Matt," Michael said, quickly. "That way you could have more room."

"Maybe," Delbin said. "And guess what else, Michael?"

"What, Delbin?"

Delbin looked like he was going to burst out of his skin. It was clear to Michael that Delbin was dying to tell him this for a while.

"I'm going to try out for the Olympics next time! I've got a trainer to help me now!"

"When I was away, my parents got a trainer for you?"

"Yes. That's one reason why they chose not to come. They didn't say anything to you because we weren't sure we would be able to get a trainer."

"That's great!"

"I plan on practicing my fielding skills a little more to develop! But I think I'll be ready by the time 2012 comes around!"

"That's a little bit of a problem. They kicked out baseball and softball for the next Olympics. Mr. Harrington told me that."

"WHAT?"

"They did, I'll explain later, though . . ."

"Is this your brother, Michael?"

Sheena had come over to talk with Michael now. Sara was now chatting with Matt while Tomas stood by the door, looking lost and standoffish.

"Delbin, this is Sheena."

Delbin looked at Sheena. "Hi Sheena," he said with complete confidence and politeness in his voice. "I heard you were good at gymnastics. I read an article about your team, and it mentioned you by name."

Sheena smiled. It was plain obvious that she thought Michael's brother was adorable. "Your brother looks a lot like you, Michael," she remarked.

"Only girls will notice that," Matt said under his breath. Tomas forced a laugh, but Sheena frowned at Matt.

"Should we go inside to the cafeteria?" Michael asked.

"There'll be more room in there."

"My parents will be in there soon," Sara said. "They went to the other side of the hotel to check it out."

"We're done with that, dear."

The group turned around and saw Mr. and Mrs. Perkins walking towards them.

"Hello," Matt and Sheena said simultaneously.

"You must be Michael's friends," Mrs. Perkins replied. "It's a pleasure to meet both of you."

After Matt and Sheena both shook hands with Mr. and Mrs. Perkins, they all walked inside the hotel to get warm; the breeze had picked up considerably while they were outside.

Sara's parents told them that they would be in their hotel room if they needed them. Then, all of the kids trooped into the cafeteria where they all sat down at one particular huge table. Sheena was giving him a time-to-spill-the-beans look, but Michael did not need her to remind him. He had planned to tell them everything as soon as they arrived to get it over and done with.

"Are you going to tell them, Michael?" Sheena queried, reading his mind.

"Tell us what?" Tomas asked.

"Yeah, tell us what?" Sara and Delbin chorused simultaneously.

"Well, I . . ."

Michael hesitated. He was not sure whether he wanted to tell them everything or not despite him planning that he was going to. He felt a little uneasy. But, after all, they did come here to support him, so he decided to be honest with them.

"Yes, there is something I've got to tell all of you . . . it is really important . . ."

And he was off, and explained everything that they did not know, and said everything that had happened during this Olympics. For about a quarter of an hour, he spoke in rapt silence, and everyone was listening to him with rapt attention. They all seemed deeply impressed and understanding at the end when he had finished. Sara, however, did have a question that even Michael could not answer.

"Do you think that the two brothers might be acting under the Chinese Governments' orders?"

Michael had no answer. He could have said something, but he did not want to lie, or give theories that might not be true. So he shrugged.

"Well, we can never be sure on anything, but I doubt it."

"Sara does have a great point, though," Matt said, giving her a significant look. "You never know. That could be true."

Michael decided to back up his assertion. "I would not bet on that. Remember, they are on the Chinese Committee. They could do what they want. They don't need permission. I think they are doing on their own accord. Mr. Goodwin thinks the same."

Delbin looked at Michael something close to wonder. "How do you get involved in all of this?" he questioned him in amazement.

"I don't know," Michael shrugged. "Trouble always finds me."

"I'll tell you why," Sheena said, waking up from her reverie slightly. "Michael got himself involved. He felt as though he had to."

"That's Michael for you!" Sara said, fondly, patting Michael on the arm.

"There might be military people who don't do what you do, Michael," Tomas piped up, grinning a little.

"Sheena?"

Sheena jumped. "What?"

"You were looking as though you were deep in thought," Sara said, gently. "Are you okay?"

"Oh, yes," Sheena said, serenely. "I was just thinking . . . we should have a picnic at my house tomorrow, just to get together. You can meet my family and siblings and everything."

"You have siblings?" Delbin asked, quickly.

"Yes," Sheena said, giving Delbin a small smile. "I have two sisters named Shawna and Ember. They are ten years old."

"That's my age!" Delbin exclaimed, looking cheerful. It was evident that he was relieved that there were kids his age to talk to.

"Then I'm sure you three will get along very well," Sheena said, smiling.

"Are you sure it could happen?" Tomas questioned sharply. "You know . . . the picnic? Your parents won't mind, right, Sheena?"

Tomas looked uncharacteristically nervous, and Michael was curious as to why, but he decided not to say anything.

"Yes, it could," Sheena said, patiently, "I just need to ask my parents."

"They'll say yes," Matt said. Then he added, "The Goodwins cook the best food ever."

"That's true," Michael commented, and Sheena blushed.

Delbin was wondering about the two siblings Sheena had said.

"Are your sisters really cute and nice?" he asked Sheena.

Sheena was about to answer when the Perkins came in a suggested that they all go to bed. Michael was surprised to see that it was already ten at night, but maybe it was not so surprising—they had been talking for a long time.

Michael stayed down with Tomas and Sara but everyone else had left to go to their hotel rooms. Sara looked at Michael.

"You have great friends, Michael," Sara whispered.

"I'm glad that everyone got along," Michael said, smiling. "That's friendly."

"We were hoping they would be nice," Sara replied. "Right, Tomas?"

Tomas looked slightly angry as he looked up, but he regained his composure and addressed his friends.

"Sara said she was hoping to talk to you the whole time before she saw Matt," Tomas replied in a low voice. "That changed her plans slightly."

"Oh, shut up," Sara said, but Michael laughed, getting the hint from Tomas.

"Well, in that case," Michael said, his eyes twinkling, "you should know, Sara, that Matt has a determined hatred of the Yankees, a fondness of the Mets, excellent at Guitar Hero, and awes over huge thrones."

"Thanks for the insight, Michael," Sara said, sarcastically, as Tomas laughed.

Michael said "see you later" to his friends and hurried up to his room. Matt answered the door and he found Delbin there as well. Delbin was reclining on the couch with his eyes closed, as though he had a strenuous day of work. He opened his eyes when Michael entered the room.

"Hey, Michael, I can sleep in here. I got permission from Sara's parents!"

"That's good."

"It'll be like a man party," Matt said.

"No, it's *Two and a Half Men*, with you being the half!" Delbin crowed.

Matt chucked his pillow at Delbin, missing his head but hitting something more fragile: the pillow sailed across the room and knocked the lampshade right off the lamp. The lamp leaned to one side, but Michael seized it before it tipped off of the polished nightstand.

"Nice one, Matt," Michael said as Delbin put the lampshade back on top of the lamp.

Michael sat down on his bed and Delbin sat on the other while Matt pulled out the pull-out bed for Delbin to make up for his near accident. Once they all had settled down on Michael's bed, Michael turned to the two of them.

"How do you like my friends, you two?"

Matt smiled. "I liked your two friends. But Tomas looked a little nervous. He seemed fine around you, but he looked out of place when we all talked as a group."

"He's just quiet," Michael said. "He's fine around Sara and me. Did you like my friends, Delbin?"

Delbin smiled as well.

"They were great, but Sheena seemed too cheerful, and she did not tell me anything about her two siblings," replied Delbin with an I-am-disappointed-about-being-refused-that-information tone.

"Sheena thought you were cute, dude," Matt told him. "I could tell. She's probably telling her sisters that right now."

Delbin looked at Michael. "I'll ask you, then, Michael. Are her siblings good-looking?"

"Well, I don't judge ten-year-old girls," Michael said, slowly.

"Ty probably does," Matt muttered under his breath viciously, but Michael ignored him.

"But let me put it this way: Shawna is Sheena at ten years old and Ember is a redhead. Does that answer your question?" asked Michael.

Delbin smiled. "Yes, it does."

Matt laughed.

"Shut up," Delbin said warningly to him. "Or I'll make fun of you in front of Sara!"

Matt stopped laughing at once. "I don't like her. She's just okay."

"Don't lie," Michael said, laughing. "I know you are lying. Matt, come on. There must be some explanation why you could not stop staring at her."

Matt laughed, as though what Michael was saying was so ridiculous. "She's not my type. She's not blond. She wasn't bad, but I was expecting better."

"You're harsh," Delbin commented. He turned to his older brother. "With his attitude, he's never going to get a girlfriend."

"What, did you expect her to be perfect?" Michael asked, climbing in his bed.

"Did you tell her anything about me?"

Matt looked worried. Delbin looked excited. Michael decided to test his conscience.

"Well, let me say this: Sara did tell me a long, time ago before I came here that if I made any friends here, she said that she won't like them if they like the Mets and enjoy gawking at huge thrones."

Matt scowled, but Delbin laughed. Matt hit him with a pillow.

"Shut up, Michael," he said, but he was smiling slightly, as he knocked Delbin into the pull-out bed. Michael could see the smile on Delbin's face, but Michael thought he had no reason to make fun of Matt. It was more or less of the same thing when he queried him about Shawna and Ember.

CHAPTER 22

USA VS. JAPAN

Michael, Matt, and Delbin dressed and showered quickly the next morning. It was a dull, gray Wednesday and it was August the twentieth. Michael went down to breakfast with Matt and Delbin, finding out from Nitro that they were playing Japan. Nitro also said how this game was very important.

"We need to win this game," Nitro said, bluntly, buttering some toast. "And you're starting today, so be warmed up as well."

"Awesome. Thanks, Nitro," Michael said.

"Enjoy your breakfast," Nitro responded pompously.

When Nitro left, Delbin stared after him. "Is his hair always green?"

"So far it has," Michael replied, taking a drink of orange juice. "Nitro isn't your average Joe, but he's a decent guy."

Not much later did Sheena and Tomas and Sara join them. They all were spreading marmalade on their toast.

"Who are you playing today, Michael?" Tomas asked, self-consciously taking a small bite of toast. "Did you find out?"

Michael took a gulp of orange juice before answering. "Yeah, I'm versing Japan."

"Aren't they good, though?" Sara asked inquisitively.

"I don't know."

"The Japanese are good," Matt said, knowledgeably. "I read an article about them. They're a decent team."

"Do you think we beat them today?" Michael questioned Matt, looking for a scouting report.

"As long as everyone does what they are supposed to, I don't see why you shouldn't come out on top," replied Matt, smoothly.

"I'll make sure I pitch well," Michael said, determinedly.

"You better," said Sheena matter-of-factly as she took a drink from her glass of orange juice. "Or I'll thrust my drinking straw up your nose!"

★ ★ ★

Michael spent the morning wandering around with his brother and friends. Michael, Matt, and Sheena gave them a tour of the facility, every arena, and even where Sheena's parents had a temporary house ("My parents like to live on the spot," Sheena explained). Then, after an hour of doing so, Sheena had to dash off to her competition for gymnastics.

"Good luck," Michael, Matt, Sara, Tomas, and Delbin wished her outside the gymnastics arena.

"Thank you, see you later," Sheena said, and she left.

Michael and Matt led the others over to a picnic area where they all bought chocolate chip ice creams, which they slurped happily as they watched people amble up and down the streets.

They met Fred, Harry, Nitro, and Ken having a combative game of cards at a nearby table but they did not stay long. Nitro turned to say "hello" to them, but stopped short and looked disappointed that Sheena wasn't with them. While he did so, Fred took the opportunity of trying to steal his cards. Nitro ended up trying to yank them back as hard as he could. Fred then let go, and Nitro flew off the bench and hit Matt in the groin with his head.

"Idiots," muttered Matt, rubbing his groin area as Ken tossed the cards into the air and the four of them battled for the cards and Fred was lying on his chest on the table, moving like a beached whale as he attempted to take Ken's cards from under his Cookie Monster hat.

"Typical Fred," Michael said, chortling.

"Who were they, though?" Sara asked.

"Some players on my team," Michael answered immediately. "You met Harry, Ken, Nitro, and Fred. Fred was the one that tried to take the cards. He's the life and soul of the team. Nitro had the green hair, Ken was the black kid, and Harry was the rather quiet one."

"Is his real name Nitro?" Tomas queried, smirking. "The green hair was odd."

"No, that is his nickname," Michael explained. "His real name is Danny, but because of his green hair, he is called Nitro. Everyone calls him that."

"Your teammates are weird people," Tomas said, fervently. "How is it possible to get along with these people?"

Michael had no answer. He thought it was a bit rich for Tomas to call his friends weird when Tomas did things that normal fourteen-year-old kids would find stupid, which included writing in a journal and playing with Legos.

At lunchtime, they headed back to the hotel to get some lunch. They all got turkey sandwiches and some Pringles from the cart and sat down to eat.

Sheena met up with them at lunchtime as well. She was still in her gymnastics outfit, but was pink in the face with pleasure. When she sat down with the rest, Michael noticed that she had a silver medal around her neck.

"I won a silver medal!" Sheena announced proudly, holding it up, even though everyone saw it already.

"Nice job," Tomas and Delbin said.

"Congratulations!" squealed Sara.

"Brilliant!" Michael and Matt beamed.

Sheena smiled at all of them. "I take pride in my performance. I never expected this. I was surprised that I won it; I thought Rachel and Kim did better than me."

"Well, I'm glad you won because I'm certainly not winning any medals with my crippled leg," Matt said, brightly. "But I don't care. Diving sucks."

They spent the rest of the lunch talking and Sheena told all of them that they were invited for a little party at the Goodwin's house.

"Good food is coming in our future!" Matt said, excitedly, and Sara laughed, but stopped when Tomas looked at her with raised eyebrows.

Michael could not wait for the picnic, but he had to get through one thing first—the baseball game. His nerves mounted as the game draw nearer. He wanted ever so desperately to pitch well for his friends.

Michael left the others after lunch to head over to the field where all of the coaches were. The rest of the team was there already. Fred was having a disagreement with Mr. Isol; Fred was holding a small cup and looking horrified.

"Put it on, O' Leary!" Mr. Isol told him sternly. "We don't want your future to be ruined!"

"I'm not putting this on, no way," Fred said, stubbornly.

"I generally prefer a lot of breathing room around my groin."

"ENOUGH!" Mr. Isol roared, so Fred, relenting, threw it into the stands.

Michael warmed up with Nitro, who seemed more nervous than ever. He kept throwing the ball away and Michael stopped some by making spectacular diving catches MLB players probably would have trouble getting.

Mr. Harrington instructed the rest to drink up and relax. Ken started a game of ultimate with his Cookie Monster hat. Harry and Lew were talking and showering an anthill with sunflower seeds. Mr. Harrington led Michael to the bullpen.

"Michael, I want you to warm up, okay?" Mr. Harrington said.

"No problem," Michael replied.

"No pressure on you, but we got to win this game, okay? Just do your best; you've already saved our team."

"Don't be, no, I haven't—"

"Mike is coming, so get ready," Mr. Harrington said, and then he left abruptly, taking Michael completely by surprise.

Mr. Oberfels and Mr. Isol observed Michael's pitching session with interest. Michael thought it went okay, but he was having trouble with his slider, which always moved too much outside. Mr. Isol openly criticized him ("Durbin, you're throwing like my nine-year-old daughter!" he said, gruffly) but Mr. Oberfels decided a better way of helping Michael out was to correct his grip.

"Grip it like this," Mr. Oberfels said, showing him by putting his two longer fingers inside the red seams of the baseball. "Now try it."

Michael did, and to his relief, he threw it outside but in the strike zone. He didn't bother pointing out to Mr. Oberfels that his grip was exactly what he showed him; it would not have made a difference anyway.

"That's better, Michael," Mr. Oberfels said.

"Only do that with left hitters, Durbin, or that will be knocked out of the park," Mr. Isol said in a gruff voice.

As usual, he was demonstrating his knack of criticizing his pitchers. Michael couldn't see why Mr. Isol was being as critical as Mrs. Cogburn, but the game they were about to play was doubly important than the others.

As a matter of fact, besides Ken and his Cookie Monster hat, mostly everyone else looked rather nervous. Fred was not joking around like usual; instead, he was always practicing his swings on the on-deck circle (though he did find amusement in using Ken's hat as a baseball).

Michael relaxed with the rest of the team for the next hour while his team and the Japanese team participated in some batting practice. It was quite fun to watch, and one of the balls ended up sailing into the dugout, almost knocking out Nitro in the process.

As the crowd settled into the stands, Michael didn't even bother trying to find his friends. Besides the fact that it was hard to find anyone in the densely packed crowd, Michael didn't want the sight of his friends to distract him from the game.

Before the game started, Mr. Harrington gave his team a pregame talk. The atmosphere was more tense4 than usual and the joking had completely subsided.

"Alright guys, listen up," Mr. Harrington said. "You know what we have to do. I want everyone focused on what they have to do. Mike, make sure you give Michael a different pitch every time. Cliff, Ken, and Samuel . . . make sure you don't play too deep, Japan does not have any power hitters . . . Fred, Harry, Xavier, and Nitro . . . I want to see all of you attack ground balls. This team hustles constantly; therefore, I want to see effort from every single one of you. The rest of you need to watch the game and not jack around. Is that clear?"

The team nodded. All of them knew that this game was no ordinary exhibition: This game would determine the fate of their team.

"Alright then—go out and play hard!"

When Michael and his team charged out onto the field, a series of deafening roars greeted them from the stands. Michael trotted over to the pitcher's mound and scooped up the baseball that was waiting for him on the mound. After warming up with five pitches, the first Japanese batter came up to the plate and Mike gave him the signal to start off with a fastball.

Michael wanted this game to go fast so he took the game at a faster pace. In fact, he was pitching so fast that the other team called timeout at least two times an inning, and they were getting seriously annoyed at Michael. Mike, knowing that the team was getting repeatedly frustrated, did not start to call any breaking pitches at all. Michael assumed he was doing this because as the Japanese team was frustrated, they would be more likely to make mistakes.

Michael felt completely in command with his pitches but he had to admit that by the fourth inning, it was becoming predictable what he was doing. The Japanese hitters were able to start connecting with the fastball and Nitro's two errors were enough to aid the Japanese team into bringing one of their men home in the fourth inning.

Michael got through five innings and only gave up one run on three hits. He struck out seven to boot and gave up no walks. Mr. Harrington was pleased with his performance, and after five innings, it was 2-1 Michael's team.

"We only need to have more offense," Mr. Harrington said to his team.

"We're trying!" Harry protested. "Why did you put me in the fourth spot, you know I suck!"

"Typical Harry," Fred said in Michael's ear. "He always has to be that poop in the toilet, doesn't he?"

"Apparently so," Michael replied, smiling a little bit; Harry had gotten the only two RBIs thus far in this pitcher's duel of a game.

Michael went out for the sixth inning and was able to shut the Japanese out one, two, and three. Michael raised his strikeout total to nine, and Mr. Isol was actually starting to admit he was good, something he assured Michael that he was trying to deny for the whole Olympic Games.

"This Durbin can actually throw the damn baseball," he growled.

To make him feel even better about himself, Michael noticed during the game that Mr. Smith was actually doing his first base coaching duties like he was supposed to. Was he watching his step now since his apology that hardly anyone truly believed? Had he really reformed? It was, indeed, hard to tell. All indications thus far were that he did, but Michael knew that Mr. Smith could not be trusted just as much as Ty could not be trusted to stick up for his teammates.

Michael watched as Nitro hit a sacrifice fly to get another run in the sixth inning and he gave Michael another run to work with going into the sixth.

Michael pitched two more innings in the game and now had ten strikeouts, but he gave up another run on two hits, and his pitch count was becoming alarmingly high. Mr. Harrington decided to pull him from the game after that.

"Michael, you have now almost ninety pitches under your belt. That's high; we do not want you to kill yourself. Remember, we may need you in the long run and we can't have you if you injure and hurt yourself."

Mr. Isol beckoned him to relax on the bench and patted him genially on the shoulder, sending Michael into the Gatorade container.

"Nice damn pitching, Durbin," Mr. Isol growled. "But it was probably one of your worst starts."

Michael sat down on the bench and talked to Nitro (who was replaced by Chad as a defensive substitute in the seventh) while he watched his team play. He was hoping that, with a 4-2 lead, as Xavier hit a rare home run, David was able to close it out with a one, two, three type inning and not give up any more runs.

David did do decent and got the first two outs but then gave up a base hit to center field. The Japanese runner sped around first and headed to second. Ken—who was too busy fiddling with a dandelion in center field—dawdled to retrieve the ball, and the Japanese runner slid neatly into second, avoiding the late tag by Xavier.

"Unbelievable," Mr. Harrington said, shaking his head in disbelief while the crowd yelled in complete astonishment.

Michael was getting nervous as David usually made things interesting, but David was able to strike the next guy out and Team

USA won the game. David got a save and Michael got another victory under his belt.

He ran out with his team and Team USA met at the pitcher's mound where they all slapped each other high-fives and celebrated their victory. Meanwhile, the Japanese team was descending into their locker room, shepherded by their coach, who looked as though he was fed ammonia.

Mr. Oberfels talked to the team in the locker room after they all traipsed back into the locker room. He was happy and he smiled as he spoke to the team, who were all grinning and joking with each other.

"Well done, all of you," Mr. Oberfels said, looking as though he were the one to stop a huge asteroid from hitting the earth. "The next game won't be until two days from now, okay? So have a good break day tomorrow and come ready to play the day after."

"Who are we playing on Friday?" Nitro asked loudly, so Mr. Oberfels could have heard him over Fred's jokes, which were very inappropriate.

"O' Leary, stop talking and listen up! We will be versing Cuba," Mr. Oberfels said. "At least I think so. But don't you worry about who we are playing. All of the teams are the same. You are all free to go after you are done changing."

Michael was the first to leave the locker room. He was pleased with his victory and nearly bumped into his friends, who were waiting for him just outside the locker room. They were all grinning from ear to ear.

"Nice job, Michael," Tomas and Sara beamed at him.

"Thanks," Michael replied, also grinning.

Sheena and Matt were giving him congratulatory smiles.

"As always, Michael beats the wind out of his opponents," Matt said in a fake commentating voice.

"You were amazing, Michael," Sheena said, beaming at him.

"Thanks," Michael said again, though turning slightly red at her praise. "Are we going up to your parents' house?"

"Yes," Sheena answered. "Delbin is waiting for us by the Bird's Nest. He had to go get something. We'll head over there, though."

"Your brother said he will praise your performance when you see him," Matt told Michael.

"All right," he said.

"Let's go," Tomas said, impatiently. It was clear that he was looking forward to eating a cooked meal. "We don't want to keep Delbin waiting."

"'Good food is waiting for us!'" Sara said in a singsong voice, quoting Matt. Tomas frowned at her.

They walked and met Delbin waiting by the Bird's Nest for them. He had a video game in his hand, plus a large bag of gummy worms that was as big as Michael's baseball mitt.

"I think I should bring something over there," Delbin said, holding up the bag. "I got this from a Beijing general store."

"That's friendly," Michael said.

"Great job, Michael, you were great," Delbin said, beaming. "You look as good as you always did."

"Thanks, Delbin. Shall we go up?"

Delbin and his friends nodded.

On the way there, they talked more about the game and Sheena told them what food was going to be available to them. Michael listened and Sheena explained how there was going to be hot dogs and burgers there, and Michael felt a rush of excitement. It wasn't a frequent event that Michael had a picnic with all of his best friends and brother.

"Hey! Sheena! I knew you were bringing them!"

And Shawna and Ember were waving towards them, and Michael knew they were also excited to find someone their own age at Beijing as well, just like his brother. Michael grinned and turned to his brother, who was smiling at the two girls. Michael knew that he would want to spend as much time with them as possible.

The group reached the girls and they were ushered in the house, only thinking about—and looking forward to—the picnic that they were about to have.

CHAPTER 23

THE YELLOW RIVER JOURNEY

Michael, Matt, Sheena, Sara, Tomas, and Delbin probably had the most enjoyable picnic in their life. They immediately began to play a violent game of kickball. Michael teamed up with Delbin, Sheena, and Tomas while the two younger Goodwin girls and Sara were on the other team with a crippled Matt. Matt could not run at all, so he kicked with his non-injured foot while Tomas volunteered to pinch-run for him. Michael's team ended up demolishing Matt's team. They still had fun, though.

Throughout the festivities, Michael noticed that Delbin was interacting well with Shawna. Michael noticed Delbin's glassy gaze while he talked to her, and Michael knew that Delbin nursed a soft spot for Sheena's younger sister. But Michael didn't care. He would actually be happy if Shawna would become as good a friend to Delbin as Sheena was to him.

Sheena was the life and soul of the party. She was the one who suggested ideas which everyone agreed to. They played several baseball matches on the Wii, and they had *Guitar Hero* contests on Expert level. Michael did not last long. He only was able to last about half the song and get only thirty percent of the notes right.

Sheena and Matt were obviously the best at it and Matt won the match with a stellar ninety-eight percent which, he said excitedly, was his best ever.

Even the Goodwin parents were joining in. Mr. Goodwin started a Madden NFL game against Michael. He told Michael that he had no pressing matters to take care of for the rest of the day.

"It's good to have some fun," Mr. Goodwin said, happily, choosing the Giants as his team.

"Mr. Goodwin, have you found out where the scroll is?" Michael asked, choosing a team at random, which was the Texans.

Mr. Goodwin stopped abruptly. "I do think I have. Remind me after this game. We'll discuss it later. Now is not the time."

Michael could agree with him. He was sure Mr. Goodwin rarely got anytime to have fun so he had no problem respecting his request to hold off on the subject.

The two of them played the game which accumulated in a 24-21 victory by Michael. He ended it with a game-winning 51 yard field goal. Everyone else was cheering for Michael and when he made the field goal, Matt did a war victory dance that ended with him tripping over the coffee table, hurting his leg even more. As everyone else laughed, Mr. Goodwin and Sara felt sympathy for him and helped him to his feet.

"Here, come in my study, Michael," Mr. Goodwin replied, after making sure Matt was fine and turning to Michael. "I'll show you."

Michael walked past Sheena and Matt, and the two were playing *Crash Bash*, the game Delbin brought; past Shawna and Ember, who were watching; and past Delbin, who was looking excited. Then Mr. Goodwin opened the door to the study and let him in.

The room was quite neat now and Michael understood why Mr. Goodwin had the rest of the night off. The computer was not on and there were only two papers on his in-tray, which looked important. Michael had a shrewd suspicion what was on the papers.

"Are those the papers that say where the scroll is?" Michael queried.

"Yes and no," Mr. Goodwin said, smiling. "It does show the exact city where it is, but the exact place in that city, it doesn't."

"Where is it, sir?" Michael asked, eagerly. "Do the brothers know about it?"

Mr. Goodwin stood up straight. "I believe that the scroll is located near the Yellow River in a place called Zhengzhou, which was the birthplace of the brothers' father."

"Are you serious?"

"I'm pretty positive," said Mr. Goodwin, his eyes gleaming fanatically. "It requires some guess work, obviously, but through consolation from my sources, I think this is the most likely place. Though it may not look like it Michael, I spent a great deal of time trying to think of possible destinations. I had Zhengzhou, Xi'an, Chengdu . . . until that is, I researched all the possible destinations more thoroughly to figure out what destination was more likely to contain the scroll."

"How did you whittle some cities down?" asked Michael.

"Well, due to the fact that this is Ying and Yang we are dealing with, I incorporated the brothers' history into my research," Mr. Goodwin explained. "Based on what I knew about the brothers, I came to the conclusion that a sacred temple in Zhengzhou is holding the scroll for the brothers. All we need to do is obtain it before Ying and Yang figure out their own father's intentions."

"Can I go with you to retrieve the scroll?" Michael queried, eagerly. "I can tomorrow, I have no game."

Mr. Goodwin looked serious, but was excited all the same. "Now, Michael, I did promise you that you can accompany me to get the scroll when we found it, but I am only bringing you on one condition and one condition only: you must obey every command that I give you, and you must obey it without question or hesitation. Do you understand me?"

"Yes, sir," Michael answered, immediately. Even if he was not going to be allowed to go, Michael had too much respect for Mr. Goodwin to disobey him.

However, Mr. Goodwin thought he answered a little too quickly for he looked skeptical.

"That means *everything*, Michael," Mr. Goodwin said, looking more serious than ever. "If I tell you to hide, you must hide. If I tell you to leave me and inform my family, you must do so. If I tell you to do crazy stuff—and you might have to—you must do it. Do you understand, Michael?"

"Yes," replied Michael patiently.

"Then I wish to leave tomorrow at precisely eight tomorrow morning. I need you to be in the parking lot of your hotel by that time. You must be ready."

"Yes, sir," Michael replied. "Am I allowed to tell Matt and Sheena and my brother all of this?"

Mr. Goodwin considered him for a moment. "You are a true friend to my daughter and Matt, Michael. Yes, you should tell them. They have a right to know. Just tell them that you are going to get the scroll. But I am going to warn you. This might be dangerous. It may be hard to get it. We may get caught and hurt, maybe even arrested. Please do not mention any of this to them. It shall only frighten them."

Michael did not think that was right, but he said, "Yes, sir."

* * *

"Are you kidding me?"

"No," Michael said seriously. "I am going with your dad tomorrow to get the scroll."

"Is it dangerous?"

"We don't know. Mr. Goodwin said it might, but he didn't give any details."

The three of them were in Michael's hotel room. Matt and Sheena were told by Michael of what would be happening tomorrow. Matt and Sheena weren't exactly assured by Michael's words. They seemed to think that the brothers might be there with machine guns and military copters.

Michael hated defying Mr. Goodwin like that, but he felt Matt and Sheena should not be concealed from what he would be facing. It was like Mr. Goodwin said—they had a right to know.

"I'll be okay, I'm with your dad," Michael reassured both of them. "I'll bring a cell phone so I can call you to update you, but don't worry. I'll be alright."

Sheena and Matt did not look reassured.

"Michael, are you going to tell your brother and Sara and Tomas this?"

"If I could," Michael said, "I will. I did not get the chance today, but I will leave them a note."

Sheena looked at him critically.

"Michael, they are your *friends*," she reminded him sternly. "I know you don't want to tell them about this because you don't want them involved. You care about their safety. But you *must* tell them, Michael. They need to know, especially your brother."

Michael sighed. He didn't want to admit it but Sheena read his emotions perfectly. He had not told his friends what he was doing because of all the reasons Sheena just said. What if the brothers found out about them?

And speaking of the notorious twins, Matt looked at Michael and asked about them. "Michael, what if the brothers are there?"

"Oh, I don't think it'll work out like that," Michael said, pleasantly. "You see, if they knew where it was, we would already know."

"You better get some sleep, then," Sheena said, anxiously. "You might be facing anything tomorrow. Good night."

Michael and Matt bade her good night as well, and then Michael drifted off into a very uneasy sleep.

It was a very weird dream. He first dreamed that he was facing fifty Chinese people with handguns. He tried to jump and avoid them but they hit him and he was—

And the scene faded out, and the next scene was Sheena walking with him on a beach with the brilliant sunset illuminating the sky—Sheena turned to face him—Michael could feel his heart beating louder—Sheena drew closer to him and—

Michael woke up with a start. He was sweating. It was only a dream, but Michael did not want those distractions. Then, he closed his eyes and fell asleep again; this time, he did not dream of Sheena.

The next morning seemed to go by fast. He woke up at seven fifteen and got dressed and showered. Matt, who Michael realized was a morning person, woke up with him.

"I should see you leave," he told Michael, when he pointed this out.

"That's great," Michael said, as they went down to breakfast. "I appreciate it."

Yawning widely, the two boys slouched into the cafeteria.

Sheena was already there with, surprisingly, her family. Mrs. Goodwin and her husband were arguing with the three girls looking embarrassed and wishing they were a part of the wall instead of the children of two bickering parents.

"Will, why are you doing this, he's too young—"

"He's not a child!" Mr. Goodwin retorted. "He's fourteen and has the right to decide for himself!"

"Will, he's only fourteen! Adults are still responsible for him and you need to understand that!"

"I do, Lily! I'll be with him; it'll be fine."

"I'm not okay with this, Will! He is still too young . . ."

"He's old enough to make his own choices, Lily! I don't know if you've noticed this or not, but Michael has matured greatly over the past few weeks!"

"Still, he needs adults to look after him and it is completely irresponsible of you to do this. If his parents knew, they would . . ."

"They probably won't care because they aren't here in the first place!" Michael said, loudly and bitterly, surprising everyone.

"Michael, are you ready?" Mr. Goodwin questioned, stopping the disagreement.

"Almost," Michael answered, taking a bowl of cereal and pouring milk into it. "Are we leaving after I'm done with breakfast?"

"Yes," Mr. Goodwin answered, "we need to get going as quickly as possible."

Michael nodded.

"Oh, and Michael," Shawna said, speaking up. "I've told Sara, Tomas, and Delbin where you are going and they said good luck and be careful."

"You did?" Michael asked, immensely grateful. "Thanks, Shawna."

Sheena gave him a come-on-dude look but Michael ignored her. His friends knew and that's all he cared about. Michael tried to eat his breakfast but he was too full of adrenaline to swallow his Frosted Flakes.

Mr. Goodwin turned to Michael only after three minutes of eating. "We better get going."

"Okay," Michael answered back, pushing his barely touched cereal bowl away from him. "I'll see you later, guys."

"Be careful, Michael!" Sheena said, anxiously. "Be safe and stick with my dad."

"Kick some butt!" roared Matt.

Michael winked at them and then followed Mr. Goodwin out to his car. They got in quickly and Mr. Goodwin started up the ignition.

"You might as well get comfortable, Michael," Mr. Goodwin replied. "It'll take about nine hours to get there and then we have to find it itself."

"When will we get back?" Michael asked.

"Early next morning, I think," Mr. Goodwin answered. "If we don't, we're behind schedule. I don't know how long finding this scroll will take."

Mr. Goodwin drove the car and Michael sat in the passenger seat, just thinking about what the scroll would look like. Certainly, it would be a scroll, and it would not be any type of rocket plan, but would it contain more information that the brothers did not even mention? And if it did, could it affect him or his friends? He hoped not but the creature in his chest roared its answer at the thought, and Michael found himself suddenly wishing he had said more than just a casual goodbye to his friends. What if he didn't come back alive? He knew the chances were slim, but he could not help being a bit nervous.

Mr. Goodwin drove, and Michael didn't ask him how far they were away. Michael didn't even bother asking him exactly they were going; he was too wrapped up into his own worrisome thoughts. He just sat there, listening to the radio Mr. Goodwin put on to make up for the lack of conversation. Michael wanted more than anything to have more than Mr. Goodwin for company. He wished his friends were here: his loyal friends, fantastic friends, his true friends, who cared about him, and he cared about.

Six hours must have passed in complete silence. The radio was still playing audibly, but Michael decided to ignore the radio. He tried to entertain himself with a magazine about sports that Mr. Goodwin provided him, but he did not have the patience or excitement. All of it was old news. So, after attempting many times to read any articles in it, he gave up. Then, he tilted back and just looked out the window, watching the landscape of China pass by him. It was not pretty, but Michael didn't feel like looking at anything pretty at the moment. All he felt was gloom. He was becoming a little unhappy at how Mr. Goodwin spoke his plan so calmly—perhaps Mrs. Goodwin was right. At first he agreed with Mr. Goodwin but maybe she was right when she said it was an irresponsible thing to do. He maybe should have had a relaxing day; he felt he deserved a break. Instead, he was working with the President of the United States Olympic Committee to thwart two notorious twins from carrying out their nefarious plans. With this mission alone he already dealt with more than his whole family put together, and he was not happy about it at all. As much as he liked helping his friends out, he felt now as though he were bound to this by invisible ropes, something that he could not wriggle out of. Michael knew it was going to be a difficult adjustment going back home to live normally with his parents—well, as normal as they strived to make his life.

His parents did not have any idea what he was dealing with, but did they honestly care? They made no effort to come and support him in the Olympics and this was his only chance. His parents did seem sorry, but still, it was not every day that your child competes for his country. A good parent will support their kid, no matter what. Michael felt that his parents were failing to accomplish that at the moment despite finding a trainer for Delbin.

Michael saw Mr. Goodwin pass the sign that read that they were in Zhengzhou.

"We're here, Michael," Mr. Goodwin replied as he drove. "We're almost there."

Pushing all of the emotions he had felt in the car ride away, he had a sudden rush of excitement. He was here. This was it. They had arrived at their destination.

"Michael, we'll be parking in a minute," Mr. Goodwin said, still concentrating on the road. "Get ready to climb out, all right?"

"Yes, sir," Michael answered, lacing up his trainers again, which had came untied during the ride.

Mr. Goodwin parked in a lot where a Chinese restaurant was and he stopped the car next to some gloomy-looking kiosks.

The two of them got out of the car, and Mr. Goodwin locked it to make sure it was secure. Michael felt a great thread of foreboding: this place looked nearly as miserable as Beijing.

"Follow me," Mr. Goodwin told Michael. "And don't stray off. This place gives me an uneasy feeling."

Michael followed Mr. Goodwin, not paying too much attention as to where he was going. The good thing to be said was that Mr. Goodwin knew exactly where he was going, as though he routinely took morning strolls around the city. Mr. Goodwin and Michael walked for about ten minutes, and then Mr. Goodwin stopped at a boatyard that looked as sturdy as a house made up Popsicle sticks. Michael was baffled. What were they doing here?

"Mr. Goodwin, sir," Michael said, keeping up with him. "Where exactly are we going?"

"Oh, I'm sorry, Michael," Mr. Goodwin answered, cheerfully. "I forgot to tell you. We have to take a boat to the other side of the city, where I think the scroll might be. It'll be quicker than walking."

Michael couldn't help feeling relieved. His legs felt like cranberry sauce.

"Sir," Michael said. "Do you mean we have to travel on the Yellow River?"

"Oh, you know about the Yellow River?" asked Mr. Goodwin, sounding delighted. "Yes, Michael we will be traveling on the Yellow River for a brief moment or two. I'll know when to stop. When we get out, we need to head for a specific location. I'll tell you about it once we've acquired a boat."

Mr. Goodwin slowly opened the black metal gate and ushered Michael onto the mini floating dock. It sagged under the weight of them both as they walked across it to find out that there was going to be a slight problem.

"Ah, there are no more boats but this," Mr. Goodwin replied, tapping a bright pink plastic boat the size of a large beanbag chair.

"Can it fit both of us?"

"It might be a tough fit," Mr. Goodwin replied, "but we'll manage."

Michael seriously doubted this as the boat looked to be made for only ages eight or lower. Looking completely fake and stupid, Michael was sure they were going to attract attention.

"Mr. Goodwin? Do you feel slightly guilty that we took a boat without permission?"

"Michael, it doesn't look like this boatyard's been used in a decade," replied Mr. Goodwin reasonably. "We'll be okay if we take it."

Michael nodded. Right now, he felt queasy and suddenly wished he could be with Sheena and Matt right now.

"Okay, Michael, get in. Watch your step and don't fall into the water, the current is pretty strong today."

Michael did so, and Mr. Goodwin then got in. There were cramped in together. Michael's knees jutted over the side of the boat, but he knew that there was no point in getting comfortable. If what Mr. Goodwin said was true, he would not be in this ridiculous position for long.

"Are we ready, Michael," Mr. Goodwin asked, "to start paddling down?"

"I think so, sir," Michael answered, trying to talk casually, but he was nervous.

Then Mr. Goodwin untied the boat from the dock and gave it a good hard push using the dock. The boat began to move at an accelerating rate down the river. Michael concentrated on the scenery and in the distance he could see the outline of a roaring tiger guarding some sacred building that looked like a Mr. Goodwin's house. Michael stared.

"What is that, sir?" Michael asked, pointing to the temple.

"I'm glad you pointed that out, Michael, because that is where we need to go. That is the Tiger Temple," Mr. Goodwin explained. "Ming—Ying and Yang's father—built this temple to provide his parents with an honorable burial. I think he had an emotional attachment to this place, so I thought we should start there."

Suddenly, the boat began to pick up speed as though it was on an interstate highway. Michael found himself gripping the sides of the boat extremely hard as the water crashed against his hands and the boat.

"Sir, the boat is going to miss the dock by the temple!" Michael shouted.

The boat indeed was spiraling out of their control. Mr. Goodwin tried to jerk it towards the dock, but it was moving too fast for him.

"Mr. Goodwin, we're not going to make it!" cried Michael as his boat hit a rock jutting out of the water, causing the boat to spin the other way. Nearly falling out of the boat, Michael gripped the back of the boat tightly.

"Do you mind getting a little wet?" shouted Mr. Goodwin as an icy wave showered them.

"No!"

"Ok, that is good. Michael, jump out of the boat and swim towards the temple!" Mr. Goodwin shouted over the roaring waves.

Michael obeyed without question and plunged into the icy river.

He heard a splash and knew that Mr. Goodwin had done the same. Drenched to the skin, he started furiously swimming to the other side. Owing to the current of the river, it was awful hard. Michael quickly swam, and pretty soon, he found himself heaving himself onto the dock.

Michael ran away from the dock, panting, and turned around. The swim, though not very long, had taken his breath away. It had been too close of a call. If they had missed their stop, it could have been catastrophic. There was a good chance the brothers and their allies could swoop down on the Tiger Temple at any moment.

"Mr. Goodwin?"

He surveyed the dock that he had just exited. He could not see Mr. Goodwin. He decided to call again, thinking that Mr. Goodwin did not hear him.

There was no answer.

"MR. GOODWIN!"

But there was still no sound but the roaring of the waves. Michael grew uneasy. Where was he?

Michael was growing more nervous by the second. If he did not come, he must be still in the river.

Michael shouted his name again, but there was still no response. Michael caught the tiger at the top of the temple with his eye, and the tiger was roaring it seemed at the approval that Mr. Goodwin did not make it to land, and that Michael Durbin was on his own.

CHAPTER 24

TIGER TEMPLE

Michael felt as he was hurtling down the river: *please be it so that he's not hurt, it's my fault if he is.*

Michael gazed back at the temple and tried to think why Mr. Goodwin told him to swim towards there. The scroll couldn't possibly be in the Tiger Temple, could it? Michael better try to look for the scroll—and more importantly, Mr. Goodwin.

Michael walked across the courtyard where only passerby stood, talking quietly. Michael wondered if they knew the scroll was there. No, he was being stupid, that couldn't possibly be true. The crowd was beginning to stare at him, due to his being alone and drenched with water. Michael did his best to ignore their questioning stares.

Michael decided the best thing to do would be to enter the temple and see if he could observe anything unusual or different. Then, from that, he might just be able to locate the scroll. That was, if Mr. Goodwin was right in saying Ming would have an attachment to the place.

Entering the temple was different, as all of the sunlight did not disappear, but there was a cold breeze in the room and the suns heat, but not light, seemed not to have reached here. It was an odd feeling.

"Wow," Michael breathed as he looked around the temple. He never had seen anything so spectacular before in his life that even topped his quality pitching.

The temple had a long red velvet rug that lay straight in the center. There was a stained glass circle in the center which showed a tiger. Then there was a gold chair and the whole room was decorated beautifully with artifacts Michael assumed had some significance to Ming's parents.

Michael walked across the room and ran his hand over the wall. He was trying to feel for any crevices where he could possibly find the scroll. However, he walked around the room twice and did not feel any crevices to think of. It was not in the wall.

Then where was it? There seemed no unusual place on the ground where it could be, and there was no cracks in the wall so how was he, Michael Durbin, supposed to be able to locate such an object? Mr. Goodwin seemed sure that it was around here somewhere, but Michael could not see anything. Michael knew he had to find Mr. Goodwin first before he looked for it. He had no shot in finding it without him.

Michael ran out of the temple, panic-stricken. He had to find him.

"MR. GOODWIN!"

Michael shouted as he ran, and many curious Chinese people were staring at him, but Michael took no notice. Michael walked to the other side of the temple, where he had not gone before. He could not see Mr. Goodwin. Michael could not bear to think that he was missing. It pained him like one thousand hot knives.

"MR. GOODWIN!"

Michael shouted again, but no response came. Michael tried at least three more times, but Mr. Goodwin did not reply back, or come to him. All was silent, except the Chinese people, whispering excitedly, and pointing at Michael as if they thought he was mad or some mildly interesting exhibit.

Ignoring them, Michael searched around the temple again, but it was no use. Mr. Goodwin was simply not to be found. Trying not to panic, Michael hurried back to the dock. He figured that maybe he could catch a glimpse of him from the dock.

Michael ran by the dock's edge, maybe hopefully seeing him swim towards him, but it did not happen. The roaring of the waves continued, but no sign of Mr. Goodwin. He obviously was not in the water.

Michael turned back and was giving up hope in finding Mr. Goodwin. He knew he could only do one thing—he would try to find the scroll by himself, and then he would have no choice but to call Blossom Suites and let his friends know what happened.

As soon as Michael reached the entrance of temple, he heard pounding footsteps. Michael whipped around to find a man that was drenched to the skin, had a brown beard, and looked anxious.

Michael never was so pleased to see this man before.

It was Mr. Goodwin.

"Michael, you're okay!" Mr. Goodwin cried, shaking his own head when he reached Michael. "I was counting on you to reach the dock."

"What happened, sir?" Michael questioned, calming himself down, but could not help keeping the relief out of his voice. "I was trying to find you!"

"The current carried me away and the boat almost knocked me out," Mr. Goodwin explained. "I was able to cling to a dock not far from the temple and head in your direction. Did you make any progress?"

"No, I was too busy looking for you."

"I appreciate your thoughtfulness, Michael. Well, we better get started. I don't want to be here all day."

"Do you think it is possible that a friend of Ming's could have helped them with this scheme?" Michael asked as they walked to the temple.

"I am not sure, Michael, but I would think not," Mr. Goodwin said, frowning. "Ming would not have told his friends of the treachery he committed. But let's not discuss this right now. All I care about right now is the scroll. It should be in this temple. Let's take a look."

The two companions walked into the temple and they looked around. As Michael had thought, nothing looked odd or out of place. Michael chanced a glance at Mr. Goodwin. He seemed to be pondering where the scroll could be. The tourists gave them weird looks and Michael was suddenly aware that their soaked appearances were sure to attract attention. Ignoring the calculating stares, Michael turned to Mr. Goodwin.

"Where do you think it might be, sir?" Michael questioned, looking at the floor.

Mr. Goodwin did not reply for a minute, but after that he smiled.

"I think I may have an idea," Mr. Goodwin said, slowly. "And I think it is in an obvious place."

"Obvious?"

Michael couldn't see what Mr. Goodwin saw. To him, this was just another ordinary temple.

"Yes, Michael, it is," Mr. Goodwin said. "Look below you. What do you see?"

Michael instantly knew it.

"Are you saying in is beneath our feet in the stained-glass center?"

"Yes, that is exactly what I'm saying," Mr. Goodwin replied. "Do you think that it is odd that no other temple in China has a stained-glass floor? All of the temples are the same for the most part—the ones that I've seen."

"But, sir," Michael protested, "There is always going to be one oddball. Do you really think the scroll is there?"

"Yes, I do," Mr. Goodwin replied. "However, I'm not too sure how we will be able to get it."

"Then we are probably wrong in thinking it is in there."

"I don't think we are, Michael," Mr. Goodwin replied, calmly. "I knew the brothers, Michael, and I could tell you that they do not hide their valuables well."

"Ming hid the scroll, not the brothers!" Michael protested.

Mr. Goodwin was looking at the stained glass circle on the floor. The other tourists and passerby were only taking one glance around it and leaving. Michael's eyes traveled across the room and he saw the throne in the temple, and he saw what was above it. Michael gaped. He could not believe that he didn't see it before. He had been too concentrated on the wall.

"The scroll is not there, sir!" Michael said, loudly.

"Then where is it, Michael?"

"It's there," Michael said, pointing to the throne.

Mr. Goodwin and Michael looked at the throne. A scroll was above the throne so anyone could see it. It looked to be in good condition and it shone gold due to the gold artifacts that surrounded it.

"Good job, Michael," Mr. Goodwin said, reaching the throne. He stared at the scroll. "I see that Ming gave his poor hiding skills to his sons."

It was perfectly blank on the side that was showing, but Michael assumed that the plan was written on the back. Michael started to feel uneasy. Why did Ming put it here, making it too easy to find?

"Mr. Goodwin—" Michael started to point out his fears, but Mr. Goodwin interjected.

"He must have hung it up like that for a reason," Mr. Goodwin replied, thoughtfully, scratching his beard. "He must have not wanted people to know about what was on it. We have to take it down. By displaying it as an ordinary artifact, no one would think anything of it."

"How are we going to take it down?" questioned Michael, staring at the scroll.

Mr. Goodwin did not answer. In seconds, he reached up and took down the scroll. He rolled it up and used one of Sheena's hair ties to keep it in that shape. He then slipped it in his pocket without anyone noticing. Michael couldn't believe how easy getting the scroll was. It almost seemed too easy, almost foreboding.

"There," he replied, smoothly as if they had just repaired a mailbox. "The Chinese apparently don't have great security here. Anyway, let's go before we attract attention. Good work, Michael."

"Can you show some identification, sir?"

Michael gulped. He whirled around to find two Chinese officials sneering at them. Michael thought they looked distinctly familiar. One of them was skinny and burly and the other was very short, and only a few inches taller than Michael.

"Identification? Why do we need that?" Mr. Goodwin asked, politely.

One official looked at Mr. Goodwin, sneering. "We saw you take down the scroll up there. Do you have authorization to do that? We were coming to take it down."

"How come?" asked Michael, trying to keep his voice polite.

"It's none of your business, kid," sneered the second official. Then, he peered into Michael's face closely and stumbling back as though Michael was covered with poison ivy. "Wait a minute. You're that Durbin kid. You're the kid that is trying to find the scroll. Who's this man with you?"

Michael refused to answer. He was not going to give them the satisfaction that they could boss them around. Mr. Goodwin spoke.

"You two must be employees for the Fireworks Factory," said Mr. Goodwin slowly. "Ying and Yang sent you here, didn't they?"

Both officials looked shocked. They recovered their poise two seconds later. "You realized that?"

Then, one official said, in a shocked voice, "I know who you are. He's Goodwin, the President of the United States Olympic Committee!"

Mr. Goodwin gave a short nod. Michael looked desperately around. He needed to find a way to get out of the situation that they were in. These two allies of Ying and Yang were obviously trying to get the scroll just like they were. It was rotten luck that they had to come on the same day.

"Give us the scroll," the shorter official snarled. "The brothers need it."

"I could give a damn what the brothers need," Mr. Goodwin retorted.

The bigger official leered towards Mr. Goodwin. "Give us the scroll, or you'll regret it!"

"Send the brothers my regards," Michael told them, turning his back on them.

"Let's go, Michael!" Mr. Goodwin cried, cottoning on.

The two of them started to sprint out of the temple, away from the officers. Michael felt himself trip and he fell to the ground. Before he knew it, the shorter official was on him and was trying to tie his arms to his back so that he could not use them to escape. The crowd was now watching with shock of what was happening.

Michael tried to call Mr. Goodwin, but he was shaking off the other official, who was attempting to subdue him. Mr. Goodwin grabbed the official by his jacket and threw him away from him at a bench, where he flipped over. The crowd gasped even louder.

The official slid on the ground, swearing. Michael felt himself being dragged across the temple. He vainly tried to free himself, but the official held him in a firm grip. Michael kicked his legs back, and he felt one of them hit him in the kneecap, and he let out a gasp of pain.

Michael saw his chance. He wrenched free and started to run to Mr. Goodwin, who was pushing the other official away. As soon as Michael reached Mr. Goodwin, both of them started to dash through the city of Zhengzhou, to retrace their route to Mr. Goodwin's vehicle, leaving the two officials and thirty thunderstruck bystanders.

"Enough of this!" one official snarled, as they started to chase after them. He pulled out his gun and aimed.

"Michael! Go to the right!" Mr. Goodwin shouted.

Michael dived right as soon as the official fired the gun. Michael felt it sail past him and hit a traffic light, which swayed precariously on the wire. Michael and Mr. Goodwin turned down onto another road Michael sensed the officials chasing them; he could hear their pounding footsteps. They turned another corner and Michael heard two gun bullets fall short of hitting them.

"Michael, follow me!" Mr. Goodwin hollered, and he led him down a little path between two buildings. As they raced down the path, the short official came into view and blocked their path of escape, with his gun pointing at them. Michael whirled around and saw the tall, burly man come into view.

The short official pulled the trigger, apparently not noticing the tall official coming from the other direction. Michael and Mr. Goodwin forced themselves to the ground, and heard the bullet hit its target, and a loud screech of pain echo through the way.

Michael felt Mr. Goodwin yanking on him to get up, and both of them started to dash the opposite way. Michael saw that the tall, burly guy was crumbled on the floor, and screaming in pain. The bullet had pierced him through his stomach.

"GET TO THE CAR, MICHAEL!" shrieked Mr. Goodwin, pointing in the distance.

Michael followed Mr. Goodwin's finger and saw to his relief that the car was waiting for them.

Michael and Mr. Goodwin dived into the car just as the shorter official pulled the trigger on them. It rebounded off the car, making a small hole.

"I don't think so," Mr. Goodwin said under his breath, and he slammed his foot on the accelerator.

The official shot three more bullets; two of them hit the car, and the third one shattered the front passenger seat window, causing Mr. Goodwin to duck slightly to avoid shards of glass. The Chinese official disappeared from view in a matter of a minute after Mr. Goodwin drove quickly away from him.

"Well, we escaped, and got the scroll," Mr. Goodwin replied, cheerfully, as he drove over ninety miles an hour to put a safe enough distance from them and the official.

Michael was silent for most of the car ride. He was still panting from their narrow escape. It was a close shave.

"That was not as bad as I would have expected," Mr. Goodwin replied, cheerfully. "I mean, we got the scroll."

"Yeah, but now the brothers know," Michael said with gritted teeth. "I'm probably going to get pummeled by them once they find me."

"Don't worry," Mr. Goodwin replied, trying to inject some concern in his voice. "We're going to make sure you do not go anywhere alone."

"What are you going to do with the scroll?" Michael queried with the air of one asking another to give him their social security number.

"I don't know," Mr. Goodwin replied, thoughtfully. "But we will think of something, I will tell you that. Anyway, we are almost back. I'm sure everyone would be relieved to see that you are okay. Michael, tell me if you can read anything on this."

He put one hand in his pocket and pulled out the scroll. Michael took it and unraveled it, eager to see what was written.

It was blank on the one side that Michael saw first. He flipped the scroll over to see that there was writing on it. It read:

This temple is known as the Tiger Temple as it Was constructed durenng the Year of the tigre. Ming, the Owner of Fireworks Factory, buit this misterious tomb and buried his parents beneath the tenple to honor their life.

Written by Sandra pics (Metot TM, 4100)

Michael was curious as to whom Sandra was, but he was unhappy with the message: this was not the scroll. Michael looked up at Mr. Goodwin.

"This is not the scroll," Michael said, heavily. "And there are a number of errors."

Mr. Goodwin looked surprised. "It's not? Really?"

"No," Michael answered. "We got it all wrong. Where could it be now?"

Mr. Goodwin sighed. "I don't know, but don't chuck it away yet. The misspellings may have a meaning to them."

"And who is Sandra?" asked Michael. "That is who wrote this. Whoever she is, she is an awful speller."

Mr. Goodwin shrugged.

Michael tried to interest himself in the baseball magazine for the rest of the ride and was pleased to hear that the Phillies were on a winning streak, almost catching up with the Mets. However, he began to feel very sleepy, and he fell asleep not long after that.

They did not arrive into until early next morning. Mr. Goodwin pulled up into the parking lot and Michael put down the magazine. He saw all his friends, Mr. Harrington, and the rest of the Goodwin's.

"What time is it, sir?" Michael asked, noticing how the sun was at the decline.

"About five forty-five in the morning," Mr. Goodwin replied, checking his watch. "We are about on time. That's good."

Michael got out of the car and all of his friends greeted him.

"How did it go?" Tomas asked abruptly, looking excited.

"Fine," Michael answered, even though he would be lying.

"You're soaked, Michael. How come you're so wet?" Sara asked, anxiously.

"Had to swim in the Yellow River," Michael answered shortly. "It was not enjoyable."

"Are you alright?" Sheena asked, looking concerned.

"Yeah, I'm alright," Michael assured her, suppressing a small smile.

"You swam in the Yellow River?" Matt, Sheena, Shawna, and Ember cried.

Michael laughed. "Yes."

"So you got the scroll?" Mrs. Goodwin and Mr. Harrington asked.

Mr. Goodwin finally came out of the car, holding the scroll. "It is not the real one."

Matt's jaw dropped. Everyone else stared at them in surprise. "It isn't the one you're looking for?"

Michael shook his head. "We have no idea where the real one is."

Mr. Goodwin related the story to the group. They looked befuddled at what had happened.

"Well, we had to use a crummy paddle boat to get where we needed to. Then we jumped in the river and swam to the Tiger Temple."

"The Tiger Temple?" Ember and Shawna gasped.

"I've never have seen it," Matt moaned enviously.

"By the way, what is so special about it?" Michael asked. "Why would—?"

"Anyway, as I was saying, we got across the river and then Michael found the 'scroll' above the throne," Mr. Goodwin said, cutting Michael off.

"You did?" Sara asked, looking at Michael, her eyes wide which made her look like a puppy begging for a walk.

Sara made it sound like it was such a big deal when it really wasn't. The scroll was in plain sight and Michael reckoned his blind grandfather could have seen it.

"Yeah," Michael answered, looking at her. Then, he added bitterly, "the one we *thought* was the one we wanted."

"And so we found ourselves face-to-face with two members of the brothers gang, but they did us no harm," Mr. Goodwin said, hastily under Mrs. Goodwin's penetrating stare.

Michael was wondering why he was bothering to not be truthful to the group. Why was it such a big deal?

"Why?" Matt asked.

"The brothers must have set that up for us," Mr. Goodwin replied, still glancing nervously at his wife, who seemed to know that her husband wasn't being entirely truthful. "But how could they have known we were going there is beyond me. I think it was just a coincidence."

"Will, of course it was not a coincidence!" Mrs. Goodwin said with an air of one being exasperated at someone for being so stupid. "They knew you were going to figure out where the scroll was and sent their henchmen after you!"

"Anyway, I better inform the Committee what happened," replied Mr. Goodwin, cutting off his wife, whose facial expression was wooden. "They have a right to know what we tried to do. Mr. Harrington, would you like to come with me?"

"Sure," Mr. Harrington answered.

And with that, the two men left, leaving Mrs. Goodwin with the kids. Sill looking incredibly furious with her husband, she turned to Michael, who backed away slightly—Mrs. Goodwin may be a nice person, but she wore a look of one avenging her brother's death. Noticing Michael's surprise at her behavior, she let the anger out as though she opened a door on her head and replaced the anger with sympathy and kindness.

"Are you hungry, Michael, dear?" Mrs. Goodwin queried. "You haven't had anything since breakfast yesterday."

Feeling ravenous, Michael nodded.

Minutes later, all of them were in the hotel. Sara's parents came too, wanting to talk to Michael but due to the fact that both had bags under their eyes and their hair stood up on end as though they had received an electrical shock, Michael knew they had just rolled out of bed.

Michael shook Mr. Perkin's hand, and thanked him for bringing his friends and brother to support him.

"You're welcome," Mr. Perkins replied, stifling a huge yawn. "My daughter felt bad for you."

"Where is Delbin, by the way?" Michael asked. "I have not seen him."

"Oh, he is in the room," Mrs. Perkins answered. "He was not feeling well. He was sleeping when you were gone."

"He'll be alright," Michael said, sounding optimistic, "Delbin always feels unwell at least once every month or so. I remember that one time when he invited his friend Roxanne over, and he showered her with his spaghetti and meatballs that he had eaten at dinner—"

"MICHAEL!" Sara, Ember, Shawna, and Sheena said, reproachfully, and Matt and Tomas laughed.

More people started to pile into the cafeteria and grab their continental breakfast. Michael's party was forced to retreat to the boundaries of the cafeteria as what seemed like half the Skippack population entered, all tousle-haired and looking like the worst idea of a zombie.

"What are you seven thinking of spending the rest of the day?" Mrs. Goodwin asked as one girl tripped over a banana peel in front of them. "Would you like a nice brunch back at the house? I can cook a ton of food."

Everyone else was all for it, so the group traipsed back to the Goodwin house where they decided to wait for Delbin to arrive, who had called Michael and informed him that he was coming. Mrs. Goodwin at first didn't like the idea of Delbin walking to her house in Beijing alone, but Michael talked her out of it—his brother may be young, but he had proved at a young age that he could handle himself.

Delbin didn't join them until a half an hour later. He looked perfectly fine as if he had never been sick. In fact, he was becoming the life and soul of the group once they all congregated in the house.

"I knew you would get it," Delbin said, thumping him on the back once he was told about what had happened in Zhengzhou. "Too bad it wasn't the real one, eh?"

"What can you do?" Michael asked, still fretting over their narrow escape.

The eight children played well into ten o' clock. Then, Mrs. Goodwin called them for a meal. They all couldn't fit at the small table only meant for four people, so they all congregated outside to eat their meal of eggs, bacon, potatoes, and orange juice. Michael thoroughly enjoyed his meal; Mrs. Goodwin once again proved her aptitude at cooking an enjoyable meal.

After they had cleared their plates (Matt's still had ketchup smeared on it), Mrs. Goodwin told them it was time for them to go back. Michael, Matt, and Sheena walked ahead of Sara, Tomas, Delbin, and Sara's parents (Ember and Shawna stayed at their house). In hushed voices, they discussed the baseball game tomorrow.

"I hope you win tomorrow," Matt commented. "Your baseball games are fun to watch."

"That would be because you like watching the Asian dancers during the mid-inning breaks," Sheena said, shrewdly.

Matt scowled, vaulting himself over a huge rock with his crutches.

"Anyway, Michael," Sheena replied, loudly, ignoring Matt. "Who are you versing tomorrow?"

"I think Cuba."

"Ah, that should be fun and games," Matt said with the air of one talking about playing with atom bombs.

When they reached the hotel, they decided to go up to their rooms and relax. Michael had planned on catching up on some sleep.

When Michael entered his room with a crippled Matt, he thought of how angry the brothers must be: their workers failed to not only retrieve the "scroll" but one of them was now dead. Little did the brothers know that the scroll was still out there, waiting to be discovered.

CHAPTER 25

GONE TOMORROW

Michael and Matt walked into the crowded cafeteria with everyone else for breakfast the next morning. After a refreshing nap, Michael felt completely awake. However, when Michael checked his cell phone for recent messages, he saw the date, and was astonished by how late in August they were. Michael was shocked to find out that there were only three full days left of the Olympics.

"It's not really a shock when you think about it," Matt reminded him as they searched for a table. "I mean, with all of the stuff that has happened."

Michael nodded. Sheena interrupted in their conversation after bringing over her breakfast (a raisin bagel with butter and a carton of skim milk) and told them about her last competition.

"Then I'm done, and all there is left is the Closing Ceremonies," Sheena said, brightly. "And they should be interesting to say the least."

"How come?" asked Michael.

"Well, with all the hysteria surrounding the brothers and the mess they left the Committee in, the Chinese Committee no longer have a planned ceremony," Sheena replied. "Dad told me. He was informed of that yesterday. From what it sounds like, it is going to be extremely chaotic. Fred and Ken will love it, Michael."

"When are the Closing Ceremonies, Sheena?" Michael questioned Sheena as they sat down at a table.

"On August the twenty-forth," she replied, spreading butter on her bagel. "Then we leave on the twenty-fifth. So . . . looking forward to your game today, Michael?"

"Er . . . kind of," Michael said, and Sheena laughed. "If we win, I think we move on in the tournament and hopefully place for a medal."

Sara, Tomas, and Delbin joined the three of them at the table later while the adults went up to get coffee.

"We finally get to see you play," Tomas replied, buttering a crumpet. "We tried watching you on television, but all they show is the stupid gymnastics."

Sheena gave Tomas an I-hope-you-take-that-back look that made Tomas recoil slightly. Blushing out of embarrassment, he muttered, "Sorry."

"Yeah, we're versing Cuba," Michael said in a slightly raised voice which made Sheena take her attention off of Tomas, who looked as though he wanted to melt into the ground like the Wicked Witch of the West.

"Is this the only game left?" Sara asked.

"I hope not."

Lunch was an enjoyable affair later in the morning. His whole team came by the table to talk to Michael, smiling with glee as they had learned yesterday how Michael's friends were coming to see him and they wanted to have the opportunity to introduce themselves, especially Fred. To nobody's surprise, Fred merely nodded at Tomas before turning to Sara and immediately offered his friendship to her ("Can I have your number?" Fred asked Sara eagerly, causing Matt and Tomas to curl their hands into fists). Thinking it would be slightly problematic if they punched Michael's teammate, Sara slipped Fred her number when the two of them weren't looking. It was only then that Fred told Michael that they were expected at the field at eleven, precisely two hours before the first pitch.

"Two hours before the game?" Tomas asked, incredulously.

"Yep," Fred said, unconcernedly. "We like to get warmed up ahead of time, you see."

"That is *ridiculous*," Tomas said.

"This isn't little league, Tomas," Sara reminded him, looking at him with a mixture of exasperation and amusement.

"Sheena, when are your competitions?" Michael asked, now pouring milk on his cereal.

"I have one at one o' clock today and then I'm done," Sheena said, looking happy that Michael was taking an interest in her athletics, particularly after Tomas had bashed it.

Michael shook his head. He was hoping to see Sheena compete again, but unfortunately her competitions coincided with his game.

"I'm sorry, Sheena. I would go if I could."

"Don't worry about it," Sheena assured him. "I appreciate the consideration."

Sara flashed Michael an exasperated and jealous look and Tomas kicked her under the table while pointing in Matt's direction. Matt immediately took his eyes off Sara and began fiddling absent-mindedly with his crutches. It was a relief when Mr. Harrington strolled by to talk to Michael as conflicts of personal interest were beginning to gather steam.

"Michael, I need to talk to you."

Michael looked up to see Mr. Harrington standing to the right of him. Michael got up and so did Delbin. To Michael's great surprise, he did not object.

"Perhaps you better come as well," Mr. Harrington said, smiling. "This affects you as well."

"What do you mean?" Michael questioned as they walked a short distance away from the rest.

Mr. Harrington turned to Delbin, smiling.

"You may have been wondering, Michael, why your parents did not come to support you throughout the Games," Mr. Harrington began, but Michael intervened.

"Yeah, I heard," Michael answered, but Mr. Harrington held his hand up. It was apparent that he wanted to say everything he planned to say without interruption.

"I called your parents before you got here," he explained. "I asked if you had any siblings interested in baseball. I was curious if any of your siblings had an aptitude for baseball. Your mom told me Delbin here was, more so than your other brother Isaac, who seemed to be like my son—not too comfortable with the competing thing. It was then I decided to put her in contacts with great trainers. Since Delbin wanted to go to Beijing, they dropped him off with the Perkins' and I gave them contacts to meet with trainers for Delbin here."

"My birthday is in June, so I could make that cut off for next Olympics. I'll be fourteen, then," Delbin explained.

"Baseball is not a sport next time," Michael reminded Delbin. He turned to Mr. Harrington. "I thought you said that."

"I'm going to try and change that," Mr. Harrington said, determinedly. "I want baseball to be a sport. We'll try to work something out, but I can't promise it. That is on the first order of business once we depart Beijing."

"Mr. Goodwin is going to try as well," Delbin explained. "But he can't promise it as well."

"By the way, sir, how did the meeting go last night?" Michael asked.

Mr. Harrington turned to him. "Well, we at first decided not to say anything about your escapade with Will until after the Olympics. However, after we decided that, a huge predicament ensued."

"What is it?" Delbin and Michael asked.

"One of our dear Committee members stole the scroll when the rest weren't looking," Mr. Harrington said, furiously.

"It's gone!" Michael gasped.

"Yes!" Mr. Harrington said, bitterly. "I know. Now the brothers are going to have a good shot at knowing that the scroll is still out there."

"It has to be Mr. Smith!" Michael fumed, angrily. "He faked his reformation!"

"You're probably right," Mr. Harrington replied, bitterly, shaking his head. "However, we do know that Mr. Smith cannot deliver it to Ying and Yang until after the baseball game. We are hoping that we can distract him to delay him handing the scroll to the brothers. We don't have much time to snatch it back before Mr. Smith can give it to the brothers. Thankfully, the brothers' distrust of Mr. Smith gives us the advantage."

So now the United States had something else to worry about now: if the brothers were able to get the scroll from Mr. Smith, they would lose their advantage in the quest to finding the scroll. Michael wondered miserably whether he would be able to breathe freely until the brothers were thwarted. He had least expected Mr. Goodwin to be careless with the scroll, but Mr. Smith's nerve enabled him to snatch it back.

After lampooning Mr. Smith savagely for a few minutes, Michael and Mr. Harrington headed over to the stadium (Delbin went back to Matt) for the baseball game. On the way there, Mr. Harrington told Michael to pretend as though they do not suspect Mr. Smith at all ("We want to make him feel comfortable so he least expects that we are up to something," Mr. Harrington said, wisely). Michael had to admit that this was not the most practical course of action but it was logical enough for him and he could see the reasoning behind it.

Once he got to the field, Michael pitched hard over the course of two hours but he was not pitching as a starter. Mr. Isol decided to bring out Justin again, banking on the hope that they would be able to use Michael for the possible Gold Medal match. Michael could also understand the rationale behind the move: Justin was undoubtedly the second most reliable pitcher after Michael.

"We'll need you in the long run," Mr. Isol growled in an undertone to Michael.

Michael enjoyed sitting on the bench, drinking Gatorade, but he was not pleased with how the game turned out to be. Mr. Isol's plan had gone horrendously wrong. Cuba absolutely crushed Justin and he only lasted three innings after giving up three quick runs. Once Justin got back in the dugout, he punched the dugout wall in anger, breaking his hand and was forced into the locker room to bandage his hand up.

The relievers were able to give Cuba another seven runs and Joe gave up a grand slam, causing him to throw a temper tantrum out on the mound, almost like a little bratty girl being denied a pony for Christmas. Meanwhile, the offense looked nearly as pathetic as a filthy pillowcase. The only show of life from Michael's team was a rare Xavier solo shot and a Nitro RBI single, which barely made it out of the infield. The final score was 10-2. Overall, it was a really brutal game and everyone trudged back into the locker room once the Cuban team ran out onto the field to celebrate looking like they all just swallowed lemons.

The coaches gave the team some news about their final game. Thankfully, they weren't eliminated from competition yet, but they could not afford another mistake.

"Okay, team," Mr. Isol said with the air of one trying to make it sound like a D on a report card was of little to no importance, "due to the fact we got our butts kicked, we will be in the Bronze Medal game."

"Who are we playing?" Nitro asked out loud.

"We will be taking on Japan," Mr. Oberfels answered him, as Mr. Harrington opened his mouth.

"That will be fun," Fred replied, as if there was nothing better in the world than looking at Japanese people. "Orientals . . . excellent . . ."

"We need to win or we leave with no medal," Mr. Isol growled. "Do you understand? The time for bullshit is over. We need to crush them or else you all are going to look like a mashed brownie once I deal with you! This bullshit ends now!"

The team nodded looking suddenly fearful. They all knew that Mr. Isol's words were empty, but it still had a powerful effect on them—Mr. Isol proved capable of defeating an army of twelve with his fists.

"Anyway," Mr. Smith replied. "Even if we don't win the medal, we still could praise anyone who gets a contract from the MLB. Is anyone trying to?"

"My brother James is," Nitro piped up. "He's finding it hard, since he got injured. He has not got many deals to work with. His injury has left skeptics believing that his injury history may be a problem in the MLB. Coach Harrington, he said he'll tell you when he agrees to a contract. It will be done by tomorrow."

"Excellent," Mr. Harrington replied, clapping his hands. "Everyone, you are free to go. Christopher, Glenn . . . Please remain behind and assist me in sweeping the dugout . . . The staff here never do it, the lazy ghouls . . ."

Michael hurried out of the locker room and ended up engaging in conversation with Nitro, who had followed him out of the locker room.

"What teams are interested in your brother, Nitro?" Michael queried interestedly.

"Not many," Nitro replied conversationally. "He told me two teams are, though. He got calls from the Tampa Bay Rays and the Texas Rangers. There may be more, though. No team has offered him a decent contract yet. However, my brother says he isn't expecting to get a decent offer so he may pull the trigger on one of those offers."

Michael found his friends waiting for him at the edge of the stadium. They all looked annoyed as if Michael denied them a trip to the ice cream parlor.

"Man, that was a brutal game," Matt said, as Michael walked right by them. Nitro left in a different direction but not before saying "Hi Sheena," as he passed, causing Matt to raise his eyebrows suspiciously.

"Tell me about it," Michael replied, wearily. "Where are we going?"

"Oh, we are going to a restaurant," Sara and Sheena replied.

"Why?"

"My dad thinks it would be nice," Sara replied.

"It would be great," Michael agreed. "I need something to look forward to."

The Perkins took all of them to a simple restaurant but it cost well over two hundred dollars for everyone. However, for Michael, Matt, Sheena, all the Goodwins, Delbin, the Perkins, Mr. Harrington, and Tomas, it was pretty good.

Despite the woeful game, Michael enjoyed it a lot. He enjoyed watching Sheena tease Matt about Sara, and Matt getting redder; Delbin talking with Shawna and Ember in a hushed voice ("Do you play any sports—?"; "Yeah, I am a gymnast and Ember likes soccer"); Mr. Harrington was talking to the adults about how the team played in today's game ("I've seen little leaguers play better than us and they get paid in ice cream cones instead of money for their efforts").

They left when it was almost nine o' clock at night. Everyone was full and sleepy that they were hardly any talking. Michael knew tomorrow it was up to him to defeat Japan and seize the bronze medal. The team taking home a medal was entirely on him, so if he lost, would it be his fault?

When Michael and Matt got into their room, they got into bed without taking off their clothes. Matt's snores told Michael he was fast asleep and before long, Michael, too, was fast asleep.

Where was the scroll, and was it still tied up in the ribbon? Their suspicions did not equal any answers, and all it did was give Michael nightmares throughout the night. He woke up at least three times during the night, drenched in sweat. He felt terrible, and the thought of whether Mr. Smith will triumph over them pierced him as if a sword had run right through him.

All Michael knew for sure was the fact that if they did not do anything about it, the brothers would receive it.

And if they did, they would be one step closer to achieving their ultimate objective.

CHAPTER 26

THE ACCOMPLICE OVERHEARD

Michael woke up on the day before the Closing Ceremonies terrible, as if he had been sick all night long. It was August the twenty-third and the last baseball game was today. Michael would be done with baseball if he could fight his way to a victory for not only his team, but his country. All of them were counting on him to produce a win.

Michael showered and persuaded a sleepy Matt to do the same. Then, after Matt had taken a shower which seemed to wake him up, the two of them walked down to breakfast, Matt slouching a little.

They must have slept too long because by the time they got down there, everyone was waiting there. Sheena and her family, Sara and her family, Tomas and Delbin, the four coaches, and Michael's teammates were all surrounding a table, looking anxious and were seemingly waiting for Michael's arrival.

"Where the hell were you, Michael?" Fred asked. "We need to get down to the field in a half hour!"

"You're joking!" Michael said, jumping as if he had received a huge electrical shock.

"No we aren't!" Nitro exclaimed. "You two have slept way too long!"

Michael glanced at his watch. He was shocked to see that Nitro and Fred were right.

"I'm sorry," Michael apologized, stifling a yawn. "I thought the game was at four!"

"It got changed," Mr. Isol growled. "The Chinese people *conveniently* told us they needed the field at four. They said something about stupid pictures and some other event! This is what happens when you have a Committee with no leader to turn to!"

He said it in such a voice that made taking pictures sound like it was only appropriate for kindergarten children.

"You're fine, right, Michael?" Mr. Harrington asked, anxiously.

"You don't look well," Sheena commented, peering into his face, looking slightly concerned.

Michael did feel terrible like he had a slight head cold, but he wasn't going to tell them that.

"I'm alright," he lied. "I'm just tired."

"Here, eat something, Michael," Mr. Goodwin said, pushing some toast towards him.

"I'm not hungry," Michael said, quickly. He honestly felt that if he attempted to eat anything he would vomit it straight back up.

"Please eat," Mrs. Goodwin wheedled him. "You need your strength."

Michael took the remaining seat and tried to eat, but it was like chewing wood. The team left and so did the coaches, leaving the Goodwins and his friends with him.

"It'll be over after today," Sara replied, while Matt said, "In about four hours, you'll have the medal."

Michael nodded. He appreciated the support his friends were giving him. He turned to Mr. Goodwin.

"Mr. Goodwin, what are we going to do about the scroll?" he asked, anxiously. "Mr. Harrington told me what happened to it."

Mr. Goodwin shook his head. "Don't worry about it. The Committee and I will take care of it. Just concentrate on pitching today."

"You'll be fine," Tomas replied, soothingly.

Michael, who suddenly felt wide awake as though he had woken up from a long hibernation, started eating his toast. Sheena looked relieved.

"So are you taking Mr. Smith into custody?" Michael asked, demolishing his toast and draining his orange juice in one gulp.

"Well," Mr. Goodwin replied, "we are going to corner him after the game. He won't argue or lie because we'll outnumber him by at least five. If he has it, we'll force him to hand it over. If not, then . . . well, we'll worry about that if it happens."

Michael wanted to point out that by that time the brothers would already know about it but decided not to. He knew Mr. Goodwin should not be contradicted right now.

"I better go," he told everyone, leaping to his feet as though he had attempted to sit on a porcupine. "They're expecting me."

"Good luck, Mikey," Tomas said, grinning.

"Good luck!" Sara and Matt said at the same time.

"You'll be fine," Sheena and her sisters said.

Then Delbin said, "We're all behind you, Michael. Make sure you trick those Japanese people with your hang glider."

Michael nodded, for he knew that Delbin was referring to his special breaking pitch that turned out to strike out half the batters he faced thus far. After a hasty wave, Michael tore out of the cafeteria, almost knocking an old lady away from her walker.

Michael dashed back to get his gear in his room. After throwing his glove, bat, batting gloves, uniform, cup, and pants pell-mell into his bag, he quickly tore back down the stairs and out of the hotel. After running across a busy road and almost getting nailed by a Chevrolet Malibu, he reached the baseball stadium, breathless and out of breath but what he saw almost made him drop his bag in surprise. All of his friends were standing casually right outside the stadium, smiling at the look of surprise on his face.

"My dad said we should come," Sheena replied. "He thinks Mr. Smith might try to harm you in any way, so we will be watching that. I'll have to leave before you start, but you'll have support."

"He does?" Michael questioned. "But Mr. Smith isn't mental. He can't get away with that in a baseball stadium in front of thousands of people."

"Yeah, maybe," Matt replied. "But he can as well. Mr. Smith knows you know about it now."

Michael left his friends and brother and headed for the locker room where his team was. All heads turned in his direction when he came in.

"Are you confident, Michael?" Mr. Harrington asked. "Are you ready?"

"Just need to warm up," Michael said, confidently.

"Hey! Michael!" Ken cried across the room. "You know that the best hitter on the Japanese team got injured? He's out for the rest of the Games!"

"You're joking, right?"

"No he's not," Fred replied. "But now that you mention it, I did hear one from some Asian guy about a blonde, a brunette, and a redhead who all go to Las Vegas . . ."

But Fred faltered under the shut-the-hell-up look that Mr. Isol was giving him. Mr. Oberfels then called Mike over.

"Here, Mike, warm him up," Mr. Oberfels replied. "Get your arm loose, and then come back."

"Don't overexert yourself!" growled Isol. "We need you well today."

Michael pitched a practice session and he thought that he and Mike were on the same page. After ten minutes, they walked back to their dugout to find the team running the bases and stretching. Michael relaxed until the game started, then he started walking to the mound when a voice called him back.

"Good luck, Michael."

Michael turned around. It was Mr. Smith, and Michael was surprised. Was Mr. Smith being genuine? Michael shook away the possibility. He knew Mr. Smith was being a phony, but he wasn't going to tell him that. Michael figured the apocalypse must have just started, because he knew Mr. Smith would wish him luck as soon as the Ying-Yang brothers showed one sign of maturity.

"Thanks, Mr. Smith," Michael replied, and then he charged out onto the field with his team.

A great roar of supporters erupted from the stands and Michael felt braver and more confident. The whole crowd seemed to be cheering for his team. He knew he could get this done. Despite his shaky start to the morning, he now felt a lot better and felt that he was going to scrape the medal for his team.

Michael was happy to find out that he was doing his best, and that the hitters on Japan could not hit to save their lives with the absence of their star player. He was able to get through four innings without a hit, and he struck out seven of them. His team, however, only supplied him with two runs thus far, and that was not nearly enough.

Michael helped himself to Gatorade on the bench and found himself sitting next to Mr. Smith.

"Nice pitching, Michael," he replied.

"Thanks," Michael said, sipping his drink.

Mr. Smith looked odd, as if he was trying to tell Michael something important. He also had a nasty grin that he did not like. "Harrington is pleased with your efforts, obviously. He was about to scratch you from the lineup."

"Why?" asked Michael.

"He thought you were under the weather," Mr. Smith explained. "He cares too much for you. However, he is pleased with how you are pitching."

Michael saw Nitro line a double to drive in another run to make it 3-0. The crowd went wild and Nitro clapped his hands enthusiastically as he reached first base.

In the stands, Sara and Matt noticed Michael talking to

Mr. Smith. Sara tapped Mr. Goodwin on the shoulder to get his attention.

"Mr. Goodwin, sir, look," Sara said, pointing to the dugout where the two of them were talking.

"What is it, Sara?" Mr. Goodwin asked.

"Mr. Smith and Michael are talking," Matt answered, before Sara did.

"It probably isn't anything to worry about," Tomas replied. "I mean, if that bloke wanted to harm Michael, he wouldn't do it when his team is in the dugout."

"I think you're right, but is it something to watch?" Sara asked.

"Yes, it is," Mr. Goodwin said. "Keep your eyes on the situation. Mr. Smith is being too friendly for my liking."

In the dugout, Michael looked at Mr. Smith, suspicious still at his behavior.

"I know you still don't trust me, Michael," Mr. Smith said, and Michael was taken aback; Mr. Smith had the ability Ying and Yang had. He could read minds pretty easily. "But I assure you I have truly reformed. I made a formal apology at the Committee meeting that Goodwin called."

That proves nothing, Michael thought. Michael could say he was a cab driver in Sin City, but does that make it true? Michael was smart enough to not take his coach seriously.

"He talked about the scroll?" Michael questioned.

Mr. Smith nodded. "It's a phony, Michael. If I know it, my sources will know it, too."

Michael wondered what he meant by sources. It seemed a little odd for Mr. Smith to be using sources right there. Then, it came to him—he was obliquely referring to the Ying-Yang brothers.

"Mr. Goodwin said the scroll was taken at the meeting," Michael said, frowning. "You don't happen to be this person, do you, Mr. Smith?"

Mr. Smith wore a twisted smile on his face. Michael did not like to see it.

"Of course not," Mr. Smith said, softly. "Of course I'm not. I told you, Durbin . . . I have changed. You better, too, or else you will end up in a similar position I am in right now."

And by that time, he had left the seat to coach first base. Michael grabbed his glove and followed, confused by Mr. Smith's parting words. What did Mr. Smith mean by that?

Michael was able to get through eight innings, only giving up a run. Mr. Isol was debating whether he should stay in the game or not.

"He should, Isol," Mr. Oberfels replied. "He's doing great."

"I think he has done his job," Mr. Smith said, seriously, "let a closer come in."

"Smith, all closers blow every damn game! They make games more of a spectacular thrilling show! I need a pitcher out there who will get the job done quickly. I'm the pitching coach," Mr. Isol replied gruffly, "and I say that this Durbin ought to be put in for the ninth."

Mr. Smith opened his mouth to retort back, but Mr. Oberfels interrupted by yelling at the team to calm down.

Michael was talking to Harry at that time, who was saying he sucked and deserved to be benched. He kept comparing himself to a stupid rabbit, and he lamented to Michael that the only reason he was here is because his father was a part of the Committee.

"I tell you, I close my eyes," Harry told Michael, "and I end up hitting it. It's like magic, I'm not good. I just have luck big time."

"Luck for you is your talent," Michael replied, wearily, who was starting to dread talking to such a negative person. "You're good, you're just—"

"Hey, Michael," Mr. Oberfels interrupted, reaching his star pitcher.

Michael looked up.

"Am I coming out for the ninth?"

"Funny you should ask that. Yes, we think you should," Mr. Isol replied. Michael knew Mr. Smith was not included in that by the muscle going in Mr. Isol's cheek. "Keep loose. We will need you to finish this off."

Michael had a seven run lead, so even if he did poor, he had pitchers to back him up. Michael swore to himself to not make this interesting.

Michael went out to pitch and for the first three batters, he struck out one, gave up a solo shot, and Nitro made a sliding catch to rob a hitter of a hit by about a hundredth of a second. He only needed one more out.

The batter, Taguchi, walked up to home plate and faced Michael, ready for a heroic comeback. However, it was in Michael's plans to not let that happen.

Mike sent Michael the first signal—a fastball.

No problem, Michael thought to himself. He beamed the pitch at the inside corner and Taguchi could not make contact with the ball, resulting in strike one.

The crowd slowly began to rise from their seats; the excitement was palpable. Mike flashed him the signal for a slider. Michael got into his delivery, and let the pitch sail as fast as a speeding car. Taguchi didn't even bother swinging at this one—the ball was already at home plate before he could get himself ready.

"STRIKE TWO!"

The crowd increasingly got louder; groups were stamping their feet, waving flags energetically. Michael couldn't help thinking that this could be it. His next pitch very well could be the last of the sport in the Olympic Games.

Michael didn't need Mike to flash him a signal—he knew what he wanted to do. Intercrossing his middle and pointer fingers on his right hand, he sent the ball sailing towards the batter. It seemed to hang in mid-air as though suspended by invisible lines but only for a second: The ball then went into a nosedive, completely throwing off Taguchi, who swung over the ball before Mike secured it with his glove before the ball hit the ground.

"STRIKE THREE!"

A tide of roars echoed and filled the stadium up. Then before he even knew what was going on, he saw his team dashing toward the mound. The coaches lifted him over the shoulders but the players jumped on them and Michael almost felt as if he had broken his arm (Cliff had accidentally stepped on it). The team was shouting themselves hoarse, and the crowd was celebrating with them. Michael even saw some Chinese citizens leaping in the air, cheering happily before the United States baseball team sank to the ground in a many-armed hug while Fred did a silly dance, shouting nonsense to no one in particular.

The sullen expression of the other teams' faces did not leave them until they stormed out of sight. At that time, Mr. Harrington, who had stormed out onto the stadium, held up the bronze medal, signifying that it was final: Team USA had won the bronze medal. Michael noticed how shiny it was as though someone had scrubbed it vigorously with steel wool.

"WE ARE HAVING A PARTY!" he yelled. "Get your stuff and let's go!"

Team USA, was still laughing and screaming, "We did it!"

Fred was doing a war dance chant that went something like "Japan sucks" but Michael couldn't be sure. Whatever it was, it was stopped quite abruptly by Mr. Oberfels.

Michael didn't get to see his friends until the team was walking to the party area. There was a building next to the baseball field, and Mr. Harrington explained that he had made arrangements to celebrate the team's success in the building whether they won or lost.

Michael's friends were congratulating him when they arrived at the building shortly after Michael's team had gotten comfortable. Inside, it was nicely made, and for being prepared at the last second, it was quite spectacular. Streamers hung from the ceiling and pictures of all the team members were pasted onto the walls with a blank piece of white construction paper below each one, leaving it up for comments. Matt explained to Michael that the place was decorated by him and a few friends.

"We did it," Matt whispered to Michael. "My dad said to form a group to get this place nicely decorated so when your team arrived, it would be all done."

"You did a nice job," Michael said, looking at the team, who were already starting to dance. Ahmad was attempting to do the salsa with little success; he merely looked like a joker trying to pull off some unfathomable trick.

"Sheena, Sara, and Tomas helped me out," Matt said. Then he smirked. "Are you going to enjoy it, Michael?"

"Yes, I will," Michael said, sitting down at a table. "How did Sheena's competition go?"

"Ask her yourself," Matt replied, still smirking. "Are you going to ask her to dance?"

Michael gave a noncommittal grunt. In truth, he would have quite liked to ask her for a dance, but he knew that plucking up the courage was something else. In the end, he decided that he wasn't going to but merely applied himself to his food and talked to his team (many of them weren't too inclined to dance). He saw Fred gripping his groin area and danced so exuberantly that people ended up getting bowled over by him like bowling pins. He watched Cliff do some really creepy dance and he saw George attempt to charm girls by reciting some pick-up lines that Fred picked out for him. Predictably, they weren't too successful as girls would call him a pig, slap him across the face, and storm off.

"Look at your friend, dude!" Ahmad yelled at Michael, pointing. He had abandoned his salsa experiment, and was merely reclining in a chair, holding a glass of what looked like urine in his hand.

Michael turned to see where Ahmad was pointing to and forced back a laugh. Matt was attempting to slow-dance with Sara but it was not going too well—his injured leg didn't seem to be up for such stressful activities such as dancing. As they moved across the floor, Matt's leg gave up on him and he fell hard to the floor, almost crushing Shawna's foot, which had been in that place merely seconds before.

"Nice one, Matty-poo!" Ken yelled. Predictably, he was waving his Cookie Monster hat at him.

Matt attempted to stagger to his feet but he fell down on his butt again. The team laughed, knowing full well that it wasn't particularly funny. Swearing, Matt gave Ken a rude hand gesture that was spotted by Mr. Harrington, who inconveniently was making his way to the table at that time.

"Control your temper, Matthew!" Mr. Harrington scolded sternly, leaving Matt looking angry and embarrassed.

A few minutes later, Michael's teammates joined the party and left him alone at his table. Feeling shy, Michael did not follow them. However, Michael was happy when Sheena came over to him a moment later.

"This is fun," she said, brushing her hair out of her face. She was a little pink. "I was just going around and . . . Michael, are you okay?"

Michael was almost falling asleep and her presence made him awake.

"Oh, I'm fine," Michael replied, looking at her. "A little tired, that's all."

"I'm not surprised," Sheena said, sympathetically, "that game must have cost you all of your energy."

"Hey, Mikey."

Tomas had come over and sat down next to him.

"How come you aren't dancing?" Michael asked.

"I was about to ask you that," Tomas replied glumly. "I asked at least five girls here and they all turned me down."

"I'm sorry, Tomas," Sheena replied, looking apologetic. "My friends are too obsessed with Michael here, I'm afraid."

Tomas sniffed loudly.

"Yeah, that's Michael for you," Tomas said, bitterly. "He was always getting the girls back at Skippack. Well, see you later."

Then he left, looking seriously annoyed.

Sheena looked at Michael expectantly, as though she was expecting him to say something to her. Completely nonplussed, he tried to think of something to say but before he could do so, they were interrupted again by Nitro.

"Hi Michael," Nitro said, abruptly. Then he looked at Sheena. "Would you like to dance with me, Sheena?"

Sheena gave Michael a quick glance before turning back to Nitro.

"Er—okay."

Sheena left Michael and started to make her way out to the floor with Nitro. Ten seconds later, they were slow-dancing (though Sheena kept glancing back at Michael the whole time). Michael couldn't help but clench his fists when he saw Nitro's facial expression. The kid wore a look as though Santa Claus left him an extra toy under his Christmas tree.

Unable to watch the pair of them any longer, Michael felt a sudden urge that he had to go to the restroom. He decided to go but Mr. Oberfels caught him halfway to the door.

"Where are you going?"

"I need to get my ball bag in the locker room," Michael lied, knowing that he needed an excuse to leave the building. "I'll be quick."

"Hurry back," Mr. Oberfels said, imploringly. "We don't want you roaming Beijing alone for very long . . ."

Michael left the party, which became extreme. The music was audible even outside of the building. He looked one last time at Sheena dancing with Nitro; Matt with Sara (they didn't even move but merely swayed on the spot to avoid injury); and Tomas with—who seemed to be being nice to him—Ember. He also saw Delbin looking at Shawna as if he was annoyed someone had taken her. She was busy dancing with a younger kid that looked to be the younger sibling of someone on his team. Michael couldn't believe how Delbin's expression completely resembled his own.

Michael walked out into the perilous grounds of Beijing, China. He only heard crickets in the air and it was cloudy still, as if a huge blanket covered the country. He walked faster, vowing to himself that when he got back, he would get out on the floor and not be a party destroyer. He would even ask Sheena to dance with him; he knew Nitro was a decent enough guy to let him have his opportunity.

Michael decided to travel into the locker room to not do what he had told Mr. Oberfels, but to use the bathroom there to make it look like he had a legitimate reason to leave. After he had finished, he suddenly remembered about Mr. Smith. He had not come to the party. Afraid that Mr. Smith was on his way to deliver the scroll to the brothers, Michael decided to go into the dugout to see if he could find any clues as to where Mr. Smith went.

Michael climbed the dugout stairs and found himself in his own dugout. There were no objects that players had forgotten to pack or clues to indicate where Mr. Smith was. However, there was an object someone had definitely forgotten, and Michael had a shrewd suspicion who.

Miraculously, the scroll was right on the bench, completely still. There was now a ribbon tied around it looking more like an ancient artifact than anything else.

Michael could have shouted out in happiness. What a stupid thief Mr. Smith was. All Michael had to do now was get this scroll to Mr. Goodwin. It would merely take five minutes.

Michael walked by the scroll and picked it up. He did not notice anything unusual about it and reckoned that Mr. Smith merely rolled it up and slipped it into his pocket. It was only convenient that he had completely forgotten that he had the scroll.

Michael was about to pocket the artifact when he heard a curt voice from behind.

"Very good, Michael. Now turn around, nice and slowly, and give that to me."

CHAPTER 27

THE PLIGHT OF THE BROTHERS

Michael felt as if he had received a huge, electric shock. Michael whirred around to see the figure of Mr. Smith, who was pointing a gun at Michael's heart.

"Mr . . . Mr. Smith," Michael spluttered, almost unable to get the words out of his mouth from the shock.

"That's right," he said, smoothly. "Now, give me the scroll, Michael. The brothers would be here any minute, and they would be pleased to see that I have succeeded at last. I told them that it was not the right scroll, but they do not believe me. I need to show them that I am telling the truth."

Despite Mr. Smith's plea, Michael wasn't going to let him do that—if he could avoid it.

"I'm not giving you the scroll," Michael replied, shaking. "You will lead me back to Mr. Goodwin and I'll come quietly with the scroll. You don't have to do this, Mr. Smith."

"It's not up to you to decide what I should or should not do," Mr. Smith insisted. "I need the scroll. The brothers promised to make me rich if I succeeded."

"Mr. Smith, you know this is wrong," Michael protested, shaking. "Don't do this."

"I have no choice!" snarled Mr. Smith, and now a flicker of fear lit up his face.

"How come you have no choice?" Michael countered. He could not think of anything except stall Mr. Smith by keeping him talking. There was no other way he could think of to get out of this. He merely was trying to buy himself more time.

"I have an agreement with the brothers," Mr. Smith said, shortly, but Michael knew there was more to it.

"Great answer. Care to elaborate?"

"No!"

"Why did you come here?" Michael asked.

"I'm not answering any more of your questions!" snapped Mr. Smith, now looking cowardly. It was plain to see that he was trembling to keep his weapon straight.

"How did you find out about the scroll?"

"No more questions, you fool!" Mr. Smith snarled. "We might not have the real scroll, but it is time we get you out of the way!"

Michael did not say anything. He was pressed against the brick dugout wall with Mr. Smith ten to fifteen feet away from him with a gun. Desperately, he tried to make conversation with the cowardly figure.

"Did anyone suspect you?"

"Your girlfriend's father kept an annoyingly close eye on me," Mr. Smith said, carelessly. "He seemed to suspect me."

"That's because I told him my suspicion about you."

Mr. Smith stopped for a moment and pointed the gun at Michael's head.

"Michael, give me the scroll now, or I shall spare your life," Mr. Smith replied as firmly as he could. "If you say no, I shall bring your body back to your girlfriend and your nasty friends."

Michael clenched his fist around the scroll, and looked at Mr. Smith. He had to do some quick thinking.

"Mr. Smith, you don't have to do this," Michael repeated.

"Give me the damn scroll, Durbin, or you will be dead!" Mr. Smith replied, now pointing the gun at Michael's heart again. "The brothers would be here any minute, and they would be pleased to see that I have completed the task! You've caused us enough trouble,

Michael Durbin! The brothers changed their minds and would rather destroy you permanently!"

"The brothers are manipulating you," retorted Michael. "They just want you to carry out their deeds!"

"I—" Mr. Smith broke off, looking uncomfortable as though he knew Michael had just defeated him in some presidential debate. "We have an accord, baseball fool!"

"Mr. Smith, I'll promise I'll clear your name if you get that gun out of my face and help us instead of them!"

"I do not make bargains, Michael!"

"This is your chance, Mr. Smith," Michael said, urgently. "You could abandon the brothers and help me, and you will be cleared. You will have a job. You will have a life. People will like you. You don't have to do this."

"I've got to do this, Michael Durbin. If I don't, the brothers will kill me. Give me the scroll."

Mr. Smith looked urgently at Michael, and Michael understood at once the conflict that was raging in Mr. Smith's head. Mr. Smith had to kill him or else he would be killed.

"You know I'm right, don't you?" Michael asked. "You could die a hero."

"I need to turn my life around. Give me the scroll!"

Michael shook his head. Mr. Smith raised the gun. Mr. Smith was clearly steering himself to press the trigger.

"Murdering fourteen-year-old athletes does not turn your life around!" Michael retorted.

"Michael, I will give you one last chance. Hand me the scroll, or I'll carry your body back to your weeping girlfriend. I'm sure she'll want to see you one last time."

Michael looked at the scroll. He had no choice; there was no way he could get out of this. He had to give it away and then alert Mr. Goodwin to hopefully stop him from giving it to the brothers.

"If you run away after you give it to me, you will die anyway," Mr. Smith replied, silkily, as if he read Michael's mind. "Give me the scroll."

Michael realized he had no choice. He held out the scroll and Mr. Smith jumped forward to take it.

Bang! Mr. Smith flung himself back and Michael noticed a silver blur coming out of nowhere and crashed into the dugout wall. Stone covered the dugout in debris.

"Ah, look, it's Durbin—"

"—With the scroll as well . . ."

Michael did not need another guess to tell who it was. Ying and Yang walked up to Mr. Smith with a swagger and sounding like they were bullfrogs sizing up a pair of juicy flies. They looked at Mr. Smith, who was getting up on his feet.

Without warning, the brothers pointed their guns at Mr. Smith's heart. Mr. Smith looked confused.

"I got Michael cornered with the scroll! Why are you pointing your guns at me for?"

"Smith, you are to shut up!" Ying snarled. "You lied to us. You said you would have the scroll and you don't. Durbin does. You . . . have . . . failed."

"I got him cornered for us!" Mr. Smith protested. "We can deal with him now!"

Michael thought that the brothers were being ridiculous that he was very much on Mr. Smith's side. Mr. Smith had him cornered after all, but glancing at the brothers' faces he could tell that they were beyond reason.

"True, Smith, you were not completely worthless," Yang sneered. "But you made promises that you failed to keep. We expected you to get the scroll and kill Durbin. You have fulfilled neither requirement."

"You will be paying the price after we deal with Durbin here," Ying replied, now turning to Michael. "Give us the scroll, Durbin, or you will receive the punishment that we are going to give Smith here. We want to be sure it is not the real one. Hand it over."

Mr. Smith moaned. Michael did not need any explanations. They were going to kill him first, then take the scroll, and kill Mr. Smith. And now, Michael needed to keep himself alive, and, however Mr. Smith had treated him, he needed to get him out alive as well. The odds, for both happening, were near impossibility. Desperate, Michael attempted to use the same technique he used on Mr. Smith to stop him from killing him—if he could keep them occupied in a conversation, help may arrive for him.

"Durbin, you are not being a good little boy," Yang said in a mocking voice. "Give me the scroll so you get to live."

"Stop lying!" Michael shouted. "You plan on killing me anyway!"

"You are alone, Durbin!" Ying snarled. "No one is here to help you. You are fighting a battle you cannot win."

"He won't be alone!"

Michael could have cheered out loud. He saw Delbin, Sheena, Matt, Mr. Goodwin, Mr. Harrington, and Mr. Isol come up right by him. Matt was leaning on his crutches with his teeth gritted in pain as if the sight he was seeing was too nauseating for him.

"You got the scroll back, Michael!" Mr. Goodwin said. "Good, that's good."

"Ah, William Goodwin," Yang sneered. "Can't say I'm pleased to see you, but I hope I find you in good condition."

"I can't say I'm too excited to be seeing you either, Yang," Mr. Goodwin replied, inclining his head. "Get away from Michael!"

The brothers laughed as though Mr. Goodwin had said an amusing joke.

"Goodwin, you will tell Michael to give us the scroll or you all will die," Yang snarled.

"He will not give you the scroll!" Matt shouted.

Ying smiled nastily. "Harrington, I have something to interest you in. Your friend Smith here has been helping me get the scroll."

"I know that," Mr. Harrington replied, nastily.

Ying pointed one gun at Michael and his friends and Yang pointed his at Mr. Smith.

"It's over," Ying replied in a menacing voice. "Mr. Smith, you are to get the scroll from them now or my bullet shall penetrate your skull and turn your brain into goo!"

Mr. Smith hesitated for only a brief moment. Then he walked over to Michael. He looked at him for a second, then said, "I'm sorry, Michael."

Mr. Smith's fist landed hard in Michael's stomach, sending him right into the dugout wall. Michael saw his friends defend him, but Michael found the scroll wrenched out of his hands by someone he could not see.

Michael was helped to his feet by Mr. Isol and saw Mr. Smith with the scroll in his hands, facing the brothers.

"I got it!" Mr. Smith replied triumphantly. "Now I can prove to you that this is not the real one."

"I'm afraid a see a snag in that, Smith," Yang said, smoothly.

Mr. Smith trembled. "You're—you're going to kill me, are you?"

The brothers let out a harsh laugh. "He's not stupid after all, is he, Yang?"

"For once in his worthless life he is not."

Mr. Harrington took three strides and stood in front of Mr. Smith.

"You will not kill him," he said, clearly to the brothers. "You will leave now. If you are lucky, the authorities might not find you."

"The authorities are in our pocket, Harrington," Yang sneered, raising the gun.

"No, they aren't anymore," Mr. Goodwin snarled. "They have been searching for you ever since you've abducted my daughter!"

Mr. Isol looked at Michael, Delbin, Sheena, and Matt. "Go on, leave."

"We can't," Delbin said.

"Go!"

Ying laughed. "If you even attempt to leave, you will die, so I would not try to."

Delbin gulped. Sheena trembled. Matt looked livid.

Michael looked at the brothers. They were pointing the guns at him.

"Michael, you have irked us for too long," Ying replied, coldly. "Too often have you infuriated me and Yang. You notice that you are too nosy to live. You have failed to be killed by my associates, but if you weren't killed by them, we would. Good-bye, Michael."

Michael did not act a moment too soon. Ying fired the gun and Michael ducked, the bullets flying over him. Michael heard a scuffling noise and saw the guns fly away from everyone. Sheena ran to him and tugged him by the arm away from the action; Matt was shielding Delbin; Mr. Isol was pummeling the brothers; Mr. Smith was just watching, scared.

The brothers picked up the guns as Mr. Isol was charging at them. The brothers dodged Mr. Isol, who dived at them and they aimed the gun at Michael.

Mr. Goodwin rammed into them with his shoulder, making their aim go awry. At that time, Mr. Smith came to them, avoiding another gun shot that sailed between his legs.

"You kids have to escape," Mr. Smith replied breathlessly. "Before Ying and Yang get you."

"Mr. Smith—?" Sheena began, but Mr. Goodwin cut her off.

"Sheena, take your friends, and go!"

Michael looked at Mr. Smith.

"I said you could do something worthwhile," Michael replied.

"I'm not doing this for you!" Mr. Smith snarled. "I was a dead duck right from the get-go for dealing with those two! I just didn't realize that until now!"

Then, with a little hesitation, he handed Michael the scroll. "Take it."

Mr. Harrington was thrown back and he crashed against the wall, and was still.

"He has the scroll! Michael has it!"

Michael hurried to the exit after his friends, but Mr. Smith accidentally tripped him. Michael fell, and Ying took Michael, and threw him back in the dugout as Michael covered up the scroll.

Sheena, Matt, and his brother were gone, probably alerting everyone. He might never see them again—

Michael and Mr. Smith stood with their backs against the dugout wall, looking transfixed at the gun that Ying was holding at them.

"Let me show you what a double play looks like," he sneered at them.

"I don't think so," Michael said in a low voice.

Ying fired the gun at him and he and Mr. Smith went in opposite directions, trying to avoid it. Michael heard it hit something as he tripped over debris. Covering his head, he saw brick falling right beside him.

Yang attempted to shoot at Michael again but Mr. Isol jumped on him from behind. Yang struggled to throw off the beastly man and with his bare hands. Mr. Isol knocked Yang out against the dugout floor and tossed him into his brother, knocking him to the ground and causing him to let go of his gun, which fell at Mr. Goodwin's feet. In one swift moment, Mr. Goodwin took the gun and with great difficulty, smashed it against the dugout, breaking it into two segments. As Mr. Isol broke Yang's gun with his bare hands, Ying laughed loudly as though he could have wished for nothing better than being cornered by his adversaries.

"I don't need a gun anymore!" he shouted. "I'm leaving!"

"What do you mean?"

Before anyone could do anything, Ying leaped to his feet and scooped up his brother. With great difficulty, he threw him into the field. Then, gracefully, he vaulted into the field before Mr. Isol could try to grab him by his ankles. The group was forced to watch as Ying scooped up his twin and dashed away from them as darkness swallowed the brothers.

Michael got gingerly to his feet. He saw Mr. Isol helping Mr. Harrington to his feet and Mr. Goodwin breathing hard, as though he had just ran a 5K.

"Is everyone okay?" Mr. Goodwin questioned.

"I'm fine," Michael said. Then he held out the scroll. "I still have it, sir."

"Give it to me later," Mr. Goodwin replied, firmly. "We need to get back to the others. Let's get out of here."

"Goodwin, where is Smith?" Mr. Isol asked. "I can't see him in this dugout."

"He must have escaped with the brothers," Mr. Goodwin replied.

"He didn't," Michael said. "He would have been killed if he even tried."

"True, Michael. I didn't think of that. So where is he? Did he leave to go somewhere else?"

"He can't have."

Mr. Harrington was looking grim. He was looking at the other three, who were all looking confused at this announcement. "What do you mean?"

"I see him," Mr. Harrington replied. "Over here. I'll show you."

The three of them followed Mr. Harrington and they stopped quite abruptly at the middle of the stairway down to the locker room.

"He's right there," Mr. Harrington said, his voice shaking. Michael looked down at the bottom of the staircase and gasped. Mr. Smith was laying there, his mouth slightly agape. He had a dark hole spreading down his front and his eyes were still open, wide in shock and horror, and the ghost of his snarl was still etched upon his face. Mr. Smith had died, cowardly trying to flee from the dugout. Michael figured he must have changed sides because help had arrived for Michael, including Mr. Isol. He died as a coward. He died as he lived.

Michael hurried to the bottom of the stairway. The three adults did the same. They were all still staring at Mr. Smith, lost for words. Michael was still finding it hard to believe that he was gone though (feeling terrible about this thought) Michael knew that due to the fact he was constantly mean to Michael and attempted to give him to the brothers, Michael's sympathy was limited for his death. He wouldn't miss him one bit.

"What are we going to do with him?" Michael queried.

"We must take him with us," Mr. Goodwin replied, heavily. "Then we must decide where he needs to go, but not certainly today."

Mr. Isol picked up the remainder of Mr. Smith's body and led the way out of the stadium. There was no noise. Nobody was even outside.

Michael felt tired. He wanted nothing else then to spend the rest of the Olympics enjoying life with his friends. He did not want to overexert himself on anything. Michael couldn't believe how quickly all the events had transpired. It seemed like no time at all passed when he was watching Nitro dance with Sheena.

Mr. Goodwin was looking at him suspiciously as they followed Mr. Isol. "Are you alright, Michael?"

Michael felt it would be better to be honest with him.

"Fine, just tired," Michael replied, stifling a yawn. "I'm getting used to this action-packed stuff by now."

"You need to rest tomorrow before the Ceremonies," Mr. Harrington advised. "Our team will be announced and I would like you there as this would be your only chance to experience it—even though it is not expected to be organized."

"Where exactly are we going?" Michael questioned.

"We are heading to your hotel," Mr. Goodwin answered. "I'm going to let everyone know what happened. Your friends are going to be worried. Your brother needs to know you're okay as well. Mr. Oberfels and my wife are with all of them, I'm sure. I'll call them and tell them to meet us there."

They walked in silence (besides Mr. Goodwin's call) for a few more minutes and soon enough, they arrived at the hotel. Michael saw his friends there, his baseball team, and his brother, and everyone he cared about. They were all looking anxious and relieved at the same time. Michael could see Nitro standing right next to Sheena as though he was determined to not give her an inch of personal space.

"Michael!"

Sara and Sheena had run over to Michael and hugged him.

"I thought you were—"

"We were worried!"

"I'm alright," Michael answered, giving both of them a hasty pat on the shoulder. "Mr. Smith isn't though."

"Why?"

Delbin, Matt, and Tomas had come over as well. The rest of the baseball team, including the Perkins family and Mr. Oberfels all looked mildly interested on what happened in the dugout.

"He's dead," Michael replied.

"No way," Matt replied, shaking his head. "How is that possible?"

"Mr. Isol brought him with us," Michael explained. "Ying shot a bullet at him when he was trying to save his own life."

"We found out very quickly that they were there to not only take care of Michael," Mr. Goodwin explained to the group, who were listening avidly. "They were there to also kill Mr. Smith and seize the scroll. They obviously had given up on Mr. Smith as a bad job. In fact, I think they wanted to kill Mr. Smith more than Michael."

"Ying and Yang treated Mr. Smith like an expendable soldier," Mr. Harrington replied gravely. "He finally realized that once the brothers cornered him. He seemed to know he had no chance of getting out his situation alive, no matter if he did what the brothers asked."

Sheena looked horrified and faced Michael. "You could have died!"

"I know," Michael said, fully realizing how close he was to death. "I didn't even think about that."

"Wait until Mom and Dad hear this, Michael!" Delbin exclaimed excitedly. "They'll be proud of what you accomplished in the past two weeks."

"I accomplished enough to last a lifetime," Michael groaned.

Everyone laughed.

CHAPTER 28

THE NEW TEXAS RANGER

Michael slept very late the next day. He did not go to bed until past midnight and he slept until almost noon next day. He felt tired, and it was hard to believe the Olympics were almost over—but that didn't mean he was happy about it.

He knew that he was going to miss Matt and Sheena. He owed both of them and their families so much. Without their kindness, Michael knew he would have been done. He only hoped that they understood he cared about them a lot—more than he could express in words.

He joined everyone at the hotel cafeteria and helped himself to a huge hot brunch which included cheesy eggs, bacon, and orange juice. For the first time this Olympics, he felt completely normal and he enjoyed his breakfast as he talked and laughed with his friends. Nitro attempted to butt into the conversation but to Michael's relief, Fred ushered him over to his table to allow Michael to talk to his friends.

Sara and Tomas gave Michael and Delbin some very important information at breakfast. Michael learned that he was to come home with the Perkins, who booked airplane tickets.

"I'll pay for mine," Michael replied. "I have money."

"You don't need to," Tomas answered.

"I know," Michael said, "but I feel I should."

After breakfast, Mr. Harrington told all of them the Closing Ceremonies are starting at eight o' clock at night.

"Make sure you are by the entrance to the Bird's Nest at that time," Mr. Harrington told Michael, who said that he would. "I want you there."

Michael spent the morning over the Goodwin's house with all his friends. It felt nice not to be involved in something so dangerous and serious for once.

"You guys will enjoy the Closing Ceremonies," Sheena informed them as they all congregated into the living room, plopping themselves on the couch. "They're fun. It won't be the same, but it'll be fun."

"Yeah," Matt said, vaguely. "Just like the Games. No one's going to look at the Olympic Games as a friendly competition anymore. The brothers changed the Games for the foreseeable future."

"I agree, Matt. To tell you the truth, I don't know whether I enjoyed this Olympics or not because of what you said," Michael replied, who was sitting next to Ember.

"WHAT?" Ember and Sara cried.

"Say what you think," Michael replied grimly, "I haven't forgotten about how much trouble the scroll got me into. And to add getting shot at, you won't forget that in a hurry."

"I guess you're right," Shawna replied.

"Where do you think the brothers are now?" Tomas queried to Michael, curiously. "They can't be roaming the streets, what with the police after them and all, right?"

Michael had been wondering the same thing but everyone was waiting for his answer, so he gave it.

"I think we can assume that they have gone into hiding," Michael said, finally. "They can never be in a position of power ever again, that's for sure. I'm sure the police are searching for the brothers . . . And the United States as well . . ."

"Michael?"

Michael whirled around. It was Mr. Goodwin.

"Can I have a word with you, Michael?"

"Sure," he replied, walking over to him after muttering a goodbye to everyone else.

Mr. Goodwin led Michael into his study where there was still the large amount of papers that cluttered up Mr. Goodwin's in-tray. Michael stepped around the overflowing trash can while Mr. Goodwin sank into his over-stuffed computer chair.

"Are you still busy?" Michael asked, appalled to see how strenuous Mr. Goodwin's job actually was.

"Unfortunately," Mr. Goodwin replied, yawning. "Being the president is a very busy job. Anyway, Michael, I wanted to talk to you."

"What about, sir?" Michael queried.

"First of all," Mr. Goodwin said, "I want to thank you. You shown your loyalty to your country by doing what you accomplished this Olympics, far more than anyone has ever done."

"Thanks," Michael replied. Then he handed over the scroll. He had brought it with him to give to Mr. Goodwin directly. "You should take this, sir."

"Thanks, Michael," Mr. Goodwin replied, taking it. "I was hoping you'd remember to bring it. We have decided to take care of the scroll in a proper manner."

"Which is what?" Michael questioned.

"We have decided to burn it at the Closing Ceremonies," Mr. Goodwin replied, "I also informed the police of the brothers. They are alerting the local police corps about them as we speak. I'm hoping that the brothers won't be able to avoid detection."

"We shouldn't burn the scroll," Michael said, seriously.

Mr. Goodwin looked surprised. "Why do you say that?"

Michael sighed. "I want to find out who this Sandra woman is. I want to find out as much information about the brothers and Mr. Smith as I can. The more we find out about them, the easier it will be to locate the real scroll. You should keep it and see if it can provide you clues or information."

Mr. Goodwin nodded slowly, smiling. He seemed to approve of Michael's thinking.

"I like that idea. I accept your word. I'll let everyone know that."

"Did the police seem confident that they could catch him?"

Mr. Goodwin shook his head. "They warned the public to keep an eye out for them, but they didn't seem too optimistic about their chances in catching them. They are not going to last too long. The police should be able to catch them in no time."

Michael, however, thought the opposite. It was true that the brothers weren't the sharpest tools in the shed, but they were admittedly more intelligent than what he and the United States were giving them credit for.

"I would not bet on that," Michael said, seriously, and, in spite of himself, he smiled. "They probably could last quite a while. I think they'll last until they find me, and by that time, they'll try to harm me. Either way, I'm sure I am going to see them again."

"Unusual prediction, Michael," Mr. Goodwin remarked. "But surely you do not want that to happen, right?"

"No, of course not," Michael said, quickly, and Mr. Goodwin laughed.

"Michael, you could go out with your friends again, I think I said everything of importance."

"Okay, sir."

Michael was at the door when Mr. Goodwin called him back. Michael turned around to see Mr. Goodwin grinning similarly to Mr. Harrington.

"If you ask me, Michael, I think my daughter would be very impressed with your actions from the past two weeks," Mr. Goodwin replied, smirking.

"Oh, shut up, sir," Michael said, and Mr. Goodwin roared with laughter as Michael closed the door and rejoined his friends.

★ ★ ★

Michael enjoyed the whole morning and part of the afternoon with his friends. They played video games for a while and then went outside and just talked. Tomas was sullen throughout the conversation and Michael felt a scrap of pity for him—he seemed to feel awkward, like he didn't fit in with the rest of them.

After eating a late dinner with his friends at a nearby McDonald's, Sheena told all of them they should start going down to the Bird's Nest.

"We don't want to be the last people there," Sheena replied.

"I'm sure we won't," Matt assured her. "There will be last minute stragglers."

All of them walked to the Bird's Nest together as one huge group. It was already dark out and light illuminated the stadium. The voices of people cheering were loud enough to reach Istanbul. Michael could never remember feeling so excited in his life, not even during the Opening Ceremonies while he was waiting for his country to be called.

"We'll be in the stands," Sara told Michael as they reached the entrance. "We can't go in there."

"See you later, Michael," Delbin said, and he scuttled off with Sara and Tomas.

The Goodwin family hurried off with them as well leaving Michael, Matt, and Sheena to walk over to find their country in a huge mass of color.

The sight of all the Olympic teams clustered together as though in some prodigious scatter plot was incredible. All the athletes were moving around, talking to each other and congratulating them on their performances. Michael, Matt, and Sheena weaved their way in between people until they heard a familiar voice over the hubbub.

"MICHAEL, OVER HERE!"

Mr. Harrington was calling him about fifty feet away. Michael squeezed his way over to his coach. Matt and Sheena followed him.

"Your friends can stay here as well," Mr. Harrington replied. "We really aren't going by teams for this one. This ceremony is disorganized based on what happened throughout the Olympics. The Chinese had a plan like they did at the Opening Ceremonies, but none of the performers were prepared completely and Ying and Yang didn't coordinate the Closing Ceremonies well."

"That's fine, it actually works out better," Michael said, cheerfully. He was glad that he could spend this ceremony with his friends that stuck with him throughout the whole entire Olympics. Matt and Sheena obviously felt the same way by the looks of their relieved faces.

"I don't want to go by my diving team," Matt answered, relieved. "They provoke me because of my age and call me a wimp for getting hurt. Also, I'm short compared to them."

"I wonder what I'll be then," Michael replied. "If you're a midget on that team, what do you think I'll be?"

"One step shorter than midget," Matt answered.

"What is that?" Sheena asked, teasingly. "Deformed?"

Matt laughed. Michael looked at her in a mock, hurtful way.

"Nah, they'll probably think I'm one of the Seven Dwarfs."

Matt laughed, but was cut off when Nitro came over to them.

"Hey Michael, guess what?"

"What?"

"My brother got signed!" Nitro said, excitedly, as if he was the one signed to a team.

"Awesome. What is the team, Nitro?"

"The Texas Rangers!" Nitro said, happily. "He got a three-year deal! I don't know how much. You can talk to him if you like. He's over here!"

Nitro led Michael, Matt, and Sheena over to where James was talking to Mr. Isol. Mr. Isol noticed the four of them coming because he said good-bye to James and walked back to Mr. Harrington. Once they reached James, he nodded at them, looking pleased.

"The Closing Ceremonies are starting in ten minutes, Nitro," James informed his brother.

"We know," Sheena replied, unexpectedly.

James looked to the right to face her. "Nitro, are these your friends?"

"Yes," Nitro said, and then he introduced the three of them. "That's Michael, Matt, and Sheena."

"Congratulations on getting that contract," Michael replied.

"Thanks," James said, grinning. "It was rather unexpected, you know. I thought my injury might hinder me from getting a contract but as I'm sure you know, life can surprise you sometimes . . . Just like seeing Nitro with friends . . ."

James stopped abruptly, knowing that he shouldn't have said the last bit. Shaking his head slightly, he looked back at Michael, giving him a look that clearly said not to mention what he had said to his brother.

"I've seen you pitch. You really put on an excellent show. You filled in my place when I got injured. I appreciate that. I really wished I could have been in the dugout with you guys."

James then turned back to Michael's friends.

"Nitro's told me about all of you," James said, pleasantly. Then he narrowed his eyes at Sheena playfully. "Especially you, Sheena."

Sheena looked surprised.

"Really?" she asked him. Matt threw Nitro a filthy look.

"Yeah. Sometimes, I have to tell him to shut up!" James replied, casting his brother an amused look and looking exactly like Mr. Goodwin when he told Michael that his daughter couldn't shut up about him.

"How big was your contract?" Matt asked, excitedly, even though Michael knew he wanted to draw the conversation away from Nitro talking about his best friend. James seemed to catch on but didn't seem to mind the changing of the subject.

"Oh, it was a three-year, twenty million dollar offer but not much of it is guaranteed," James replied casually, as if everyone got twenty million dollars on a regular basis. "I think it is a lot, but the other teams only offered me five hundred thousand with nothing guaranteed, so I went with the Rangers. They're banking on the hope that my stats in Athens would show up for them. I'm getting my uniform tonight."

"What number are you going with?" Sheena asked.

"Forty-seven," James answered. "I was going to have thirty-seven, but someone on the Rangers already has that number, so I had to switch."

Michael noticed while he was talking to James that a group of four girls which he recognized as the girls Sheena had talked to when they first arrived in China were ogling at him as if they never saw something more awe-inspiring. They were pointing and giggling at Michael, which Michael found extremely annoying and unfair. Michael found himself wishing that giggling was to be made illegal.

Sheena, noticing this as well, said, "Get used to it."

"I've noticed," Michael replied, bitterly.

"Those girls are on my gymnastics team," Sheena replied, "all they talk about is you. I've told them about you, so they are basically worshiping you now."

"I'm used to it," Michael said, darkly, even though he was glad that they didn't hate him; the Ying-Yang brothers were enough.

An announcement suddenly crackled over the Bird's Nest and a loud, booming voice echoed throughout the stadium.

"LADIES AND GENTLEMEN, I WANT TO CORDIALLY WELCOME YOU TO THE CLOSING CEREMONIES OF THE 2008 SUMMER GAMES AT BEIJING!"

After the crowd began to cheer even more boisterously, Michael found himself walking out onto the stadium for the Closing Ceremonies.

It was incredible for the amount of noise that the stadium made. Everyone was up on their feet, screaming, hollering, and stamping their feet. Michael kept bumping into people as he looked around the stadium, wanting to catch in all the sights. He found himself wishing that he had six more eyes. Everywhere he looked, something riveting was occurring. Whether it was a dazzling firework (coming from the Fireworks Factory which Michael supposed was now controlled by the Chinese Government) or an athlete talking to a reporter, Michael couldn't help but feel a rush of adrenaline pumping inside of him through some kind of invisible hose.

"This is *unbelievable*," beamed Matt, his mouth agape at a juggler throwing what looked like Chinese swords in the air. "This is something I've been waiting my whole life to see."

Michael noticed that all of the countries were pouring into the stadium interacting with one another. Reporters were running around the stadium, circling for their player. Fireworks spectacularly shown in the Bird's Nest, and that by itself, was quite a show altogether.

Michael walked with Sheena and Matt, celebrating with the rest. They met several athletes that they once competed against and saw Matt's trainer looking like Gloomy Gus with his hands stuffed deep into his jeans pockets (they joined a group of Indian athletes to avoid detection at Matt's insistence). As all of this was going on, the gold medal finalists were being called up to the stage to receive their medal.

"Man, do I wish I could be up there," Michael said, wistfully as a Kenyan athlete made their way up the stage.

"Me too," Sheena replied. "But what I really wish for is for no reporters to interview me."

"Too late for that," Matt said.

A woman with a long wrinkly neck and wispy-looking hair walked right up to them. She had a belly that made it look like she was pregnant but this was impossible: She looked to be someone's great-grandmother. With her physical features being taken into account, not only did Michael deduce that this was one ugly woman, but she resembled a vulture that had snacked on one too many dead animals.

"Would it be alright if I could interview Michael for a few minutes?" she asked.

"Of course," Michael answered. "I'll see you two later—"

"Don't say anything stupid," Matt advised him.

"Follow me, dear," the reporter said, ushering him away from his friends, who had turned away from him and started talking with Cliff and Samuel.

The reporter led him over to the edge of the stadium where there was no people and faced him, looking business-like.

"My name is Patricia Dawkins, Michael Durbin," the reporter said, smiling. "I was wondering if I could ask you some questions about the Olympics."

"No problem," Michael answered, feeling slightly nervous.

"How was your experience at this Olympics? Would you say it was enjoyable, memorable?" Dawkins queried.

"It was definitely memorable. I was able to have success as an athlete and was able to meet some new great friends," Michael replied.

"Can you tell me who your new friends are?" Dawkins asked.

"Matt Harrington and Sheena Goodwin."

"What sports did they participate in?"

"Well, Sheena did gymnastics and Matt did diving," Michael answered.

"I've heard rumors about you how you went and discovered the ancient scroll. Can you confide in me if that was actually true?"

Michael thought that was okay to answer. He was reminded irresistibly of Mr. Goodwin and himself running through Zhengzhou, dodging gunfire and hopping into a plastic pink boat.

"Yes, all of it is true. It was no easy task to collect the scroll, though."

"One last question: Do you feel that the Ying-Yang brothers will be caught?"

Michael thought carefully on this question. He did not want to send the world into a panic, but thought it was best to tell to say what he really thought.

"I really think they will definitely not be caught."

Dawkins looked shocked. "You really think so?"

"It's funny, but I think they'll stay out of trouble," Michael replied. "They're clever enough to stay out of sight from the police. That is what I can guarantee you and everyone else."

"What do you plan on doing after you get home?"

"I'd say the sky's the limit," Michael said, seriously.

"Thank you for your time, Michael. Have a great rest of the Olympics."

"Thank you."

Michael was walking back into the thick of things when two more reporters—a portly white man and a skinny black woman—accosted him and blocked his path to his friends. Michael looked at them. The white male looked as though he had been hit over the head with a poker.

"Hey guys, I already got interviewed," Michael said in a casual voice. "Can you please—?"

"Not so fast, Mikey," the white man replied. After exchanging glances with the black woman, he added, "Miss Delacour thinks you're being rude."

Michael couldn't believe how reporters could be so annoying. All he wanted to do now was enjoy the Closing Ceremonies with his friends. This was the only opportunity he had to experience them.

"Well, tell Miss Delacour that I was just interviewed by Dawkins, and I'm done talking," Michael replied, losing his patience and tried to walk away but the two reporters closed in on him.

"Dawkins is senile and unreliable as a reporter. Marty and I decide when you're done talking," Miss Delacour said, giving Michael a look of deep disgust, "not you, Michael."

"We like you, Mikey," Marty added. "Hate to see you not go home without giving your admirers an inside look at the teen they are idolizing."

"We want to give the public what they want," Miss Delacour said, leering at Michael. "And they want to know about your relationship with Sheena Goodwin."

Michael swore inwardly. The last thing he wanted to do was to reveal his personal life with two selfish reporters. Why couldn't they let him enjoy the Closing Ceremonies? Michael looked at the two rude reporters.

"No comment," Michael said, and he once again attempted to move past them, but the two would not budge.

"Mikey," the white man said in a mocking voice. "Come on, man. Just give us the goods, and we'll back off. Just tell us: Are you attracted to Sheena Goodwin?"

"Guys, I have to go back to my life—" Michael started to say but he was cut off.

"What, you have to go see your girlfriend and your crippled Harrington friend?" Marty asked. Anger throbbed in Michael's veins about the jibe made about Matt's condition. "You have to go live a normal life and hang out with your friends who don't even care about you? Buddy, what kind of life is that?"

"It's one you reporters are depriving me off," Michael retorted, turning his back on the two reporters.

However, he had walked two paces when he heard a threat uttered by Miss Delacour and then a louder voice.

"Hey!"

Michael whirled around. He saw the two annoying pests right behind him and a few yards away were Mr. Harrington and Mr. Isol, both of them with their arms folded.

"What are you doing?" Mr. Harrington asked.

"What are *you* doing?" Miss Delacour asked in a low voice.

"How about you two screw off before I toss you out of this stadium?" thundered Mr. Isol.

The reporters looked as though they were going to put up a fight, but after considering Mr. Isol's size, both of them turned to Michael.

"See you soon, Mikey," the white man said, threateningly, and the two of them disappeared.

Michael walked over to his two coaches. He didn't like the sound of the "See you soon, Mikey" but he was grateful to be shot of them.

"Thanks for everything," Michael replied.

"I know how it feels when two reporters don't know when to shut up," Mr. Harrington said seriously. "It's happened to Isol, right, Lyle?"

"Yeah," Mr. Isol replied, gruffly, "they didn't speak another word for a week after I gave them a sneak peek at who they were dealing with!"

"Well, thanks again," Michael said, thinking that the next time he was approached by a reporter, he would take a trip to the bathroom. "See you later . . ."

Michael went back and found Matt eavesdropping on a conversation where two men were arguing with one another about who was better. A very pretty woman was watching them, giggling.

"You know I am a star quarterback in the Australian Football League!" one man with acne all over his face said. "I threw for an average of three touchdowns a game—"

"No you aren't. You're a garbage collector!" the other man yelled, who was rather dark. "I am a lawyer bringing in an inordinate sum of money!"

"Bullshit!" the first man replied. "You flunked out of school after getting a twenty in your English class!"

"Hey, you know that I got a 2400 on my SAT!" Matt yelled, and the woman laughed even harder.

"Honestly, Matt," Michael said, dragging him away. "Why did you have to say that?"

"I couldn't help myself," he said, grumpily. "Why were you so late getting back?"

"I ran into two reporters and they became pestilential," Michael replied, honestly.

Matt scowled.

"Tools those reporters can be."

"Where is Sheena, by the way?" Michael asked, now noticing she was not here.

"She got interviewed," Matt replied. "She should be coming . . . oh, there she is."

Sheena was running towards them through a dense crowd of British athletes.

"How did your interview go?" asked Michael curiously.

"Oh, it was alright," Sheena replied. "The reporter got annoying because I would not go into full depth of what happened in Fireworks Factory, so the reporter started asking me if you were my boyfriend. At that point, Mr. Oberfels came and led me away from the reporter."

"And what did you say?" Matt asked, excitedly.

"I did say you were my friend. I'm not sure she believed me, though."

"She must be taking Ty's comments as the truth," Michael said, dispassionately. "The same thing happened to me except that Mr. Harrington and Mr. Isol got me out of it."

The three of them walked around for a little bit longer. They talked to some people they went against and were interrogated by some reporters. Though none of them got as angry as Marty and Miss Delacour when Michael refused to entertain the notion about Sheena and himself, Michael still found it irritating that the reporters could not find a more interesting topic to talk to him about.

"Do you like Sheena Goodwin?"

"How is Sheena's relationship with you?"

"Do you like her?"

"Is she your girlfriend?"

"Do you think she is pretty?"

At that point, Michael was able to escape from them by saying that he had to use the restroom but instead went over to where Nitro, his friends, and James were standing.

"The MLB ceremony is starting," Nitro said. "They are announcing the players that were signed. Mr. Harrington and the other baseball coaches insisted that this should be a last-minute addition to the program."

"That's exciting," Michael answered, thinking that Mr. Harrington made the right decision.

"Pierre Garson from France! He was selected by the Seattle Mariners, is a pitcher, and will wear number thirty-six."

The crowd cheered as Pierre walked with a swagger up to the podium, and receive his jersey.

The next person—by the name of Ramses Darwin—was unceremoniously greeted but he too walked up calmly, and accepted his new uniform with the Phillies.

"I heard of that kid," James replied in an undertone. "I heard he could pitch over one hundred miles and he never lost a game in his career!"

"What was his ERA?" Michael queried.

James shrugged as though his ERA was an insignificant statistic.

When James heard his name called, he walked up while getting the loudest cheer of them all. Michael, Matt, Sheena, and Nitro clapped loudly, and they were the last to stop clapping after he took his uniform.

The ceremony ended about ten minutes after that and orchestras and bands were now making their way out onto the stage to play. The athletes joined in the dancing and pretty soon the whole Bird's Nest was dancing, even the fans in the seats.

Michael, Matt, and Sheena joined in as well. Michael was comfortably aware that this was one of the first times he could have fun without worrying about anything like his nerves, the brothers, or the scroll.

Michael saw Fred take the microphone out of someone's hand at the end of a song and started singing. He was not actually too bad. Everyone laughed, and so did Michael, Matt, and Sheena.

"I'm joining Fred," Matt replied, and he left on his crutches, leaving Sheena and Michael alone.

"He's going to make a fool of himself," Sheena replied, grinning.

"Probably," Michael said, nodding.

They watched as Matt joined Fred in singing. More dancers came and laughed as the two sang. Matt sounded inadequate—his voice was like a particularly noisy vacuum cleaner.

Michael turned to Sheena. "Should we join them?"

Sheena met his eyes, and smiled. "Yes, I was thinking the same thing."

The two friends joined the group where Matt and Fred were starting a line. Michael and Sheena became a part of it. Then, pretty soon, Michael's teammates joined, and even foreign players decided to get in on the fun. Everyone was joining the line as Fred led it around the Bird's Nest, pumping his fist victoriously in the air.

Michael couldn't help grinning at the thought that Sara and Tomas could not join in on the fun. All they could do was sit in the stands, watching the ceremonies. Michael knew Sara would willingly give away all her pocket money for a chance to be with Michael and the other athletes.

The Closing Ceremonies lasted a long time. Michael enjoyed it immensely, but more than anything, he wanted to go to bed. He was exhausted from the past two weeks, and felt tired.

He felt an odd sense of loss, too, because tomorrow he would be leaving two of his best friends in the world, who stuck with him throughout the troubled times of this Olympics. He did not know if he would see them again for a long time.

Matt and Sheena were not just friends to Michael. He thought they were more than just best friends. He himself could not quite explain it, but there was something between them that was different between Sara and Tomas. It was an odd feeling, something he had never ever felt in his life. The experiences he had with Matt and Sheena he could not duplicate with Sara and Tomas.

Spectacular fireworks were now blasting through the skies of Beijing. The crowd gasped and gaped at the spectacular sight. Michael could not help cheering as well. Matt and Sheena were right by him, cheering with him.

Then music started to play again and it gradually became louder. Songs changed after every two minutes or so. Michael recognized many of them, but abstained from singing along with his friends, thinking grimly to himself that the last thing he needed was for another stupid reporter to publish an article about his singing ability.

However, the display was interrupted by a loud noise. Sheena plucked his sleeve and pointed him in the right direction to where the noise was coming from.

A huge van was moving into the Bird's Nest. A ton of people were following its progress as it made its way slowly into the stadium, inching along like a caterpillar. Michael could make out the words as it stopped right in front of the stadium.

London 2012

People were now filing out of the van, yelling, singing, and dancing with the rest of the athletes.

"This is truly unbelievable," Sheena breathed.

"Yeah," Michael said in agreement. "Too bad I won't be there in 2012."

"Hey, guys, look at the scoreboard!" Matt cried, pointing to the right of them.

All three of them turned their heads and looked at the scoreboard. It was easy to make out what it was showing.

It was Michael talking to Dawkins. He was saying what great friends he had in Matt and Sheena. The crowd instantly said "AW!" very loudly, making Michael feel embarrassed but pleased all the same.

Matt and Sheena looked at him, beaming. They all put their arms around each other and watched the remainder of the fireworks.

Michael knew he would never forget tonight. He finally was able to spend a problem-free moment with his best friends, and it wrapped up a thrilling Olympics. However, he was relieved to go home. He went through too much in two weeks, more than he had in his whole life.

Michael knew that he would have to face leaving his friends tomorrow, but for now, he laughed with them, enjoying the last golden peace moment of the Beijing 2008 Olympics. Even though Michael knew the Closing Ceremonies were not usually like this, he still thought it was better than searching for a scroll, avoiding two evil twins, and the weapons that they possessed.

CHAPTER 29

MICHAEL: THE OLYMPIAN

Michael had a short sleep due to the fact he stayed up so late during the night. He was a little exhausted from the night, and he was dragging as he packed away all of his things. It took a while to do so, since Matt had strewn his cherished items all over the place. He was to go home with Delbin, Sara, and Tomas at noon. They wanted to relax in Beijing for a few hours before boarding the plane.

Michael felt extremely miserable. He didn't want to leave Matt and Sheena behind. Those were his two best friends who had helped him through the Olympics. Michael knew he would miss them for the coming days; he only hoped that they would miss him as much.

But Michael was not the only one with preoccupied thoughts: Matt seemed unhappy as well. He was dragging as he packed up as well. The two boys barely talked to each other, tired from the Closing Ceremonies.

"Do you think we'll be able to talk to each other again?" Matt asked as he folded his underwear and placed it in his suitcase.

"Of course, Matt," Michael said, laughing. "I'll give you my e-mail and phone number and address. You can mail me letters, call me, or e-mail me."

"You're giving them to Sheena as well?"

"Certainly I will."

"You know, Michael, I think Sheena would like that," Matt said, seriously.

Michael did not answer but resumed packing. Matt didn't seem to be expecting an answer because he continued packing as well (he now was folding up his socks, which were now dirty and stretched-out).

Nine o' clock came and both boys were walking downstairs to the cafeteria where they would meet everyone else. Michael was allowed to enjoy one last breakfast with Matt and Sheena and then it was time for him to head to the airport.

Michael was able to carry his stuff down with him. Matt, however, was not so fortunate. He had not brought about five or six bags with him that he had to struggle with. Michael offered to help, as he only had three, but Matt said he was alright. Even with a crippled leg, Matt was still mobile and he was able to balance his stuff along with his crutches to the elevator.

Once the doors opened, they lugged all of their gear to the cafeteria where they found Sheena and her family there with Michael's three coaches.

"I guess that the Perkins, Delbin and Tomas are not here yet?" Michael asked, taking a seat next to Sheena.

"Not yet," Sheena replied. "Delbin had a little something to do."

"What exactly was it?" Matt questioned.

"He didn't want you guys to know," Shawna answered, taking everyone by surprise.

"How do you know?" Ember asked.

Shawna grinned. "He told me, but told me not to tell anyone else."

"Why?" Michael asked, ready to berate his brother for kissing up to Shawna when he came back.

Shawna shrugged.

"How are you, Michael?" Mr. Goodwin asked, coming over to shake Michael's hand.

"Fine, sir," Michael answered.

"No, you're not," Mr. Isol said, gruffly. "Not after what those—"

"Mr. Isol," Mrs. Goodwin said, warningly.

"—Chinese—"

"ISOL!" Mr. Harrington warned him.

Ember giggled.

"Oh, there they are!" Sheena said, pointing.

Delbin was walking towards them with Sara and Tomas. To Michael's surprise, Delbin was carrying the Zhengzhou scroll.

"How did you get that?" Michael asked, amazed.

"Thought you might want to keep this," Delbin said, holding it out. "You know, as a souvenir."

"But I thought the Committee was—"

"We decided it belongs to you," Mr. Goodwin replied, smiling, "if you want it. There's nothing on it, of course, but you still can have it."

Michael grinned. "I'll take it. For all the happy memories that came with it, you know."

Everyone laughed at Michael's comment.

It was an enjoyable breakfast despite the fact that everyone was leaving. Sara's parents came in as well and it was like another party. Michael looked at Delbin, who was telling a joke to Ember and Shawna, and they laughed, causing the customers at the other table to eye them angrily.

Then, at long last, the time had arrived for him to leave Beijing. Michael tried to tell the adults about checking out, but Mr. Harrington stopped him.

"We already took care of that," he replied. "There is no need to worry about it."

"Mr. Harrington, is this really my only Olympics?" Michael asked. He had been battling with himself to be able to discuss the matter calmly.

"We'll see," Mr. Harrington replied, gravely. "I'm going to try to bring it back, but you never know. I will try to bring it to the 2012 Olympics."

"And what happens if we don't?" Michael asked.

Mr. Harrington gave Michael a small smile. "What will come, will come. And then we'll conquer it when it finally does. But we must be patient."

And Michael knew he was right.

The transportation was already taken cared of. Michael would go with the Goodwin family and Matt in one car while Delbin, Tomas, the three Perkins, Mr. Harrington, Mr. Oberfels, and Mr. Isol went in the other one.

"Spend time with your friends; you won't be able to see every day," Sara told Michael.

"Yeah," Tomas said, smirking, "but don't give Sara Matt's contact information. Her parents already don't like her cell phone bill."

Sara flashed him a dirty look, and Tomas did have a steely glint in his eye, just like the one Michael admired in Mrs. Cogburn. In any case, Michael was glad that his friends were letting him be with Matt and Sheena for the last hour or so. It was a tactful thing his friends could do.

Michael packed his gear in the trunk of the car. Matt and Sheena were getting home differently, so they helped carry Michael's gear to the car. Then, Michael climbed into the back seat with Matt and Sheena.

Mr. Goodwin was the last one to get into the car. He apparently had to dash back to the house to grab his cell phone, which he said he needed in case of an emergency at work. It was obvious that he didn't really want to; he conveniently dropped it twice in a row.

"It's all B.S., really," Mr. Goodwin replied, hopping into the car, finally pocketing his cell phone.

"Tell me about it," Mrs. Goodwin grumbled.

The ride to the airport was not far away. In fact, it was about ten minutes away. Michael was able, however, able to have a conversation with his friends.

"I have to give you two my e-mail, phone number, and address," Michael answered, "so that you can contact me whenever you want."

"Good, I'll give you my phone number as well," Sheena said, looking pleased. "But I think we'll be seeing each other sooner than you think."

"Really?"

"I'm sure of it," Sheena said, confidently.

Michael wondered whether she already arranged something but he decided not to comment on her remarks.

"Well, I'll be seeing you anyway," Matt said to Sheena. "Our parents usually have dinner parties."

"I know I'll see you," Sheena said, laughing. "But Michael was whom I was mentioning."

"I might try to invite you two to my school," Michael said, "I think my class in general would like to see who I befriended over the course of the Olympics."

Both Matt and Sheena looked at each other, wearing looks that indicated that they were appreciative of Michael's gesture.

"Michael, I'm just curious," Matt said, abruptly as they were pulling into the parking garage and darkness swallowed them up. "Do you think your parents would be proud of what you did?"

"They should," Sheena said, defensively, before Michael could answer. "You probably accomplished more than they did their entire lives. It still strikes me as odd that they didn't come and watch you, though. Your brother did."

"I have another brother as well," Michael said, realizing suddenly that he never mentioned anything about his brother, Isaac. "And he didn't come."

Matt and Sheena couldn't seem to think of a reply for this, so they just shrugged.

Mr. Goodwin parked the car and they all got out of the car. After taking out all of his suitcases, Michael, with help from Matt and Sheena, carried his gear into the airport.

Inside the airport, a bunch a people in alien costumes were walking up and down, holding out boxes for people. They were obviously collecting for something. Mr. Harrington found their antics amusing.

"Welcome to nutjob city," Mr. Harrington replied, pointing at the crazy people and trying not to laugh.

"What do you suppose they're collecting for?" Shawna asked.

"Don't know . . . and I don't care."

Airport inspection took a long time. They joined the shortest line where they found Sara, Delbin, Tomas, and everyone else, so at least they had people to talk to, but they were still unbelievably bored.

"They need to figure out a better way to do this," Shawna said, glumly, as they moved up a foot.

"There is no better way," Mr. Goodwin said in an undertone. "Anyway, if he misses his flight, it's no big deal, eh?"

Mr. Goodwin looked at Matt and Sheena and gave them a very small wink.

After a half an hour, they were able to get out of the deadly boring inspection line and make their way to where Michael's flight was. He would be taking a direct flight straight to Philadelphia.

Mr. Isol decided to treat everyone to some Burger King burgers while they waited for Michael's plane. He had to buy himself two Big Macs and a large French fry container just for himself while everyone sufficed with only one hamburger. However, everyone was grateful for Mr. Isol's generosity.

While they ate in the terminal, Michael noticed that many athletes who were walking to find their own flight were acknowledging him with a wave or a nod as they passed. Michael saw the same batter he struck out when he played Japan and a group of British gymnasts waved at him. When he waved back, the girls turned around with their faces in their hands, apparently embarrassed. Matt sniggered.

"Those gymnastics girls were hitting on you, Mikey," he whispered.

Michael and Sheena both kicked him at the same time, nailing his only good leg. While Matt moaned in agony, Delbin handed Michael a cell phone.

"Call Mom and Dad," Delbin said. "They should know when you are to be home."

Michael excused himself and dialed his home phone number on the cell phone. He heard it ring once, and then a voice echoed through the phone.

"Hello?"

"Isaac, is that you?"

"Yeah. How are you, Michael? How was Beijing?"

"Very eventful," Michael answered.

"Are you at the airport now?"

"Yes. My plane is arriving shortly."

"Ok, Michael. I'll tell Mom and Dad that you're coming home. They are doing food shopping at the moment. They are very proud of you. We heard about you on the news. We saw a few highlights of your pitching. You were awesome, Michael."

"Thanks. See you later, Isaac."

"Bye, Michael."

Michael hung up and closed the cell phone, feeling happy that his parents actually did enjoy having him over in Beijing, competing.

Matt and Sheena were not there when Michael came back. Everyone else was, though. They smiled as Michael walked toward them.

"I think your flight is about to board," Mr. Goodwin said as an announcement was made, alerting all passengers to make their way towards the passageway between the plane and the airport for the flight to Philadelphia.

Michael was shocked and alarmed.

"Really?"

"Yes," Mrs. Goodwin said, hugging Michael. "Keep in touch, Michael."

"Bye, Michael!" Shawna and Ember said, grinning at him sadly.

"See you, Durbin," Mr. Isol said, gruffly.

"See you," Mr. Oberfels said in farewell.

Michael then turned to Mr. Harrington and Mr. Goodwin. They were the two most important people that he would have never got through the Olympics without. They had helped him become a true Olympian and confront the evil Ying-Yang brothers. Michael knew he would be forever grateful for their advice and kindness.

"Take care, Michael. Be sure to give your contact information to my daughter," Mr. Goodwin said with a glint of amusement in his eyes.

"And to my son, as well," Mr. Harrington said, shaking Michael's hand. "And keep practicing."

"Where are they?"

"Over there," Delbin said, pointing at a table next to the Burger King Mr. Isol purchased burgers from.

Michael walked to the direction Delbin was pointing in and indeed, he saw Sheena and Matt there, writing it seemed.

Michael approached them.

"Hi, guys."

"Michael, good, I want your contact information," Sheena said, breathlessly. Then, she handed him two slips of paper. "This is mine and Matt's."

Michael quickly scribbled his phone number, e-mail, and address on two pieces of paper that Matt handed him.

"Here. Make sure you call me or something. I need someone to talk to over the break."

"See you, Michael," Matt said, shaking his hand and clapping him on the back.

Michael then looked at Sheena, who smiled, and swiftly walked forward and hugged him. "Bye, Michael. Keep in touch, please, okay?"

"I'll call every day if you want me to," Michael said, hugging her back.

"Hey, Michael," Matt said as though a sudden thought occurred to him. "Can you get me Sara's contact information as well?"

Michael smiled as he let go of Sheena.

"Tomas may not like it, but I'll try."

Michael waved his hand in farewell and he gathered his gear, and made his way to the airplane, passing other athletes from other nations as he handed the attendant his boarding pass and exited through the chute to the plane.

As Michael found a seat on the plane by himself, his mind wandered back to the brothers. He still had many questions that needed answers. Where were the brothers now? Why did Mr. Smith insist that he had to follow the brothers' orders? Where was the real scroll?

Then he remembered what Mr. Harrington had told him.

There was nothing to worry about yet.

And Michael knew Mr. Harrington was right. He had no reason to be worried.

The plane started to fly down the runway, and as the plane lifted into the sky, Michael was riding off into the clouds like an Olympian, where the Gods could congratulate him at last.

WETZEL'S FINAL NOTE

I hope that you enjoyed reading the first installment of the *Michael Durbin* franchise. I had fun creating my characters and developing a story, but trust me, finishing this book was the most difficult part of the process.

I feel that I owe all of you an explanation on how I came to write this book. I first got the idea when I was twelve years of age. The Beijing Olympics arrived, which brought excitement to everyone across the world. Everyone looks forward to this event and it serves as a great time to establish ties between nations and have fun while hard-working athletes represent their country.

I started following the Olympics since the Opening Ceremony and watched mainly swimming and gymnastics competitions because those were the two main events that were often shown on television. Throughout watching the Olympics, I began to formulate a preliminary plan on a possible novel. I always had the ambition to become an author since I was in the second grade. However, with my thirteenth birthday coming close, I thought it was about time I start taking my ambition seriously. Within the first few days, my main characters were formed. I decided to have two of the main characters a swimmer and a gymnast because they were always on television like I previously said. I came to create the two role characters, Matthew Harrington and Sheena Goodwin before I created the most important figure in my novel. I decided early on that Matt would represent the faithful and funny sidekick of my protagonist. I envisioned Sheena as a nice, proper girl who would play as the main protagonist's love interest because nowadays, that is what is going to spark the audience's interest.

I did a little research on the Olympics and the arenas that were in Beijing like the Bird's Nest. My dad told me that baseball and softball were making its final appearance in the Olympics, and I thought that the predicament was sure to anger baseball fans and the athletes that participated in those sports. I spent a great deal of thought on this problem, and decided that having a baseball player as my main character would set up a possible sequel well and also form another conflict that would add intrigue to my book. I came to create Michael Durbin, the hero in my novel.

After my three main characters were developed, I found it easier to construct more characters. I decided to make as many connections with the main characters as I could. I made Matt's father (Mr. Harrington) be Michael's baseball manager. Then, to make it more interesting, I created Sheena's father (Mr. Goodwin), and appointed him the President of the United States Olympic Committee. After that, I constructed the rest of their families, making Matt an only child, and Sheena and Michael having two siblings (funny enough, Michael has two brothers and Sheena two sisters).

Then, I still was missing an important piece of a novel. I needed to create the enemies in this book. Ying and Yang, two Chinese-American twins, were born. After that, I decided to make up the baseball team's roster with the other coaches. Mr. Isol represents the asset to the American side, because of his size. Mr. Oberfels represents the seemingly innocent coach who was dragged into this by his friends. Then, to add a twist to this novel, I created Mr. Smith as the undercover agent for the two brothers.

Originally, Sara Perkins and Tomas Isolant were not going to be as important as I made them. I originally never intended for them to go to Beijing. However, I decided to give my main character some support in the Olympics, realizing that athletes rarely go without some family member present to watch them.

I filled out the rest of the baseball team, and I then concentrated on the plot. I had some difficulty making all the pieces fit together. I was very impulsive when I was twelve and thirteen and I learned an important lesson to bear in mind for future writing projects. I discovered the importance of completely planning a novel out before writing it.

I finished the first copy of the book on September 27th, 2009, when I was thirteen years old. Then, I realized that I made some huge errors that affected the plot. I went back and fixed those, and I got the plot straightened out on January 12th, 2010. Lastly, I went back one more time to add more figurative language and details, and I kept re-reading it until I felt comfortable sending the book to be published. I realized that it was going to take time until I felt comfortable sending my book out for people to browse at their leisure.

I hope to continue making more books with Michael, Matt, and Sheena and I can promise you that these three characters will return as soon as I finish the second book. As of now, I am in the middle of writing it, but I will not reveal any details yet until I feel it is necessary. Thank you for reading my novel and I hope you consider reading my books in the future.

Sincerely yours,

Billy Wetzel